ISHI

ISHI

GLEN PETERS

GLENPETERS.INFO

Copyright © Glen Peters 2022

The right of Glen Peters to be identified as the author of this work
has been asserted.

All rights reserved.

No part of this book may be reproduced, stored in a retrieval system, or transmitted in any form or by any means (electronic, mechanical, photocopying, recording or otherwise) without the prior written permission of the author, except in cases of brief quotations embodied in reviews or articles.
It may not be edited, amended, lent, resold, hired out, distributed or otherwise circulated without the publisher's written permission.

This book is a work of fiction. Except in the case of historical fact, names, characters, places, and incidents either are products of the author's imagination or are used fictitiously.
Any resemblance to actual persons, living or dead, events, or locales is entirely coincidental.

Permission can be obtained from glenpeters.info

ISBN: 978-1-7387709-0-8

Canadian Intellectual Property Office
Registration number: 1181249

Published by Glen Peters

Editor: Jessica McAleney

Cover design, illustration & interior formatting
Mark Thomas / Coverness.com

Through sobs, Ishi uttered what she had already realized immediately yesterday even when arriving at the airport. "I shouldn't have looked for you…"

CHAPTER 1

The air was still.

The bright three-quarter moon emerged again from behind another cloud. The leaves and branches of the poplar bushes once more rimmed silvery against the moonlight; this small East German farm seemed calm and peaceful. But, inside the humble farmhouse, a storm of urgency and frenzied nerves frantically blew.

Horst and Dagmar Gruber had long pleaded to God for children yet, year after year, they had been unsuccessful. However, just after midnight, on May 2, 1988 — four days late — Dagmar's water broke!

Horst quickly saddled up. Through the dark, he rode his mare the two kilometers to the edge of Vacha — to the home of the midwife. Aroused from her sleep, the heavy-set woman immediately, though grouchily, prepped; hastily lumbered outside; and hoisted herself up on the horse. She held tightly to Horst as they galloped along the night road back to the farmhouse.

Now, just after two o'clock in the morning, the little farmhouse was a hive of emotions and urgent activity.

"Rinse this!" the midwife commanded. And, keeping her focus on Dagmar, she held the bloody towel out behind her. Horst grabbed it. In his nervous excitement, Horst eagerly obeyed all the demands of the midwife for more towels, fresh basins of warm water, and whatever else he was ordered to do. "I need better light!" the midwife complained loudly.

Immediately, Horst ran out to the barn and, gathering up three more lanterns in his arms, rushed back to the house. The light from the extra lanterns bettered the situation.

The energy in the house was charged and palpable!

As minutes seemed to stretch unbearably long, Horst eagerly anticipated hearing the sound of a baby's wailing at any moment. Time ticked torturously slow. The midwife worked feverishly, occasionally ordering Horst for more new towels and water, but also — intentionally — blocking Horst from the view. Horst began to sense that it was all taking too long.

"Aaaagh!" Dagmar's groans and wails of pain filled the small house as the midwife repeatedly tried to reassure her.

"Push, Dagmar!" Her tone was strong and confident. "Just push … And breathe … Push! Take a breath … Push!"

Finally, the baby was out! The midwife bent closer to the infant, tending to it desperately. Horst stepped up to see. But there were no baby's cries.

"Is the b-b-baby alright?" Horst asked fearfully.

The midwife turned to meet his eyes. She then turned back to look at Dagmar — exhausted. There were no words. The baby was stillborn.

CHAPTER 2

Sonya had been ecstatic when their baby was born! They named her Isabella. Sonya, almost immediately, nicknamed her Ishi. Born in 1985 in Tel Aviv, Israel, Ishi became her mother's joy.

Sonya Katz was born Sonya Braun in Schenklengsfeld, West Germany in 1959. Now, at twenty-nine, her life had already presented interesting twists and turns. Since her teenage years, Sonya had a love for fabrics and rugs. She landed a job in a local textile mill at the age of nineteen and rose quickly up the ladder. Within four years, she became Assistant Superintendent at the mill. At twenty-four, she was scouted by the textile distributor, Dorfan Textiles, based in Munich, and decided to make the move to the big city in 1983. She soon found herself on the sales-marketing side of Dorfan Textiles and a year later, at the age of twenty-five, she represented Dorfan Textiles at a tradeshow in Venice, Italy. As it happened, Joseph Katz was also in Venice.

Joseph Katz was born in 1955 at Jaffa, Greater Tel Aviv, Israel. While in Venice, he was in meetings with potential furniture wholesale clients. He had inherited Katz Furniture from his now deceased parents, and he had grown the already-renowned company into one of the three most prominent furniture companies in the region.

They met, quite accidentally, while exploring the tourist attractions in their free time. Each had decided to go to the famed San Marco Square, and it was there that Sonya noticed the handsome man — his thick, black hair appealingly disheveled. He noticed her, too. They flirted. And it did not take long to find themselves dining together. Sonya fell hard and fast.

The next four months were a whirlwind of travels to see each other: three trips to Munich for Joseph and two trips to Tel Aviv for Sonya. By Autumn, she was pregnant. The surprise, though welcomed, necessitated fast and sweeping decisions. Sonya Braun and Joseph Katz became engaged for two short months, and married in November 1984.

Joseph knew he could promise to provide for a wonderful life in Tel Aviv for Sonya. Sonya recognized the opportunity to continue developing her expertise with fabrics and design through her new husband's company. So, Sonya made the move, without reservation, to her new life in Israel.

*

The bright July afternoon sun glinted off the water of the Mediterranean Sea — about forty-five kilometers off the Israeli coast near Tel Aviv. A 71-foot Marquis 690 Fly rested stationary on the calmness; the water's reflection sparkled its brilliance on the vessel. The luxury yacht was a veritable home-away-from-home for Joseph and Sonya Katz. Every three months, they found themselves enjoying the spacious staterooms and warm opulence of its teak and cherry Italian design as they cruised in comfort.

Joseph was on the bridge checking his charts to ensure there were no anchoring restrictions whilst, simultaneously, determining the quality of the seabed before dropping anchor to the water line. Remotely controlled from the helm, Joseph engaged the windlass and released the anchor housed in its cubby in the hull. Joseph had dropped anchor in this location many times before, so he trusted his calculations; still, he let the anchor chain out one-third at a time to allow the boat to straighten at each interval.

On the yacht's main deck, Sonya played with their three-year-old daughter, Ishi. Because these yachting excursions had become a quarterly occurrence for the Katz family, Sonya had made sure to furnish little Ishi with a variety of activities and toys to keep her happily occupied. Ishi's clear favorite, of all her on-board things, was the gigantic two-story-plus-attic dollhouse. When the weather was nice, Sonya would carry the dollhouse out onto the main deck where Ishi, with Sonya kneeling beside her, would play for hours. While standing on her tiptoes, it still took the full stretch of little Ishi's arm to place the doll-baby on the top level where she had set up the miniature furniture to create the nursery — detailed in pink wallpaper sprinkled with tiny yellow flowers.

As Joseph descended the three steps down to the main deck, he glanced to his right to view, expectedly, a smaller powerboat fast approaching. It carried two middle-aged men. The one seated was rather handsome, clean-shaven, and fit. And, as the boat came closer, he stood and placed two briefcases on the edge. The other man was the driver and, as if a planned opposite, had long, unwashed hair with a beer belly that pushed up against the wheel. This man, at the controls, cut the boat's engine, turned the wheel, and expertly drifted the boat to the side of the yacht.

The pilot remained at the wheel — an AK47 machine gun slung over his left shoulder — while the handsome man lifted the two briefcases up to Joseph. Leaning over the edge of the yacht, Joseph took a briefcase in each hand and hoisted them onto the vessel. Without any exchange of words, the powerboat revved back up and quickly left. Joseph immediately took the briefcases down below to the staterooms.

Ishi watched the powerboat jet away while Sonya, remaining focused on Ishi, tried to distract her back into their pretend storyline.

Almost immediately, Joseph reappeared from below, turned, and ascended the three steps back up to the bridge. Here, he scanned the instrument console and took the necessary procedural steps to raise the anchor and return it to its housing. After checking several more instruments until he heard the three successive beeps indicating that the anchor was raised. Then, moving the throttle control lever upwards, Joseph engaged the two engines. There was a powerful rumble deep in the hull — increasing as the giant vessel moved ahead. Joseph steered the yacht in a slow half-arc northward to the open sea. They were heading for Cyprus.

As always, when sailing to Cyprus, Joseph maneuvered around the east of the island, to north of the island, and then carried on west. Following a course ninety kilometers south of Turkey's coast, the Katz family would make their first fuel stop, of many, at Bodrum, Turkey. Having made this trip every three months, Joseph navigated the waters masterfully. The entire trip to Monte

Carlo's port was just over fourteen hundred nautical miles and lasted eight days. Joseph would captain the yacht most of the time, but Sonya would trade him off long enough to allow him a full six hours of sleep each day. As usual, their trip would end by settling their luxury yacht amongst the magnificent seacraft of the port.

*

Ingrid Braun, Sonya's mother, remained back home in West Germany. Having lost her father to pneumonia when she was just a young teen, Sonya cherished her relationship with her mom and missed her terribly. Joseph brought Ingrid to Tel Aviv for their wedding ceremony, but Sonya and Ingrid had not seen each other in the three years since. And so, Oma Ingrid would have to wait to meet her granddaughter, Ishi.

Ingrid lived on an acreage — bequeathed to her just before Sonya's move to Israel. It was on the southern outskirts of the town of Philippsthal and was only thirty-five kilometers from where Sonya grew up. Ingrid could enjoy the acreage life while still preserving her lifelong relationships with her friends in Schenklengsfeld.

Her modest three-room shanty sat atop a gentle rise with her twenty acres sprawled around it. It all was comfortable enough for Ingrid. The farm was quaint, complete with a manual-pump fresh water well and a charming, yet rather substantial, chicken coop housing thirty laying hens. A neighboring farmer leased her land to grow alfalfa for his livestock. Ingrid felt blessed to be walking distance from him, as well as the neighbor on her other side — and to be able to count them as friends.

 When sitting outside on her front porch, shelling peas, or reading, Ingrid would look past her chicken coop toward the forest. Although somewhat in the distance, she could easily see the border tower, the guard's hut sitting awkwardly atop its tall, spindled supports that splayed beneath. It loomed as some kind of giant wooden creature whose legs could just start moving at any moment to carry it away. The extended platform square at the base of the hut was bordered with a simple railing and Ingrid would sometimes see the guard leaning against as if surveying his kingdom below. But the image disgusted her! In Ingrid's mind, the border that split Germany represented only pain and division. So, she would intentionally redirect her focus back to her peas or her reading — not giving any further attention to such hostile thoughts.

*

There was a strong side breeze as they sailed farther northward toward Crete. The breeze, along with the swift sailing yacht created too much of a mist for Ishi and Sonya's dollhouse playing. So, Sonya quickly packed up the miniature tea set, and some other extraneous items, tucked them back into the dollhouse, and closed it up. Then, wrapping both arms around it as best she could, Sonya heaved the dollhouse up and walked with it toward the stairs that led below — the dollhouse just barely fitting through the stairwell. Ishi, quickly snatching up a few Barbies, followed her mom.

Joseph and Sonya lived a life of luxury. To those on the outside, it appeared that Katz Furniture was successful to a measure that afforded Joseph and Sonya an enviable amount of wealth. To those on the inside, the reality was very different and a well-kept secret. The furniture company was not succeeding. Joseph had been unable to bring in an adequate volume of clients — a troubling downward trend that had begun long before Joseph and Sonya had ever met.

CHAPTER 3

The yacht sped along its route toward Monte Carlo while, in the galley below, Sonya was preparing lunch. She had created a salad of mixed greens to pair with their usual lox and cheese. With everything neatly assembled, and the table set for three, she looked up the steps toward the deck. It crossed her mind to trade Joseph off so he could eat first. But she lingered on the second step on the way up to tell him and, instead, sat down to watch Ishi play in her safe little world of pretend.

The tension and pressure of their daily lives were never far from Sonya's mind. In fact, they permeated every moment and even tarnished the very few times she felt free to enjoy her adorable Ishi — her only light in the darkness of duplicity. Yes, she lived a life of excessive abundance and wanted for nothing when it came to material wealth. But black clouds of corruption were ever present. Sonya felt trapped. This life of crime, this life of constantly looking over her shoulder, this life of twisted insides was not what she signed up for. She was embarrassed that she never knew this man before she married him. She had been tricked and betrayed. So, day in, day out, Sonya battled depression and despair, reserving the heaviness of silent tears when away from Ishi's little eyes and ears. And she, most certainly, would not allow herself to show Joseph how much she struggled. He did not deserve the satisfaction. Sonya was alone.

*

Katz Furniture had been a reliably established company for many years. They manufactured custom orders for clients and delivered their product not only within Israel but beyond its borders as well. Business negotiations proved fruitful within Syria, Jordan, and the Palestinian territories.

Unbeknownst to Joseph, all these travels caught the attention of the PLO who established regular surveillance and analysis of his comings and goings. And, over the years, its agents manipulated many of these occasions to establish communication. Palestinian leadership learned that Joseph was certainly no Israeli loyalist. They also became acutely aware of his burden of massive debt. Thus, the Palestinian Liberation Organization surmised that Joseph Katz could, more-than-likely, be used to their advantage. They would appeal to his less-than-ideal political leanings and exploit his financial vulnerability.

Joseph embarked on a business trip to As Suwayda, Syria in 1983; he had high hopes of landing a well-known buyer with very deep pockets. They were engrossed in a closed-door meeting when it was abruptly interrupted. Benjamin Sharod, the Deputy to the Israeli Minister of Finance, simply walked in, unannounced, as if he had been invited. He was a heavy-set man of about 6'1", and his confidence sparked the energy in the room. Joseph recognized him immediately and was both shocked and confused at the sight of the prominent Israeli politician in foreign territory.

Sharod turned and locked the door behind him. In a richly resonant voice, the Deputy informed Joseph that he was aware of his debts to Israel's Hapoalim Bank due to Katz Furniture's sea of debt. While ignoring the third man in the room, Sharod continued to report, flatly, factually, and in great detail, what the PLO had observed over the years. The Deputy paused and looked over to the buyer with enough commanding intent that the buyer at once knew to leave the room. He stood and nodded quickly to both parties. He fumbled awkwardly with the door but was sure to promptly close it upon exiting. Once again, Sharod re-engaged the lock. The Deputy then turned back to Joseph and asked if he wished him to continue. Sensing a way out of his financial mire, Joseph replied, "Yes. I do." He felt a shade embarrassed by the sound of his own eager and somewhat desperate tone.

Deputy Sharod proceeded to unfold the details surrounding the complexity of an established infiltration into Israel's purse — where funds were skimmed from Israel's state revenues and rerouted to Palestine since 1981. Sharod divulged that he, as Deputy, along with the Minister of Finance, were agents working for the Palestinian movement.

Joseph was impressed that the scheme had been in operation and gone undiscovered for the past two years. "That doesn't sound like anything that wouldn't be quickly discovered in an audit," he prodded.

Sharod explained that budgetary payments to Infrastructure in Israel were made quarterly through agent Yitzhak Biton, governor in charge of the bank's head office at Kiryat HaMemshala in Jerusalem as well as Avraham Azoulai, COO of the bank's branch office in Tel Aviv. At this point, Benjamin Sharod paused again to determine if Joseph was digesting the information and following the intricacy of machinations. The Deputy explained that they would be utilizing Joseph's business travels to transport the money. He noted that the financial rewards would not only rescue Katz Furniture and redeem the honour of Joseph's family name, but, also, provide for an exceedingly generous profit. Sharod wasn't asking.

Joseph rationalized that he owed nothing to Israel and, avariciously, he coveted the ideas of wealth and importance. And so, he quickly traded any potential national loyalties and moral boundaries for the furtive contract to, essentially, be a mule for the PLO.

"You can not just change your mind. Do you understand?" Sharod was anything but subtle with his threatening undertone.

Joseph nodded. "Yes, I do." He did an internal roll of his eyes at his own repetitive response to the Deputy's questions.

"Be very sure that you do." Sharod continued coldly, "We do not tolerate misunderstandings; the transports will be your priority; communication will be kept minimal and efficient."

Joseph left the unexpected meeting feeling that he had done the right thing. *I can take my family name and polish it to reveal its true exceptional status.* He knew exactly what he was getting into, and he welcomed it. *I was always meant to be important — more than just another owner of one more furniture company in the region.* He didn't aspire to be just the "best in the business"; that was his father's dream. He chuffed to himself at the thought. Joseph recalled the hard times when his family was barely getting by; he remembered his father's frustration, coupled with the long hours he would work, and all just to please a stranger. Yet, Joseph did become the best in the business — just not the Katz family business. His whole life changed, and it was all under the guise of furniture dealings. For every transport of money, there was a handsome profit. And, for every profit, there was a need in Joseph for people to see his success. He proudly exuded an air of arrogance and could think of nothing he needed in his life. A year later, he would meet Sonya.

Six months into their marriage, Sonya was appreciating the grand life afforded her by the clear success of her husband's company. The ability to live freely without the thought of cost was a very new concept to her; it was certainly not what she was used to growing up in Schenklengsfeld. Sonya was eight months pregnant when her new husband blindsided her with the news: their good fortune was not a result of hard work and honest transactions; instead, Katz Furniture was just a front and, to Sonya, the luxury she appreciated now seemed a lie.

"No," she screamed in defiance. "How can this be? How could you not tell me? How could you be so willingly deceitful?"

"Don't be so dramatic," he mocked. "You do not seem to mind our life's advantages. Did you really think that all this came from buying and selling furniture?!"

"I should have known that there's something else about you!" she snarled. Sonya was realizing that the little voice inside her for the past six months had been trying to unveil the truth. She had wanted, so desperately, to give this man and their relationship the benefit of the doubt. She wanted to excuse his holier-than-thou attitudes and his condescension toward her as his working too hard, expecting too much of himself, and wanting to provide the best of life for her and their baby. "All that pompous show-boating you do," she lashed, "All that silent brooding when I'm expected to just leave you alone to your oh-so-important business; it was all just you being devoted to - to these people. People who are clearly more important to you than we are!" She held her belly and turned slightly on an angle. In that moment, any clouded thought regarding her relationship had been cleared. It was obvious what she had to do for herself and her baby. She, at once, felt free. Yes, the little voice had told her. She just didn't listen well enough to trust it.

"I'm leaving," she said, surprised at the venom with which she colored her tone. She was impressed with her own resolve. "You are a pretender. You are a nothing! You are a traitor to your own country! You can not be a father; you can not be a husband," she laughed with intentionally quick barbs. "You are such a –"

A brutal backhand landed hard on her face. It knocked her to the ground and left her winded and in shock. She froze.

"Not only will you stay and cooperate," he said sternly, "you will not create any trouble." Joseph was catching his own breath. He was taken aback by his outburst. *She forced it; she knew I wasn't going to just allow her to talk to me like that. Who does she think she is, so easily crossing the line? Why is she so unappreciative?* "You will carry on as if nothing has changed and you will tell no one. And …" He paused here as if it was vital to find exactly the right sentiment. "You will be grateful." He brushed his hair off his face and, as he did so, he glanced at his knuckles to see if there was a mark. He did a quick snap down of his shirt, turned, and walked away — trying to commit to dominating the moment. *I hope she is okay,* he thought.

*

Sonya hated the whole 1.5-million-dollar yacht. She balked at its distasteful design. Of course, despite her expertise, she had spurned Joseph's invitation to be part of its overhaul; she now took pleasure in watching him give poor and un-informed decisions to the many questions posed by the man he had hired to do what she had refused. Every three months she dealt with the same routine from Tel Aviv to Monte Carlo. Once in harbor, Joseph always instructed that she and Ishi stay on the boat. And so, Sonya tried to create little games for them to play to fill the two days they were kept there, like prisoners. Joseph, in the meantime, would fly to Geneva with briefcases full of bank notes for deposit into a numbered account. The PLO took it from there.

When Joseph returned to the boat, he resumed his manner of tolerating his inconvenient passengers. Joseph did not at all attempt to hide his regret at having a family. He shunned and rejected them. And he resented Ishi especially. Sonya saw it, felt it, and it broke her heart.

CHAPTER 4

She rubbed the last bit of sunscreen onto Ishi's little bare arms, and then, side-by-side they both jumped up the steps from the cabin to the yacht's deck — counting as they went. They would jump onto the first step and Ishi would shout, "One!" look up at her mom, and eagerly wait for her response. Sonya would then have to describe an animal, in clothing, to make Ishi giggle.

"One pink giraffe wearing sixteen neck-ties in sixteen different shades of green!" Sonya would do her best to sound enthusiastic about the game that they played umpteen times a day. Ishi's reactions always rewarded her efforts.

"Two!"

"Two rhinocerouseseseses wearing woolly red sweaters!"

"Three!"

"Three snakes slipping out of their silky silver slacks!"

"Aaaaaaannnd Four!"

"Four cuddly possums wearing pajamas the wrong way 'round, hanging upside down from the clothesline, with their noses poking through the bum flaps!" Sonya always made an extra silly remark on the fourth and final step.

"Mommy!" Ishi gasped in glee. "You said bum!" They both laughed and Sonya gave little Ishi a little, playful hip bump.

Ishi was proudly carrying her little badminton racquet and couldn't wait to play. As Sonya got to the top step, the bright afternoon sun blinded her momentarily. She put a hand up to shade her eyes. She gazed up at the beauty of Monte Carlo built up and around the mountainsides. As many times as she viewed its magnificence, it never ceased to impress her. Ishi tugged on her mother's tank top to come and teach her how to bat a birdie. Sonya was very patient as she stood behind Ishi, released the birdie with her left hand and then, hand-over-hand, Sonya and Ishi swung at the birdie with the right. Ishi struggled to do it, but was very persistent. However, she would get frustrated that she never made contact with the birdie without her mommy's help. Sonya would encourage her daughter to try again and reassured her that they could do it hand-over-hand for as long as it took.

Every once in a while, Ishi's attention was drawn to her dollhouse, and she would drop her racquet to go and check on her "baby". Sonya watched as Ishi attended to the little doll. "It's okay, Tia," Ishi soothed in her best mommy voice, "Daddy will be home soon." And then, Ishi would run back to her mom to attempt to conquer the first step of badminton. "She's so sweet," Sonya thought as she observed her daughter adoringly. "She is so … innocent."

While Joseph was away for his couple of days in Switzerland during each excursion, Sonya was content to spend quality time with her Ishi. There was very little Sonya could control in her life and she was determined to raise Ishi the way her mother had raised her — with undivided attention, and kindness, and respect ever-present. It was important to Sonya that she use every playtime, every game, every interaction as an opportunity to plant seeds of confidence and independence. She wanted Ishi to grow up feeling a solid foundation of unconditional love. Clearly, Ishi was not to receive this bonding from her father. Sonya took full advantage of the times when he wasn't around to make his snide comments — that is, the few times he bothered to do even *that*. Just one more day and Joseph would return. And, once again, they would resume their usual facade and their game of keeping up appearances. Joseph would take her to their customary five-star restaurant near the casino and, on the way home, they would perhaps stop at his favorite clothing establishment. It remained open late exclusively for Joseph. He would make an appointment to be fitted for his suits, ensuring he would be the only patron there. The staff would fawn all over him and Joseph would soak up all the attention while Sonya would read Ishi a book or three in their private little armchair corner. Then they would return to the yacht for one more night in the harbor before their eight-day trip back to Tel Aviv. The routine was very predictable. An easy predictable. Sonya would remind herself that, at the very least, predictable meant no surprises.

Suddenly Ishi dropped her toy badminton racquet and ran again to the dollhouse. "Oma needs to bake!" Ishi reached for a Barbie with short hair and placed her at the stove in the dollhouse kitchen. Sonya was stunned with surprise; Ishi never mentioned Oma! Of course, Sonya had talked to Ishi about Oma many times — retelling childhood memories of licking the jam off her fingers while making Krapfen with her mother. She made an effort to describe her mother to Ishi and to try and create a relationship through stories.

As Ishi had never met her Oma, Sonya assumed that it would be next to impossible for her to grasp the concept of this phantom family that lived so far away. But, clearly, the details of how Sonya would bake with her mother had left an impression. "Oh dear," Ishi said giggling, "You have sugar on your cheek." Sonya watched as Ishi used the Barbie's hand to wipe Tia's face. It warmed Sonya's heart and she felt the tears well in her eyes. She missed her mom palpably. She longed for her mother to meet and know her precious Ishi. *How they would love each other!* she thought. *Ishi needs to meet her. I need to see her!* Sonya decided to demand it of Joseph as soon as he returned. *Ishi will meet her Oma.* Sonya resolved to make it happen.

The following afternoon when Joseph returned, Sonya chose her moment carefully and simply stated that they were going to spend a few days visiting her mother at her acreage by Philippsthal — all three of them.

"Like hell we are!" Joseph snapped, not sure which was worse: the thought of the visit or the way Sonya thought she could just make that kind of unilateral decision. He quickly answered his own question; it was the latter. *Why does she insist on provoking me?*

"Your daughter has never met her Oma. My mother has never met her only granddaughter. And, I —"

"I don't care," Joseph cut in. "If I don't get back to Tel Aviv on time, I'm going to fall behind on the builds for Jaffa and Cairo. And that is unacceptable."

"No you won't," Sonya protested. "Matthew is entirely capable of handling it — all of it. He'll keep the wheels turning. You deserve some time away. I know it isn't the time away you would choose for yourself, but your daughter needs this, Joseph. She needs this." Sonya decided that the best tactic to employ first would be to appeal to his ego and then to his sense of fatherhood. She was quite sure there was very little, if any, sense of duty to his family but she needed to try honey before vinegar. "And it's really not fair to my mother. It is not fair to Ishi! Or, to me! Besides, —"

"Forget 'besides'! We're not going. It's not going to happen. You are forgetting your place, wife." Joseph liked to weaponize the word with an intent to condescend. In his head, he remembered how humiliating it was when his father would call him "boy". "You don't get to make these kinds of demands."

"Let me finish please, Joseph," Sonya continued, "I was going to say that if we stay away from my mom any longer, she may start to pry." Sonya knew to take the final tactic — any suggestion that his real enterprise would be adversely affected. "It's been three years and people connected to her may plant seeds that it seems odd she has not been invited here nor have we been there. The longer we keep her and her granddaughter apart, the more we invite unwanted questions from who knows who."

"Fine. You can go then." Joseph reasoned that she may have a point. The last thing he needed was to field questions from his mother-in-law. *I do see that a visit to Oma is necessary for your daughter … and mine.* "You may book a flight back to Germany for you and Ishi."

"We're not going without you!" Sonya was losing her patience. "My mother needs to see a family intact — a family that isn't disintegrating. Unless you're afraid to see my mother?" Sonya added just the right amount of antagonizing. She was intentionally pushing his buttons; in particular, she knew the exact button she was aiming for. She added a level of anger, controlled anger enough to manipulate him. "Joseph. Joseph, look at me. For once, I am not asking."

This caught Joseph somewhat off-guard. He was impressed with how she was playing her cards. It reminded him of the independent Sonya he fell in love with at San Marco Square. *Fine, I'll let her have this win. She may just be right. This one headache might save me a few more down the road.* "Alright. We can go. But not on this trip. It's too late now. We will go immediately after the next transfer."

"Another three months?! No, I'm not waiting another three months. If you make me wait another three months, I cannot promise - that I won't do something we will both regret." She hoped this would hang in the air. And it did.

Joseph had seen glimpses of this Sonya before and knew not to underestimate this side of her. She'd made trouble for him before. It was never anything he couldn't handle, of course, but still … "Fine. I'll have the flights booked first thing in the morning and we can pretend that you won this one."

"It wasn't about me winning, Joseph. Thank you. Ishi will be so excited." Sonya turned away from him. *Yes, Joseph, it is about me. Finally, no longer acquiescing at the sacrifice of my daughter.*

That very evening, the arrangements were made.

CHAPTER 5

A little brown Border Terrier perched on the arm of Oma's wingback chair; his tail wagged a mile-a-minute as he sensed the anticipation in the air. He stared out the window scanning for anything that moved. "They'll be here soon, Honish," Oma said as she played with the soft underside of his small, floppy ears. "You are going to have so much fun with Ishi!" Honish panted excitedly in agreement. *I don't even know if Joseph likes dogs*, Oma thought to herself. She had not seen Sonya and Joseph since the wedding and Sonya did not tend to share much about their life. *Ishi*, she thought, *I finally get to hug my precious granddaughter!*

A white Skoda sedan appeared from around the corner — making its way up the inclined dirt driveway. Honish started in with his low protective growl. "They're here!" said Oma. And, with that, Honish launched himself off the chair and cheerily yipped as he raced for the door. "Shush now, Honish," Oma said as she quickly shuffled up behind him. "Honish! Sh! Quiet!" she commanded. When she opened the door, Oma watched as the driver's side door flew open and her daughter, her beloved Sonya, raced to hug her. They embraced, holding each other tightly, as tears of joy freely flowed. Until that moment, neither of them had really understood how much they had longed for this reunion. Releasing from the embrace, they took a moment to drink each other in. Sonya then turned to beckon over her family. She couldn't wait for sweet Ishi to meet her Oma in person.

A reluctant Joseph opened the passenger side door and stood behind it — as if partly in protection and partly pausing to gear up. *I wonder what Ishi is thinking right now*, he thought. *This is all so strange to her. She doesn't know this woman.* Joseph felt a small, strange tinge of guilt conscious of the long separation that was largely his doing.

Sonya, realizing that Ishi was not sure what she was supposed to do, stepped to the car, and opened her door. Ishi looked up at her mother with bright, questioning eyes. Sonya smiled warmly and squatted down to talk with her.

"Do you need to sit here together with me for a moment?" Sonya had learned that Ishi could be simultaneously curious, excited, and cautious and needed a little patience sometimes — allowing her to digest new situations.

Ishi, trying to display courage, looking past her mother and toward the older woman, shook her head.

"Go and hug your Oma," Joseph said sharply to her, trying to deflect from his own hesitation. Sonya shot him a glance of *don't command her like that!*

"Not every encounter with a new person needs to be so dramatic. She needs to learn to not be fearful of everything and everyone," he continued.

"It's not a fear," Sonya explained, "she's just three. It's new, that's all." Joseph sighed and reached for his fedora that he placed on the dash while they were traveling. He ran his hand through thick hair, to tame the curls, and confidently placed his hat — readying himself with a deep, low breath.

Sonya took Ishi's hand, uncurled her little fingers, and kissed it in the center of her palm. They both smiled their knowing smiles at the game. "Are you ready?" Sonya asked. Ishi nodded and scooched herself off the seat. Holding her mother's hand, Ishi's eyes glanced from her Oma to the dog and back again. Ishi had decided that she felt stronger walking as close to her mother as she possibly could — partially behind her whilst pressed into her right hip. Sonya walked awkwardly toward her mother while trying to encourage her daughter to walk beside her.

Meanwhile, Honish had become quite distracted from the whole situation as he lay in the grass licking an old, wet, bone that he held between his paws. But as Ishi reached Oma, his ears perked up in interest in the strange little human's arrival.

Oma bent toward Ishi; her hands clasped slightly against her thighs. "And you must be Rachel?" she asked with a little sly smile. Ishi nuzzled into her mom. "No? Hmm, oh, that's right. You are Sarah." Oma tapped one finger on her lips and put on her best thinking face. "Charlotte? Maya?" Ishi giggled and tugged on her mother's dress — signaling Sonya to bend down so that her daughter could whisper in her ear.

"Tell her I'm Ishi," she tittered.

"Why don't you tell her?"

"I want *you* to. She knows I'm Ishi, right?"

"Of course, she does. Oma likes to play little games just like we do." Sonya gently squeezed her daughter's hand, smiled proudly, and royally announced, "This is your granddaughter, Ishi - Ishi, this is my mother. And your Oma." Ishi came out from her hiding space with a big grin on her face as she looked up at her Oma.

Oma squatted with her arms open wide. Ishi looked at her mom and Sonya nodded. The granddaughter willingly walked into Oma's embrace and was wrapped in squeezing love. And then, almost immediately, Ishi stayed at her Oma's side and took her hand as if they'd been friends for years. "Who's that?" Ishi asked, pointing to the dog.

"Well, that is Honish. He's a little busy right now concentrating on his bone."

"That looks gross."

Oma laughed. "Well, it's seen better days but, to Honish, it's as good as it was on day one."

Joseph watched the scene while still standing behind his car door. *I wonder how much Sonya has told her*, he thought. He snapped his shirt down, as he always did when confronting any situation, put on his best smile, and walked, hand out-stretched, toward his mother-in-law. Just as he got near, a sudden wind gust whipped his fedora off his head — as if out of a comical movie scene. It caught the eye of Honish who thought it flew by, intentionally, for him to fetch. Both Honish and Ishi tried to chase it down. The dog was successful. He picked it up by its brim and proudly marched it toward the front door. *Damn it!* Joseph was worried about the marks that might result from the little dog's teeth.

"Honish," Oma commanded. "Bring it here!" She patted her leg as part of the instruction. Honish did as he was trained to do and sat at Oma's feet. "Drop it," she said firmly. Honish obeyed and Oma quickly scooped up the hat, giving it a thorough once-over. She picked off a piece of dried grass, blew away the dust and, carefully, returned it to Joseph. "A bit windy today," she said.

Joseph, having foregone the handshake, took the hat and, unapologetically, checked it for damage. "It's lovely to see you again, Ingrid," he managed, with a smile.

"Dearest Joseph," Oma said as she hugged him close. She patted him on the upper arms with a you're-such-a-good-boy gesture. "Let's get your things inside now." She opened the door with Ishi at her side. "I apologize for the size, Joseph. It's a perfect fit for me and Honish but, I'm afraid, it's going to be a little close quarters for the five of us.

Why do people do that? thought Joseph. *Counting the dog as "one of us".* He did his usual internal eye roll.

"Luckily," Oma continued proudly, "we have lots of wide-open space to enjoy. Shall we take a tour? I want to show my granddaughter all the places she can explore with Honish." Oma playfully poked Ishi in the tummy as she spoke.

Oma took her family all around her kingdom right to the edge of the property. "Here you can look to the north toward Phillipsthal," she had been holding onto Sonya's arm and took a moment to pull her closer. *So many memories back at our home in Schenklengsfeld,* she thought. "And to the east you can see that wretched wooden guard tower." Sonya's mother had told her that this was the only part of her property that she did not care for. It bothered Ingrid to the core. It felt like a stain on an otherwise beautiful fabric of countryside. "And look at this." Oma switched gears and was pointing out the endless carpet of brightly colored wildflowers on the surrounding pastures.

Three hours later, they found themselves sitting in the quaint country living room enjoying a light lunch followed by coffee and biscuits. Joseph had dutifully participated in answering questions about the furniture business and their regular sea journeys. Sonya noted that it seemed as if he almost enjoyed the banter. *This is the Joseph I remember,* she thought. *He is trying. I wonder if he's seeing that we all need this. Maybe he just needed to be reminded.* However, it was not long after this observation that Sonya sensed a shift in Joseph's mood; he had grown notably quieter. Joseph was, indeed, getting antsy.

"Did you know," Sonya interrupted her mother's story, "that Oma has a wonderfully busy chicken coop?" She intentionally baited Ishi's excitement. "You've never seen a chicken coop; would you like to go and see it?"

Oma was only too glad to oblige; she loved to showcase her chickens. Sonya, Oma, and Ishi all jumped up to embark on the adventure with Joseph begrudgingly bringing up the rear. Sonya let Ishi go ahead with her mother and waited for Joseph to catch up. She walked beside him for a while. They were both silent. In one instance, she linked her arm through his and squeezed it a little. It was her way of thanking him for the moment. He looked at her — at first, a little taken-aback and then, he allowed the beginnings of a smile. He remembered how she could melt him. He was thinking about something to say to her when she let go to catch up with Ishi.

When they reached the coop, numerous chickens scratched around in the outside enclosure. Ishi was fascinated! She giggled uproariously as she reached her little fingers through the wire fence to try and touch the silly, busy creatures. Sonya and Oma laughed at her squeals. Even Joseph smiled at his daughter's innocent delight. "Do you want to see if there's an egg?" Oma asked.

"Yes! Yes, please," Ishi exclaimed, her eyes lighting up. Sonya was impressed that her little daughter remembered her manners even in all the excitement.

Oma took Ishi's hand and lifted the latch of the little wooden gate; Joseph closed it behind the three. The house was too small for them all to fit and Joseph preferred to remain outside anyway. Ishi was all-at-once overwhelmed by the chickens surrounding her. Oma quickly scooped her up and carried her on her hip as she opened the brooding house door — ducking as she entered. It was, of course, much calmer inside as only seven chickens sat quietly brooding. "Are you okay to go down now?" asked Oma. Ishi nodded. Oma set her down and Ishi took her mother's hand while inching closer to the nesting boxes.

"Are they sleeping, Oma?" she whispered.

"Well, these are the hens - the female chickens - and they are sitting on their eggs to keep them warm."

"Are there babies in the eggs?" Sonya and her mother exchanged a look both knowing that a simple answer would be best.

"Not in these ones, dear. These ones are for us to eat. Shall we see if we can find one?"

Ishi nodded.

"Okay, let's see." Oma bent down to lift Ishi up to a third-tier box where a fat, rust-red hen sat brooding. "I'll lift the hen a little, and you feel underneath, okay."

"No. Wait. Will it bite me?" Ishi asked hesitantly.

"Oh no, sweetheart, it won't bite you." Oma lifted the hen. "See … now just put your hand under and feel around."

Ishi looked at her mom and Sonya nodded encouragingly. So, she put out her little fist ready to snatch it back if she needed to. She was surprised how warm it felt underneath the chicken. "I can't find the egg, Oma. Where is it?"

"Well, that's just the thing; it's like an Easter Egg hunt every time I come to collect eggs; I never know where I'm going to find them." Oma could see that Ishi was a little disappointed. "Do you want to check the others for me?"

"Yes, please," said Ishi. "I'm good at it now."

"Yes, dear, you are," Oma affirmed. She looked at Sonya and mouthed, *she's so adorable.*

Sonya smiled knowingly and appreciatively. She loved seeing how quickly Ishi had bonded with her mother. *This is exactly how I pictured it would be,* she thought.

Oma carried Ishi to another nesting box at the end of the second tier. "Okay, so I'll just lift her up and you reach —"

"I know, Oma," interrupted Ishi confidently.

Oma laughed. "Oh yes, you do, my little Ishi. You are now my official egg collector."

Ishi reached out to feel under the hen. "Oma, Oma, I found one. This one has one! What … Oma — there's two. I can feel two of them." Ishi was absolutely astonished, and with great excitement, she pulled her hand out to reveal her prize.

"Ooh, careful! Don't drop it. Be —"

"Here. You take this one, mama. I have to get the other one." Sonya, more or less, caught the egg from Ishi. Ishi was just beside herself with delight as she reached in for the second egg. "Mama, mama, here, take the other one. Oma, we should check the others, too. Can we check the others, Oma?"

"Yes, child," said Oma, laughing. "They're not going anywhere."

They checked under the other hens and, each time, Ishi was thrilled to find another reward. And, each time, she unintentionally made her mother catch them. And, each time, she beamed proudly at her Oma. And, once they were all gathered, they re-joined Joseph outside.

"It sounds like you were successful, Ishi," Joseph said.

"Daddy, I am the best egg collectioner —"

"Collector," he corrected with a smile.

"Collector. And Oma said I can be her official collector. And I want to come out everyday and maybe I can try by myself and maybe I can have a chicken coop at home."

Ingrid, Sonya, and Joseph all shared a smile. "May I carry that for you?" Joseph asked Sonya.

"Most certainly, sir," she replied in a flirtatious tone. *Who are you?* she thought. She knew it wouldn't last. An afternoon like this was few and far between and she rarely, if ever — saw this Joseph now. But she would enjoy what she could when she had the chance to do so.

"Alright," said Oma, "Let's head back to the house for supper. When's the last time you had one of my suppers, my Sonya?"

"Far too long ago, mama." Sonya realized what she had said aloud. And she took a quick glance to check on Joseph's reaction. She breathed a small sigh of relief that he hadn't pounced on the comment with a threatening look.

After a hearty supper of dumplings, sauerkraut, sausage, followed by a somewhat-dense coffee cake, they stayed seated at the table to visit for a while. Sonya was pleased to see Joseph putting forth an effort to engage her mother in conversation. They continued to discuss the furniture world, their life in Tel Aviv, Oma's experiences moving from town to the acreage, and many stories of Ishi.

Ishi had long left the adults at the table but not before Oma had presented her with dolls from Sonya's childhood. Oma had been excited to share them with her and, prior to her arrival, had pulled out boxes to search for them. Ishi immediately chose one doll out of the three as her favorite. "That's Suzy," Sonya told her. "Suzy was *my* favorite doll when I was a little girl." Ishi was enamored with the doll and was happy to introduce her to Honish. The little Border Terrier was equally happy to have all the attention.

Dusk arrived, and by nine o'clock, the sun was setting. Joseph had excused himself from the visiting, at least an hour earlier, claiming that he needed to review business papers. Resigning to Oma's big, soft armchair, Joseph unpacked papers out of his attaché and had them strewn on his lap.

The following day, the little family settled into their activities. Sonya and her mother chatted while they cooked in the kitchen. Joseph sat absorbed in his papers. And Ishi enjoyed her dolls while she played outside with Honish — that is, until it was time for a mid-afternoon nap. Ishi complained that she wasn't tired but, after being told she could snuggle with Honish, she succumbed, and fell asleep before Honish had even completed his naptime ritual of circling his spot on the bed. And, when Ishi awoke, she got right back to the business of playing the day away.

Late afternoon came, and Oma had enticed Ishi to go for a walk to gather some of the wildflowers to make a centerpiece for the supper table.

"Can mommy and Honish come too?"

"Of course they can, dear." Oma thought it odd that she didn't mention inviting her father. *Perhaps she instinctively knows that he is busy with his work,* she pondered. And thought nothing more of it. When they returned, however, just before the supper hour, Ingrid did notice that Joseph seemed somewhat agitated. She took Ishi into the kitchen to find a vase for their bouquet and tried not to eavesdrop as Sonya squatted beside Joseph's chair for a private conversation.

"Mommy - mommy? Come see," Ishi called.

"I will, sweetheart - in a minute, sweetheart."

Sensing that Sonya and Joseph were having a necessary discussion, Oma decided to take Ishi back outside. "Shall we go and see if Bertha has laid anything, Ishi?"

"Who's Bertha?"

"Our favorite rust-red hen," Oma said, with a wink.

"Do they all have names, Oma?"

"Hmm - unfortunately, I haven't had time to name them all. Do you think you could help me with that?"

"Yes, please. I'm really good at making up names. And I'm really good at finding eggs."

"Yes, you are, sweetheart. Okay — Honish? Honish come," Oma called out.

When Oma, Ishi, and Honish returned to the house, Ishi bravely struggling with the weight of the ice cream pail half full of eggs, Ingrid felt that there was something brewing between her daughter and son-in-law.

"Mom, we hope it's not an inconvenience, but Joseph and I thought we might drive into town for a few hours?"

"Oh ... okay," Oma responded with understanding. "And supper?"

Sonya continued, "I know we've made a lot of food; we'll eat a lot of it tomorrow, I'm sure, but I think we're going to find a good pub and have supper there for tonight." Sonya glanced back at Joseph and then caught her mother's eye with a we-need-some-time-together look.

"Oh, that's a good idea," Ingrid said, rescuing her daughter from having to explain herself. "Joseph should have a traditional, authentic pub experience here."

Sonya smiled a thankful smile. "We were hoping that it wouldn't be too much to ask if you'd watch Ishi for a few hours?"

"Oh, I'd be delighted!" Ingrid was thrilled at the idea of her first opportunity, at long last, to babysit her very own grandchild.

"Oma is going to babysit me?"

"Yes," said Sonya, kneeling in front of her daughter. Then she whispered in her ear, "Oma is getting a bit old and needs some help. Do you think you can help take care of her while Mommy and Daddy go out for a while?"

Ishi nodded. And Sonya gave her a big, squishy smooch on the cheek.

"Thanks, mom," Sonya said, giving Ingrid a quick hug.

"Oh, it's my pleasure. Now you two go and have a nice time. Ishi and I are fine here. I'm sure Ishi will take good care of me." Oma winked at her granddaughter.

Sonya and Joseph each grabbed a coat and headed off to town.

Ishi was an absolute darling and Oma was enjoying every second with her precious granddaughter. With some instruction, she helped her Oma set the table. For Ishi, this was like a gigantic version of playing dollhouse. She carefully placed the forks and knives beside the two plates and was quick to ask for a dish set for her favorite doll at the table, too. Oma obliged and then placed two cushions on the third chair so that Suzy would sit high enough to be seen above the tabletop. After supper, Oma invited Ishi to come sit on her lap in the big soft armchair. Oma had leaned a couple of photo albums against the chair side and, taking the first photo album, showed Ishi photos of when Sonya was little.

"And here she is with her new lunchbox. She had just learned to pack it herself and she was so proud."

"What did she pack?"

"In her lunchbox? Well, let's see. If I remember correctly, her favorite sandwich was cheese and onion and that got wrapped in parchment paper. And, of course, she put cookies in there, and … I think she used to put in a whole carrot, too."

"But onions make mommy cry," said a confused Ishi.

"Well, these were already cut for her," explained Oma. "But you're right, onions sure do make us cry."

"That's because the chlemicals get in our eyeball."

"My," laughed Oma, "You are such a smart little girl!"

Of course, Ishi had many questions and comments about all the photographs but soon began to tire of it. "Suzy and I are going to play now," Ishi suddenly announced matter-of-factly. She slid off the chair and onto the large area rug. Over the next hour, Ishi pretended that she, and, Suzy, and Honish were wildflower hunting — using all the colors of the carpet. Although no longer a puppy, Honish was excited with the activity now in the house and he was eager to please the little girl. He dashed back and forth from Ishi to various spots in the room — grabbing up a slipper and bringing it to Ishi, then grabbing up another slipper and depositing it near the fireplace, then dashing in and out of Oma's bedroom, and then back to Ishi and Suzy, all in excitement to be part of the action. "Not the blue ones," Ishi warned the other two. "They were poisoned by the bad witch."

Ingrid flipped through the pages of the photo albums while listening to her granddaughter's vivid imagination. Her heart was warm and full.

CHAPTER 6

Joseph and Sonya sat at a small table in the middle of the local Wirtschaft. It was fairly quiet that evening with only five other patrons; three obvious regulars sat at the large Stammtisch and two tourists sat on the stools, engaging the Barmann with questions about the places in Phillipsthal they should not miss.

Joseph and Sonya had finished their meal; Joseph had washed his down with a Pils while Sonya awkwardly nursed a glass of wine. Their worn faces and cold energy revealed that their conversation over the past hour had been a sour one. Joseph slid his chair out, stood, and offered the Barfrau a partial wave.

"Check?" she assumed.

"No. Telephone?"

"Ah, yes, sure," the lady pointed toward a dark, short corridor that led to the washrooms. "In the hall."

Joseph nodded and, with the intent to check in with the manager-on-duty at the Tel Aviv plant, headed to where he was directed.

Knowing that such a phone call might take at least twenty minutes, Sonya pulled out a small notepad from her purse. The pen required a deeper scrounging. She then sat back, crossing one leg over the other, and began writing ideas for tomorrow's activities.

*

A clean-shaven German military man, in his early forties, sat in his guard tower on his reliable wooden chair — solid and sturdy. His legs were crossed, with his heavy-booted feet, and he had propped them on the small, square, metal table in front of him. Strategically positioned, along the wall opposite the door, sat an unmade cot with its bedding balled and crumpled. Along the same wall, in the right corner, was a small table just big enough for a wash basin and a pitcher. And, in the left corner, a radio sat atop a mini fridge. The guard relaxed as he listened to a rock music station playing, unobtrusively, in the background.

A 303 single shot rifle leant against the metal table and a Bayard M1908 pistol lay beside the heel of the guard's boot. The 303 could bring down a bear or moose with one shot, and, historically, was one of several rifles of choice for military duty away from the front lines of actual battle. The guard's rifle had a bullet chambered and ready. The pistol was loaded and was ready for action, too — not necessarily for any person daring to breach the intimidating mesh-wire four-meter-high fence that separated West Germany from East Germany, but for one of his fun pastime activities. He kept himself entertained sniping small animals such as coyotes, rabbits, and wild boar, while, simultaneously, satisfying his need for an adrenaline surge.

The single door of his modest, square guard tower room was a framed full-length window. All the other windows on every wall were large and set low. Even when reclining in his go-to position, the guard could easily see past the surrounding planked walkway all the way down to the fence. The only part of the fence that the guard could not keep an eye on was the portion immediately below him — only that small fifteen-meter radius directly underneath the tower. During his nineteen months at this post, he had not encountered any attempts to breach the border fence, so the guard satisfied his duties with an occasional lazy walk outside onto the planked perimeter to look below.

He dug his rolling pack out of his shirt pocket, pulled his boots off the table, sat forward, and unfolded the small kit. After opening the little, round metal canister of tobacco, he pulled out a sheet of rolling paper. Then, with his right forefinger in a tapping motion, he coaxed a measured amount of tobacco onto the paper. Adept at this routine, he had quickly rolled his cigarette, licked it to seal, and put it between his lips. The only other item regularly sitting on the ottoman-table was a box of matches. In fluid movements, the guard had the cigarette lit, returned his boots onto the table, and reclined once again into the stiff wooden chair.

*

"Where the hell are you?" Deputy Benjamin Sharod growled into the phone.

"I am exactly where I said I'd be," Joseph snapped back. He was standing in the short hall by the pub's phone, but now, on his cell phone for this call.

"You said you'd be gone up there for two days. I don't like —"

"I said …" Joseph sighed impatiently, "I said three days. Three."

"Well, get back on that yacht of yours now," snarled Sharod. "I thought you had a firmer grasp on the gravity of the situation … Cut your little cursed pleasure trip short!"

In response, the Deputy heard a punctuated click as Joseph abruptly ended the call.

*

Ishi had easily filled the evening with her creative play. *She has such an imagination*, thought Oma. Suzy and Honish were her companions of choice and Ishi instructed them in their roles, creating the script of the Witch and the Wildflowers as she went. Oma sat comfortably in her big armchair, feeling relaxed and fully content. She was smiling to herself as she watched her granddaughter pretend and, even as she began to nod off, the smile was still present. In a few minutes, she was sound asleep — the fresh, warm evening air gently breezing through the window.

Honish could be somewhat of an escape artist, so to have the window fully open was certainly an exception to the rule for Ingrid. Typically, the window was only up just enough to allow the summer air to refresh the house. Ingrid had also learned, the hard way, not to leave anything under the window. Honish was smart enough to use anything close by as a booster allowing him to stand on it, get his head through the opening, and nudge the window up until he could fit through. This day, there was so much cooking and baking that the house heated up to an uncomfortable temperature, so Ingrid thought it wise to slide it all the way up. Moreover, Sonya and Ingrid were lost in conversation while the second-last batch of muffins baked in the oven. And, since they weren't watching the time, they were a little too overdone — leaving a burnt odor clinging to the interior air. Yet another reason to welcome in the outside breeze.

For the past two days, Joseph and Sonya's suitcases had been set against the wall beneath the window — there was nowhere else to put them, really. They were out of the way there and had just become part of the furniture. Unnoticeable.

Quite suddenly and unexpectedly, in the middle of Ishi's game, Honish took advantage of the recent addition to the room. He dashed toward the open window, leapt up on the suitcase, and through the window he went! Ishi couldn't understand why he was leaving. She decided she needed to follow him to find out where he was going. She quickly ran over to the suitcase, climbed on top of it, and crawled out the open window calling after her adventurous friend.

It was late dusk and already quite dark. Oma dozed on.

As usual, when he had previously made a successful escape, Honish scampered directly for the chicken coop. But — rabbit! Surprised by the sudden appearance of a dog, it jumped up and bounded eastward down the acreage slope. Honish excitedly gave chase!

Ishi had landed on her feet and then tumbled forward into the dusty yard outside of the window. She stood, turned, and caught sight of the chase. "Honish!" Ishi called. "Honish. Wait! Stop!" She chased after her friend as fast as her little legs could go.

The rabbit bolted eastward reaching the bottom of the long acreage decline and then, farther on toward trees that held promise of cover.

Although it was quite dark, the dog had no problem keeping track of the rabbit -- staying with it as it dodged impulsively to different diagonal trails. Ishi, however, found it more challenging to follow Honish in the dark.

She called again, "Honish!" Honish would stop at the sound of Ishi's voice, wheel around to look, and respond with an excited bark -- as if narrating the chase to Ishi as he went. But, after barely a pause, he would resume his pursuit of the rabbit. Ishi just followed his bark as best she could.

By now, the rabbit was quite far ahead of Honish and Ishi. It approached the small forest of trees set just on the other side of the far-reaching mesh-wire fence. The fence, however, presented no obstacle. The rabbit landed at a spot where, clearly, small animals had burrowed before -- a countless number of them had depressed the ground there over time. A perfect getaway.

The rabbit had gone unseen by the guard, as did Honish. It was not as easy for the little dog to flatten underneath the fence; his back end required some effort in maneuvering. Consequently, Ishi had made it there just in time to see her playmate push through to the other side -- lifting up the bottom wires as he did so. Without hesitation, Ishi followed. This time, the back-to-back commotion captured the guard's attention as well as his assumptive intrigue.

It was too dark and about forty metres away. The guard could not see exactly what it was, but he was sure it would make for a good sniping target. He jumped to his feet and opted to grab the pistol over the rifle; he didn't want his little guilty pleasure to scare the neighbors into curiosity. Any report from the 303 firing would definitely get the attention from the acreages nearby. *Damn, it's too dark,* he thought. "Shit!" The animal was gone. He stepped out onto the walkway and scanned down toward the spot where he'd seen the movement.

The rabbit had already disappeared into the forest. Honish had lost its scent and quickly wandered different directions amongst the trees, nose to the ground, trying to pick it up again. He barked sharply and Ishi, having followed Honish into the forest, finally caught up with her now tired little four-legged companion. He seemed to have given up on the rabbit. Ishi was looking up at the stars; she had never seen so many.

Having had his fill of adventure, Honish, quite suddenly, dashed away back toward the fence to return home. Ishi tried to follow. "Wait. Honish! Honish?!" She had completely lost sight of the dog and could not hear him either. The trees seemed to envelop her in absolute darkness. She started to feel very lost. And alone.

Crack!

A yelpy dog whine.

Ishi was startled by the short, loud bang. And she thought the yelp sounded like Honish. The sudden noise, no sight of Honish, and standing there in the darkness paralyzed her with fear. "Honish!" she yelled. She ran a few steps into the dark in one direction, tripping over a branch. "Honish!" she cried. Honish!" She could taste her salty tears as she tried to rub her eyes thinking she would see better. She ran in another direction and snagged her dress on the bark of a tree. She tried to free herself but, as she did, her hand slipped and the bark scraped into her soft little palm and her leg. Ishi was gasping and sobbing now. She couldn't see a single thing. "Honish!? Mommy! Mommy! …"

CHAPTER 7

Only three kilometers apart, the once neighboring towns of Vacha and Philippsthal were separated by a border fence that divided East Germany and West Germany. A two-kilometer dirt road ran from the East German town of Vacha to the barrier. It had been paved by the Directorate-General of the Federal Trunk Road Authority in 1986 — as if to signify the road to the fence, and the fence itself, was both important and permanent. The road turned north and continued along the entirety of the fence.

Just a nine-minute walk west from Vacha was the Gruber farmyard. It was framed, at its back and sides, by a small forest. The woodland, unconcerned with the political fence, stretched from Gruber's farm, through the barrier, and to the town of Philippsthal immediately on the West Germany side.

Over the years, Horst and Dagmar Gruber poured devoted, ardent care on their little family of animals: three milk cows, one gentle mare, fourteen pigs in an outside pen, and a chicken-filled coop. On the east side, along with the animals, sat a small red barn, with a lean-to, covering a mound of hay and a small bale stack. They proudly cultivated fourteen acres of barley, and two acres of alfalfa. At the west side of the grass-dirt yard, opposite from the barn and pens, sat a quaint, daffodil yellow, three-room farmhouse. Behind the farmhouse, between it and the woods, was a substantial vegetable and flower garden. Both Horst and Dagmar took a notable amount of time and attention tending to it.

The Grubers always began their day with an early breakfast together. With a full belly, and a kiss for his wife, Horst would pull on his rubber boots and would make his way outside for morning chores.

This day, as he walked across the yard toward the fence to the pig pen, he glanced toward the cows, noticing that their attention was focused on the lean-to and the straw bales. Usually, the cows waited, impatiently, for the hay that he forked over the fence for them each morning. "Skunk in the bales?" Horst asked them. He didn't smell skunk though. Horst redirected his stride toward the small bale stack — cautiously aware that he would certainly not want to startle any black-and-white critter capable of spraying him. He stared at the bale stack for a few moments. There was no noticeable rustling. So, he redirected his attention back to the squealing pigs who were eager to receive their banquet of mash.

Horst carried five pales of chop from the small barn through part of the pig's enclosure and dumped them evenly along the pig troughs. "There ya go," he told them, as he left to go and satisfy the cows.

Walking around the lean-to, he found his pitchfork and began heaving the hay to the three waiting cows. He monitored the amount of hay he pitched over the fence as he wanted the cows to stay hungry for their barley. In a couple of hours, Horst would coax them into the barn — each to their respective stall for milking. Thus, the usual routine unfolded; every morning Horst facilitated the same daily drill.

After delivering the hay, Horst stowed the pitchfork — punching it into the side of a straw bale. Two days earlier, he had yanked out a few bales from the middle of the stack, leaving a holed center. Now, in the space that was left, something caught his eye.

"What in the world —"

Her little legs were bent in a fetal position as she huddled to keep warm.

"What in heaven's name —" Horst was still trying to process what he was seeing. Immediately, he pulled two more bales away from above the crawlspace — being careful to keep the remaining bales interlocked enough to not cave in.

Completely dumbfounded, Horst wondered what he should do next. She was very still, and he feared the worst. As he pulled the bales away, a little brown-haired girl in a pretty blue dress, bare legs, and pink shoes lay on her side with her arms wrapped around her knees. There was dried blood on her little hand and on her leg. She started to wake.

"I'm cold," she whispered faintly. She'd found the little shelter in the dark hours and curled up as best she could. Now she looked up at the man studying her. Her eyes squinted in the sun. Her face was red from crying and her skin was rashed from the stubbly bed. Her hair was clumpy and dusted with bits of straw and her dress was torn.

"You are l-l-lost, little one. What is y-y-your name?" Horst asked tenderly. His stutter usually became prominent when he was in an unfamiliar situation.

Ishi didn't understand German. She just stared back at the man - bewildered and frightened. "I want to go home," she cried, trying to make an even tighter ball of her little body.

Horst didn't understand her Hebrew. "It's okay, sweetheart," Horst tried again. "Where did you c-come from? You are s-s-safe now," Horst tried to reassure her and reached out a gentle hand, but she drew back in fear of the stranger.

Ishi's only response was a whimper while she wept.

She needs Dagmar, thought Horst. *I need Dagmar.* "Stay here," he told the little girl. "I'll be r-right back with my w-w-wife." He motioned as he spoke with both palms facing out. Horst slowly backed up a few steps and then raced back to the house -- as best he could in his big, cumbersome rubber boots. Blasting through the door, Horst shocked Dagmar who was sweeping in the middle of the living room.

"There's a girl! In the bale s-stack. There's a g-girl in the bale s-stack!"

Dagmar just stared at Horst - seeing and hearing the panic but not at all comprehending. "What do you —"

"She's in the bales. I don't know … It's a little g-girl," Horst tripped over his words in his panic.

"Breathe, my love," Dagmar said, trying to calm him. "Now, tell me, Horst, what did you see?" But her usual method of demonstrating deep breaths did not encourage him to pause this time.

"Come! Come see!" Horst did not wait for Dagmar to understand. He spun around and headed, hurriedly, back toward the barn. Horst just assumed Dagmar would follow and, indeed, she did. Broom still in hand and slippers on her feet, she tried to keep up with her husband. Arriving at the bale stack, Dagmar studied the girl. A bewildered incredulity left her speechless.

"I was just feeding the c-cows, and —"

Ishi, shivering and beside herself, looked at the woman.

"Oh sweetheart," Dagmar finally spoke with an intentional soft and sympathetic tone.

Nothing.

"Who are you?" Where is your mommy? How about your daddy? Here, come here." Dagmar extended a hand in hopes that the little girl might feel safe enough to take it.

Ishi, very scared and confused, didn't have the energy to move. She pleaded with the woman, "I want my mommy."

Horst, thinking that he might be a cause of fright for the little girl, backed away several steps. But Ishi continued to cry. After a few moments of Dagmar trying to engage the little girl, she retreated to where her husband stood.

"What should we do?" Horst asked. "She's so s-scared! How do we find out wh-wh-where she comes from?"

Dagmar decided to be more assertive. "She clearly needs to get warm. I need to clean her up — and she's probably starving." She stepped back to the little girl, leaned down, and gently scooped her up in her arms. "Let's go into the house, little one."

Once at home, Dagmar gently placed the little girl on the couch. Horst found a blanket to wrap around her shoulders. He brought Dagmar a large bowl of warm, soapy water and a cloth. Dagmar knelt in front of the little girl and, with the washing bowl beside her, began to wipe the dried blood from the girl's little palm. She attempted to ask her questions — anything that might help them figure out where she came from — but it was futile considering the language barrier and Ishi's complete lack of energy. Instead of pushing any further, Dagmar had Horst bring her a cup of warm tomato soup. And, as Ishi sipped it and dipped the occasional cracker, Dagmar put her arm around her to try to reassure that she was safe. After feeling the tension in Ishi release somewhat, Dagmar thought it best to get her rest. "I'm going to tuck her into our bed for a while," she told Horst, who had been watching and listening from the kitchen.

Ishi immediately closed her eyes. *Poor little thing,* thought Dagmar as she ensured the blanket was tucked around her. Horst had followed them into the bedroom carrying a small stuffed bunny. He put his arm around Dagmar as he handed it to her. Dagmar held it, with both hands, and stared at it awhile. She then looked up at Horst with tears in her eyes and yet, a grateful smile. She lifted Ishi's blanket and slipped it under her arm. Together, Horst and Dagmar watched her sleep and as Ishi's body relaxed, so, too, did sighs of relief come from the couple.

"How will we f-find out who she is -- where she is from?" Horst whispered.

Dagmar took his hand and led him out to the living room.

"What do we do next?" Horst asked, looking to Dagmar for the answers. Dagmar was silent. Horst, sensing the complexity of her emotions, kissed her on the forehead. "My sweet wife, we can take some time for all this to settle. We don't need to make any decisions right n-now. She is safe."

Horst headed back outside to finish his chores but noted, as he closed the door behind him, that Dagmar was returning to where the little girl slept. He sighed to himself as he quietly latched the door.

Horst filled the chickens' self feeders with chop mixed with supplement and then filled their water troughs from the nearby hand-pump well. The water troughs were truck tires he'd cut in half and laid on the ground in the outside enclosure — ideal for the chickens. He looked at the troughs and shook his head, *I know how to operate a farmyard,* he thought, *but Dagmar will be the one to know what to do in this situation. She will figure out how to help that poor little girl.* He then went into the chicken coop to gather eggs — ducking through the door to avoid hitting his head on the bare, dusty rafters.

As Horst entered the house with a plastic ice-cream pail half full of eggs, he found his wife on her knees in the living room. Her forehead rested on a sofa cushion, her hands extended above her head, fingers interlaced. *"Is she praying?*" he wondered. He was unsure of how to react to the unusual sight.

Dagmar eventually noticed her husband watching her. She got to her feet and fixed her skirt. "It's an answer," she said, coming to stand in front of him and grabbing his hand. "She is an answer to our prayers, my love." Dagmar's face was glowing as she smiled up at him.

Horst did not immediately understand but he could feel a hurt in his heart. "Dagmar," Horst responded, "what are you s-saying?" Horst felt uneasy with what he was beginning to understand. Dagmar squeezed his hand to her heart and then walked away with a determined step — back to the sleeping girl. "Dagmar?"

CHAPTER 8

Joseph walked along the second-floor gangway and then descended the corrugated metal stairs to the main assembly floor — a large room, forty by forty meters. He'd had the cork floor installed a few years earlier to ensure an ergonomic comfort for the workers that stood long hours in their role. Closest to the stairs, and about a third of the room, displayed one long row of connected tables that were divided, equally, by a large shelving bin about four meters in height. Rolls of fabrics — a multitude of colors — were stored there. Chair legs, wooden sofa skeletons, unfinished tabletops, and other items laid on the first half of the table-row showing a progression of woodworking from sanding to staining. The second half of the table-row laid out the developing fabric process from cutting to actual application — direct to cushions and then onto furniture. The rest of the room featured three designated areas for furniture assembly, whether table, chair, or sectional sofa.

Joseph walked, purposefully, toward Sonya who was looking over the shoulder of a worker at the fabric table. Sonya was pointing to a board of fabric swatches as they were attempting to choose the best color and texture for a specific piece. As soon as she heard Joseph approach, she stood up to receive the expected business particulars.

"We just finished the paperwork for Hassam," he stated.

"So, does that mean that their deposit is paid up? Should we start on their order?" she asked.

"Yes." Joseph silently evaluated Sonya's face and energy; she was always tired now. Tired, sad, and ashen-looking. Ishi had been missing for two months. Joseph had a period of mourning, of course, but had shifted back to business at this point. There was nothing more to be done. *She needs to let it go now,* he thought. *Accept the reality for what it is.* Joseph had allowed his heart to harden where Ishi was concerned. She had been in their lives for three years and, looking back, the birth of their daughter had destroyed their marriage. She had become the only important thing in Sonya's life and her sole focus. Joseph decided it was best to return to the way life was before Ishi; when it was just the two of them. *I need to remind her,* he thought. *Remind her that she can still love me, and I can be enough.* He did not like to see Sonya so devoid of life. "How are you feeling?" Joseph asked, knowing the answer.

Sonya looked at Joseph with a mixture of incredulity and slight disdain. *Seriously?!* She thought to herself. "Oh, just fine, Joseph," she said with biting sarcasm. "What could possibly be bothering me?" Realizing, very quickly, that using a facetious tone never ended well with Joseph, she retreated the attack and, intentionally, back-pedaled as she had done so many times before. "I'm sorry," she sighed, "I'm just so tired. I'm going to leave early today." She took Joseph's arm and led him away from the table. Sonya had mastered the art of placating Joseph. "I am never far from bursting into tears," she said quietly. "And the staff is always walking on eggshells — never knowing if they should ask about her or not."

They won't, thought Joseph. A month before, he sent a mass confidential memo to his whole staff stating that his wife was not to be asked about their daughter — that the matter was closed and needed to be put to bed.

After Ishi could not be found anywhere on her mother's land, a massive search was undertaken. Sonya was, of course, beside herself. Everyone around her was preaching positivity and she hated them for it, for not allowing her to show the searing pain. And yet, her mind was playing games with her. She began to believe that if she didn't appear positive, and Ishi wasn't found, it would be entirely her fault. After two weeks of following every lead, pursuing every abduction theory, and employing the scent dogs to all surrounding properties, the Landespolizei regretfully informed the family that they had turned up nothing — nothing at all but a dead dog.

Sonya broke.

She was decimated. She was completely empty and full of pain at the same time. She stayed in bed, silent, for days on end with a blur of voices talking at her and insisting that she eat. At one point, she thought how funny it would be to just eat everything in sight to spite them.

Now, two months after the pub night that destroyed her life, Sonya had no capacity to manage her thoughts and emotions. Her heart was a million shards of broken pieces — each piece a memory, a question, a fantasy, a prediction — all seeming to cut into the other and slicing her insides the more she tried to swallow them down. And her mother. The unforgivable things she yelled at her mother. It made her stomach turn to think of how she blamed her. She winced at the sight of her mother's face singed in her mind's eye. Nothing but guilt burned into her conscience. *Oh mama, I'm so sorry! I know it wasn't your fault.* Sonya's thoughts smothered her by day and taunted her by night, rendering most nights sleepless or, at best, a restless four hours. *What happened to my baby?!*

*

JANUARY 1990 — ONE AND A HALF YEARS LATER.

Ingrid Braun lay on her back in her bed. Her white-haired head was propped up by several pillows. She opened her eyes and stared at the ceiling. Then, reaching to the nightstand beside her, she grabbed the oxygen mask and placed it over her nose and mouth. Switching hands to hold the mask in place, she reached over and turned the small, blue wheel at the top of the oxygen tank. With oxygen now flowing, she rested back down into her pillows.

Oma Braun had aged a decade over the past one and a half years. Guilt and shame ravaged her psyche and devastated her body from the inside out. She could hear Ishi's little voice: *"Not the blue ones ... They were poisoned by the Bad Witch."* She shook her head as if it would shake the memory free. She fought against all assumptions about her missing granddaughter knowing that the worst possible outcome was probably the most likely. Ingrid did her best to seek solace in her faith — to trust that God would return Ishi to her heart broken Sonya. Although Sonya had forgiven her, she would never forgive herself. Never. It was the eternal price she would willingly pay to assuage the immense burden of guilt. She reached a hand to the oxygen tank and turned the wheel slightly more closed — the high flow noise was giving her a headache. *Trust,* she told herself. "Faith," she sighed aloud. There was still a strong determination in Ingrid to believe that Ishi might be found.

Nearly every time the local doctor made a house call, Ingrid would ask him, "Have I ever told you about my granddaughter? Oh, she had such an imagination. The games that little one would create ... she went missing, you know. I was out on a date with my husband and —" Sometimes, Ingrid's dementia would conflate events or even have her believe that she was a different character in that night's story. The doctor always calmed her with warm smiles and encouragement, knowing the dementia was taking its hold, with quickening pace, on the dear, heart-broken old woman.

Ingrid heard the familiar knock on the door, and then listened for the door to open as the doctor let himself in. She heard him stomp his boots on the mat to shake off the snow.

"Hello," the friendly young doctor's voice called in a happy, sing-songy manner. "It's me, Frau Braun." Momentarily, in socked feet, the doctor appeared at the side of her bed with a replacement oxygen tank in one hand and the traditional black leather doctor's bag in the other. "How are you feeling?"

She removed the mask to answer, "Same."

The doctor competently changed the fittings to the new tank. Then, he reached into his bag and produced a small container of medicine. "A new supply of pills, Frau Braun," he said, while screwing the cap off and peeling away the seal. "Has Diane been by with lunch yet?" he asked.

"No. I'm not hungry anyway." She stiffly hoisted herself up into a sitting position. "Were you able to get my money? He told me all I needed was that form."

Ingrid had decided to withdraw all seventy-three hundred euros from her bank account in Philippsthal. Knowing that it would be extremely difficult for her to complete the task, she had arranged that the doctor stop by the bank and pick up the applicable proxy form. Also a certified Notary, the doctor brought the form he'd been given to the previous visit. Ingrid signed it, and he notarized it — thereby giving the doctor the authority to withdraw from her account.

He reached into his bag and withdrew two bundles of euros each wrapped with an adhesive paper band. He set the money on the nightstand. With brow furrowed, the doctor asked again, "Are you certain you don't want help with that?"

Ingrid had previously explained to the doctor that her money was of no use to her, and that she had decided to divide it, as gifts, to family members.

Considering her dementia, the doctor felt somewhat uneasy about her plan so, inquired about the family members and if they had asked for money. She emphatically assured him that they had not. When he tried to collect more details to round out an assessment of the situation, his questions were answered, quite curtly. "That's not your concern, young man!" As can be the case with dementia, the doctor was confident that Ingrid's financial literacy remained intact, and she was still rather astute with money matters. Her dementia seemed to only attack her emotional cognizance and, even then, he usually noticed it more when she'd had very little social interaction.

"Three hundred of that is yours," she told him, with a smile. "For helping me."

"That's very thoughtful, Frau Braun, but I'm happy to help. Besides, I can't accept gifts from patients. You're not trying to get me in trouble, are you?" He gave her a wink and a grin.

Later that same day, Diane came by to tend to Ingrid's household tasks: dishes, sweeping, dusting, and anything else that needed to be addressed. Just after Diane left, Ingrid got to work. She moved from her bed to her big armchair taking time to be thankful for her mobility, limited as it was, and her reasonable balance. She just had to be sure to take her time.

Ingrid sat with pen in hand and a notepad on her lap. Both small side tables, flanking the armchair, were full of euro bundles, two white plastic grocery store bags, string, packing tape, light twine, a felt marker, and a roll of wax paper that had unrolled from the small table and onto the carpet. The oxygen tank sat beside the chair, and Ingrid's oxygen mask rested on the top of it. She wrote:

Dearest Isabella — my sweet Ishi,

I have lived under a mountain of guilt and shame since I lost you. Each day I have prayed for you and I continue to keep hope that you will make your way back to us. Should the day come where you find yourself back here looking for answers, please know that I have given you all I own. I imagine that I will no longer be here to see your beautiful face and hold you in my arms, so this is what I can do to show you my love. I hope this humble acreage, where you left with Honish so many years ago, will bring you some peace in your years and it has for me — that is, until that tragic night. I have had no peace since. It is important to me that you are the only person who receives this bequest. I have not even told your dear mother. As you will learn, and may have already, your father is not a good person; I want to make sure he can not touch what is meant solely for you. And here, too, you will find my cash savings. I know it can not make up for that horrible night — for falling asleep. I have nightmares about what you must have gone through and how you must have felt, sweet girl. I am so sorry, my dear Ishi. So very sorry. All I have is yours. I love you always.
Your Oma, Ingrid Braun.

She carefully tore that sheet from the notepad, folded it into quarters, and began writing on a new sheet: *Ishi my dear granddaughter; I pray you remember how you loved gathering eggs with me. That would make me so happy. If so, all is 'well'. Just look!'* Ingrid folded this sheet in half. She then wrapped the cash, along with the longer note, in the plastic bags; bundling it in two layers of wax paper, she then tied it, securely, with the string. The one-meter rope was attached to the package as this is how she planned to lower it beneath the platform of the hand pump. Once satisfied that she had prepared for the task at hand, Ingrid bundled up for the outside quest, being careful to take her time so as not to exhaust herself before she even made it to the well.

Had the doctor foreseen Ingrid's plan, he may not have agreed to it or, inadvertently, encourage it. Ingrid could only focus on how this intention eased the burden of her guilt by providing for her little Ishi. The idea struck her as the only way she could get money to her granddaughter whom, with each passing day, she convinced herself would return to where it all went wrong. Ingrid Braun had always been a clever woman, but the dementia did compromise her ability to process, accurately, the very poor odds that her plan would work.

With her oxygen tank dangling from her left hand and the package in her right, Ingrid trudged out into the bright snow. She reached the platform of the hand-pump well, she kicked most of the snow away with her boots, and placed down her items so her gloved hands were free to brush off the rest. She knelt beside one particular board, that she knew to be loose, and heaved on the end with both hands — attempting to pull it up towards her. But she hadn't anticipated that the ground would be frozen and, so too, the board. She pulled and grunted simultaneously with all the effort she could muster. Undeterred from the operation, she tried again and again — resting when she needed, putting the oxygen mask to her face. Exhausted, she tried one last time, yanking up the end of it. This time her efforts paid off and, with the board finally detaching from its frozen bed, she tumbled backwards. Ingrid laughed in delight at the accomplishment as she crawled back onto the platform. She lowered the package into the well and, making a knotted loop in the rope, she hooked it over the end of a rebar that jutted out of the concrete below. Lowering the board back into place hid the rope completely. Pleased with the outcome, Ingrid sat on the platform and took a few more healthy gulps of air through her mask before making her way to the chicken coop.

She hadn't been in this small building for more than a year — not since she gave away the last of her hens. She waved the cobwebs away as she entered, nearly being overcome by the thick and musty ammonia-air. Again, a few more full breaths. Ingrid proceeded to the nesting box, that was once Bertha's favorite, and, pulling the felt marker from her coat pocket, she wrote 'ISHI' on the front of it. Ingrid then unzipped her coat, reached into an inside pocket, and pulled out the shorter note. Pulling up the dusty old straw, she placed the note into the box, and let the straw back down to conceal it.

By the time Ingrid shuffled back to the house, she was completely spent. *Now, I must pray and pray,* she dedicated, as she crawled back into her cozy bed.

CHAPTER 9

TEN YEARS LATER, SEPTEMBER 2000.

Beethoven's Symphony No 6 in F major began very quietly. The volume of the music slowly increased. Sonya's eyes opened as her head remained on the pillow. The Bose Wave player that sat on the mantel above the fireplace five feet from the foot of Sonya's bed gradually increased the volume as Sonya's wake-up call. Her head still sideways deep in the feather pillow, Sonya looked toward the glass sliding patio doors and out into the small garden that was already alive with sunlight and flitting sparrows.

As Sonya trundled down the hall of their luxurious contemporary bungalow to the kitchen to make coffee, she realized that she needed to pee. She turned and retreated back to her bedroom and the ensuite. As she entered the ensuite, she saw herself in the large mirror before sitting down on the toilet. In her tussled brown hair, she noticed more gray that had annoyingly appeared. After flushing the toilet, she washed her hands and face, then examined herself more in the mirror. Sonya frowned, not at her decision to cut her hair to shoulder length several months earlier, but at the obvious aging in her eyes. It wasn't just the dark discoloration beneath her eyes. She ran her fingertips gently across the dark skin below her eyes. They seemed to be getting smaller. *I guess there's no treatment for that.* Sonya again headed toward the kitchen to make coffee. As she walked down the hall, she passed the open door to Joseph's bedroom. As usual, the bed was made, and Joseph was not there. Every weekday, Joseph got up earlier than Sonya, and headed to the office.

Arriving at the kitchen, she stepped over to the coffee bar, reached up to open the top cupboard door, and lifted down a tin of Verona dark roast coffee.

Her cell phone chirped! She grabbed it off its perch on the charger. "Morning," she answered dully.

Joseph's voice, "Get up!"

She snapped back, "I'm up."

"How soon are you coming in?" Joseph's voice carried a slightly urgent tone.

Sonya glanced at the silver star wall clock. The hands revealed 7:24. "I can be there, uhh, by nine."

"Okay, come straight to my office!"

"What's up?"

"Another delivery to Zarqa. You, this time."

"Why me?" Sonya's brows furrowed.

"I'll explain when you get here," Joseph abbreviated the call by hanging up.

As Sonya pulled her silver Audi A4 up to the front doors, she stepped out of the car and greeted the valet briefly as the valet stepped into the car to park it.

As she opened Joseph's office door and entered, Joseph was ending a phone call, and waved her in. She sat down facing him across his desk. "Why me?"

Joseph replied, "You and Matt."

"Why me?" Sonya repeated.

"Benjamin told me this morning that I'm too regular riding along on these shipments, and he's worried that it's beginning to draw suspicion."

"Ben came here! Tell me that Ben didn't come …" Sonya's face showed terrified expression.

"No, no. I met him at a car park. Stayed inside the cars," Joseph calmed her down. "Then I went to meet Yitzhak Biton's courier in the street behind the bank. He gave me both briefcases."

Sonya didn't like this. From the beginning many years ago, Sonya despised the entire situation, always dreaming of an escape. After the tragic events over eleven years ago … Then, considering her poor mother's guilt-ridden existence until her passing less than three years after Ishi's disappearance, Sonya had been able to think of almost nothing else but how to escape this insane life in Israel.

Recently, the risks had been escalating. Benjamin Sharod, the former Deputy to the Finance Minister, after the sudden passing of the Finance Minister, had been promoted into the roll of Finance Minister. And Sharod had recently been pressing Joseph and Sonya, besides running money on their usual Monte Carlo route, to run money directly into Jordan and Syria using the guise of furniture deliveries.

During a carefully encrypted three-way phone call between General Arruk, Benjamin Sharod, and Joseph Katz, Arruk had explained and stressed, "Urgent situations regarding the PLO's position with Israel requires action. Faster action! And faster funding that couldn't wait for the typical quarterly Geneva instalments!"

Joseph had pushed back hard, emphasizing to Arruk and Sharod that this was not what Joseph had originally agreed to.

But Ben had shut Joseph down with his big, controlled voice, "You'll thank me in the end. You'll be rich beyond your wildest dreams."

Nevertheless, Joseph had continued to protest during a three-way phone call.

General Arruk countered with a sinister four-word reply, "You will do this!" leaving no room for negotiation.

Naively Joseph angrily retorted, "You broke your damned promises already you snake. And now you think I'll just do anything you want! Go fuck yourself Arruk! I didn't sign up for this level of risk."

Sharod instantly interjected, "Joseph, Joseph, calm down Joseph,"

Arruk wasn't as delicate. "Joseph Katz you Jewish worm, you'll be sorry you talked to me in such a manner." Then Arruk had hung up.

"It is insane!" Sonya was terrified. "The risks are …" She put her face in her palms.

"It's in the left arm of the Arya Modular," Joseph stated.

"Matt driving? Or is there a third?"

"Matt will drive."

"I can't go!" Sonya was firm. "I have a doctor's appointment tomorrow."

"You will go!" Joseph's eyes narrowed.

"Damn you," Sonya spat the words at Joseph as she stood to leave. "I'm not going to do this." She was furious now, and marched toward the door.

"You will do this," Joseph replied matter-of-factly.

*

The white and green Mercedes twenty-passenger bus rolled down the final block of Völkershäuser Strasse, and turned left into the large, paved parking lot of the Johann-Gottfried School. With a squeal revealing that the bus's brakes soon needed attention, the bus doors folded open, and teens began to pour out. Among those teens was a pretty, slender brown-haired fifteen-year-old Ishi. She stepped down onto the parking lot and, laughing and bantering with two girlfriends, walked toward the school.

"Can you come over later?" Julia asked Ishi.

"Is Tomas going to be there?"

Her girlfriend gave Ishi a playful little shove, "No, silly!"

As they stepped up the two concrete steps to the front school doors, the other girlfriend Julia challenged, "Ishi, you don't have to always ask your parents every time."

"Yes, I do," Ishi answered as they disappeared through the doors into the school.

*

Rather than sitting, Horst stood as he drove a small W-6 International tractor pulling a swather through the two-acre alfalfa field. He stood so that he could more easily spot stones hiding in the alfalfa that could damage the swather.

This was the second of two cuttings this year, and the swaths were full. The weather had been perfect.

Horst sat down and stepped on the clutch, grabbed the shifter that rose between his legs from the metal floor, and shoved it into the neutral position. He grabbed his cane that was tucked beside the seat, and laboriously dismounted the small tractor. Then, with the aid of his cane, he walked to a spot four meters in front of the swather paddles and leaned down to inspect the weight of a big stone. Knowing that he'd need both hands, he let his cane fall. He squatted and lifted the stone. With hands full, Horst was unable to bend down to retrieve his cane. So, he very slowly and carefully trudged around to the rear of the swather and placed the stone beside several other smaller stones on a flat metal table of the rear of the swather. He'd dump these stones onto the stone pile later when he was finished swathing. He then returned to fetch his cane and returned to the tractor.

The past decade had been kind to Horst and Dagmar. Crops had been consistently good enough to supply feed for his small livestock variety. Horst's and Dagmar's health had been relatively good except for his bum knee that he injured during a trip and fall in the pigpen while loading pigs five years ago. But most of all, the joy of having a daughter, the deep satisfaction of being able to parent, that, just that alone has made each day of the past decade seem sunnier.

After adopting the little mystery girl, Horst and Dagmar stayed careful to never tell anyone that she was anyone other than their own natural child. Because their little farm was somewhat isolated, and because they'd never been very social with neighboring farmers or townsfolk, they were able to avoid questions when they did come. And of those several prodding questions that arose from time to time, Horst and Dagmar simply lied and explained that it was a home birth, one they had always prayed for.

It took Ishi only a couple of years for memories of her former life to evaporate. Coddled and comforted in her new home, Ishi soon believed that this was her true original home. As she learned to speak German and forgot any Hebrew, Ishi was entirely satisfied that Horst and Dagmar were her loving natural parents. Isabella Gruber. In a relatively short time after her discovery in the bale stack, Ishi had conveyed to Horst and Dagmar that her real name was Isabella, but that most people called her Ishi. As for her previous family name, as a three-year-old, Ishi didn't know.

Horst and Dagmar were so proud of Ishi's academic achievements too. Ishi was now in grade ten, and her report cards always proved that she was worthy of her parents' pride. However, occasional school field trips always made the Grubers a bit nervous. Ishi's track and field events made the Grubers even more nervous. Ishi's athletic accomplishments, especially in short and long-distance running, should have made her parents proud. Instead, they worried more about the extra attention Ishi's achievements might bring.

Over the past eleven years after each school day, Ishi had been delivered by bus to the end of the Gruber gravel-dirt driveway. Then after walking home up the driveway, Ishi would spend the rest of her day either doing homework or helping around the farm or writing poems, something at which she was actually very talented. It was inevitable though. Horst and Dagmar knew it. Ishi was growing into an age of wanting to date, to meet boys, to socialize more with her girlfriends, and to sometimes stay out evenings for those reasons. Horst and Dagmar knew that there was no way they could avoid the fact of Ishi's age and growing appetites.

CHAPTER 10

By 1981, at the age of twenty-one, Akeem Almasi had successfully run covert missions of destruction into the heart of Jerusalem's west side. As a young man, Akeem Almasi, using an alias, had been accepted in 1980 into the prestigious Jerusalem University College for studies in journalism. From that perch — over the course of ten months — he was able to mastermind four successful bombings in busy Jerusalem locations that included public markets, cafés, and synagogues.

Akeem Almasi was extricated back home to the West Bank in mid-1981. Recognizing his talent and achievements, he was immediately promoted by the fledgling intelligence arm of the PLO as a covert operative — a spy. Now, in the Autumn of 2000, Akeem Almasi's phone rang at least once each week as PLO's second in command, General Arruk, called on him for strategic advice.

*

From the park bench where Sonya sat to rest, she watched two joggers approach along the path to her right. She clutched her grip a bit tighter on the leash to Pippen — her four-legged Cocker Spaniel companion — lest the pet, in her puppyish eagerness, should be tempted to follow the passing joggers. Sonya had been jogging, too, but not as fluidly as many other joggers such as these two that just passed by.

At forty-one, Sonya felt somewhat embarrassed that already, at this relatively young age, her physical abilities were confiscating things — as natural to her as jogging — as more challenging. *But damn it!* She was determined to keep trying. *It's just that things have been so hard,* Sonya's mind would repeat.

Sonya gazed forward over the wide strip of grass, and across the beach, to the sparkling blue Mediterranean water. As beautiful as the Mediterranean was, Sonya harbored mixed feelings about that sea because it represented the hated quarterly journeys of crime. It represented the times spent aboard the yacht — with Ishi and without Ishi. Sonya's mixed feelings were daily and constant. In an effort to cope with her entire situation, she had become emotionally numb in most ways. As a result, she had avoided making friends, avoided many social events, avoided any further efforts trying to connect with that monster called Joseph — her evil husband. Sonya had, essentially, disconnected — period. She had never, in her younger years, been an extrovert per se but now, she knew that she definitely fit the definition of an introvert.

A middle-aged couple walked slowly along the path to Sonya's left. At approximately fifteen meters from Sonya, they came to a stop, and faced each other — as their voices raised into an argument. The woman was blonde with shoulder-length hair and a strange body with legs that were disproportionately short for her long torso. As her very skinny male companion appeared to be berating her for something, she was busy scrolling on her cell phone. Momentarily, she found what she was looking for and faced the phone screen toward her companion. Seemingly without consideration that Sonya could hear her, she snarled at the male, "You bastard!" Then she stomped off in the same direction from which they came. After a small delay, the male trailed after her.

"Okay," Sonya announced to Pippen, "Let's go!" She forced herself back up off the bench and began to jog again. Pippen, with her floppy ears, happily ran as far ahead as the leash would permit. As Sonya and Pippen passed the couple that had been arguing, a sudden musical tone announced a phone call. She stopped jogging, unzipped her fanny pack at her waist, and brought her phone to her ear. "Hello?" She noticed the couple noticing her answering the cell phone, so she turned her body away from them to ensure that they didn't hear her words.

"Where are you?" Joseph's voice was sharp.

"Jogging."

"Come to the office!" Joseph's voice commanded.

"Joseph, it's Sunday."

"Doesn't matter. It's important. How soon can you be here?"

Sonya sighed in distress. "When I'm done jogging, I can swing by on my way home."

"Come now!" Joseph's voice commanded.

"Why—"

Joseph cut her off, "Come now! Don't ask why!"

Having arrived at the office, Sonya freed Pippen from the leash and Joseph pointed a commanding finger at the chair for Sonya to sit down across from his desk. For no reason, except to display defiance, Sonya remained standing as she glared at Joseph.

"We're heading to Damascus tomorrow morning. Ben called me just two hours ago with last-minute instructions."

"No way! Not a chance!" She immediately stepped toward Pippen again — intending to reattach the leash and then exit the office. Sonya was furious!

"Sonya, I don't want this either."

"Then say no." Sonya tried to calm her voice. "By the way, who is 'we'?"

Joseph reached beside his chair into his briefcase, withdrew a file folder, and tossed it onto his desk. "We is we. Me and you."

Sonya's eyes widened with shock. "Nobody else with us?" Sonya's voice was a mixture of seething and trembling. "Why? I'm not doing it! No way. I'm not … this is crazy. This is too far. I'm—"

Joseph interjected, "I'll tell you what Ben told me. C'mon, just sit for a minute."

Sonya relinquished her defiant posture enough to sit down. She sat starkly straight in the chair — defiant, resistant, nervous, and frightened. "Why us? Why you and me? Why not Matthew, or Matthew and me?" Sonya didn't like the unusual orders.

"Five billion Syrian pounds is why. And government documents. Sonya, that's eight million euros — nearly ten million dollars. We get a percentage, don't forget."

"I don't care. I don't care if it's all the money in the universe. You know, as well as I do, that you're already flagged at the border, and it is highly unusual and suspicious that you and me — the two owners of the company — are doing the slave labor of running deliveries. No way, Joseph!"

"But —"

"But nothing!" Sonya shouted over him. "You'll end up getting arrested. Then I'll get arrested! We'll get searched. And busted. Then I'll end up in prison, too, if not executed. No way!"

"There's more," Joseph spoke softer.

Sonya just glared at Joseph.

"There's more," Joseph repeated. When no more words came from Sonya, Joseph continued. "Ben told me that, after this delivery, he wants to sit down with us and discuss an exit plan."

Sonya took a few moments to absorb Joseph's last words. "Exit?"

"Yes. An exit from this entire thing. Retirement. In luxury, Sonya." Joseph awaited her response.

After fifteen seconds, she spoke, "Does Matthew know?"

"Not yet. I'll update him next. Not about the exit."

Sonya remained seated, sinking back into the chair — somewhat into a posture of deflation.

"Honey, we don't have the option to say no. You realize that, right?"

Sonya had no more words. She just looked, blankly, off to the side — her thoughts so overwhelming that they no longer formed coherently. "This is where we die," she mumbled under her breath.

Joseph was already punching in Matthew's number. "Matthew! Are you alone? Can you talk?"

As Joseph began speaking with Matthew, Sonya muttered sourly, "… and don't call me Honey."

*

Joseph sat behind the large steering wheel of the white Renault Midlum 12-ton truck as they progressed east toward the Syrian border. The truck was loaded with a variety of furniture including sofas, armchairs, dressers, nightstands, coffee tables, and more. Throughout the night, Sonya, Joseph, and Matthew had modified a compartment behind the right half of the dashboard — to hold the documents and 3 billion Syrian pounds. The secret compartment was not large enough to contain everything. So, because the money was being delivered in two different currencies, Syrian pounds and euros, both the driver's and passenger's seat backs were modified to contain soft pouches with the five million euros. For an added emergency measure, a Walther PP handgun was put into the dropdown ceiling compartment mid-cab — that would ordinarily contain documents such as shipment manifests and truck permits. So that the pistol wouldn't fall out, or be obvious upon visual inspection, Joseph had installed a Velcro strap, as wide as the gun, to conceal it and to hold it against the very top of the compartment.

Years earlier, Joseph had asked Benjamin Sharod why money transfers couldn't be done electronically — with encryption. Ben had explained that absolutely every electronic communication in and out of Israel, involving currencies over thirty thousand shekels, was scrutinized. It was a law in Israel. And, if any such transaction was encrypted in any way different than the nation's banks' standards, the scrutiny increased tenfold. The risk was too great, and failure would almost be guaranteed.

Sonya, having been up all night, should have been tired. But her mind raced. None of this seemed right. Besides the insane risk of this delivery with Joseph, who might easily be flagged at the upcoming border station, the entire thing seemed off — seemed weird.

Joseph and Sonya continuously both monitored their mirrors and nervously scanned as far as they could see on the road ahead. Since passing through the small town of Chorazim, fifteen minutes ago, Sonya had noticed — in her mirror — a grey vehicle, some distance behind their truck. Once they had turned east onto highway 91, and the grey vehicle also turned east, she pointed it out to Joseph. "Looks like a Range Rover," Joseph had commented. At one point, the SUV had followed them a little bit closer but, over the past five kilometers or so, it had fallen further back. Nevertheless, both Sonya and Joseph kept their eyes on it in their mirrors. "Likely nothing," Joseph said to break the tension, referring to the Range Rover. Sonya felt a knot tying tighter in her stomach. Still keeping an eye on the vehicle behind them, she saw it turn left off the highway onto a side road and disappear from her mirror. "It turned off," she updated Joseph.

"Are we going to have an escort after the DMZ?" Sonya asked.

They were now halfway between Mishmar and Gadot — two towns merely a kilometer and a half apart from each other. Looking to her right, out of her passenger's side window to the south, Sonya saw where the flat fields drop off into a ravine half a kilometer away.

"Ben guaranteed it. But only after I demanded it," Joseph's voice was edgy.

As they passed through Gadot, Sonya could see ahead of them where the highway's upcoming curve to the south would lead them steeply down into the Jordan River valley. She had never been on this road before, but she saw, from the map on her phone, that they would descend down into the river valley for approximately half a kilometer, then hairpin to the left, and cross a bridge over the Jordan River one kilometer before reaching the DMZ line. Across the DMZ line, they will drive for thirty minutes to the war-ruined former capital city and now, sparsely populated city of Al Qunaitra. It is there that they will arrive at the border checkpoint.

Each of the four times Sonya had delivered a shipment out of Israel by driving north of the Westbank and across the border into Jordan on their way to Amman, she had seen the remarkable contrast of agriculture on the Israel side versus the uncultivated scrubland immediately across the border. Even though she did not have strong Israeli patriotism — due to the fact that she was German born and, even more so, punctuated by her fierce desire to escape the Middle East altogether —seeing the obvious agricultural productivity contrast did give her some sense of pride in what the Israeli people could do. She recognized the small, odd wave of pride each time, wondered about the feeling, and then justified it by reminding herself, *I have lived in Israel for a decade and a half, after all.*

They drove down the steep decline, around the hairpin, and, as the big truck rumbled onto the bridge, Sonya read the large bronze sign pinned to the right side concrete bridge post inscribed in both Hebrew and English: Gesher

Benot Ya'akov Bridge. Looking south, down the Jordan River, she noticed three children playing on a large, flat, homemade wooden raft. The raft was slowly floating southward with the river and Sonya saw that the floating raft would, momentarily, softly crash into two motorboats moored at a small dock. The truck was across, and they began to ascend steeply out of the river valley.

As they continued along the 91 northeast past three villages, each approximately one kilometer apart, Joseph suddenly announced, "He's back!"

Sonya glanced at Joseph and saw that he was looking in his mirror. Immediately, she looked at her mirror. The grey Range Rover was, again, behind them. Her eyebrows frowned. "That couldn't be our escort, could it?"

"No way. No chance a Syrian escort would start off on the Israel side."

They drove on. The terrain was so flat that, even from two kilometers, they could begin to see the small buildings ahead that made up the border checkpoint. They also saw that the grey SUV had accelerated and was immediately behind the truck. Sonya was terrified. "Something is wrong! Turn around! Joseph, stop. Turn around!"

"We can't. They've already seen us." Joseph tried to speak calmly — pointing his finger toward the border.

"Joseph! Stop! Joseph, stop," Sonya was nearly yelling. "It's all wrong!" They were now within one kilometer of the border, and Joseph let his foot off the gas.

"It's okay. It has to be okay. It's all coordinated," Joseph thought, out loud. "Ben has this figured out."

As the truck slowed, the grey SUV quickly passed and, once in front of the truck, slammed on the brakes. Joseph instantly slammed on the truck's brakes, but the weight of the load caused the big truck to hit the back of the grey SUV, slightly, before coming to a stop. A mere few hundred meters from the checkpoint now, Sonya looked at an assembly of uniformed men standing on the road there watching them from a distance. Suddenly, to the north, on a dirt road, both Joseph and Sonya noticed a black SUV approaching them at high speed in a cloud of dust. "Shit!" Joseph threw the shifter into reverse. But, before he could get the truck into reverse, the female driver of the grey SUV and a male passenger exited their vehicle — both with handguns. They immediately pointed the guns at the truck cab and began approaching. Sonya instantly recognized the short-legged, long-torsoed woman. "It's Mossad! I know that woman. Go! Go! Get us out of here!"

The black SUV arrived and screeched to a stop on the pavement — the cloud of dust following and enveloping all three vehicles. Joseph engaged the reverse gear. The truck lurched backward. Joseph cranked the steering wheel and the truck nearly tipped over as it veered sharply to the left ditch. Sonya screamed as the truck rocked and then, settled quickly back onto all four wheels.

Through the clearing dust, they could both see that the two men from the black SUV were also armed — one with a machine gun. All four assailants ran toward the truck with weapons up and aimed. They yelled orders at Joseph and Sonya. Sonya could only assume that the orders were to get out of the truck. Joseph struggled, and failed, to get the truck shifted back into a forward gear. In panic, Sonya threw open her door and jumped out to run. As she jumped out, she yelled to Joseph, "Get out! They'll kill—" Her words were drowned out by distant, rapid machine gunfire. As she ran down the highway and toward a ditch, trying to keep the truck between herself and the assailants, she glanced back over her shoulder and saw Joseph jumping down out of the cab through the passenger's door. He ran — following her. More machine gun fire. *From a distance?* That didn't make sense to Sonya as she ran. Then she heard return machine gun fire, from nearby, and realized that the distant border patrol and the Mossad assailants were exchanging gunfire — although, at a distance that made the gunfire ineffectual and, mostly, just threats.

As Sonya raced off the pavement, and downward into the shallow ditch, she tripped and fell forward — sliding on her stomach and face along dry rubble and stiff dry grass. There was a deafening explosion! A split-second later, a rush of searing hot air blasted past Sonya. Laying on her stomach, Sonya turned to see their big delivery truck, mostly the box of the truck, dissolving in flames from the explosion. The explosion impact had launched Joseph into the air and he landed in a crumple on the pavement. Sonya's first thought, *A bomb in our truck? There was a bomb in—* Swish! Another explosion, on the other side of the burning truck. It suddenly occurred to Sonya that one of the SUVs had been blown up. The jet-sounding swish was from torpedoes. She scrambled to her feet and, while trying to see through the smoking and burning truck to evaluate the threat of her exposure, ran up out of the ditch to Joseph. He was writhing in agony, but alive. Sonya was relieved. From his position curled on his side, Joseph raised his head, slightly, to look back at the mayhem. "The money," Joseph wheezed. Sonya, confused, just stared back at Joseph as he turned his head toward her. "Get the money!"

Sonya stared at him, unable to organize her thoughts. Then she reached down and carefully turned Joseph onto his back, drawing wails of pain from him. "Where are you injured?"

Joseph replied, through gritted teeth, "I don't know."

Sonya quickly examined him and the pavement for blood. She saw none.

"Get the money!" Joseph's voice was stronger now.

"And then what? How?"

Joseph could see past the burning wreckages from his vantage point low at pavement level. He examined the scene for two more seconds. Sonya stood back up and put her bloodied scraped hands to her face in the despair of not knowing what to do. "There's no one there," Joseph concluded, still looking underneath and past the burning truck. He attempted to stand up, and failed, but screamed in pain as he put both of his hands on his left hip.

Sonya looked toward the truck. The truck box was almost fully in flames, but the cab was still mostly intact. The entire cab bent forward, unnaturally, and doors hung open. Suddenly, without giving it more thought, she raced along the pavement back to the truck. Arriving at the truck, she felt the intense heat of the fire. Holding her shirt up as a curtain to the flames, she quickly looked through the front of the slanted cab trying to see through to the other side. All she could see was the front half of what looked to be an intact grey SUV. She quickly stepped to the front of the truck and inched across along the front bumper to get a better look.

The black SUV was totally engulfed in flames and smoke. To her horror, she saw two bodies lying beyond the burning black SUV — both bodies incinerated and lifeless. And Sonya could see the group of soldiers, a few hundred meters away, shouting at each other with animated arm gestures, grouping, and beginning to load into a topless Jeep. A desperate idea came to Sonya. She retreated, quickly, to the passenger's side, around the hanging open door, and stepped on the now-angled gas tank to climb up into the sweltering hot cab.

The heat of the inferno, just to her left, caused her to retreat back down, twice, before she tried again to climb up — this time holding her shirt up as a shield. Quickly, she looked around for a knife. Already knowing she wouldn't find a knife, she looked at the broken mirror glass. Then, she spotted a piece of broken mirror glass laying on the door sill right beside her foot. Knowing that the glass would be too sharp to handle, Sonya quickly peeled her shirt off. Wrapping the shirt around her hand, she grabbed the glass shard and, quickly, began cutting the seat back apart.

Sonya was too panicked in the moment to think of doubts. Between slicing actions, she glanced back to see Joseph attempting to stand again. Then she looked through the driver's blown-out window and saw that the soldiers were almost completely loaded into the Jeep. They were attempting to also load in a handheld rocket launcher — the rocket launcher that certainly had created these explosions. Sonya hurried! Her hands shook in desperation more than fright. Pulling the vinyl forward, she extracted four attaché-sized soft pouches and tossed them down to the asphalt. As she looked down where the pouches landed, she saw the gas tank. *Oh!* The wave of realization caused her to nearly pass out! *The gas tanks!* Realizing that both tanks, on either side of the cab could explode at any moment, Sonya gasped and jumped clear and down to the road. In her jump, she placed a hand onto the door frame and instantly screamed in pain. Collapsing to her knees, beside the pouches, she quickly examined her hand. The burn marks were straight white lines where the doorframe burned her skin. Disregarding the pain, she tried to grab all four pouches — fumbling one and then two.

With two pouches, Sonya raced around the front of the truck toward the grey SUV. As she ran, she saw that the distant Jeep was now turning and starting to move toward her. She realized that she was now exposed to that approaching Jeep. As she plopped the pouches onto the SUV's front passenger seat, she quickly glanced to ensure that the keys were there. They were! Sonya looked back up to measure the arrival of the Syrian border guards. She had time! Her right hand throbbing with searing pain, she dashed back to the remaining two pouches, grabbed them up, despite the pain of grabbing them, raced back to the grey vehicle — this time around to the driver's side open door, and jumped in. As she landed into the seat, she realized the crunch of broken glass that she just sat on. She turned the key and threw it into gear. As the SUV began to move, Sonya confirmed the source of the broken glass by seeing that most of the SUV's windows had been blown out.

To get the SUV around the burning truck would be easy. But, with Sonya now aware of the threat of explosions from the gas tanks, she made a wider arc around that required her to drive partly into the ditch and then back up. As she drove back up from the ditch, she heard machine gun fire and several startling sharp thuds on the rear side of the SUV. Although the approaching Jeep was an imminent threat, Sonya was too frightened and too filled with adrenaline to assess the odds of escape. She was back on the pavement now and approaching Joseph. She was too hurried to be aware of her momentary advantage of being entirely shielded from further gunfire by the big burning truck.

As she pulled up so that the SUV passenger door was alongside Joseph, she screamed, "Get in!" Immediately, realizing that he could not get in, she jumped out, very quickly, without remembering to put the shifter into park. The vehicle began to move forward. Realizing her mistake, Sonya jumped back into the glass-filled seat and slammed the shifter into park. With the gritting sound of the abuse of the transmission, the SUV stopped abruptly. Sonya then ran around to the passenger's side and, with all her energy and piercing pain in her right hand, lifted Joseph up. With combined effort, Joseph opened the passenger door only to see the passenger seat piled with pouches on top of broken glass. They quickly shuffled to the rear passenger door, opened it, and, although the seat was covered with broken glass, Sonya helped Joseph fall backward into the vehicle and onto the bench seat.

The sound of the approaching military Jeep could be heard over the burning truck and the engine of their own vehicle as Sonya scrambled back around, jumped in, and stomped down on the gas pedal! The same moment that Sonya closed her door, a gas tank exploded behind them. The swoosh of instant hot air blasted through the grey SUV's broken windows blowing Sonya's hair forward onto her sweat-covered face. Sonya immediately swept away the hair that stuck to her sweaty face. They raced forward down the highway in the direction from which they came. Momentarily, she heard another explosion behind them, knowing that it was the second gas tank. Sonya glanced up to the unbroken rear-view mirror and saw that the Jeep had driven around the burning truck and was chasing after them. The military Jeep was too far behind for guns to be effective. As Sonya looked more carefully, to her horror, she saw the rocket launcher come into view above the height of the Jeep's windscreen. "Oh!"

"What's happening?" Joseph called from his laying position in the back seat.

"They're chasing us. With a rocket launcher."

"Fuck!"

Then Sonya saw a grey object in front of them flying low in their direction. "Helicopter!" Sonya yelled in horror. "Military," Sonya updated Joseph, as the helicopter and the grey SUV quickly closed distance. *But there's nowhere else to go, to turn.* Resigned to their fate, she kept the gas pedal to the floor. To her amazement, the grey military helicopter passed over them and out of her periphery. She glanced up to the rear-view mirror and saw that the Jeep full of border soldiers had already turned around and was racing away in the opposite direction. She drove on — constantly monitoring anything in her rear-view mirror.

Approximately twenty seconds later, as Sonya and Joseph advanced further away down the highway, she saw the helicopter landing at the location of the burning truck. She kept driving. Instinctively, she used her arm to wipe the sweat from her face — sweat that was continually blinding her by running into her eyes — she realized that her arm was sleeveless. Her shirt was still wrapped around her left hand. Using her agonizing burnt right hand, she unraveled the shirt from her left hand and wiped her face. Then she glanced back to check on Joseph. He seemed okay but was wearing a continuous expression of agony.

It was a nerve-racking twenty-five minutes of driving back west along highway 91 and then, south, down the major highway 90. Approximately two minutes south along highway 90, upon seeing a rest stop mostly hidden by bushes, she pulled in and stopped, leaving the vehicle idling. Sonya stepped, mechanically, out of the vehicle and pulled her dirty and crumpled shirt back on. She opened the rear door and, as much as possible, scraped glass out from under Joseph.

Beginning again, south down highway 90, they almost immediately approached the city of Rosh Pina; she couldn't stand the risk of exposure any longer. "I'm pulling off," she told Joseph.

"Where are we?" Joseph shouted over the sound of the wind blowing through the open side and back windows.

"Rosh Pina."

Sonya exited west into the city, and then continued along the main street through the small city — all the while studying signs and buildings for any medical clinic or at least a pharmacy. Seeing none, she drove on — noticing that the vehicle was increasingly saggy and not firm on the road. Sonya suspected a flat tire. Continuing through to the outskirts on the west side of Rosh Pina, the vehicle's tracking on the road felt completely sloshy. She decided to take a right turn into a mostly empty campground parking lot that stretched widely along the Rosh Pina River. The exit was none too soon. As she parked at the campground, and stepped out of the vehicle, she saw that both rear tires were nearly flat. *Likely a result of the heat of the black SUV explosion and fire,* she assumed. Sonya assessed that both tires were already too flat to drive any further.

"Sonya, where are we?"

"Just outside west of the city. Both rear tires are melted. One of them is almost completely flat."

"Shit."

Sonya stepped to the rear door and opened it. "How much pain?"

"Enough." Joseph was trying to sit up, his face betraying the pain involved in the effort. After two tries, Joseph succeeded in sitting up. "Look what I found." He held up a Glock 19 9mm semi-automatic pistol. "It was laying under the driver's seat." Sonya frowned as Joseph tucked it into his belt.

Ten minutes later, Sonya had handed Joseph two of the pouches. Together, they'd been counting euro bundles. They both frequently scanned the area for other people. "One and a quarter million per pouch," Sonya reported.

"Just as it should be."

Sonya, unable to make the past hour make sense, had begun to connect some dots. "It was a set up," she glared at Joseph. "They were going to take us at the border."

Joseph retorted, "What are you talking about, how do you—"

"That was Ben's exit plan for us. I've been thinking about it since you told me about the so-called exit plan. There is no exit for us." Joseph just stared, numbly. Sonya continued, "How could they just say thanks and goodbye? We know too much."

Joseph pondered Sonya's words. "They wouldn't blow up all that money and the documents."

"I don't think that was their plan. I think Benjamin Sharod and his gang wanted us to cross into Syria, then take the truck, and kill us. By the way," she pointed her nose indicating toward the SUV's missing glass, "we're pretty conspicuous with these windows blown out! Not to mention the bullet holes and flat tires."

"You don't know that!" Joseph contested. "I mean, why would they ... What about the others?" Joseph's thoughts dangled.

Sonya suddenly felt incredibly tired. "I don't know."

A wave of anger swept over Joseph as he recalled Sonya's earlier words, *It's Mossad! I know that woman.* "What did you mean when you said you know her? How do you know her?"

A black Range Rover SUV pulled off highway 90 into Rosh Pina and drove west along Ma'ale Gei Oni Street. The single male occupant's head rotated back and forth examining every parking lot as he drove.

Having determined that Joseph's hip was dislocated, Sonya, after scouring the riverbank, found a sturdy branch, and returned with it to the SUV. Joseph, using his fingers, pruned the branch as clean as possible in a hurry. He stepped out of the vehicle, putting his weight on the crutch. "Aaghhhhh!" Instantly worried about the volume of Joseph's cry of pain, Sonya looked along the dirt parking lot at a young couple that sat propped against the hood of their BMW, eating something. They were far enough away to likely not hear Joseph.

"We have to hide the pouches," Sonya stated.

Joseph glared at her. "Why? Why would we leave it for someone else to find? Are you completely daft?"

Sonya snorted back, "Whose vehicle do you think we're in?"

"I don't know," Joseph snapped back.

"Well," Sonya answered, as she stepped back around the rear of the vehicle and looked at the Israel license plates, "I doubt our Syrian escorts drive around with Israel license plates on their vehicles." She paused to try to connect more dots, remembering the familiar woman with the disproportionate body. "I think—" she began.

"I think I have to piss." Leaning hard on the crutch, leaving a trail of expletives due to the pain, Joseph began to walk toward a small group of bushes nearer to the riverbank.

Sonya continued, "I think we'd been made for a while. They had us under surveillance. That explains the woman."

As Joseph progressed with groans toward the bushes, he called back over his shoulder, "Then why wouldn't they just arrest us?"

Sonya had an ah-hah moment! "Trying to catch us red-handed. That's what they were trying to do!" It was all too much too fast. "I don't know. Maybe they … I don't know." Joseph disappeared behind the nearest bush twelve meters away.

Sonya called, "So what do we do now?"

"I don't fucking know!"

"Well, we have to get away from this vehicle," Sonya shouted back. "I'll call a taxi." She reached to her pants pocket and, immediately, felt that her phone wasn't there. A flush of panic crossed her face. "It's in the truck," she quickly assumed in despair. Sonya quickly bent down into the grey SUV to scour under the seats in desperation for her phone — not expecting to find it. As she looked under the seats, she noticed the BMW, and the young couple, exiting the parking lot. She sighed in relief.

As Sonya was searching under the seats, a black Range Rover slowly, and quietly, pulled off the main street and into the campground parking lot. The driver, identifying the damaged grey SUV immediately, pulled up straight toward it, and stopped. Sonya, hearing the vehicle, pulled herself back out of her search, and looked around. Her heart stopped cold as a man stepped out of the black vehicle, pistol raised and trained on Sonya's head. He stepped forward cautiously. "Do not move!" He stepped closer. "Put your hands in the air! Now!" he shouted.

Sonya, too scared to speak, raised her hands.

"Where is your husband?" The man was a fit mid-thirties agent. Sonya was sure he was Mossad or Shin Bet. "Where," the man raised his voice, "is your husband?"

Sonya's voice trembled as she tried desperately to lie confidently, "I'm alone. I have no husband."

The man took a step closer, "We know who you are Sonya Katz. Where is your husband?"

Sonya's legs threatened to give out. She answered in a whimper, "He was killed in the explosion."

The man, gun evenly trained on Sonya's head, asked with a commanding voice, "You will tell me who hired you, Sonya Katz." The man, gun still trained on Sonya, stepped backward until he could reach into his vehicle. He leaned in slightly and produced a police style radio handset. "We know who you are, Sonya Katz. But we don't know who your Israeli connect—" He caught himself giving away too much. "Who do you work for?" He pushed a button on the handset, and began to speak, "Wills, Agent Shora here. I—"

A sudden shot! The agent's immediate expression was of shock as his gun flipped up and out of his grip, a bullet tearing a hole into his heart. The agent collapsed onto the dirt parking lot, lifeless. Joseph stood, mostly concealed by the bush, gun still raised, shocked by what he had just done.

CHAPTER 11

Joseph had always kept the yacht moored at Jaffa Port instead of the Tel Aviv Marina — to keep away from associations of notables that always use Tel Aviv Marina because of its glamour factor, and the luxurious Hilton Hotel, and high-end restaurants there.

They couldn't risk stopping by the house. They couldn't risk airports. Joseph and Sonya, Sonya at the wheel, intended to drive straight to their yacht. They realized that it would only be a matter of a short time before the black Range Rover they'd borrowed from the slain Mossad agent would be identified. They could only assume that every available police service in Israel, and every Mossad and Shin Bet agent would be doing the utmost to find this black SUV. Time was definitely of the essence.

"They don't know about Benjamin," Sonya reminded Joseph, several times, as they drove the two hours down highway 90, then west on the 77, then south on the main highway 6 to Tel Aviv. The prayer in Sonya's mind, the only desperate prayer that mattered now, was that the incident at the Rosh Pina Campground was not discovered quickly. "We should've put him in the river." She had dragged the dead agent's body into the tall grass along the riverbank, but Sonya worried that it was too discoverable. "He was on the radio. They will have heard. They'll know." She felt sick to her stomach. As they drove, determinedly within the speed limit, Joseph's utterances were merely desperate profane mutterings. Sonya was silent. But the pressure was terrible!

They stopped, very quickly, as they were driving through Tel Aviv. Sonya, having seen a pharmacy, ran inside and purchased three containers of Extra-Strength Tylenol, cream and gauze and wrap for her burned hand, and a cane.

As she exited the pharmacy, she saw a clothing shop a few doors down. Quickly, she walked there and bought a shirt for both Joseph and herself. She had also quickly scanned there for sport jackets for each of them but saw none. By the time they neared the harbor, the Tylenol had already helped Joseph. But he was still very much in discomfort.

Sonya and Joseph were desperate to park as close to the yacht as possible. "Park as close as possible!" Joseph commanded.

"Hey, I have an idea! I'll try to park as close to the yacht as possible." Sonya's bitter sarcasm was toned with fury.

As Sonya steered the SUV through the parking lot toward their moorage spot, Joseph said, "Try to park in between lots of vehicles." Sonya suddenly saw an available spot and lurched the vehicle to the left and into the space. "Aaghh," Joseph yelled in pain. "Fuck!"

Joseph was physically useless to help carry anything. He could only limp himself to the yacht with the new cane. Sonya knew that, after her repeated dashes from the black SUV to the yacht with the four heavy Euro-laden pouches, she would have to, as quickly as possible, prepare the boat for sailing. That would require running the bilge pump, idling the engines for a two-minute warm-up, untying the dock lines, confirming the zero-speed stabilizers, and bringing the anchors up. Neither she nor Joseph remembered how much fuel was in the tanks, but they agreed that it likely wasn't much.

Within ten minutes, after struggling with his balance on the passerelle, Joseph was aboard. He slowly, and carefully, laid down on a cushioned bench on the main deck, letting the cane tumble down to the deck floor beside him as he groaned and groaned.

Sonya had had many years of learning to pilot this very large boat. Fully capable, and as soon as she saw that Joseph was aboard, she throttled up slightly, put the shifter in reverse, and backed out. The Harbormaster's old, cracked voice came onto the radio speakers, "Report, please!"

Oh, Sonya remembered, *I need to report out.* She stepped to the left side of the silver and black leather steering wheel and grabbed the VHF radio hand unit. "Isabella Two on exit. Twelve to twenty-four hours. No waypoint." As she pushed the gear shifter into forward, she reached for the throttle and nudged it up slightly.

"Confirmed. Pleasant sailing," came the Harbormaster's response.

The yacht stopped its backward motion, and smoothly transitioned to a slow forward motion. "Damn it," Sonya grumbled quietly. Ordinarily, she was a big supporter of the marina's very slow speed limits but — today — these were painful limits.

As they had driven between Rosh Pina and Tel Aviv, Joseph and Sonya both agreed that the Wardieh Marina at Beirut, Lebanon, would be the best place to moor the yacht. From that marina, Sonya calculated that it would be a twenty-five-minute taxi ride, south, along the 51 through Beirut to the Beirut-Rafic Hariri airport. The sailing from Tel Aviv to Beirut was one hundred and ten nautical miles. In good, normal conditions, Joseph would often run Isabella Two at a top cruising speed of thirty-five knots. Today, Sonya held the speed quite consistently at forty knots, reducing the travel time to only three hours.

During those three hours, while Joseph swallowed more Tylenol and yelled occasional curses about their situation up toward the bridge, Sonya kept both the 2-way radio and the AM radio turned up to see if there would be any mention of them — or any mention of the explosions at the Syrian border. There was no mention of either. And so, Sonya's stomach and head hurt with pressure of not knowing if they were in the clear, somewhat, or if Mossad or Shin Bet was on top of them, or if they'd simply be apprehended at either the Wardieh Marina at Beirut or at the airport.

She found it easy to tune Joseph out. The insane pace of events had her mind in a whirlwind state that had no room for measuring her hate for the man that had created all of this for their tragic marriage, for her life. From time to time, the realization of the past eight hours swept over Sonya like shockingly cold, crashing waves. They had been the target for assassination. They had witnessed at least four others get killed — incinerated. And they had murdered an Israeli agent. *No*, she reconsidered, *Joseph murdered the agent.* Nevertheless, trying to pass off the killing to Joseph gave her no sense of consolation or relief, even if she hated her husband viciously. Her stinging left cheek caused her to touch her finger to it. The earlier headlong fall into the ditch had scratched her cheek but, thankfully, it hadn't broken skin or caused bleeding.

Hours later they arrived at Beirut-Rafic Hariri airport, exited the taxi, and Sonya, arms full of pouches, immediately walked past two armed guards at the entrance and into the terminal to find a motorized valet for Joseph. As she walked, she sneaked glances up toward the high ceiling to try to spot surveillance cameras. She saw many cameras but realized that looking toward the cameras would only create suspicion. She was determined to not look up at all. "So tired!" she said muttered as she walked. She found a row of chained-together scooters. Approaching the attendant at the kiosk, she rented a four-seater — using Euro bills only — and drove it back to the doors that Joseph had hobbled up to. Painfully, he got into the passenger's seat. In a sudden, panicked voice, Joseph exclaimed, "Where are the pouches?"

"On the floor."

Joseph, proving his exhaustion, looked around on the terminal floor and then back at Sonya confused and worried.

"Behind you. In the scooter." Sonya glanced at Joseph just in time to see him squeeze his eyes closed as a sign of exhausted relief.

They wheeled close enough to the ticket counters to read the incoming and outgoing flights on the massive black electronic wall behind and above the ticket counters. During their flight from Rosh Pina to the yacht, Joseph and Sonya had discussed possible destinations — between sporadic bursts of recapping the events in an effort to try to understand some of it. Some of those bursts were full of panic. Some were full of anger.

They had mentioned Germany, but Sonya said that Germany would be too obvious for searchers, given her heritage. Joseph had agreed. South American cities were mentioned. Having heard too many negative things about crime in Brazil and Colombia, Sonya stated her distaste for those choices. But Quito, Rio De Janeiro, and Lima were possibilities. Anywhere in the UK or the United States were quickly dismissed. Joseph stated, emphatically, that those countries' ties with Israel were too close. Montreal, Canada was mentioned as a possibility. They had not decided on a destination. Sonya had suggested that they should quickly assess based on next flights out, upon arriving at the airport. So here they sat, five million euros on the scooter floor behind them, two countries searching for them, and without a chosen destination to flee to.

Miami to Havana would leave in four hours. "That's too long," Sonya stated. Marseille, France would leave in two hours and twenty minutes.

"Too long," they said, nearly in unison.

"Christ!" Joseph was panicking. Chicago to Vancouver leaving in thirty-five minutes. "That's the one," Sonya pointed out. "Vancouver through Chicago leaving right away!"

"Vancouver?" Joseph wasn't sure. "Canada?"

"Yes," Sonya replied. "I've read a number of times that Canada will let nearly anyone in. They don't scrutinize like some other countries."

Joseph was hesitant. "It's not Vancouver that concerns me. It's going through Chicago."

Sonya stepped out of the scooter. "Give me your passport!" Joseph produced a passport from his shirt pocket and handed it to Sonya. She walked toward the ticket counter. She suddenly became aware of the sweat running down from her forehead toward her eyes. She wiped it away quickly.

*

The mood was dark and intense at Kiryat Arba Regional Council Building in Hebron, Palestine. Major-General Tariq Al Khalil stood at the head of a small boardroom table, leaning forward with long fingers spread like tripods on the table. His deeply lined, stern face glared, in anger, at the four other uniformed turbaned men sitting on both sides, two per side.

"Trying is not good enough!" he shouted, with rage, at sixty-two-year-old General Arruk who sat furthest from him on his right. Arruk peered at his younger boss, his glass eye fixed, his real eye narrowed, the deep lines on his very dark brown forehead furrowed, "Yes, Major-General—"

"Shut up!" screamed Al Khalil. "No words! I know what happened. You've explained it four or five times. I want them found. Now!"

A younger man, nearest on the left side of the table, dared to speak. "Major-General, if you will allow me, we are employing absolutely every resource.

And, I should add, we have the advantage of gleaning the intel from Israel's side through Benjamin Sharod."

Major-General Tariq Al Khalil spat on the table in fury, "Sharod will be blown. Benjamin Sharod will be a damned target if we don't find those two now! The whole network will be blown!"

General Arruk, elbows on the long table, leaned his pointy chin on his thumbs, taking some moments to restrain his hatred of the Major-General. Then he turned his narrow face with his glass eye, and a sunken small eye, toward Major-General Tariq Al Khalil and said, "We have all our friends in the area on alert. All the ports. The airports."

"How far?" Tariq asked sharply.

General Arruk answered quickly, "All the way up the coast to Turkey and to the Saudis."

Major-General Tariq Al Khalil sat down, folded his hands on the table in front of him, seemed to study his hands, then said, "We don't know enough about those two Katzes. Learn more! Learn more! Learn everything!"

Arruk snarled, "That Joseph Katz was a mistake right from the start. He's nothing but a Jewish demon. I'll find him and kill him myself, with great pleasure. With my own bare hands."

Major-General Tariq Al Khalil stared at General Arruk. "Get it done then!"

Arruk replied, "I think Akeem Almasi should be in leadership on this."

*

Because of Joseph's injury, Sonya had made sure to buy all three seats in the row. That would allow Joseph room to spread out, as needed, to accommodate and, hopefully, alleviate somewhat the painful hip. Because they had no other luggage, Sonya carried three pouches and Joseph carried one pouch, saving the other hand for the cane. Once they were airborne, the relief of their successful escape was so overwhelming that neither Sonya nor Joseph said anything. They just sank into their seats. As soon as Sonja saw only water down out of her little window, she pulled the blind down, reclined the seat the small amount that it would allow, and was quickly asleep. It had been more than twenty-four hours of sleep-deprived hell.

Her sleep was fractured. She woke up several times over the next few hours. Each time, she looked over to Joseph and saw that he was fully asleep. She again closed her eyes. During her sleep, Sonya's dreams were bizarre, and included odd mixtures of driving a burning army tank over dead bodies while trying to drive away from gunfire, parking the tank in their garage and then going inside to tend to pots and pans that were beginning to boil over on the stove, and rushing into the back yard to her mother's chicken coop to gather eggs. Most emotional of all, in her bizarre dreams, was Ishi waiting for her in the chicken coop, eager to help gather eggs. *I'm a good collectioner!* She woke up distraught from the crazy dreams, and clueless about how far along they were in their flight; she could not, and would not, close her eyes again.

Suddenly, Joseph bursts awake shouting "Where are you going?" swatting at the seatback in front of him. His words were the final remnants of a dream. He fully opened his eyes, realized his environment, and calmed down. Sonya quickly glanced around to see who had noticed. Nobody had. Both Sonya and Joseph were fully awake now. With groans and moans of pain, Joseph craned himself out of his seat to check the overhead compartment that contained the four pouches. Momentarily satisfied that everything was okay, with Sonya rising and stepping aside, he carefully returned into his seat, moaning expletives.

CHAPTER 12

Near the center of a row of pea green metal school lockers, Ishi stood at her locker, the door open. She was pushing her thick, grade 11, yellow algebra textbook into the very full compartment. To her right, she noticed Rebecca approaching her.

"I just heard," Rebecca announced in hushed excitement. "Christian is coming to Julia's party!"

"I know," answered Ishi with a coy smile.

Rebecca was slightly taken aback, "Ishi, how do you always know everything before me?"

Ishi clanked the metal locker door closed, spun the dial lock, and turned to her best friend, grinning, "I have spies working for me." She narrowed her eyes and glanced left and right playfully.

"I hate you," Rebecca pouted. The girls began to walk away down the hall together.

"I guess I'm going home," Ishi offered.

"What about volleyball?"

"Moved to Monday."

The brakes squealed as the small green and white school bus stopped at the end of the Gruber driveway. Momentarily, Ishi stepped out of the bus — several books tucked under an arm. As the bus left, Ishi turned halfway around and waved at the remaining students. She then sauntered toward the yard. After only several steps, she bent down to tie a shoelace, then continued walking.

After one and a half hours of struggling to do homework at the kitchen table, annoyed by the distraction of the TV game shows that her father was watching, she finally gave up and moved into the bedroom. It was the only bedroom in the three room, humble house.

Almost sixteen years earlier, by the time Ishi had been part of the Gruber family for a year, Horst and Dagmar had built an actual wall — separating the fairly large room into two spaces. The wall didn't go the entire length of the big bedroom but, instead, stopped a meter and a half short of the area by the door so that both spaces could freely use the door. It did, however, afford Ishi some privacy. The divided spaces still each held enough room for a double bed and a dresser.

Ishi began to undress and began to prepare to crawl into her cozy bed. In a long, warm night sweater, Ishi emerged again from the bedroom to go to the bathroom. As she passed through the kitchen, she glanced at her mother who was sitting on the sofa beside her dad. As her mom and dad watched TV, her mom was busy husking corn — throwing the husks into a large plastic pail. It was obvious that the jerking motions, made by the husking, annoyed Ishi's dad but he tolerated it. Ishi adored her mom for many many reasons. *Dad's such a gem,* Ishi swooned.

The next afternoon, all three of theCed Grubers were in the large vegetable garden behind the daffodil-yellow house. Ishi and her mom gathered potatoes into brown metal four-gallon pails. Her dad, half a potato row ahead of them, dug up with a spade — faster than they could keep up. Ishi straightened up, her pail full. "I have to get ready to go," she informed her mom.

From her stooped position, her mom asked, "Should papa drive you?"

"No, I'll take the bike. It's okay."

Dagmar straightened up and looked at her daughter. "But it'll be dark by the time you come home!"

Ishi lifted the full pail with a grunt and began walking toward the house. "It's okay. It's only a ten-minute ride."

Julia's family's two-story home, situated at the outskirts of Vacha, was very luxurious compared to Ishi's home. And it afforded lots of space for a good party. Ishi had never been jealous of the difference between their obvious financial situation. She adored Julia. Julia, Lucy, and Rebecca had always been the three friends that Ishi could tell anything to. All four girls shared many tears of sadness and laughter together. They had shared the most intimate secrets and wishes during their many school day afternoons sitting on the grass beside the school football field, watching the schoolboys as the boys played football.

Ishi sat on the second bottom step of the stairs by the living room. She had a can of Pepsi in one hand and a small paper plate of various cheeses in the other hand. Suddenly, the doorbell rang. Simultaneously, the door swung open. Dan and Christian entered — having rung the doorbell but not waiting for Julia. Ishi brightened!

"We heard there's free beer here," Dan's voice was loud and jovial.

Julia, standing in the middle of the living room chatting with two other girls, turned to Dan and Christian.

Light-heartedly, Rebecca called out from out of sight in the kitchen, "The only free beer for you is beer that you bring."

Dan was the more boisterous of the two. Christian was naturally more reserved. Ishi always liked that about Christian. They all attended school together, so nobody was unfamiliar with each other's personalities. Nevertheless, even though Ishi and Christian had been friends forever, Ishi found that she almost always became a little bit shy around him. She glanced from Christian to Julia. Julia was glancing back at Ishi with a wry smile. Lately, Ishi and Christian had been spending more time together and the crush they had on each other was becoming obvious. They found ways to pair up at events.

Sometimes lately, Christian would ride his bike up to Ishi's driveway. Ishi would see him there, would walk to the end of the driveway, and they would chat and laugh for fifteen or twenty minutes. Sometimes their end-of-the-driveway-mini-dates went so long that Ishi's mom would come out onto the porch, wave a tea towel to get the attention of the two teenagers, then call either for Ishi to come in and do her homework or sometimes invite Christian to come to the house for some snacks.

Shy or not, Christian saw Ishi as soon as he entered Julia's house. He approached and planted himself on the step beside her.

"Want some?" Ishi offered him some of her cheese.

Christian, in an effort to be a gentleman, replied, "Thanks. I'll get a plate." He stood back up and entered the kitchen. "Want anything?"

Just as someone turned the volume of the music up, as an afterthought, Ishi called after Christian, "Can you bring me some grapes?"

"Done and done," his voice nearly drowned out by the music.

It was eleven-thirty and Ishi was putting her coat on, while squeezing in some last few words with Rebecca at the door. Both Christian and another classmate, Eddie, stepped up behind Rebecca. Christian stepped past Rebecca and approached Ishi.

"Bike?" Rebecca assumed questioningly to Ishi.

"I'll come with," Christian quickly offered.

Ishi was slightly confused. "What do you mean? You rode here, too?"

Christian smiled broadly. "No, you ride. I'll walk. Or jog."

Ishi was astonished. "What?"

"It's dark out there. And cold." He already had one foot through the doorway, while sliding his jacket on, as he turned and called, "Thanks Julia! Loved the tiramisu!"

As Ishi mounted her bicycle, she looked at Christian, "It's twenty minutes on foot. More! Each way!"

Christian had already begun jogging. He called over his shoulder, "More, if you don't get going." He laughed. "Come on!"

Ishi began to pedal after her friend and tried to conceal a very satisfied smile.

It was a fairly bright night. Ishi and Christian were halfway to Ishi's home. Christian, exhausted, couldn't jog any farther. He began to walk instead. Ishi stopped and got off her bike to walk alongside Christian.

"Why are you escorting me? The party is still going, you know."

Christian stumbled a bit with his response, "Because. It's dark. I don't know. And all the monsters in the woods." He pointed scanning with his finger while grinning. They arrived at Ishi's driveway. Christian said, "Okay, I think I'm good to jog again." He turned and began to jog back to Vacha.

Ishi stood there watching him begin to disappear into the dark. She called, "Thanks! Careful of the monsters!"

Immediately, Christian turned around and ran back to Ishi. Ishi was confused. Christian slowed to a walk, then stepped up to Ishi and kissed her quickly and lightly on her lips. Christian then spun around and jogged away. Ishi just stood there, surprised, a wave of happy electricity passing through her.

*

A uniformed Palestinian hurried through a room of workstations, approximately half of them manned. As he rounded the last desk, his jacket brushed papers off the desk to the floor, drawing a guffaw from the middle-aged stern woman at her typewriter there. The officer continued on through an open office door — with his left hand pulling the door to swing closed behind him. Inside the office at a paper-strewn desk, General Arruk looked up, in stern surprise, at the officer who had just blown into his office.

"They had a daughter," the winded officer announced. "The Katzes had a daughter."

General Arruk just stared, his good eye widening in interest, waiting for more.

"And," the officer continued, "the daughter went missing in 1988. In Germany."

"Sit! Sit!" General Arruk was suddenly very accommodating as he motioned to the empty chair. As the officer sat down, General Arruk asked, "Brother, is she still missing? Is she alive? Dead?"

The still-winded officer held up an open palm facing the General as a way of communicating that he needed to catch his breath. "We don't know."

"So how did you learn this? This is interesting news!"

The officer answered nervously and eagerly, "The office searched every publication going back decades. They found, at least, three stories describing how Joseph and Sonya Katz's daughter went missing during a trip to Germany in 1988. We're still studying for more details."

General Arruk leaned forward, his face becoming more grim. His one good eye narrowed and focused on the young officer. "Manifests? Travel manifest?

I want an update. Now! I want to know if those two are still in Israel or not."

The officer's expression became a bit more sheepish. "Nothing. We've heard from everyone. But the Lebanese are not telling us anything — as usual."

General Arruk leaned back again, in his swivel chair, swiveled away from the officer to gaze out of his large window. "Nineteen eighty-eight. Three. She'd be, uhh, sixteen now?"

"Likely fifteen, General." The officer waited for his stern superior, with the arched long nose and the war-scarred face, to say something more.

"They are cursed by Allah," Arruk finally muttered, "those idiots in Lebanon!"

*

Matthew Mizrahi's family had a history of heart problems. While Matt had always been thankful that cancer, diabetes, and other ailments were not common in his lineage, he was well aware of the genetic heart curse. Three out of four of his grandparents died of heart failure. Two of his beloved uncles died of heart attacks while just in their fifties. And, only two years ago, his own father had a triple bypass that extended his father's life, but made it more tentative.

Matt looked at his lean, dark-skinned body in the mirrored sliding double-door of his closet. With the vertical blinds of his bedroom closed, and with only the yellowish light from the two bedside lamps, his white boxers made his skin appear even darker. He held his hand to his chest just above his heart. *That's where the pain is.* Matt murmured, frowning.

He walked to the bedroom's wood-framed glass door that led to a small balcony, grabbed the vertical rod that controlled the blinds on the glass portion of the door, and turned the blinds into an open position. November sunlight immediately brightened the room. Realizing that he might be viewed in his undressed state or perhaps viewed by wrong eyes, Matt turned the blinds closed again, stepped back away from the balcony door, and walked across the bedroom. He pushed open the sliding pocket door to the bathroom intending to shower.

It had been two months since Matt's world turned upside down — two months since Joseph and Sonya were killed in the missile attack at the Syrian border, and two months since Matt quit his job at Katz Furniture and fled. In a state of pure fear of being blown as a participant helping Joseph and Sonya help the PLO, he had quickly given up his rented apartment at Tel Aviv's city center and moved to Kuşadasi at Turkey's west coast.

He'd been to Kuşadasi twice before, both times on holiday trips. Matt had been impressed by the mix of Moslem culture and Western-styled openness that created a mosaic of people that Matt was sure he could hide in. So, without giving anyone including his landlord any notice, Matt withdrew all his savings, bribed a merchant ship's Captain to let him onboard, bid his world goodbye, and disappeared.

*

Within days after Joseph and Sonya going missing, Benjamin Sharod instructed the Israel Government, considering the large debts owed by Katz Furniture, to take control of the company. An appointed general manager stepped in to take over Katz Furniture two days after all the news channels described the tragedy at the border. The new general manager explained to the thirty-six staff at Katz Furniture that the company would be under new ownership and new management.

Benjamin Sharod, well aware of Matthew Mizrahi's involvement in the activities of the PLO through the Katzes, made several weak attempts to find him. Having been reassured by Joseph multiple times in the past that Matthew Mizrahi was never exposed to details or names of their sources in the Israel government, Sharod felt mildly satisfied that Matthew Mizrahi was not a great threat. Nevertheless, Benjamin Sharod informed his handlers in the PLO, at the Kiryat Arba Regional Council Building in Hebron, of the possibility that Matthew Mizrahi might have information that could lead them to Joseph and Sonya Katz.

The PLO weren't the only ones now looking for Matthew Mizrahi. Both of Israel's secret service agencies, Shin Bet and Mossad, had had Joseph and Sonya Katz on their radar for months prior to the catastrophe at the Syrian border. Shin Bet had, tragically, botched the attempt to catch them red-handed at the Syrian border, getting four of their agents killed. Shin Bet had hoped to bring Joseph and Sonya in for interrogation. And they also flagged the quick departure of Matthew Mizrahi from Katz Furniture as highly suspicious, convincing Jonathan Ben Dod, Mossad's Director, that Matthew Mizrahi was tied in. While Shin Bet's focus was more on internal Israeli affairs, Mossad's tentacles immediately stretched throughout the Middle East and Europe in an effort to find the former Katz Furniture shipping and receiving manager.

*

"She's alive!" General Arruk announced on his phone. "Get over here! We found the daughter. The daughter is alive!"

*

Major-General Tariq Al Khalil, General Arruk, Akeem Almasi, and two turbaned, bearded, middle-aged men in civilian clothing sat around the small boardroom table at the Kiryat Arba Regional Council Building.

"As you already know," Tariq Al Khalil said, "we can not let the Katzes continue to blow in the wind even after all this time. They know too much and can expose Benjamin Sharod, and our Israeli bankers, at any time — destroying everything."

General Arruk lit a cigarette and waited for the Major-General's next words.

"We know, through Benjamin, that Mossad has not located them yet." Major-General Tariq Al Khalil looked at each of the four men, one at a time. "You know what's at stake here."

One of the two men wearing civilian clothing said, "We do."

Major-General Tariq Al Khalil pushed his chair back and stood. He stepped to the window and gazed through it. "As you know, we don't have the complex international reach that other intelligence agencies do. Brothers, we have a new opportunity here. We need that daughter to find her parents." He turned back to the four men. "Our funding depends on it! The security of our network depends on it." As an afterthought, he added, calmly, "Benjamin Sharod and his two agents at the bank will remain in place for now."

*

The pain in Matt's chest lessened slightly as he showered. After his shower, as he shaved off two days of stubble, he made a mental note to pick up more aspirin later in the afternoon when he'd go out to find a doviz kiosk to change some currency.

In the two months that Matt has been in Kuşadasi, he hadn't dared leave his small, rented flat — except only a handful of times when he, carefully, walked to a food shop one block away. He bought laundry detergent there, too, and had been washing his laundry in the shower and sink. During those small shopping trips, Matt paid with the only type of money he had on him, Euros. But, in an effort to not draw attention to himself, he knew that he had to start paying with Turkish liras. And that required converting some Euros over.

After brushing his teeth, he put the brush down beside the toothpaste next to the small clock radio that sat on the counter beside the sink. The radio was plugged in far from the bed, a trick Matt learned long ago to make it impossible to hit the snooze button. He looked at the radio and considered turning on some kind of quiet music station. But he was not in the mood for music, any music. Seized by fear, he hadn't been in the mood for music, or for anything other than survival basics, during the two months of hiding.

Matt stepped out of the bathroom and froze! A man, dressed totally in black with a black balaclava. sat on the end of his bed holding a Glock 9mm handgun — the business end pointed at Matt's face. Matt's reflex was to step backwards into the bathroom. As he began to move, the man in black said, in commanding Hebrew, "Don't! Do not move!"

*

"Slow down!" General Arruk was listening to the panicky report over the phone from Benjamin Sharod. "You're talking too fast. Now first—"

"Mossad has Matthew Mizrahi. They found him in Turkey. Kuşadasi." General Arruk cursed, "Ayreh Feek! Benjamin. Hold it! You assured me that he's clueless."

"And I have no access," Sharod continued, his anger apparent in his voice. "We needed to find him first!"

General Arruk let Sharod's tone of accusation dangle as he leaned back in his chair, thinking, not speaking. After drawing a deep breath, General

Arruk responded, "I'm not terribly surprised. We don't have the resources that Mossad has."

Benjamin Sharod's voice rose again, "I said Mizrahi likely doesn't know anything. Likely. But he might. I could already be blown for all I know. General, I have to exfiltrate. Now!"

General Arruk's voice was steady but forceful, "You will stay right where you are, Benjamin Sharod! We have our plan, and it will succeed." He reached for the pack of Camels on his desk and lit one, breathed in, and then exhaled as he listened to a string of anxiety-filled "Fuck! I'm fucked! I'm dead!" shouted out on the other end of the phone. General Arruk asked, "Where are you?"

Arruk thinks I'm being overheard. Benjamin answered, "I'm in my home office."

"Okay then. Stay where you are for a day. Call in sick or something. Get a doctor to come by and write up a report that you're sick with … oh, a stomach bug or something. I'll get Major-General Tariq Al Khalil into a meeting in the next hour, and we'll call you with instructions within two hours."

CHAPTER 13

Although a PLO operative, Benjamin Sharod had a twelve-year-old daughter and an Israeli wife. He met his wife, Deena, during his fifth year living in Tel Aviv and during his first campaign while he was attempting to be elected as Regional Counsellor for Infrastructure and Finance of Haifa.

Israeli-born, Benjamin Sharod had a seething hatred for one thing in the world and an unquenchable love for one thing in the world. He despised his own government in Israel. Israel had given his family no honor, or compensation, when his father and brother were killed in the Six-day War in 1967 when he was only twenty-six. While a stipend and a one-time compensation was paid to all other non-Palestinian families so they could at least afford to bury their dead, Benjamin and his mother were refused because of his mother's family ties to Palestine. As a result, they were forced to take menial jobs for mere survival. At the age of twenty-six, when Benjamin's peers were excelling in their careers, his dignity was severely damaged. Although he rose up through the ranks at an accounting firm, enough to buy the firm within a decade, his fury at Israel was set in stone, although publicly buried.

Benjamin Sharod had a love for one thing in the world. Himself. He could envision nothing else except a position of power and influence. Although his public candor was always fair and good, his ultimate objective was power — power at any cost.

And so, when Benjamin Sharod was covertly approached by the PLO, shortly after he was elected as Regional Counsellor for Infrastructure and Finance of Haifa, he listened. And when he learned of the financial reward for his services, if he could attain a higher position in government, he was all in.

All in, with no real love for the PLO, and certainly no love for Israel. This was all, unapologetically, about money and power.

Sharod had run massive and expensive election campaigns. How he was able to afford such campaigning was never explained nor ever investigated. The extravagant spending did in-fact help him win the election. Sharod, with his business skills and interpersonal charm, had quickly gained the attention of a wider audience throughout Israel by creating some innovative initiatives for the common Israeli.

Within two years, Sharod was tapped by the retiring Deputy of Finance in the National Government to vie for his position, considering that the then Deputy of Finance was elderly and seeking retirement. This was precisely what Benjamin Sharod, and his secret overlords in Hebron, were hoping for. Perfect! Eight months later, after another massive and expensive campaign, Sharod won the vote and became Deputy Director to the Minister of Finance. Now, three and a half years later, Sharod was, himself, the trusted Minister of Finance. As a PLO mole with a lot to deliver, he ran two agents installed as governors at Israeli banks, and, until recently, also ran Joseph and Sonya Katz. Now Benjamin Sharod had a lot to lose. Deena and his daughter, Rosa, had been along for the entire ride but were, at no time, aware of his true loyalties. And now, it might all blow up — thanks to Joseph and Sonya Katz.

Benjamin visited the restroom after the family's supper. No sooner had he perched his big body on the porcelain, then Deena called, "Honey, it's for you."

"What's for me?"

"The phone," Deena called through the door of the main floor half-bath.

She only heard him grunt out "God damn it" and quickly wrestle with his pants and belt. Flushing, he bolted out of the restroom and headed for the short stairs that led him up to his office. "I'll take it in my office."

At his desk, without taking time to sit, he grabbed up the phone, waited a beat to confirm, audibly, that Deena had hung up the other phone, and answered, "Sharod."

The female voice on the phone flatly said, "Server four eight seven six."

They both hung up.

Benjamin reached for the mobile phone in his pocket, dialed the code given to him, and, momentarily, heard three electronic beeps. He then dialed a number.

"Benjamin," Major-General Tariq Al Khalil's voice was big and calm.

"Major-General."

Tariq Al Khalil spoke immediately, "Benjamin, you can calm down. We think we have this Matthew Mizrahi situation in hand."

Benjamin's brows furrowed. "What do you mean, 'in hand'?"

Tariq Al Khalil continued, "Well, Benjamin, it's going to require you to do some quick digging. Put your cursed bourbon down and get your brains going on this!"

Benjamin sat.

Tariq Al Khalil continued, "We are aware of two of Mossad's safe houses. We also know that there are likely more that we are unaware of."

Benjamin waited for more. Suddenly, Benjamin was struck with a question, "If you knew about two of Mossad's safe houses, why haven't you done something to destroy—"

"Because, Benjamin Sharod, we've been waiting for a rainy day."

Benjamin waited for more.

Tariq Al Khalil added, "I believe today qualifies as a rainy day."

"Yes, it fucking does," Benjamin blurted out.

"You, Benjamin Sharod, will control your tongue! You talk like an infidel."

After a quiet moment, Benjamin replied, "Yes Major-General."

Tariq Al Khalil continued, "Mossad safe houses must be paid for somehow. You have access to all the financial information. Grab a pencil. I'll tell you, right now, the addresses of the two known safe houses. We need you to dig deep into the numbers and discover which numbers correlate to those addresses. Then, using that information, determine if there are more safe houses, and where."

Benjamin pulled open a drawer and extracted a pen. He put it back and extracted a pencil. Not finding any paper on his desk, he dug a scrap of paper out of his trash can beside the desk. Then he said, "Okay, I'm ready."

*

Matthew knew he was in a basement. Besides the cold dampness of the room, even with the sac over his head, he could hear the squeaks of rats running along the walls near him. He laid on a cold concrete floor, terrified. He didn't know how long he'd been here. He had gained consciousness only a few minutes ago. He felt some hunger pangs though and assumed that he hadn't eaten in quite a while. His hands were cuffed to a metal pipe that ran horizontally along the bottom of a wall. The position of his cuffed hands made it impossible for Matthew to sit up. And that made the existence of rats much more ominous. In the few minutes that he had been conscious, he had heard the rats scurry very close up to his hooded head. He imagined how, at any moment, they would begin chewing through the fabric hood.

I don't even know if it's the same day, he wondered. *Why, if I've been captive for half a day, or a day, or two days, I don't need to piss?* At that same moment, he felt the soaked area of his pants. Then he smelled it, too. *Someone put my pants and a t-shirt on me!*

Suddenly, he heard a faint growl on the floor above him, and the patter of a big dog walking across the floor. Momentarily, he heard the noises of a door opening and the thuds of boots walking in on the floor above. The shuffle of footfalls told Matthew that more than one person had entered. The walking ceased, and muffled voices could be heard. But the floor above Matthew insulated him from being able to discern the words or even the language. A cell phone electronic tone! "Yes," a voice answered, in accented English. That's all Matthew could make out. The rest of the phone conversation was too quiet to hear any details.

The door to the basement opened, and Matthew heard the heavy thuds of two sets of boots walking down the steps into the room and then toward him.

"Oh look," exclaimed a whiney-pitched voice in Hebrew, "he couldn't find the toilet."

Laughter.

"Well," a deeper voice replied, in a deadpan flat tone, "you forgot to show him where the toilet is."

Matthew heard a metal scraping as an object, like a chair, dragged across the concrete floor in his direction. Then the hood was yanked off his head. The two ceiling lights that hung down, equally spaced in the cold empty basement room, blinded Matthew instantly. It took ten seconds of squinting before Matthew could see clearly enough to look at the faces of the two men. As Matthew focused, the bigger man took a seat on the metal chair that sat approximately three meters from where Matthew laid on the floor cuffed to the pipe.

"Where am I?" Matthew's heart raced as he tried to remain somewhat calm. "Who are you?"

The leaner man, with the shrill nasal voice, replied with a smirk, "I'm Tom. And this is Jerry. We'll be your hosts today. Our aim is to serve."

Matthew felt his blood run cold. The bigger man just sat gazing at Matthew.

The lean man continued, "You, Matthew Mizrahi, are the newest contestant in our little game show we like to call, What Will He Tell Us?"

Matthew's terrified face betrayed his total fear. The little man stepped close so that his metal-toe boots were inches away from Matthew's head. From directly above, the man added, "We need you to tell us who you answer to. We need you to tell us where Joseph and Sonya Katz are. We need you to tell us who your mole is in Israel's government." He turned and stepped back beside the chair where his partner sat. "See, simple questions."

Matthew responded in confused surprise, "The Katzes are dead. They died!"

"Uh uh. Nope."

Matthew was in shock! "Sure they did. It was all over the news."

As the bigger man stood and began to walk over to a darker corner of the basement, the little man said, "Ummm, good try Matthew Mizrahi. But, so far, you're not winning in this little game show." He smirked.

The bigger man bent down, picked something up, and began back toward Matthew. He carried a cage. Matthew's heart stopped and he nearly fainted as he saw the wire cage with several rats inside. "No! No, no," Matthew stammered, "You can't! I don't know anything. They're dead. I thought they died."

The bigger man finally spoke. "Let me explain how this works," he said, motioning toward the cage. "These rats haven't eaten anything in quite a while. They're hungry." He set the cage down near Matthew's urine-stained pants.

"The Katzes died. I thought they were dead!" Matthew screamed.

The bigger man continued, "Shh, shh, let me finish. You see, the bottom of this cage is just a bit of tin that slides out. We set the cage on your stomach, and—"

Matthew twisted and writhed in his horizontal position, screaming, "I don't have the information you think I have!"

The little man spoke up, "Question number two for contestant Matthew Mizrahi. Who do you answer to?"

Matthew immediately blurted out, "Nobody. I did answer to Joseph. But, as soon as he was dead, I ran."

"No, no. Maybe you misunderstood. Who do you answer to now?"

Matthew was at a loss to understand the question.

"That's okay," the little man said with a sigh as he sat down on the chair. "We're not in a rush. Maybe you just forgot. Take your time."

Matthew blurted out, "Nobody. It was Joseph. I ran. There is nobody else. I swear to God almighty!"

"Oh, don't swear like that," the little man chuckled. "Not in Israel, anyway."

"We're in—?" Matthew realized that they'd brought him all the way back to Israel. That explained his hunger.

The big man bent down and picked the cage up. "Okay, it's lunch time in the cage," he said flatly. The skinny man sat down on the chair.

"No! No!" Matthew writhed backward, harder against the horizontal pipe.

"Jerry! Jerry," the little man interjected. "Just hold up a minute. We haven't even given our contestant the third skill-testing question." The little man, with the whiney voice, stood and stepped up to Matthew, this time stepping partly onto his face with a big boot pressing down on Matthew's cheek. "Okay, Matthew Mizrahi, question number three. Who is your agent in parliament?" After a few seconds, he removed the boot.

Matthew answered immediately. "I don't know. I never knew. I know he's in there. But that's all I know. I never knew. Joseph never told—"

"Okay," the little man turned to his associate, "maybe it is feeding time in the cage." He looked back at Matthew's horror-filled face. "Do you think Matthew has the guts for this part of our little game show?" The little man laughed at his own pun. Then, without warning, he wheeled around swinging his leg with a full kick to Matthew's stomach. Matthew nearly fainted with pain. Three seconds later, Matthew's head was impacted with the full force of another booted kick. The pain was complete and unexplainable! Matthew was on the verge of passing out, but he didn't. He felt his legs being grabbed and dragged toward the center of the room. With his hands cuffed now above his head attached to the pipe, his shoulders nearing a position of dislocating and his body stretched into the room, one of the men stepped onto his legs, one boot per leg. Matthew was completely drained of energy. He cried, tears gushing down his bruised face, "I don't know. I don't know any of those things. I don't know. Please!"

The bigger man, with no expression, slowly let the cage down onto Matthew's stomach. He then pulled it back off and set it aside. "Oh, it's likely better if—" He reached down and yanked Matthews dirty sweat-soaked t-shirt up. He then reached again for the cage and lowered the cold metal of it down onto Matthew's skin.

"Turns out," the little man continued speaking while standing on Matthew's legs, "that you're not winning in our little game show."

Matthew was nearly unconscious now as he heard the little man's words. "I don't know," Matthew squeezed the words out. "I just don't know. Any of those things. I don't know."

The bigger man began to slide out the cage's metal bottom sheet. The little man chuckled, "Too bad your memory is so bad, Matthew Mizrahi. But think! Think fast! Who is your agent in parliament? Come on, man! The rats are hungry."

The cage bottom was completely out now, and the rats were beginning to sniff and nibble at the exposed skin. Matthew shrieked and screamed, writhing desperately. "I don't know!"

A mobile ring was barely audible through Matthew's screaming. The little man dug into the front pocket of his pants, producing the cell phone. He brought it up to his ear, and heard a wildly frantic voice, "Get out of there! Incoming mi—" The lean man began to look upward and heard a split-second whining sound, and then the explosion and blinding white ended everything.

CHAPTER 14

It was a drizzly early March afternoon in North Vancouver.
Carla Fostadt had just finished her laundry at the small laundry mat at West 15th Street. Just in time, too, because her dog groomer said he'd be finished grooming her Bolognese by three o'clock. After picking up Brewster, six minutes late, and then quickly returning to the laundromat to pick up her laundry, Carla needed to drive up to Lonsdale to fetch her nine-year-old daughter from school by 3:30pm.

Carla hurried out into the drizzle to her blue Kia Spectra that was parked on the street directly outside the laundromat. She set her full laundry basket on the car top and quickly opened the rear door before the laundry got too wet. Then she placed the laundry basket onto the rear seat beside Brewster, ran around to the driver's side and jumped in. Within seconds, Carla was driving, eastward, two blocks intending to turn north onto Lonsdale.

As she approached the lighted intersection, she glanced at her dashboard clock. 3:28pm. *I'm late.* She grimaced, *but tolerably late.* She looked up just in time to see that the light was already amber. "Auhg!" Not knowing how long the light had been amber, she decided to go for it. Then, reconsidering, she hit her brakes. Crash! Carla's head lurched backward against her headrest as the Kia lurched forward. Some of the laundry spilled into the front seat between the middle console. Brewster was tossed from the front passenger seat onto the floor where he responded with two scared yaps.

Shocked, Carla glanced up to her rear-view mirror to see the front grill of a white Ford SUV. "No," she half-yelled! She glanced at her side mirror and saw a middle-aged man getting out of the SUV. He was approaching, and obviously angry. Carla, somewhat dazed and scared, remained sitting with the window closed.

The man, his dark wavy hair glistening wet from the light rain, rapped hard on her window. Carla just sat there looking forward trying to think. The man rapped the window harder, yelling "What the fuck? Bitch, open your window!" Carla complied and opened her window halfway. "You slammed on your brakes; you idiot!"

The man took a few steps toward the back of the car to assess the damage. Carla slowly got out of her car, still dazed and confused. Brewster immediately tried to spill out of the car with Carla, but she quickly forcefully shoved him back inside where he obediently stayed. She had never been involved in a car accident, so she had no idea what was involved now. She looked at the man, who was bending over to more carefully assess the damage, looking closely at both his white Ford Explorer and the damaged Kia.

A woman got out of the SUV's passenger side, popped up an umbrella, and walked to the front of the SUV, also looking at the damage. Carla and the woman looked at each other. The woman could see that the younger woman's eyes were already brimming with tears, and that she was a mixture of emotions of fear and panic.

The man looked at Carla. "What the fuck were you thinking?"

Carla looked at him and then at the woman. "I'm sorry. I was—"

The woman cut in, "Sweetie, come over here. The woman took several steps toward the front of the Kia in a gesture for Carla to come over there where she was. Carla did.

"It's okay," the woman said, as she saw Carla's tears flowing. "Come here."

Carla stepped under the umbrella close to the woman who had an arm extended. The woman embraced the crying girl. "It's minor. It's no big deal." The woman released Carla from the embrace.

Carla suddenly remembered, "I have to call the school. My daughter!" Carla opened up the passenger door. Not seeing her phone in the center console slot where it should be, she searched the floor and found it. The woman looked up at the man. "How bad is it?"

With a dark expression, the man relented somewhat. "Just the bumpers mostly."

Carla suggested, "I guess we're supposed to exchange information. Or … do we call the police?"

The woman quickly asked the man, "Will it drive?"

"Of course it will drive. Can't you hear? Just the bumpers, I said."

The woman turned back to Carla. "Give me a minute while I talk to my husband, okay." She walked around the front of the Kia to her husband. Both squeezing to shelter under the big umbrella, they began talking when the woman turned back toward Carla. "Take a minute to call your school! We'll figure this out. You'll be driving. Just a bit late, that's all."

As Carla made her phone call, Rebecca and David discussed the situation.

"We can't let her call the police," David stated.

Rebecca nodded in agreement. *Why did you have to act like such a caveman?*

"In fact, we can't stay here a minute longer," David added.

"I agree. How bad is it?"

David looked again at the crumpled bumpers, the Kia having the greater damage. "One, two thousand. Maybe less."

"Why did you have to be such an ass to her?" With no response from David, Rebecca then asked, quietly, "How much do you have on you?"

"Around twenty-two hundred."

Rebecca added, "And I have about eleven hundred."

David began walking toward the front of the Kia and Carla. Carla had just finished her phone call, and wiped rainwater from her face.

"Let me!" Rebecca intervened, pulling back on David's arm. As David relented, Rebecca stepped toward Carla.

Rebecca began, "You'll be on your way in a minute." Intending to warm up the situation, she held out her hand. "What's your name?"

"Carla." Carla shook the woman's hand.

"Hi Carla," Rebecca said warmly. "I'm Rebecca. And that's David," she said, gesturing toward her husband. "Please forgive him. He's a hot head. Loses his temper fast."

Carla offered a nervous, forced chuckle in response.

Rebecca continued, "Carla, if we involve insurance, we're just going to make this all bigger and more expensive. David thinks that the damage on your car is under a thousand dollars. But we feel bad for you, too. So, we're going to make sure you're okay and give you three thousand. It's our way of saying sorry."

Carla looked at her in astonishment.

Rebecca continued, "It's all we have on us right now. This way we can both go on with our day. We're running a bit late, too."

Carla's mind raced. She didn't know what to think or believe. Carla stepped to the rear of the car to again view her rear bumper. It really didn't seem all that terrible except, yes, it seemed obvious that the bumper will need to be replaced. "How much are bumpers?" Carla asked.

David replied, "For that car, likely around eight hundred. Maybe nine hundred."

Carla didn't look at the man who was, just a few minutes ago, calling her a bitch and an idiot. But she decided to believe him. She looked back up at Rebecca and stepped toward her. "Okay. Three thousand. I'll accept. I mean, I don't know."

*

One and a half years earlier, Sonya and Joseph had not flown to Vancouver via Chicago. It had dawned on them, during the flight across the Atlantic, that they would be too easy to track if they stuck with that flight plan.

After nervously clearing Customs at Chicago O'Hare and changing sixteen thousand euros into approximately twenty thousand American dollars, they booked a separate flight to Seattle. The new plan was to buy a car in Seattle and drive the final two hours up to Vancouver.

In Seattle, buying a used car, without divulging much personal information, was easy enough. The complication, however, came in the registering and insuring of it. They also realized that the risk was too great to drive across the border with so much cash. A random car search would ruin everything.

Sonya and Joseph rented a townhouse in Everett, just north of Seattle, a place where they could squat undetected while they planned their next move.

One month in Everett turned into two, and then into five months. During this time, Joseph received treatment for his hip. Sonya's burned hand healed. And Joseph explored Seattle's dark side to try to source someone who could create new identifications for them. Both Sonya and Joseph, separately, also found various discreet currency converters to change euros into American and Canadian dollars. The currency conversions were done in amounts under one hundred thousand at a time, to hopefully avoid raising any flags.

It was a wet day at the end of January when Joseph came through the townhouse door to show the newly acquired passports, and Canadian social insurance cards, and birth certificates to Sonya. From that day on, they were David and Rebecca Weiss. Immediately, they registered their white Ford Explorer and replaced stolen license plates with properly registered and insured plates.

During those five months, prior to getting their new IDs, Sonya and Joseph had made two trips driving north to Bellingham. Armed with spades, in three separate wooded remote areas between Bellingham and Ferndale just north of Bellingham, they buried three of the pouches — each deep enough that no animal would forage down and dig them up. Of the seven million, four hundred, and ninety-two thousand dollars buried, they took two-hundred and fifty thousand with them. With that, and now armed with proper ID, they opened joint bank accounts at three separate banks including Wells Fargo, Bank of America, and Citigroup Bank in Everett depositing ninety-seven thousand dollars at each bank.

Sonya and Joseph each kept nine thousand dollars on them, an amount small enough that they wouldn't need to declare it when crossing the Canadian border.

On the 23rd of February 2001, David and Rebecca Weiss, with minimal essentials, crossed the Peace Arch border into Canada and entered Greater Vancouver. It took them three days of staying in a nondescript Travelodge in Burnaby until they found the rental house that suited them.

The newish fifteen-hundred square foot bungalow on Badger Road, at Deep Cove on the north shore, offered David and Rebecca Weiss relative anonymity. The home featured a nice view of Deep Cove harbor to the east from the expansive main floor back deck, and a thick mountainside forest directly across the street to the west. Below the deck, at the walkout lower level, the lawn remained flat for sixteen feet into the back yard and then sloped steeply downward another twenty-four feet where a semicircle of overgrown shrubs backstopped and ended the property. The monthly rent was slightly high for the area, but both David and Rebecca agreed that renting, as opposed to buying, would keep them off any radars for now.

One of the first things David and Rebecca did, after moving into their rented house, was renovate a wall in their master bedroom's gigantic walk-in closet. Because that particular wall divided the master ensuite from the closet, and because the sink vanities sat against that wall on the bathroom side, the modification that David and Rebecca made was a wall cavity accessible through the vanity door at the back of the vanity space and jutting into the walk-in closet space. The perfect size for a hidden safe. Anyone opening the vanity doors would see only four-inch shelves for toiletries, not realizing that the shelves could slide sideways into the adjacent space. On the closet side, they placed an oversized air-exchange vent to disguise and justify the square protrusion into the closet.

The strategy that David and Rebecca agreed on, after much arguing, was for them to individually make shopping trips across the border every month. Each trip would involve David or Rebecca digging up and retrieving three-hundred thousand dollars, depositing ninety-seven thousand at each of the three banks, and coming back into Canada carrying nine thousand dollars. According to their calculations, with this strategy, they could move all the hidden money in approximately a year. The banked money would be moved through bank transfers and through Forex. As the money would arrive in the Royal Bank in Canada, David and Rebecca would consistently withdraw two of every three dollars and put it into their safe.

The stress involved in keeping a low profile and, regimentally, moving the money across the border was cause for regular bad moods. For Rebecca, a bad mood caused her to become withdrawn and quiet. For David, a bad mood involved getting loud and abusive. That abuse more and more came in the form of throwing things, sometimes throwing things at Rebecca. During the many flare-ups between Rebecca and David, David regularly slapped or punched Rebecca.

The resentment by Rebecca became such that she could no longer sleep in the same bed as David. And so, just as what had previously transpired between them in Tel Aviv, she moved into one of the two other bedrooms. David retaliated against that, too, ordering Rebecca to move back into the master bedroom. She did not comply. It was a stand-off, a pressure-filled stand-off that seeped into every part of daily activities.

Meals were without conversation. And regular household discussions, such as the need to go for groceries, almost always generated verbal denigration from David. The words that David chose to describe Rebecca became crueler and more vulgar by the day.

Added to the abusive environment, both Rebecca and David lived in constant paranoia of being discovered. Every knock at their door, every trip out, every phone call, everything had both of them on edge. That is how they lived during the year that it took to finish transferring the money across the border.

CHAPTER 15

SEVEN YEARS EARLIER, MARCH 1994

Just a few minutes past 8:00am, one kilometer east of the Israel border in the West Bank town, Qibya, Mohammad Bakir trudged the last few steps to his small home — carrying a heavy cloth sack of flour over his shoulder. As he entered the open door, he saw Saadia — his wife — who, anticipating his arrival with flour, had pulled out two large bottom drawers of the kitchen cabinets. Seeing her husband enter, she hurried over to him to help him take the very heavy sack off his back. Together, they carried the sack to the open bins.

As Saadia pulled at the rope knot to untie the sack's top, Mohammad looked over his shoulder and saw the eight-year-old twin daughters sitting together at a desk, by the window at the living room side of the space — each writing, diligently doing their schoolwork.

"Where's Azim?" Mohammad asked his wife. "He can help you with this."

Finally successful untying the knot, Saadia answered, "Azim took the garbage out."

Qibya, not having the luxury of house-to-house garbage pick-up, required all residents, from each of its nine streets, to take their garbage to a container at the end of each street.

With the sack of flour open, both Mohammad and Saadia lifted and began to pour the contents into the first of the two bins. As they poured, Saadia commented, "He's taking long. Should have been back by now." Having poured half the flour into the first bin, Saadia said, "I'll go see where he got off to." Leaving Mohammad with the now lighter sack, she stepped out through the door into the bright morning sun. Saadia looked up along the yellow dirt street, shaded her eyes with her hand, but didn't see Azim. "Azim!" she called. "Hurry up!" No response. She began walking in the direction of the street's garbage container that was just out of sight around the bend. Suddenly, she heard a split-second whining whistle. And then a deafening explosion! Instantly, searing air hurled her forward off her feet into the air. Rocks, sand, and various debris flew against and past her as she fell, skidding face down, on the street.

The cloud of dust hung in the air for several moments — so thick that Saadia didn't see the bloody dirt beside where she lay. Groaning, she turned onto her side. Then she noticed the bloody dirt. And she saw the gash where a shard of glass had embedded into the back of her right arm just above her elbow. Then, she felt the stings on the back of her legs. And her head! She put a hand to feel the back of her head. Her hair was matted with dirt, but she didn't feel anything cutting her head. She looked at her hand to see if it revealed any blood from touching the back of her head. No blood. Only then, Saadia's ability to think returned.

In horror, she realized that it was a bomb or a missile. Immediately, it struck her that it happened behind her. Her house! *Mohammad! The girls!* Shock and panic stunned her as she raised herself to her knees and looked back toward her home. "Nooooo!" she screamed. Painfully, she raised to her feet, forgetting momentarily about the shard of glass in her arm and needles in the back of her legs. Her house, and the house on the other side, were shrouded in a thick cloud of smoke and flames. As she could see through the ugly shroud, they were gone. Saadia wailed in horror!

As she struggled to her feet and began to stumble forward, several other people appeared around her. She continued to stumble forward toward the burning mess. A teenager raced past her, screaming in terror as he ran, "Noooo!" It took Saadia several moments to recognize the teenager as Azim, her son. He reached the house ahead of her but stopped thirty feet away because of the heat of the severely raging fires. "Mama!" he screamed. "Papa!"

Saadia tried to call out to Azim as she ran toward him, but only dry crackles came from her mouth now. She tried again, "Azim! Azim!" Hearing his name called, he turned around and saw Saadia approaching. "Mama!" The horrified twelve-year-old turned and ran to her and was about to embrace her when he saw the stream of blood running down her arm — down along her skirt and leg. His eyes widened in horror. Immediately, he identified the glass shard protruding from the back of her upper arm. He grabbed it and yanked it out. Saadia cried in pain! Blood instantly gushed faster from Saadia's wound.

A neighbor, having run up to the pair, whipped off his kibber that he was wearing over his ankle-length thobe. He quickly wrapped the kibber around the bleeding gash. Immediately, he realized that he wrapped it too loosely, so he removed it, the cloth now already partly blood-soaked, and began to wrap it again more tightly. But, as he tried, Saadia screamed more and shuffled closer to her burning destroyed home. "Mohammad! My babies!" She approached as closely as the cruel cloud of dust and burning smoke would allow, then collapsed to her knees, wailing. As she had been moving, the neighbor had been continuing to try to reapply the kibber as dressing for Saadia's arm.

As both Saadia and Azim wailed in horror, others standing outside of the other destroyed house had also gathered and were screaming and wailing.

*

Many years earlier, after the 1970 Jordanian Civil War — also referred to as Black September — the rift between the Palestinian leadership and the Kingdom of Jordan had continued to widen. The Arab League affirmed the right of the Palestinian people to self-determination. The Arab League also affirmed the right of the Palestinian people to establish an independent national authority under the command of the Palestine Liberation Organization.

In the three years that followed that errant Israeli retaliatory strike in 1994 that killed Saadia's husband and daughters, Palestinian Liberation Organization officers recognized her agony and her anger. Both Saadia and Azim had developed a blood-thirsty fury against Israel. In 1997, a friend of her deceased husband — an officer of medium rank with the PLO in Hebron —

suggested to Saadia Bakir that he would have a clerical position for her at the PLO headquarters. Soon afterwards, steps were taken to groom a very-willing Azim for small covert missions just past the Israeli-Palestinian border.

*

With his long and impressive resume in covert missions and spycraft, Akeem Almasi, already in PLO leadership regarding the Katz situation, was tapped once again in April 2001 by General Arruk for the most complex covert mission of his career. He was charged with the task of selecting a wife and selecting a son that could pass for age eighteen. Both agents would need to be well-trusted agents. All three of them would need to immerse themselves into the study of German to the extent that, by mid-summer, all three of them would need to be fluent — completely fluent with no perceivable Arab accent.

Akeem Almasi chose carefully. And he was satisfied with his selection of Saadia Bakir and her nineteen-year-old son Azim. Akeem Almasi had had various encounters with both Saadia and Azim over the past several years, and was impressed at both their intellect and their eagerness to contribute to PLO's cause. Filled with a spirit of vengeance, although intimidated by the foreign nature of the mission, both Saadia and Azim Bakir eagerly agreed to participate.

Five months after General Arruk brought Akeem Almasi into this endeavor, the PLO, aided with some intel from Moscow, had successfully taken out the two known and one newly discovered Mossad safe houses with missiles — thereby eliminating the possibility of any details of their mole, Benjamin Sharod, being gleaned from Matthew Mizrahi. However, in that event they had also eliminated the person with potential information that might have led them to the Katz couple. Nobody in the PLO could be certain that Matthew Mizrahi had such knowledge. Both Arruk and Almasi doubted it. Nevertheless, now that lead was dead. And so, desperation forced the PLO to focus on their only remaining potential lead, Isabella Gruber. Attention was now poured onto spurring that long-lost daughter, Isabella, to lead them to her parents.

From mid-April to August 18, 2001, nearly every day was filled for Akeem Almasi, Saadia Bakir, and Azim Bakir with orientation, arms training, trade craft, and language training by Major-General Tariq Al Khalil, General Arruk, and other agents. The entire scenario, regarding Joseph and Sonya Katz, was explained to Akeem, Saadia, and Azim. The final four weeks of their training took place in Munich, Germany so that the three agents could legitimize their familiarity with German lifestyle and mannerisms and better learn language colloquialisms.

*

For nearly two decades since 1981, Benjamin Sharod, as Deputy Finance Minister, had run the two PLO agents at Israeli banks: Yitzhak Biton, governor in charge of the bank's head office at Kiryat HaMemshala in Jerusalem; and Avraham Azoulai, COO of the bank's branch office in Tel Aviv. With both of these banks designated to manage government funds payments to pre-budgeted infrastructure projects throughout Israel, both agents were committed to continuing the exercise of gleaning funds, doctoring audits and reports, and funneling the funds to Palestine.

In October 2000, there had been a cabinet shuffle in Israel. Sharod was moved to Minister of Infrastructure, a move he had anticipated. However, instead of staying on in a new role as Minister of Infrastructure, Benjamin Sharod publicly sank into a very luxurious retirement in Tel Aviv, and covertly continued to act as the Controller for those two agent bankers.

PLO's funding largely depended on keeping the entire long-lasting scheme secure. The absolute highest priority continued to be to find Joseph and Sonya Katz and to eliminate them. Any lead, however weak, was important enough to follow-up on.

The locating of Isabella Katz, now known as Isabella Gruber, by the PLO intelligence office was significant. Now it would be up to Akeem Almasi and Saadia and Azim Bakir, to bring that daughter to search for her real parents — and quickly.

Their mission would involve posing as a new family at Vacha, Germany. They will be Israeli-born, immigrants decades ago to Germany. Their names will be Shimon, Miriam, and Sebastian Adri. They will own and operate a grocery store — one that will normally require Akeem to travel sometimes.

Azim was charged with getting very close to Isabella Katz — even romantically if that's what it would require.

And so, on August 21, 2001, the Adri family moved to Vacha just in time for twenty-year-old Sebastian to enter grade twelve posing as a seventeen-year-old.

CHAPTER 16

It was a warm and slightly breezy August afternoon in Vacha, Germany. A large moving van reported its beep-beep, repetitively, as it backed up at an angle across Georg-Witzel Strasse — the rear dual tires climbing up over the curb and crossing the sidewalk. The truck driver intended to get the rear of the truck as close as possible to the front steps leading up into the two-story house. As the truck reached its landing spot, a middle-aged man and woman stepped out of the house, down the three stone steps, and stood to the side on the lawn. It was obvious that the couple were the new homeowners.

A small group, of five neighbors, had gathered nearby on the sidewalk watching the proceedings. The large leprechaun-green name and logo — Starz Umzüge Moving — covered most of the truck's white box. The neighbors all recognized it as one of the nation's prominent moving companies.

Sebastian was upstairs in his completely empty new bedroom. He looked out through the window down to where the two movers in the green and white company uniforms had begun to open the truck's rear door and pull out the ramp.

*

Seventeen-year-old Ishi knelt on the beige linoleum hallway floor at her metal locker, the locker door open, as she was struggling to place items into the bottom of it.

"You have the same locker as last year," Julia said, as she approached, happily — her long blonde ponytail bouncing with her steps.

"Yeah," Ishi answered, "I hope I get the same desk in home room, too."

"I hope we all do."

The grade twelve students were getting oriented at their desks. Some sat. Some were standing at their desks. A few were milling in and out of the classroom. Ishi glanced at the clock at the back of the classroom and realized that there were only eleven minutes remaining until the electronic buzzer would make its muted short buzz announcing the beginning of class.

Ms. Schneider hadn't appeared yet. Ishi was already seated. She lifted up her desktop and, pulling out a fuchsia-colored scrunchy, pulled her long brunette hair back behind her head and applied the scrunchy to hold it there in a ponytail.

At the same time, Ishi's eyes widened slightly as she watched a new boy enter the classroom. The new boy was medium height — fit — with black hair and beautiful black eyes, and altogether hot! He carried a stylish small brown leather duffle bag. Ishi looked across the classroom at Rebecca. Simultaneously, both Rebecca and Julia looked to Ishi with a *Wow, who is that?* look!

Ten seconds later, Christian entered the room with Peter and Eddie. Christian and his friends were jostling each other and laughing. Momentarily, Christian looked toward his desk, stepped toward it, and threw a smiling glance over to Ishi. Ishi returned the small smile. She turned her gaze back to the new boy, who was referring to a note in his hand, and then counted the desks in the second row in an effort to locate his. Ishi glanced back at Christian, then at Julia — who was watching the new boy with admiration. Ishi then looked back at the new boy as he sat down at his desk and began to unload several books into his desk.

Thud! Every head in the classroom swiveled to see what made the noise on the window. Dan, a very skinny, tall boy ran over from the back of the classroom, peered through the window, and down. "A bird," he announced.

"Oh," inserted another voice from the classroom, "that's going to give him a headache."

There were several chuckles.

*

Ishi and her parents sat at the supper table halfway through the meal.

"There's a new family in town," Ishi said.

"Oh!" exclaimed Dagmar.

"Frank Yatke was telling me this m-morning," Horst added. "Meat. Deli. Apparently, they want to open a m-meat shop or a grocery store or s-something."

"Oh," said Dagmar, "that would be good!"

Ishi took another two bites of scalloped potatoes. "Their kid is in grade twelve."

Dagmar was intrigued, "Did you meet him?"

"Duh," Ishi replied, sarcastically, her mouth full as she spoke, "there are only thirty-eight in my class."

Horst asked, "So, you m-met him?"

Ishi just looked up at her father with an *I already said yes* look.

The shocking events in New York just weeks earlier - on September 11 - had riveted everybody to their TVs for many hours through the past weeks. However, over six thousand kilometers away from the collapse of the World Trade towers, and two and a half weeks later, life carried on in the middle of Germany.

Three hours of Christian Neufeld's late afternoons and early evenings were often taken up with hard work. His father, a mason, employed Christian for three hours after school, most weekdays, to help lay bricks. That involved carrying many bags of cement, shoveling a lot of sand into the small cement mixer to create mortar, and moving countless amounts of bricks to each exact spot where his father placed them. The work also rewarded him with a wage, a wage that furnished Christian with the ability to buy his own 1996 maroon-colored Volkswagen Jetta, the thing he did the week he turned eighteen. To make this all work, Christian's family supper with his younger sister and his parents usually occurred no earlier than 7:30 each evening. They were all accustomed to the routine.

Similarly, Sebastian's help was also required by Adri Foods each weekday after school. One month prior to moving the family to Vacha, Shimon Adri finalized the purchase of a one-story commercial building at the corner where the two highways that run into Vacha intersect.

Previously, the building had housed a hardware store, so it already had the cash register systems in place. With just under two months of renovations, that included the installation of a freezer room, shelves, display refrigeration units, an interior decorating redo, and the import of food, Adri Foods was open. It was immediately popular. Part of the intrigue, for locals, was that Adri Foods also offered Middle Eastern foods and a deli counter that served hot irresistible shawarma, sabich pita wraps, and various types of kebabs. This was new and tantalizing for the Germans in Vacha.

Because Adri Foods was hiring at least one fulltime and two part-time staff, a first target had been grade 12 students. News of the job opportunity spread immediately throughout the school during the first week of classes in September. Sebastian approached Ishi directly and mentioned to her that he thought she'd be a good fit at Adri Foods. After a conversation between Ishi and her parents, they had all quickly agreed that the opportunity would be very good for Ishi to earn some money for herself and her future schooling.

Ishi caught on quickly to the cash registers and the work of stocking shelves. Miriam Adri managed the deli and the preparation of hot foods. Shimon, overseeing the entire business, focused on food orders, marketing, and general management. And Sebastian stayed busy managing the back room and stocking shelves.

But today was Sunday. All shops were closed. With warm fall temperatures, Ishi, Sebastian, Julia, Rebecca, and Christian were driving one hour south to Fulda for the open-air rock festival. With both rear windows open on Christian's maroon Jetta, the long hair of the three girls that occupied the rear seat blew around wildly. Christian and Sebastian had turned the music loud. There was a lot of shouting over the music and a lot of laughter. It was a great day to be alive!

As a city at least twenty times the size of Vacha, Fulda presented an excitement for Ishi. She had been there twice before with her parents when they were buying feed supplements and shopping for furniture, but this was the first time with her friends.

Struggling to find a spot for the Jetta at the parkplatz at Alter Käsbach Park, near the athletic fields, Christian finally succeeded. From there, totes in hand

and slung over shoulders, the five excited young adults walked into the park and toward the throngs of people milling about near the Fulda riverbank. Julia had the forethought to bring blankets, and she walked with both tucked under her arms.

Ishi saw two stages set up with tall criss-cross aluminum rigging for lights. No bands had started yet. There were at least eight or nine food vendors set up around the perimeter of this area of the park and, immediately, Ishi wondered if Adri Foods should have tried to be involved.

"I think we should be here," Ishi said to Sebastian, while pointing out the vendors.

"Absolutely!" Sebastian saw the opportunity, too.

Ishi added, "We'd make a killing!"

They found a suitable spot on the grass to settle in, and all five plopped down onto two large blankets that Julia had spread out. With considerate strategy, both Julia and Rebecca sat apart from and in front of Christian so that Ishi could sit beside him. Also strategically, both Julia and Rebecca were keen on sitting beside Sebastian, and each sat on either side of him.

"Becky, you knit that dorky hat yourself?" Christian, sitting mostly behind Rebecca, chided, playfully, at the knit beanie that Rebecca was wearing.

"Ha, hah, smart ass," Rebecca retorted, "my grandmother knit it for me while sitting around her gramophone." She whipped off her hat and threw it back at Christian.

"I'm going to look at the food," Sebastian said as he stood.

"I'll come with you." Ishi quickly stood up, too.

Christian watched as Ishi and Sebastian walked away chatting. Christian continued to watch Sebastian's and Ishi's playful chat and laughter as they walked, feeling a wave of jealousy well up in him. He immediately stood up. "I'm going to check out the food, too," he announced to Julia and Rebecca. Christian jogged to catch up with Ishi and Sebastian.

Dusk set in. Each stage alternated with performers, and a punk-rock band now played on the stage to the right. The silver and blue spikey-haired lead singer bent forward as if with stomach cramps as he squelched out his lines.

Ishi and Julia had just visited the line of Porta-Potties at the rear of the park and approached the blankets to rejoin their friends. Christian, having earlier piled up the totes to create something to recline against, awaited Ishi's return. She sat down in front of him between his outstretched legs, and leaned back against him. Sebastian and Rebecca both lay on their sides facing each other, playing rummy. Sebastian hadn't ever played rummy, but caught on quickly.

Ten minutes later, as Sebastian and Rebecca's game ended, Ishi moved toward them. "Can I play?" she asked. "There's no way you'll beat me," she added playfully, challenging Sebastian. Christian watched for a minute, and then closed his eyes, and rested his head back in pseudo sleep taking in the music.

It was just past midnight as Christian delivered Ishi to her front door.

As she began to open the car door, Christian said, "Hey, Ishi, I'm starting to look at schools."

"It's only October." She waited for his next words.

"I've been looking at the Hans-Böckler in Frankfurt for computer sciences."

Ishi looked at him, waiting for more.

"Have you thought about school? What you want? Where? I know it's still a ways off, but—"

Ishi answered slowly and thoughtfully, "I don't have a clue what I want to go to school for. So, it's hard to even look."

Christian replied, "Oh, I know. I was just wondering. Early bird gets the worm. Oh, hold it! I think that's an expression about getting up early. Anyway—"

Ishi looked at him, quizzically. "What brings this on, now?"

"Well, I think it'd be super if we'd choose the same city. Don't you?"

Ishi pushed the car door open. "I don't know if I'm even going to school right away." She put a leg outside. "Thanks for driving."

Quickly, Christian asked, "But, I don't mean you have to decide. I'm just saying—"

Ishi stepped out and looked toward her house. "I might stay at the store and earn more money first." She closed the door and began toward the front door. "G'night. So much fun!" she chimed back to Christian as he watched her through his open window.

"Good night! Thanks for today," he replied. His brows furrowed as he drove away down the Gruber driveway. The vibrancy that Ishi showed toward him for years was quickly becoming duller. Duller, ever since Sebastian showed up. "I'm just saying—" Christian repeated in a mutter to himself. "What a stupid thing to say!"

*

"Ishi!" Miriam called to Ishi as a customer exited the store. It was still mid-day, but with no customers in the store, at the moment, Miriam saw an opportunity to teach Ishi some deli skills.

Ishi looked at Miriam and walked from the cash counter to the deli. "Yes?"

Miriam smiled invitingly. "We have a little chance now for me to teach you how to make shawarma. Let's try!" Miriam quickly handed Ishi a white full-length apron, slipped it over Ishi's head, and said, "Turn! I'll tie it." Ishi turned around as Miriam quickly tied the apron at the back.

"Okay." Miriam pulled the metal hood up and off the large round chuck of processed pork that had been slowly turning on the vertical rotisserie. "You've seen me trim it many times. Now you try!" Miriam picked a knife up off the counter and handed it to Ishi. "Here's the plate." Miriam snatched a plate from a nearby stack of plates.

Ishi took the plate in her left hand and, with her right hand, began shaving the pork from top to bottom in long, even strokes. Using a technique that Ishi had observed Miriam and Sebastian do, she trimmed even cuts, letting each thin pork slice fall onto the plate.

"Nicely done!" Miriam exclaimed. With enough slices soon piled on the plate, Miriam continued, "Okay. Now the pita. You get it from here," she opened a round wooden canister, the size and look of a hat box, and, using tongs, took out an unbaked pita. "You take this pita, and … make sure it's set to three hundred," adjusting the knob on the counter-top grilling oven, "just put it in there for two minutes. Of course, you'd do this first so that it bakes while you cut the meat."

A bell dinged as Sebastian came through the front door into the store.

"Did you find them?" Miriam asked.

"Yes," Sebastian answered. "But they were all in the field, so I brought it to them there."

Miriam looked surprised and doubtful. "Really? But—"

"It's okay. They wanted it there. They wanted to have lunch in the field with their tractor and baler."

Sebastian and Ishi exchanged warm smiles.

"Ah hah," Sebastian smiled broader, "learning a new skill!"

Ishi chuckled slightly. "Trying."

It was 8 o'clock. Ishi was busy doing cash-out at the till. Miriam walked to the front door and turned the lock. As she flipped the Open-Closed sign around, she asked, "Ishi, would you like to come over for dinner on Friday? Ingrid and Karissa will be closing, and we thought it would be nice if you'd be our guest."

Ishi quickly scribbled a number on a paper, then looked up. "I don't think I can on Friday. It's my dad's birthday, and we have a dinner for him at home."

Miriam thought quickly. "Well then, how about Sunday? I'll introduce you to a full Israeli meal at our house."

"Okay. Sure. Of course, I need to ask my mom."

"Of course."

That Sunday, before getting on her bike and riding the ten minutes to the Adri home for dinner, Ishi took quite a lot of extra time to braid her long brown hair into one loose braid that hung to one side. She had never done that before, but, having done it, she proudly observed herself in the mirror. It really suited her! She reminded herself of some Jewish girls that she'd seen pictures of in history books over the years.

The meal was nearly done. The warmth and friendliness around the Adri table with Shimon, Miriam, and Sebastian together, along with the good and interesting food, had given Ishi a sense of full satisfaction. Ishi noted, again, during her visit, something she had noticed with the Adris at the store. Their speech was very straight. Very proper. They almost never used slang. *Huh,*

Ishi thought, *some families are just more formal, I guess.*

"Ishi, do you have any baby pictures? I'm sure you must have many." Miriam slid her chair out, walked to another room, and, momentarily, returned with a photo album. "Here, I want to show you what Sebastian looked like when he was a baby."

Sebastian sighed in refute. "Oh mom, do you have to?"

As Miriam moved several dishes out of the way, and placed the photo album on the table in front of Ishi, she replied to her son, "Why not?"

Ishi turned page slowly after page, looking at photos of a young Sebastian in various scenarios. Turning a page to a larger photo of Sebastian, at the age of approximately five, Shimon reached across and pointed his finger to Sebastian's head, laughing. "Look at his hair!" Shimon laughed louder. "He got a hold of my electric shaver that day." Miriam laughed, too. Sebastian just sat, embarrassed.

"Next time, you should bring photos if you can," Sebastian challenged Ishi.

Ishi hesitated slightly. "Next time?"

Miriam jumped in, "Oh, we should do this often! And your parents should come, too."

Ishi pondered. "I guess I'd have to look for my photos." She was a little bit bewildered because she couldn't remember seeing too many photos of her when she was young. "My parents didn't really have a camera; well, not a very good camera when I was young. So—"

"Oh sweetie, I'm sure you'll find some. Bring what you can," Miriam encouraged.

After dinner, as Sebastian showed Ishi some framed family photos on several walls, they progressed along the hall toward the living room where Shimon was now sitting in a big armchair watching a nature show on TV. Ishi noticed two rolled-up mats beside the TV. "What's that for?" Ishi was simply curious why two mats were stored beside the TV. "Do your parents do yoga?"

"Oh, those are our prayer mats," Sebastian quickly answered. Instantly, he wanted to take his words back!

Shimon's head snapped around to look at Sebastian!

Immediately, Sebastian corrected himself, "Uh, I mean, those are just mats. Extra door mats."

Shimon added, "We were just too lazy to put them into storage yet."

Ishi was satisfied. "I see."

Shimon was already on his feet to clear the mats out of the room.

It was dark as Ishi and Sebastian sat on the front steps of Sebastian's home. A sconce, on each side of the front door, illuminated the front stone steps, the sidewalk that led to the street, and the grey stone one-meter-tall bird bath at the middle of the left half of the lawn.

Sebastian asked, "You don't have any brothers or sisters? I mean, I've met your parents at the store. But I've never seen any brothers or sis—"

"No," Ishi answered. "I think my parents wanted more children. They never really wanted to talk about it. I did hear mom say one time though, that she had some complications when I was born."

"Oh?"

Ishi suddenly stood up. "I should go. It's already dark, and I don't want my parents to worry."

Sebastian stood up too. "How far?"

"Only ten minutes by bike. Pretty short."

"Well then, I'll ride with you. I'll get my bike. Hang on!" He darted around the house, into the black, reappearing thirty seconds later walking his new-looking white bicycle. "Let's go!"

CHAPTER 17

Even though they could cushion their life with luxurious comfort, materially, over the course of a year and a half in Vancouver, they lived almost fully separate lives under one roof. They ate separately. They could not stand being in the same room with each other.

Eventually, David had increased his occasional social steps out to the local pub, Fat Friar's, to watch sporting events. Rebecca had become more and more involved with social activities in the nearby North Shore Alliance Church, first being enticed by a volunteer opportunity for a neighborhood food drive for the homeless, and then other activities such as local sailing events and hiking up the grind on Grouse Mountain with some of the women from the church. Over time, David developed several buddies and Rebecca developed some girlfriends.

The thirteen years since the disappearance of Rebecca's darling daughter, Ishi, caused Rebecca to walk more slumped, to be notably more introverted, and to be generally gloomier. There were countless days and nights when Rebecca remembered those three years with Ishi, and wept. And Rebecca wept for her poor mother who had worn the guilt and had died sad and burdened. For Rebecca, this was a private pain. She couldn't talk about it with any other person.

Besides their estrangement, David did not share, at all, Rebecca's emotions regarding Ishi. An issue that cut Rebecca the deepest, more than any other physical or verbal violence, was that every time Rebecca would put up a framed photo of Ishi, David would remove it. David had never wanted Isabella in the first place. And, in the three years that she was in their lives,

David had been subtly, and often not-so-subtly, sour about it.

In an effort to create some companionship at home, Rebecca adopted a puppy.

Suzanna, one of Rebecca's acquaintances from church, had a Maltese that had birthed five puppies. While Suzanna's Maltese wasn't a purebred, the puppies were in demand and valuable. Rebecca had mentioned to David that she wanted to have a dog. David's curt response was only "Why?" Rebecca could have explained to David that it was for companionship or as an extra security alarm in the home, but the relationship was so dead that Rebecca didn't bother explaining. She knew that he would shoot down the idea anyway. So, she simply went ahead and bought one of Suzanna's puppies.

Rebecca named the adorable, white, fluffy puppy, Lily. It offered immediate joy to Rebecca. Besides being astonishingly cute, being a two-month-old puppy meant that it required lots of attention. Rebecca found that the time spent in training, cuddling, feeding, and playing with Lily was a valuable distraction to her otherwise dour days. Instead of relying on boring television and re-cleaning an already spotless home, Rebecca now had some purpose — even if it was just to raise Lily correctly.

When David wasn't out drinking, he gave Lily no attention. It was clear that the dog was an irritant for David. Lily's barking was met with cursing and often objects being hurled at her by David. During the first several weeks, whenever Lily would be in David's path, David would merely kick the dog away. As those kicks grew more severe, Lily did quickly learn to not get in David's way.

Over the past year and a half, David and Rebecca had been getting by with only the white Ford Explorer that they'd bought in Seattle and driven up to Vancouver. But, increasingly, their separate lives, the inconvenience of taxis, and their growing individual social excursions brought a very real need for another vehicle.

David's hip had continued to plague him ever since the injury at the Syrian border. Doctors that treated him in Seattle told him that the iliofemoral ligament, which connects the pelvis to the femur at the front of the joint, had been torn, and the femur ball had been wrenched out of the socket. The iliofemoral ligament keeps the hip from hyper-extension, however even though doctors in Seattle had reset David's hip, osteoarthritis had increased. He walked with a significant limp and was now often reliant on a cane. It had come to a point where he was looking at no other option but a hip replacement. The prospect of a hip replacement was, in David's opinion, a positive. He would, hopefully, be in less pain, be free of the damned cane, and perhaps soon even learn to golf and join his beer buddies in the activities that they talked about endlessly.

Having parked the SUV in the attached garage, David walked through the door into the mudroom. Leaning his cane against the wall, with a grunt, he sat on an upholstered bench to untie his shoes. As he untied his shoes, he heard Rebecca on the phone with someone.

Rebecca, having heard David enter from the garage, opened the sliding glass door and stepped from the breakfast nook onto the large deck. Lily quickly scooted outside with her as she slid the door closed behind her. It was a calm April afternoon, and she gazed east to the pristine beauty of Deep Cove as she continued her phone conversation. "So, as I was saying, I mentioned it to Debbie, and she wants to, too." *Murphy's Law! As soon as I'm on the phone, he comes home.*

David, now in the kitchen, tossed some Lexus and Jeep brochures onto the island and, placing his cane on the island, turned to the fridge. After only a few seconds of looking into the fridge, he straightened up and yelled at Rebecca through the closed glass door, "We're out of food!"

Rebecca, hearing him yell, turned to glance back at him. She then returned her gaze to the cove.

"Why didn't you buy groceries?" David shouted again.

Assuming that Suzanna could hear David's ranting, Rebecca said, "I guess you can hear that David is home. Oh joy, oh bliss."

David grabbed his cane and marched over to the door sliding it open. "What the fuck? Are you completely useless?"

Rebecca quickly said to Suzanna, "I gotta go. Sorry. I'll call you later."

David was stepping out onto the patio now. He yelled, "I'm fucking hungry. What am I supposed to eat?"

Rebecca responded firmly, "I wanted to use the vehicle to get groceries. So, I was waiting for you to get ho—"

"You didn't need to wait. Instead of your gossip-fests on your phone all day, you could call a taxi, and —"

"I'm not gossiping. And there is food. And you could have taken food out of the freezer, too. You're not five years old. Or are you?" Rebecca was angry now.

David stepped closer, his face red with rage. Lily, sensing a threat, scampered between Rebecca and David, barking shrilly and furiously at David.

David yelled over the barking, "You think you can talk to me that way? You bitch!" As Rebecca retreated a step, David grabbed the phone from her hand. He hurled the phone over the deck railing. She spun around to see the phone disappearing down the steeply sloped backyard lawn tumbling and finally sliding into a small bush far below. She spun back around and tried to push her way past David. Bracing his hands against her shoulders, he stopped her.

"Don't touch me!" Rebecca hissed as she struggled to get past him. After a moment of struggling, she tried to sidestep him.

Lily was growling and barking wildly now. As Rebecca managed to step past David, David, enraged, swung his cane and hit the dog hard. Lily's whelp of pain caused Rebecca to turn to see what David had done. Lily had tumbled over along the deck floor from the force of the blow. As the little, white, pain-stricken dog regained her footing, David stepped forward and with an even stronger swing, hit the dog again bringing on screeching yelps of pain from the little Maltese. Rebecca rushed to Lily's aid. Before Rebecca could reach her dog, David bent down, snatched up the dog with one hand, and hurled her over the deck railing, too.

Screaming, Rebecca ran to the railing in time to see Lily landing twelve feet below and then tumbling summersaulting in a melee of white fur down the steep lawn slope and crash into the first of small bushes. Rebecca turned and raced for the stairs to the lower level and the bottom doors to the back yard.

*

Dusk was setting in as Shimon Adri slowed his rental Skoda and pulled off the quiet Kresnice Parkway into a mostly dark parking lot, lit only by one streetlight at its entrance. The parking lot sits beside the Sava River in Ljubljana, Slovenia. Shimon Adri had come here to Sava Specialty Meats to negotiate a wholesale purchase for Adri Foods.

Akeem Almasi stepped out of his car and stretched his legs. Between the drive to Frankfurt, the flight to Ljubljana, the infuriating argument at the car rental desk, and the twenty-minute driving around a little bit lost to finally get here, Akeem's day had become a long one. His typical handsome, positive expression was now a tired, impatient one.

Patches of snow still lay on parts of the parking lot and the riverbank, leftover from last week's unusually rare April snowfall in Slovenia. He glanced at his watch. He'd rest up at the hotel tonight and be fine for his meeting at Sava Meats at 9:00 in the morning. But now, the digital window on his wristwatch read 8:43pm. His contact was three minutes late. That worried Akeem, who worked in a clandestine world in which details and perfect punctuality matter a lot. *Where are you?*

Seconds later, a bicyclist approached on the jogging path along the riverbank — dodging a few patches of crusty snow. As the bicyclist arrived at the mostly unlit parking lot, the too obviously overweight rider in loud red and blue spandex veered into the parking lot and straight toward Shimon. Stopping only long enough to put one foot down on the parking lot dirt to steady himself, without a single word, the rider reached over his shoulder with one arm, pulled a manila envelope up and out of his backpack, and handed it to Shimon.

"Is that it?" Akeem looked, inquisitively, at the young man's face, noticing the lack of any facial hair except very thick, dark eyebrows that extended over both eyes nearly without a gap.

"No," the bicyclist answered, "there's a message."

Akeem just stared at him, waited to hear it.

"General Arruk is getting nervous. Very nervous. He tells you to turn up the heat. Speed it up!" With that, the bicyclist sped off on down the jogging path in the same direction that he was originally going.

Akeem got back into his car, started it, and turned the heater one notch higher. He opened the envelope and drew out a sheet of paper filled with

Arabic handwriting. Before reading it, he dumped the other contents onto the passenger seat — seeing an assortment of a dozen or so photos. He grabbed up one of the photos. It was too dark, now, to see well, so he reached up above his head and, after searching with his hand for a few moments, located the light button.

With the interior light on, he looked at the photos. They were images of Sonya Katz, with the young daughter, aboard a luxury yacht in a harbor, a modest acreage and house, an elderly woman standing beside a chicken coop, another photo on the yacht of Sonya Katz and Ishi playing with a dollhouse, a studio family photo of Sonya and Joseph Katz with baby Ishi on Sonya's knee, a couple of aerial photos from the Gruber farm to the Philippsthal acreage, Sonya and Joseph Katz posing for a photo outside Katz Furniture entrance, Sonya in a jogging outfit sitting on a park bench with a little dog on the bench beside her, and more.

Akeem took the sheet of paper that had "3 khatawat (3 steps)" scribbled as a top line. After reading the paper, carefully, the PLO spy stepped out of the car again. He reached for a cigarette, lit it, and then lit the paper, letting it drop to the ground — watching it to ensure that it burned completely.

CHAPTER 18

Ishi walked to the end of the driveway. Arriving there a few minutes early for the bus, she watched her father as he roared in a straight line pulling a 36-foot-wide sprayer with the small cab-less W6 International tractor on the small, barley field. It was May 12, and Horst got an early start with spraying because of the lack of wind in these spring mornings — wind that otherwise could compromise the even delivery of the weed-fighting herbicide.

As Ishi sat near the front of the small school bus, her mind was on the graduation dress that she'd need in just three short weeks. Her mother had offered to make one for her. But Ishi worried that her mom's product would end up looking too hokey. Of the money she had earned at Adri Foods, Ishi had carefully saved nearly two-hundred and fifty euros for this exact reason. But she'd need to somehow get to Fulda or Erfurt to shop for one.

Algebra. The final class of the day. Ishi was so bored in this Algebra class, a subject that was very easy for her. She didn't understand why Herr Schmidtke couldn't ever let the class go early — like many other teachers did with Friday's last classes.

Finally, the bell rang. Ishi, having already closed and stacked her two books, stood immediately and headed for her locker.

Ishi stepped out through the school's heavy, open front doors and down three steps to the front sidewalk. The two white and green buses were already half-finished loading, but Ishi wouldn't be taking the bus. Her shift at Adri Foods started in one hour. It was a long Whit Holiday weekend, so Adri Foods was expected to be extra busy.

"Hey!"

Ishi turned to see Christian approaching through the doorway behind her. She turned and smiled. "Hey you."

Approaching, Christian said, "I guess it'll be a big weekend at Adri's. They're closed on Monday, right?"

"Yeah."

"What are you doing on Monday? I was thinking that a few of us, or maybe just you and me, could go to the weir at Dorndorf. Go fishing. Swimming. Whatever. Just hang."

The Dorndorf weir, less than a fifteen-minute drive east from Vacha, was a regular destination for many young people during warmer months. Besides the fishing and swimming, that particular spot had become a known outdoor party location. Over the years, the villagers of Dorndorf had put up several stinks over the gatherings, mostly about trash left on the site. But all in all, the gatherings had been well-behaved and were harming nobody. Several visits from the local police to the site, to check up on the goings-ons had confirmed that there was really nothing of concern.

Surely the weir would be full of young people this weekend, especially considering the warm weather.

"Actually," Ishi responded, "I'm trying to get down to Fulda or to Erfurt. Monday is really the only chance I have to shop for a graduation dress."

"Yeah, Lucy was talking about that, too."

"Oh, I haven't really talked to her about—"

"I know!" Christian had an idea. "How about the three of us go to Erfurt during the day, and hold it. Are shops even open?"

"Yeah, I checked. Offices are closed, but shops are open."

"So then, let's go to Erfurt during the day, and stop at the weir on our way back."

Ishi liked this idea. "Sure! Your car, right?"

"Yep." Christian smiled. "Mi Jetta, su Jetta."

*

Dagmar was vacuuming as Ishi washed the breakfast dishes. Ishi groaned at her mother's poor singing over the loud vacuum cleaner, but was inwardly happy that her mother was happy enough to sing as she worked.

A car horn sounded outside.

Dagmar had seen Christian's car arrive just as the horn honked. "They're here sweetheart! Go! I'll finish."

Ishi quickly dried her hands off on a tea towel. "Thanks, mama."

Ishi rushed into the bedroom, grabbed a sweater, high-heeled shoes, and her purse. Carrying those items, she quickly ran to the front door, opened it, and waved to the car to let them know that she's coming, and then slipped her feet into untied sneakers.

"Here!" Dagmar was approaching Ishi with a plastic bag — holding it out to her daughter. "Fruit. Something for you and Christian and Lucy so you don't spend all your money on fast food." Dagmar's voice carried a note of caring pleasantness.

As Ishi ran out to the car with her arms full, she saw Christian, Lucy, and, to her surprise, Sebastian! Lucy and Sebastian were in the back seat. Christian reached across from the driver's seat and pushed the front door open for Ishi.

As Ishi got in, she exclaimed to Sebastian, "I didn't know you were coming. I thought you had something with your family today."

Sebastian chimed his response, "Ha! Got out of it. Would rather be with you guys."

Lucy added with a notable juicy tone, "I'd rather you be with us, too."

Ishi looked around at Lucy as Christian began driving. *Really, Luce? No discretion?*

As they drove, Sebastian asked, "How far is Erfurt?"

Lucy responded, "You've never been?"

"Lucy," Sebastian replied, "I've only lived here for nine months. I'm not a shopaholic like you." He jested as he playfully over exaggerated a photo-model pose.

"Hey!" She playfully pushed him. They jostled momentarily. Ishi and Christian both noted the chemistry in the back seat.

After a moment, Sebastian retracted and became intentionally less playful. As he turned to gaze out of the window, he asked, "How does your father—?

Hey, Ishi! How does your father do everything by himself on that farm?"

Christian answered for Ishi. "What? Have you ever seen how hard Ishi can work? Man! She's a true blue farming machine!"

Ishi laughed at this. Looking back toward Sebastian, she answered, "My mom and I help. It works, somehow."

Lucy asked, "You milk, too?"

"Not usually. But I have. It's kinda fun. The cows love being milked."

Christian added, "Yeah, I've heard that. My uncle used to have a radio hanging in his barn. He said that, when he milks, the cows would actually sway to the music."

Sebastian asked, "Do you do that? A radio?"

"Ha ha," Ishi laughed. "No. But maybe we should."

Christian added, "Yeah, play Scorpions. No, Metallica, and the cows will give you cottage cheese."

Laughter!

"Motown," Lucy added, "and you could get chocolate milk."

More laughter!

Sebastian didn't understand. "Motown?"

Lucy explained, "Soul. Groovy. Black."

Sebastian was still confused.

Lucy continued, "Sometimes smooth," as she slid a hand along her long leg in a sultry manner, an action that Sebastian could see but was out of sight from the front seat.

It was clear, to Sebastian, that Lucy was making moves on him — even this early on a Monday morning. In any ordinary circumstance, Sebastian would have welcomed the advancements from the very gorgeous, tall, slender brunette. But Sebastian was also very aware that positive responses to Lucy would curtail his mission objective to endear Ishi to him.

Sebastian said, "Hey Ishi, I heard that our mothers talked, and set up a dinner at our house for Friday. Did you know?"

Ishi didn't know. "Oh. Good. But what about my shift?"

"Taken care of."

Arriving at the center of Erfurt, Christian parked at Schlösserstrasse within easy walking distance of many shops. As the four poured out of the car, Lucy suggested, "Ishi, I know all the shops. Let's go! The boys can entertain themselves." Ishi agreed. Locked arm in arm, the two girls immediately walked, happily, up the street.

"Well," started Christian, "what shall we do?"

Sebastian was hit with a sudden realization that it might be many hours that he'd need to spend with Christian. Sebastian didn't dislike Christian. It was just that he'd never made a friend of him. "Ummm, I don't know," answered Sebastian. "How long do you think they'll be?"

Christian took a moment to think. "I don't have a clue. Dress shopping? Oh, it could be three or four hours, I'll bet."

Sebastian's face showed his displeasure.

Christian suggested, "Hey, I know a cool pub about two blocks from here. It's called Ubersee. Wanna check it out?"

Sebastian looked at his watch. "At ten-thirty in the morning?"

Christian's face showed that he hadn't thought about the early hour. "Well," Christian was thinking, "hmmm, well, we could go to the main square and just hang out. See what's there. It's a few blocks that way," Christian suggested, pointing.

Sebastian was indifferent. "Okay."

Just as Christian had predicted, most shops were open. Ishi and Lucy found a very good shop with lots of formal dresses.

Lucy already had her dress, so she didn't need to shop. Ishi had already tried on two dresses that she kind of liked. She was in a dressing room, fitting into dress number three, as Lucy sat in a chair waiting for Ishi to emerge and model it for her.

Lucy asked, "What are you going to do about Sebastian?"

"What do you mean?" Ishi responded from the fitting room.

"Oh come on, Ishi! It's obvious how attracted he is to you."

Ishi responded between huffs and puffs as she tried to get the dress on, "Luce, you're mental. Sebastian likes *you*."

Lucy replied quietly to herself, "If only." Then louder, "Are you totally blind?"

Ishi asked, "Even if it were true, which it's not, what do you mean what am I going to do?" *What am I going to do?* She toyed with the thought. *What girl doesn't find him totally hot?*

Ishi emerged from the dressing room as Lucy replied, "I mean, what about Christian? Oh, wow! Ish, that's the one! Turn! Turn!"

Ishi turned around, modeling.

Lucy gasped, "Oh, Ishi, I love the sheen panel on the back. The scarlet red is gorgeous. Suits you so good! Oh, wow, Ishi!"

As Ishi stepped over to analyze herself in a full-length mirror, she asked, "What do you mean, what about Christian?"

"You guys have been a, uhmm, a thing for so long—"

"A thing? We're not a thing."

Lucy tried to clarify, "You are so a thing! Christian thinks so."

"We're good friends." Ishi knew she was bidding for neutrality and felt a pang of guilt in her dishonesty.

"I'll say!"

Ishi began walking around the store.

Lucy asked, "What are you doing?"

"I want to see what it feels like, you know, to walk around in," Ishi explained as she strolled, proudly, up an aisle and then down another aisle, raising her hands ballerina-style above her head and doing a happy show-off twirl.

Lucy maneuvered so that she could analyze her girlfriend approaching down the second aisle. "Wow!"

Ishi's happy expression turned slightly more solemn as she said, "Two forty. That taps me out completely."

"Yeah, but it's totally worth it, Ish."

The girls exited the shop, excitedly, and came to a stop.

Lucy asked, "Did they say where they were going?"

"No," it dawned on Ishi. "I'll call Christian." As she pulled her phone out of her purse, and as she began to enter Christian's number, she said, "You like him, don't you."

"Like who?"

As Ishi put the phone to her ear, she said, "Sebastian. Duhh!"

As Ishi waited for Christian to answer, Lucy silently mouthed the words, "Well, hot!"

"Oh hi, Christian," Ishi chirped, "we're done. Where are you?" Ishi listened as Christian explained.

As Ishi tucked her phone back away, Lucy said, "Sebastian totally has it for you."

Ishi replied, "I doubt it."

"He does," Lucy punctuated.

"For you, you mean," Ishi corrected her friend, knowing Lucy might be right.

"Ishi, it's obvious. Everyone sees it."

Ishi changed the subject by saying, "They're at the square watching a chalk artist. Let's go!"

As they began toward the main square, Lucy said, "I'm happy."

"Why? Why are you so happy?"

"I'm happy for you."

As they walked on, Ishi frowned, not sure how to take Lucy's words.

They'd gone for lunch at Viba Confiserie-Café. And now mid-afternoon, they were on their drive back to Vacha. This time Lucy sat up front with Christian, and Ishi was in the back seat with Sebastian — the big shopping bag with the dress between them.

Ishi really was attracted to Sebastian. It was a tricky situation because Christian had been such a close friend for years with sometimes hints of romantic sparks, and Ishi was fully aware of Christian's strong feelings for her. She had strong feelings for Christian, too. She remembered that they'd kissed, twice. She also knew that she had always ducked out of any conversations with Christian in which he seemed to be leading the conversation toward commitment or at least something more. Ishi wasn't sure why she had resisted Christian. Nevertheless, it had become more complicated now because of her attraction to Sebastian.

While Christian and Lucy were quite jabberish along the way, both Ishi and Sebastian were slightly shy and slightly uncomfortable. Ishi wasn't aware, however, that Sebastian was anything but shy. It was the act that Sebastian had chosen for a bit, in order to send Ishi two messages.

Sebastian offered Ishi an occasional adoring look that communicated, clearly, that he liked her. And Sebastian remained slightly withheld to communicate to Ishi that he wasn't going to push, hoping that would impress her.

Finally, Ishi broke the silence. "Did you bring your swim, umm, swimming—" she didn't know exactly what to call it, "swim stuff?"

Christian and Lucy, overhearing, laughed.

"Swimming trunks," Lucy declared, giggling.

"Shorts. Swimming shorts," Christian corrected Lucy, laughing. "They're big shorts. That's all."

Ishi replied, "Okay, okay. Swimming shorts or whatever."

Sebastian answered, "Yeah, they're in the back."

Lucy twisted around to look at Ishi. "Did you?"

Ishi realized that she completely forgot to bring her bikini. "Oh, I completely forgot. Crap!"

Christian offered, "It's only fifteen minutes to get them. I can drive you home quickly."

Ishi corrected Christian, "Half an hour both ways. No, that's okay. Drat!"

Christian responded, "That's no problem. What's half an hour?"

Sebastian quipped, "Who needs a swimsuit anyway? Ha ha! Swim in your undies. Maybe nobody will notice the difference."

Ishi looked at Sebastian's grin -- and liked its playfulness. "You wish," she flirted.

Sebastian mouthed the words to Ishi silently, "I do." He grinned.

Ishi felt a blush in her cheeks, and as she quickly looked away, she felt a small wave of electricity pass through her. Ishi caught Christian's eyes in his rear-view mirror. "No Chris, it's okay. I don't need to swim.

It'll be fun anyway." Lucy chirped up, "We can fish for a while anyway. From the weir."

Ishi quickly agreed. "Yeah. Just hang out. It'll be good!"

It was just after 4:00pm, in the warm May afternoon, when they arrived at the weir. They immediately saw the throngs of young people — many were swimming, some were kicking a soccer ball around. There were many blankets strewn about on the pebbly shore, anchored down with coolers of various bright colors.

Quickly, Christian popped the trunk open, and Lucy, Christian, and Sebastian pulled beach totes out. Sebastian then pulled out one last, apparently heavy, tote. Grinning, he held it open toward Ishi for her to look into it. She looked, and saw two bottles of red wine, one bottle of vodka, and at least six or seven or eight cans of Kromback and Warsteiner beer. Lucy also peered into the sack. "Wow!"

If Sebastian would've been true to his faith in normal circumstances, the last thing he would've brought would've been alcohol, any alcohol. But he was on a mission. And, as such, he and his two associates, using the family name Adri, were convinced that the Koran instructs to do what is necessary.

Five hours later, after sunlight gave way to moonlight and the light of campfires, a few people were still splashing around in the water. The several boomboxes that were on the shore had been coordinatively tuned to the same Erfurt-based hip hop radio station.

Both of Christian's and Lucy's large beach blankets had been joined to form a very large blanket. Lucy laid on her side, a slender arm propping up her head. She was still in her bikini, but with an unbuttoned shirt covering her torso. She had consumed a lot of alcohol, and flirted gladly with two boys and with Sebastian who also laid on that corner of the large blanket. All three young men were shirtless and in their dripping wet swimming shorts.

Christian was sitting on the opposite corner of the blanket with Ishi for a while. But he had accepted an invitation from his good friend, Peter, to go for a few dives off the weir, leaving Ishi sitting alone.

Sebastian, while pretending to drink alcohol liberally, had actually instead drunk very little. The moment he noticed that Christian left Ishi, he seized the opportunity. Standing up, he stepped over to Ishi, and laid down where she sat on the blanket. Immediately, Sebastian recognized that Ishi was feeling the effects of wine and had loosened up. He picked up the bottle that Ishi had next to her, and looking at it, saw that it was nearly empty. He smiled at her, took the bottle to his lips, and pretended to chug a big gulp. Ishi giggled, a little bit drunk. Ishi noticed that Sebastian was even more beautiful in the environment that was lit only by a few small campfires in various nearby places.

Sebastian had just sat down beside Ishi when a new slower song began from all the coordinated boomboxes. It was a local favorite. He jumped back up to his feet and began to sway in a slow dance.

"Dance with me!" Sebastian invited Ishi.

Ishi replied with a sheepish smile, "Oh no. I can't." *Oh, I want to!*

"Come on!" Sebastian coaxed. He reached a hand down.

Relenting, Ishi took his hand and let Sebastian pull her to her feet. Holding each other at arm's length, they swayed to the music.

Christian had just climbed back onto the weir from a dive. He wiped water from his face and looked over to see Ishi dancing with Sebastian. He scowled.

Ishi bathed in the romantic experience of dancing with Sebastian in the firelight. She had enough wine in her to dull her, to dull her enough to forget entirely about Christian. Slowly and carefully, Sebastian pulled Ishi a little closer to him. Ishi saw Sebastian's handsome, dark-skinned chest inches in front of her. She let herself be pulled up against it as they swayed to the music. The sensation of her body, her chest physically touching that of another person was excitingly new! She liked it.

When the song finished, sensing that he had taken this far enough for now, Sebastian gently prodded Ishi away. He then took a step toward Ishi, kissed her on the cheek, and jogged to the water, splashing his way into it. He knew that he had, strategically, left Ishi wanting more. And, he also knew that, if he had not cut away, he might risk confrontation with Christian.

The fifteen-minute ride home was quite quiet. Ishi, in the front passenger's seat, was slouched against the door — half asleep, quite drunk, and foggily emotionally conflicted.

Lucy was tired and drunk, too, but managed to toss out some happy quips about how much fun it was. Christian and Sebastian, both completely sober, didn't speak.

Christian, considering Ishi's state, decided to take her home first. Arriving at Ishi's front door, Christian began to take his seatbelt off, but Sebastian had already jumped out to help Ishi. Christian popped the trunk, and Sebastian retrieved Ishi's bags. Christian could only watch.

CHAPTER 19

A thick-bodied, blonde thirty-six-year-old woman took a coffee that had just been handed over to her, by the vendor, in a trendy coffee shop. She turned and saw an empty table, in the far corner, near where the coffee shop's floor-to-ceiling accordion divider separated the smallish coffee shop from a much larger bookstore. As the woman moved toward her chosen seat, two teenage girls, unaware of the woman, beat her to it. The woman stopped and searched again for another table where she could open her laptop away from prying eyes. Opting for a table near the glass entry door, in the other opposite corner from her originally chosen table, she settled in, and pulled her laptop out of a satchel. She placed it on the table beside her coffee and opened it.

The last half of May here in Everett, Washington was so nice! As the woman Leah Fromm sat with her coffee and laptop, she enjoyed the wonderful aroma from the three big planters of flora that were situated just outside the open glass door of the coffee shop. After entering her password to bring her screen alive, she clicked on a link that asked for a code. She entered the code. Another small window appeared asking for a second code. Leah entered that. She was now completely secure while using the coffee shop's public Wi-Fi.

She clicked on a button labelled 'Contact'. A small chat window appeared. Momentarily, a text appeared from the user on the other end, "Iden". Leah typed in "t-o-t-o-n-8-8-z".

"Hi Toto. Update?"

"Yes," Leah typed. "Progress. All use of names Joseph, Sonya, and Katz ended Feb 2001. Their Everett apartment lease ended that same month."

"How is that progress? We already knew most of that."

Leah typed, "I found the make and license plate numbers of their purchased vehicle on their lease agreement — indicated for parking purposes. Tapping into vehicle databases today for anything on that vehicle: registration; sale. If they still have that vehicle and have re-registered it, or sold it to themselves, their new identities, it'll show up." Leah took a satisfied sip of her coffee.

Responding text, "How soon will you have the data results?"

"By tomorrow," Leah typed. Then she clicked 'End'.

Mossad recruited Leslie Parskiman when she was twenty-eight years old. She had been working as a journalist for Reuters News Agency — as a foreign correspondent in St Petersburg, Russia. Mossad's attention was originally raised by Parskiman's frustration from accepted anti-Semitic narratives that were often condoned by many mainstream news agencies. One year after the death of Parskiman's last remaining parent — her mother, who died of natural causes — Leslie Parskiman had, clearly, become depressed and frustrated. That depression led her to opioids and the beginning of a downward spiral. But Mossad had seen her investigative talent.

Agreeing with Mossad's offer, after a series of secret meetings, Leslie Parskiman joined a ski group touring to Rosa Khutor — a popular ski resort in Russia near the Black Sea. During her time there, and while back-country skiing, a small avalanche was triggered. Leslie Parskiman's body was never recovered.

She spent the next two and a half years in Tel Aviv learning trade craft and multiple languages. In 1998, Leah Fromm, with the code name Toto, was commissioned to her first mission in the field for Mossad. And now, three years later, Toto was the point agent tracking the mysterious Katz couple.

*

When Rebecca had raced outside to the steeply sloped backyard to retrieve her shocked little Maltese puppy and phone, David had yelled at her from the deck above, "And if you keep up your shit attitude with me, I'll throw you off the deck, too."

That had done it! The final straw! Rebecca gathered up her scared but not-seriously damaged puppy, located her phone in the grass, struggled back up the steeply sloped lawn, and entered the lower level of the house. There, she sat down into an armchair, panting from the exertion. She coddled the frightened puppy on her lap and examined her. She took a couple of minutes to pluck the dry grass and twigs out of Lily's fur, cooing comforting expressions to her precious little Lily. "Ohh, sweetie. It's okay. You're okay. Here, let me get this grass off of you. Ohhh, my baby ..." Then Rebecca collected herself and, cradling Lily, she walked resolutely upstairs through the mudroom and into the garage. She got into the Ford Explorer, opened the garage door — expecting, at any moment, that David would come bursting toward her from inside — and she backed out.

David had been in the master bedroom washroom when Rebecca left, so he didn't notice until he heard the garage door closing. He ran to the garage to see it empty.

Rebecca's phone rang. She didn't answer. It rang again. She didn't answer. Texts began to arrive. Concerned that David might think that she'd made a permanent run for it, she pulled over and texted him back. "I'll be back. Need a few hours." Then she put the phone down on her lap, put her face in her palms, and sobbed.

After several minutes, more collected, Rebecca called Suzanna.

Suzanna answered, "Hi Rebecca. I was just thinking about you. How are you?"

Rebecca hesitated, momentarily, as she had just found a tissue and was wiping her nose. "Hi Suzanna. Not good. Can I come over? I need to talk."

Suzanna replied, "What happened? Of course, sweetie. I'm not home though. Just coming out of the grocery store. I'll be there in fifteen minutes. Is that okay?"

"Oh sure," Rebecca answered. "I'll meet you there. Suzanna; thank you!"

David, with his anger on a low boil, decided to go for a walk. His walk took him the two and a half blocks down to the harbor. He walked onto one of the boardwalks among the boats, then stood and gazed out over the water. He wondered how it all came to this. *What a messed-up existence!* He thought about Tel Aviv. On his phone he searched the Internet for photos of Katz Furniture.

Of the dozen or so photos that appeared, four of them seemed to look recent. *Who knows how old these photos are?* Two of the photos showed new model cars in the parking lot, so he assumed that the photos were quite recent and that the business was still in operation. Clicking the phone screen off, he gazed over the water again. Bringing the phone screen alive again, he punched in Rebecca's number. It rang with no answer, again only going to voicemail.

Rebecca and Suzanna sat at the table in Suzanna's breakfast nook. Rebecca's face was red, her eyes swollen from crying. Suzanna reached across and topped up Rebecca's tea.

"Did you ever plan to have children?" Suzanna queried gingerly, assuming that this might be a sensitive topic.

Rebecca's cell phone chirped. She looked at it, and touched the 'End' button, stopping the chirping. Rebecca took a few thoughtful moments to sip the tea, put it down, and raised her eyes to Suzanna's eyes. "We had a child," Rebecca finally admitted.

Suzanna was surprised! "You did? Where is-- What happened?"

Rebecca wondered how she could tell Suzanna anything about Ishi without giving too much away. "She went missing. When she was three."

"Oh Rebecca! That's awful. Missing? Abducted?"

Rebecca explained, "My mother was babysitting. She was outside playing, and—"

"So, you have a daughter somewhere right now. How long ago was this?"

Rebecca's cell phone delivered a tone indicating a voice message. She ignored it and put the phone to the side. "Sorry." She then looked at Suzanna, paused, and said, "Fourteen and a half years ago." She took her tea again, sipped, then added, "Nobody knows if she's alive."

Suzanna's expression exuded compassion. "Oh Rebecca, sweetheart!" She got out of her chair, stepped around the table to Rebecca, and hugged her.

Rebecca broke back into tears. Even though she was sobbing, it felt so good to finally share it with someone despite the risk!

As Suzanna sat back down, she said, "Three – and fourteen. And so, she'd be seventeen or eighteen now. What's her name?"

"Suzy, I don't even know if she's alive."

Suzanna replied, with a hopeful tone, "Well, odds are that she is."

"Isabella. We called her Ishi for short." Rebecca realized that she was risking now by divulging any of this information, even to Suzanna.

Suzanna asked, "Have you ... Stupid question! Sure, you've searched for her. Have you done an ancestral DNA search?"

Rebecca was becoming uncomfortable that this conversation might disclose too much. Her cell phone delivered another tone indicating a text message. She lied, "David always refused."

"You should do it anyway," Suzanna suggested. "And, yes, of course you can stay here as long as you need to. Mark won't mind at all."

"Thank you. I'll just need long enough until I can find a place."

"Do you have pictures? Of course, you have pictures. What am I thinking?"

Rebecca held her teacup to her lips without sipping, "Somewhere. Not on me." Rebecca reached for her phone and read the text message from David. *I'm sorry.* Slightly surprised at David's apology, she put the phone back down.

Rebecca realized that, only one and a half years into their fugitive situation, it might create a messy danger to split from David — despite the horrible environment at home.

Suzanna got up and walked to the fridge, opening it. "You hungry? I have a ton of food now. Some grapes?"

After giving the bunch of grapes a quick rinse in the island sink and then placing them in a pretty bowl, she stepped back to the little breakfast nook table. Each woman nibbled on a grape.

"I think I'll go home," Rebecca said.

"Becky, you don't have to. We have lots of room."

"I really appreciate it, Suzy. But, no, I'll go and see if I can make peace."

Suzanna's brows knitted. "You sure?"

Rebecca grabbed another tissue and cleaned up her face. "No. But I'll try."

"Wha--?" Suzanna looked into Rebecca's eyes, confused. "Becky. Okay. I'll be right by my phone, okay."

"Okay."

As Rebecca drove home, the thought of an ancestral DNA registry filled her mind. Halfway home, Rebecca pulled over, took her phone, and took several minutes searching the Internet for a local ancestral DNA registry. She quickly found two. Choosing the one that looked good, and had an office on the North Shore, she memorized the phone number, then dialed.

*

Christian wasn't happy that Sebastian was moving on Ishi. And he was deflated that Ishi was playing along. Sure, Christian and Ishi had never declared a boyfriend-girlfriend relationship, but over the past years as such close friends that had many inflections of romance, he thought it was obvious. He was not sure what to do though. As one measure, he offered to drive Ishi home from school — each day that she didn't have an Adri Foods shift— instead of her taking the bus. She had agreed.

This was one of those days. The Jetta stopped on the clumpy grassy-dirt yard in front of the Gruber house beside Gruber's sand-colored 1996 Volvo sedan.

In an effort to keep Ishi from getting out of the car immediately, Christian tried to engage in conversation. "Did you … the council, confirm the band for the dance?"

"Not quite yet. We're trying to decide between Lemon and The Roos. I'm hoping for The Roos."

"Yeah, way better!"

"And more expensive."

"So?"

Ishi explained, "We've already nearly blown our budget on the dinner and decorations."

Christian looked at the cows in a small pasture near the barn. "Do you still milk?"

"Sometimes. Not often anymore. I'm too busy. Dad or mom do it."

"I'd like to try it," Christian mused. "Do you think I could try it sometime?"

Ishi snickered. "Sure, ha ha … I can see you all nervous that the cow will kick you."

"If you can do it, I can do it."

Ishi added, "Oh yeah! Well, how about when the cow swings its tail, dripping with shit and piss, across your face while you're milking? Can you handle that?"

Christian's mouth dropped open. "That happens?"

Ishi laughed. "Yeah, sometimes."

Christian made a sour face. "Eeeeesh! I'd still try it though."

*

Akeem and Azim knelt beside each other on their prayer mats, each bent forward with their foreheads near the floor. The drapes were pulled closed in the Adri living room as they performed the Asr — the afternoon prayer.

Finishing, they each rolled up their mats. As Akeem removed the kufi cap from his head, he handed his rolled-up mat to Azim. "This time, make sure they are put away in the back closet!" Akeem realized that he was beginning to actually feel like Azim's father. Strangely, he was warm to this sensation.

"Come on now," Saadia called from the kitchen. "They will be here in less than an hour. Go upstairs and get changed!"

"Come in! Come in!" Miriam, Shimon standing behind her, opened the door for Horst, Dagmar, and Ishi.

Dagmar was holding a wide glass vase full of a colorful variety of salvia, yarrow, gazania hybrids, and dahlias. "Thank you. Hello," Dagmar and Horst chimed together as the three of them entered Adri's front door. Dagmar, immediately, held the flowers out to Miriam. "These are from my garden."

"Oh! Oh, you shouldn't have," Miriam took them with a wide smile.

"Oh yes, I should have. There are a lot more where they came from."

Shimon welcomed, with a hand gesture, "Welcome to our home. I'm glad you came."

The early June warm temperatures negated any need for outerwear, so there were no jackets to shed. Walking through the entry, toward the living room of the classic Victorian-styled home, all three Grubers marvelled at the ornate chandelier, drapery, the cherry hardwood floor, and the beautifully framed photos on the wall. Horst and Ishi looked closer at the photos as they stepped toward the sunken living room and its massive fireplace and the lively crackling fire. The photos were of Adri's younger days in Frankfurt — one of Sebastian playing in a soccer match as a young teenager, and one of the Adri Foods shop in Stuttgart. It was not possible for any viewer of the photos to see that they all were photoshopped.

"Aaand, this was your shop in S-S-Stuttgart?" Horst pointed a finger at the framed photo.

"Ah, yes," Shimon answered. "We did okay there. But you know, big city, too much competition. Taxes."

Miriam chimed in, "Definitely a smart move to come to Vacha."

Sebastian appeared, coming down the wide beautiful stairs.

He looked at Ishi first, "Hi, Ishi."

All three Grubers looked at him as he reached the bottom and stepped down into the living room. Ishi was astonished how handsome Sebastian looked this evening. "Hi," she shyly squeaked out.

Dagmar greeted him cheerfully, "Oh, hello Sebastian. Don't you look handsome in that burgundy shirt!"

All having thoroughly enjoyed dinner's main courses, Miriam scurried to remove the main course dishes and bring dishes of desserts to the table. She asked Horst and Dagmar, "So, where are your folks? I beg your pardon if they've passed. I don't mean to be disrespectful. Are they still with us?"

Dagmar answered, "Oh, yes, sadly, all four of our parents have passed."

Miriam immediately replied, "Oh, I'm so sorry for asking."

Horst said, "It's n-nothing to be sorry about. It's life."

Dagmar added, "Both our fathers died in the war. It's not a good story, actually. My mother lived in convalescence, in Heidelberg, and Horst's was in Mannheim. Handy! We could often make trips and see them both easily."

Shimon asked, "Was it your plan to have one child? Did you think of having more?"

Miriam quickly referred to Ishi, "Did you ever want a brother or a sister?"

Ishi answered, "Umm? Not really. I never really thought about it. I had my school friends."

Dagmar interjected quickly, "We thought about it."

Horst added, "It takes m-money to bring a child up, right. That's s-something we've n-never had a lot of."

Dagmar finished his thought, "And, we wanted to give Ishi everything she deserved."

Ishi frowned slightly — in embarrassment at the sudden attention put on her wellbeing.

Suddenly, Sebastian asked Ishi, "Your middle name? Do you have a middle—?"

Dagmar quickly jumped in, "She never needed one. Her true name, Isabella, is so beautiful on its own, we thought it didn't need support." Dagmar laughed a little to communicate satisfaction with her answer.

Sebastian had begun to read irritation on Ishi's face from all the grilling about Gruber family history. He jumped to his feet to help clear away the last of the dirty main course dishes as Miriam set two crystal platters of desserts on the table. The platters were full of kunafah and shaabiyat — specialty Middle Eastern desserts that were unfamiliar to the Grubers.

"Oh, wow!" Horst exclaimed.

Dagmar added, "Oh my!"

Ishi asked, "What are they? I have seen those in the store. Those are kunafah, right?" she pointed at a dish.

Shimon explained, "These are popular in the Middle East. We learned them from our parents." He pointed at one dish. "You are correct. This is kunafah. It's rosewater syrup with cheeses, ricotta, made with kataifi dough." He pointed at the other platter. "This is shaabiyat. Filo pastry with sweet cream, sort of like a puff pastry."

Miriam looked at Dagmar. "I might be able to bake, but I've never been good in the garden. Maybe you'd allow me to come see your garden one day?"

"Oh sure! I'm no master gardener. But any time."

Horst added, "Hey, you'd m-make a good weeding team. We n-need all the help we can get." He laughed as some chuckles joined his laughter.

"Here, you just use your fingers for these," Shimon instructed, as he plucked a kunafah off the platter. As he grabbed the kunafah, it fell apart. "Ya aimra'at-- 'ahdar mughrf," he barked at Miriam! Immediately, realizing that he spoke in Arabic, he said, apologetically, "Oh, sorry. Some of—"

"… some of his parent's expressions," Miriam quickly interrupted, to explain, while getting up to fetch a serving spatula.

Shimon added, "In their language. Of course, we learned some of it as kids." He glanced up to the Grubers to gauge their reaction, hoping they couldn't tell Arabic from Hebrew.

The three Grubers were more surprised by Shimon's denigrating tone toward his wife than the language. Horst offered, "W-we understand."

The sun had set. As the two couples sat in the living room visiting, Sebastian had led Ishi out onto the front small porch. Each in cushioned deck chairs, positioned as close together as the wide wooden chair arms would allow, they faced the quiet well-lit street.

Ishi, enamored by her handsome classmate, started with small talk. She put her hand on her stomach, "I'm so full!"

"Yeah, me, too. I ate too much."

"But it was all so good," Ishi puffed out her cheeks to exaggerate her full stomach! Then she threw Sebastian a little smile. "Your parents are so great!"

"So are yours. And so are you."

Ishi was taken off guard by the compliment. She glanced back at Sebastian with surprise. Sebastian shifted in his chair cushions, nervously. He said, "Ishi, I want to ask you a question."

"Sure!"

"It's sort of a big question."

Ishi was a little bit nervous. "Okay?"

Sebastian shifted to look directly at her.

Ishi prodded nervously, "What? Ask!"

Sebastian said, "I know you and Christian have been friends forever. And I don't want to make him mad." Ishi felt a blush coming up her face but didn't know where Sebastian was going with this. It dawned on her -- just as he asked, "Will you be my date for graduation?"

Ishi looked at his eyes, marvelling, but momentarily, without words. Her mind was instantly a mixture of racing half-thoughts, quick calculations, and excitement.

"Hey, maybe you already committed to—"

"No. No other commitments." She quickly thought of Christian. *How would he take this?* She considered quickly, *But Christian could've asked me. He hasn't.* She looked down at her hands in her lap as she peeled at a fingernail flaw. Then she looked back at Sebastian. "Yes!" She gave him a big smile.

Sebastian sank back into his deck chair, in relief. "Oh, wow!" Sebastian breathed out. "I thought you were going to say no." A broad smile stretched across his handsome face as he gazed at Ishi.

To punctuate her answer, Ishi placed her arm across Sebastian's chair arm, letting him know, by her posture, that she is open to him. Sebastian put his hand on her arm for a few seconds. She didn't pull back. Then he pulled the arm, and Ishi, toward him and they hugged warmly, but somewhat awkwardly, while still each sitting in their chairs.

*

Ishi's hands, each wrapped around a cow's teat, squeezed rhythmically in downward motions — the stream of milk, from each teat, shooting down into the silver metal pail. The black angus, held in place by a vertical stanchion around her neck, munched comfortably on loose hay in the trough. Ishi looked up at Christian as she milked. Christian stood, watching and learning, from several feet on the other side of a long four-inch deep and ten-inch-wide concrete gutter — watching and learning.

"It's easy," Ishi explained. "See! And the cow likes it."

Christian asked nervously, "But what if the cow kicks?"

Grabbing the little stool by one leg, and the pail in the other hand, Ishi extracted herself from the cow and stepped across the gutter, handing the pail and stool to Christian. "Don't be nervous," Ishi instructed.

"But—" Christian resisted.

"But nothing! Just go for it! If you act nervous, the cow might get nervous, too."

Christian stepped, warily, across the gutter and placed the stool down. Sitting gingerly on it, he placed the pail under the black cow's udder.

Ishi said, "She might move her feet or give little kicks sometimes. Just act as if you're in control. Put your left knee against her leg, between her leg and the pail, like I did."

Christian reached for a teat, carefully wrapped his hand around it, then did the same with his other hand on another teat, noting the strange and new sensation of touching the unfamiliar warm skin of the teats.

"Okay, now just squeeze downward. Not too hard. Not too soft."

Christian began. The cow shuffled a little bit, stepping her nearest hoof forward a few inches. Christian instantly jerked backward, afraid.

"No, don't let the cow dictate. Just use your knee and put pressure against the cow's leg. Coax it back with your knee."

Christian obeyed, prying his knee carefully against the cow's leg. Compliantly, she moved her leg back and away.

"Yeah, just like that."

As Christian began again to squeeze the teats, milk streamed down into the pail. Christian was clearly elated as he glanced a half-smile of satisfaction toward Ishi.

Ishi added, "Don't be afraid to cozy in. Put your forehead against the cow a bit!"

Christian had the hang of it. For several minutes, he had a nice rhythm going. The pail was almost a third full.

Ishi had stepped back to sit on an empty upside-down five-gallon pail to watch. Nervously, she said, "Christian, I have something to tell you."

Christian was fully invested in his work now. "What?"

"It's about graduation."

Christian didn't respond as he continued his rhythm. *Oh, no!*

"Uhmmm," Ishi's nerves rose, "I said yes to Sebastian."

Christian didn't look up. "Yes, what?"

Oh, no! What have I done? "Yes, to being his grad date."

At this, Christian stopped milking. After staring down into the pail for several moments, he grabbed the pail and the stool and removed himself from the cow, stepping across the gutter. He put the pail and stool down and stared, blankly, at the nearest of the small square dirty windows in the little barn.

Ishi prodded fearfully, "What, Christian? What are you thinking?"

Christian didn't look at her. A moment later, he hoisted himself up backward to sit on the top of three horizontal planks of a pen's fence. "Did you ask him? Or did he ask you?" Christian's tone was calm but, clearly showed hurt.

"He asked me."

"And you said yes," Christian added, with a hint of snideness.

"Yeah."

Suddenly, Christian jumped back down to his feet, and walked toward the big open barn door. "Okay, milking lesson done for today. I gotta go."

As Christian strode out of the barn, and toward his Jetta, Ishi jogged out of the barn after him. "Christian, I'm sorry," she called after him as he reached his car. "I—"

"That's okay," he said, as he opened his car door to get in. "I wasn't fast enou … You make a nice couple."

Instantly, Ishi's heart dropped. She felt horrible. *Did I make a terrible mistake?* Ishi wanted to say something more but didn't know what to say.

The car started and, as Christian circled around the yard to leave, his open car window passed near to Ishi. He stopped. As the yard's dust caught up and passed the car, Christian looked down at his lap, apparently thinking. He looked up and then at Ishi. "Ishi, if you're happy, then, I'm happy. Or, at least, I'll try to be, okay?"

Ishi was lost for words. Christian drove off, dust rising behind his vehicle. Ishi watched, conflicted, sad. She wasn't sure, now, if she did the right thing by saying yes to Sebastian. But she was sure that she had really hurt one of her closest friends.

CHAPTER 20

Akeem and Azim emerged out of Ingrid Braun's old, abandoned house into the very grey, cloudy afternoon. Azim had papers in his hand. They began walking toward the chicken coop, but the sudden start of rain caused them to retreat back into the house. As they re-entered the house, Akeem's phone buzzed.

"Yes," he answered, in Arabic, recognizing the source of the call on the call display.

Akeem switched the phone to speaker as the terse voice, on the other end, asked, "So, anything that we missed?"

Akeem looked at the papers in Azim's hand while answering, "No. There are only several notices from local utilities for electricity. But they are years old. Nothing noteworthy about them."

"Akeem Almasi, you better turn up the pressure. We're running out of time. Benjamin Sharod says that Mossad is watching his house day and night. He's sure his phones are tapped. Akeem! Are you hearing me?" the voice shouted, angrily.

"Yes, General. We are—"

"Speed it up! If Mossad arrests Sharod, makes him talk, that's the end of our funding! And, if that Jewish devil, Joseph Katz, wherever he is, talks and reveals our bankers, well—"

"General Arruk, there's no guarantee that the girl will go searching—"

"Make her search! You've been there ten months already. Make her do it, or you'll wish you did!" He hung up.

Azim looked at Akeem's worried face. As Azim tossed the useless papers onto the kitchen counter, he reassured Akeem "Graduation is in four days. The day after will be the day."

Akeem started walking toward the door. "I wish it was tomorrow, brother." As an after-thought, Akeem pointed at the discarded papers that Azim had thrown back on the counter. "No, bring those!"

As they both prepared to run through the rain, Azim reminded Akeem, "We both know that the Grubers aren't travelling to Manheim and Stuttgart until the day after the graduation."

As they hurried into the car, Akeem acknowledged, "I know."

The black BMW drove away.

*

In the dark, Jonathan Ben Dod sat quietly in his grey Jeep Wrangler, his eyes on the two vehicles parked nearly a block down the quiet upper-class Tel Aviv residential street. He didn't need to sit here watching his Mossad watchers keep eyes and ears on Benjamin Sharod. But he found that he thought clearer, and strategized better, when he was actually physically watching the action or — in this case — the non-action.

He had been sitting too long. He opened his door and stepped out. Ben Dod was extraordinarily tall among his Israeli peers — at 198 centimeters. His complete lack of hair and his oblong-shaped head made him appear even taller. He placed his hands on the roof of his Jeep and stretched back his legs one at a time. He turned around and bent down trying to touch his toes. As tall as he was, Ben Dod did that easily, reminding himself that his morning stretches were working and needed to continue.

Mossad and Shin Bet both had plenty of intel about the comings and goings of the Katz couple through France in the 90s, specifically through Monte Carlo — comings and goings that synchronized too well, timewise, with financial discrepancies in Israel's government coffers. So far, both intelligence agencies had enough to throw the noose around Benjamin Sharod. But they were eager to learn the channels and his accomplices in Israel. And so, here sat Jonathan Ben Dod and his watchers.

His phone buzzed quietly. "Yes?" He put the phone to his ear. He heard two electronic clicks and then a male voice, "Iden s-i-f-t-e-r--4-5-t."

"Iden confirmed," Ben Dod responded. "Go ahead, Sifter!"

The voice reported, "I can confirm activity at Vacha around the PLO agents there."

Ben Dod asked, "What kind of activity?"

"General Arruk, here in Hebron, was in conversation with the agents in Vacha stressing a go-ahead quickly on a plan of action."

"Do you know the plan of action? I'm assuming it relates to the Katz girl."

"No. All I know is that they are taking some action, in three days, that will pressure the girl to do something. And, as before, they reminded the agents of their fear of Benjamin Sharod being uncovered. Of course, we already know what we know about Benjamin Sharod. But I still have no names of his accomplices."

Ben Dod replied snidely, "Why are you educating me on the same thing I educated you on? Something wrong with your memory there, Sifter?"

"I apologize, sir. Being thorough, I guess."

"Is their cover in Vacha still operating as Adri Foods? Is it still just the Adri family or did they bring in others?"

"Yes, Adri family. No others that I'm aware of."

"Alright." Ben Dod made a quick decision. "I'll have Toto redeployed there tonight. And I'll send someone to help her."

"In what capacity? What will be her story?"

Ben Dod paused to think. "I don't know yet. Leave it to me." He clicked 'end' on the phone and inserted his long body back into the Jeep.

Jonathan Ben Dod, Director of Mossad, was confident that he was positioned far enough away from his agents' vehicles that they couldn't have seen the dim light of his cell phone. He didn't want his agents to lose morale by knowing they're being scrutinized.

*

Lights were on at only two places at the Kiryat Arba Regional Council Building at Hebron, Palestine. A large floodlight was on at the entrance where armed guards were stationed, two guards inside and two outside at the compound gate guard booth. And there was a light on in the second-floor office of Major-General Tariq Al Khalil.

He sat at his large plain desk, with a cell phone laying on the desk in front of him, speaker on. "If you don't finish this tonight," Tariq Al Khalil growled, wiping a bead of sweat from his forehead, "you will be damned in the eyes of Allah, in my eyes, not to mention the fate of your wife and children! I do not care if he's being watched. I do not care if he has grown wings and is circling the Earth. You will erase Sharod tonight before Mossad takes him! Do I make myself clear?"

Two male voices replied in unison, "Yes Major-General."

Tariq Al Khalil's stomach was upset. He stood up and shouted at his phone, "We don't know how much that Katz couple knows, if they can name the bankers. I'm sure they can. We'll find them. And tonight, we'll be done with this loose end, Sharod, before Mossad gets at him. Get it done!"

The intimidated voices replied, "Yes Major-General. We have already begun tonight's plan."

"Which is?"

One of the voices explained, "We learned the door code. The wife and daughter are at a school function this evening. They will return home to find him gone. We have prepared a letter, with a good signature, explaining his sudden flight to Palestine."

"Without making a noise," Tariq Al Khalil emphasized. "The house is bugged by Mossad."

The other voice replied, "Yes Major-General, without making ... without us making a noise."

Feeling a strong wave of nausea, Tariq Al Khalil sat back down. "Report when you've finished."

Both voices replied, "Should be within an hour. Fi sabil Allah!"

Tariq Al Khalil yelled back, "Screw the path of God shit. Just get it done!" He jabbed his finger on the 'End' button, sat down, and placed a hand on his wrenching upset stomach. *Flu?* Sweat was beginning to form on his face. *Was it something I ate?*

Inside the opulent study of Benjamin Sharod, one of the two PLO agents hit the 'end call' button on the cell phone that laid face up on Sharod's desk. Sharod looked at both of the agents, smirking. Then, looking up and around the office, he asked again, "You are sure you swept every bug in here?"

Both agents nodded. "Yes," replied one of the agents, "those Mossad spooks out there will be dying to know why no noise is coming from your study."

Sharod grinned, "Oh, they'll think I'm reading."

Sharod took his phone and entered a phone number, then set it back on the desk — with the speaker on. After an electronic tone and two clicks, Sharod touched two more keys to complete the connection.

"And?" General Arruk's voice was curious.

Sharod spoke, "All set here. Moving in five minutes. And you?"

General Arruk replied, "Tariq Al Khalil took enough in with his supper, enough to kill an elephant. Benjamin Sharod, by tomorrow you will be sitting in my chair."

"And," Sharod added, "you'll be sitting in Tariq's chair. Well planned, my brother!"

Arruk asked, "When are you leaving?"

Both agents piped up, "Right now, General Arruk."

Sharod stood up from his desk to make his secret exit from Israel. Just as he was going to tap the 'end call' button, he said one more thing. "General Arruk, that Katz couple is the only remaining loose end. They must be eliminated at all costs!"

"Tell me something I don't know," Arruk rasped a reply snidely and loudly, "Yes. Top priority. We must keep the funding channel alive."

Sharod repeated, louder, "Immediately!" He clicked the 'end call' button.

The two agents, and Sharod, walked very quietly out of the study, down a short hall, through the kitchen, and toward the heavy oak and glass back door. One of the agents quickly punched the code into the alarm panel beside the door, and turned the gold door handle down, opening the door quietly.

*

It was early evening at Fat Friar's, a local pub situated near the water at Deep Cove. David, and three other men, were perched against the heavy wooden bar with their eyes glued on the three TV monitors mounted in a row on the wall above the back of the bar's glassware and bottles of many various liquid offerings. The Patriots were losing to the Chiefs, but it was close — with just over three minutes left in the game. All four men were Chiefs' fans. David had taken a real shine to American football, and the NFL, since arriving less than two years ago.

Rolly, a big-bearded jovial man, sat next to David. They'd become friends as pub-buddies. Rolly's usual attire was as though he was on his way to a logging camp, but David knew that it simply suited his casual gruff style. The ability to relax here had done David a world of good.

As the game cut to a commercial break, Rolly nodded to the bartender — indicating another round for him and David. He turned slightly to David, "Patch things up at home?"

David had divulged, with Rolly, here at the bar a week earlier. "Yeah," David answered. "I'm a shit head. Just gotta check my own temperature once-in-a-while."

Rolly asked, skeptically, "It was all you? Don't think so."

"Doesn't matter. We called a truce."

"Buddy, us dudes always take the blame. I'm sure she's not perfect. My old lady sure isn't."

David sighed, "Yeah, she's not perfect." As the new beer was set in front of him, he took a swig. "Sure hate that damned yappy little dog though!" *I'd love to just kill that stupid dog.*

As David and Rolly were chatting, a woman entered the pub from the door directly behind where the four men were sitting. She stepped toward the bar and called, "Joseph!" David's heart stopped! Because of the volume of the TVs, the woman assumed that she had not been heard. "Joseph! Joseph, can't you—" David was seized with fear and, instantly, prepared his body to make a run for it. He grabbed his cane.

The bartender saw her and walked to a part of the bar to the side of the four men, and motioned her to come closer, holding his ear as an indication of not hearing her well.

David had his cane, in hand, and had begun to slide off one side of his barstool. The woman arrived at the bar immediately beside him, and said to the bartender, "Joseph, can't you give Shandra at least one night off tomorrow? It's her damned birthday."

Joseph, the bartender, replied, shouting over the volume of the TVs, "It's also a damned Friday. We're going to be packed in here." The bartender returned to his work. David's heart started to beat again.

The woman shouted, "Joseph, she only has a birthday once a year. You have lots of Fridays." The woman was angry in defence of her daughter.

The game was back from a commercial break as Joseph shouted back, "If Shandra can cover her shift, she can go." The woman paused to consider, then turned and left.

"S'matter with you?" Rolly was assessing David.

David took another gulp of his beer. "Oh, suddenly got a pain in my hip. It comes and goes, you know." He replaced the cane to the coat hook under the bar.

In the parking lot lit by two streetlamps, David's new black Infiniti was parked, cross-angled, taking up two stalls. As he approached it, he noticed a note tucked under his windshield wiper. He grabbed it and read it as he opened his door to get in. He tossed it on the parking lot pavement and drove away.

Arriving at his driveway, he pushed the remote to open the double garage door. As it opened, he saw that Rebecca's white Ford Explorer was gone. David scowled.

As David walked through the mudroom toward the kitchen, he saw a note on the island. He looked down to see only three handwritten words 'out for awhile'. He grabbed the note, crumpled it and tossed it back on the island surface. Walking around the island, he bent down to the beer and wine fridge, and extracted a can of pale ale. Pulling the tab open with a crack and hissing sound, he took a long gulp, then set the can down and walked through the master bedroom door and turned right into the ensuite. He opened the vanity door, bent down, pushed the mock shelves aside and spun the lock wheel forward, then back, then forward. Pulling the safe door open, he peered inside. It looked like everything was intact. He closed the safe, spun the dial, and walked out of the ensuite.

Rebecca sat behind the steering wheel looking down the mountain slope on the magnificent high-angle night view of Vancouver. The white SUV was parked at the lip of a small area created as a viewpoint on the North Shore halfway up Grouse Mountain. With no streetlamps here, and only a sliver of moon, it was dark. The vehicle was turned off.

Earlier today she had gone to the office on Lonsdale Avenue, gave her saliva sample, her actual name, her new name, her parents' names as registered in Germany, and began a registry for an ancestral DNA genetic search but didn't complete it because of all the potential implications it could have. The very sweet young woman helping her at that office obviously had seen many indecisive customers before. As Rebecca had hesitated and explained that she wasn't sure, and needed to sleep on it, the young woman had completely understood. She said, "We have everything we need here from you, physically. You'll be sent an email. You can complete the registration there if you decide to go ahead with it."

Rebecca, racked with nerves, had thanked the young woman, and started to leave, but turned back to the young woman with a question. "How confidential is this?" Logic was already telling her the answer as she asked the question.

"Oh, Missus—" the young woman glanced again at the paper forms in her hand, "Missus Wiess. It stays safe with us."

As the young woman had offered a reassuring smile, Rebecca already knew the dangerous answer. *It couldn't possibly remain purely confidential, or the worldwide search wouldn't work, would it!* She turned again and left, exhausted from emotion.

As she sat at her perch in the night, thoughts flooded her mind. Rebecca was trying hard to apply rationale, but emotions kept piling into her mind when she tried to weigh everything logically. *What if the DNA-genetic search* blows their cover? What's the worst? It's been a few years. Maybe they gave up looking?*

Rebecca had never been more than a social smoker, sharing a cigarette with friends in Tel Aviv during social occasions, and even then, rarely. But on her way to this perch this evening, she had stopped at a 7-11 and bought a pack of Marlboros. *Anything to calm me a bit,* she justified. She pulled one out of the pack now, turned the key enough to enable her to lower her window all the way, turned the key back off, and, taking the lighter she had also bought at 7-11, lit the cigarette.

What will the future look like if I keep things as they are? She exhaled. *Lonely. Lonely and sad. All that money is good for nothing. Lily isn't nearly enough. My casual friendship with Suzanna and the others is torture, not because they're not nice friends, but because they are living their lives. Unlike me in my prison, they are living with fullness right in front of me. Can't fault them. But I can't take it anymore, hiding forever. Not living.*

Rebecca took her phone from the cupholder, in the console, and entered the code to bring it to life. *What would David do to me if he found out? Quite literally possibly kill me,* she considered, gravely. Drawing and exhaling again on the cigarette, she tapped her email icon and opened up the Family Tree email. The large button in the body of the email read 'Confirm Registration'. *I could be taken back to Israel and put in jail for the rest of my life for treason.* Her hands shook.

There was nowhere to butt out the cigarette. She didn't see anyone around, so she tossed it onto the pavement beside the SUV. Rebecca watched the lights of a large cruise ship entering the harbor far below.

But, then again, if Ishi is somehow still alive somewhere, I might find her. That thought did it! She tapped the 'Confirm Registration' button. Another window immediately appeared on the phone screen with many words but with the most prominent large bold words 'Registration Complete. Thank you.' A sudden wave of panic hit Rebecca. She threw her phone onto the passenger's seat and, with shaking hands, pulled out another cigarette.

CHAPTER 21

Leah Fromm's pudgy white hand guided the steering wheel of the red Skoda hatchback. Mossad had provided her with this car when her flight arrived in Frankfurt earlier that morning. She pulled the car over, to a parked position at the curb, immediately, after passing through the first intersection leading her from highway 84 into the south end of Vacha. She pulled up the map app on her phone and confirmed her route to the Sankt-Annenweg 30 Hotel, where a reservation awaited her. She pulled back onto the road and drove another minute and saw the hotel ahead on her left. Pulling into the parking lot and driving alongside the hotel, she was happy to find that the parking lot continued and wrapped around a little more behind the cream-colored stuccoed three-story building. She parked there, glad to be able to park her vehicle out of sight from the street.

She pulled her phone from her handbag, typed in a code to wake it up, and then typed in a phone number. Seeing that the connection was made, she typed in another code and waited a few seconds. Momentarily, the phone reported back a ding confirming the connection. A message box appeared. She typed in 'Landed 1'. Ten seconds later, a text response appeared below her text. '2 landed 15:24'. She hit the 'Disconnect' button ending that connection, then touched the 'end call' button, and put her phone back into her handbag.

*

Christian and Lucy sat against the hood of his car sharing French fries that they bought at a shop up the street. They were parked tucked in behind Adri Foods, in the shade of the building, to escape the burning hot June sun. They chatted and laughed as they waited for Julia to arrive.

A minute later, a white rusted Volvo approached from the rear of the parking lot. The section of the parking lot behind Adri Foods was unpaved packed dirt with gravel, but packed so hard that the approaching Volvo kicked up no dust. The Volvo stopped. The driver's door swung open, with a creak, and Eddie jumped out, his fuchsia-red mohawk and wide smile accentuating his apparent energy level. Julia got out of the passenger's side, reached back to flip forward the seat, and Cara, Julia's younger fifteen-year-old sister, emerged too. As they walked up to Christian and Lucy, Julia said, "I heard!"

Lucy replied, "Yep."

Eddie asked, "Heard what?"

Julia explained, "Christian and Lucy are dates for grad tomorrow."

Eddie leapt in front of Christian and Lucy, crouched slightly while mimicking holding a camera and taking photos, "The paparazzi is here for the famous couple!" making camera clicking motions with his finger. He laughed at his own antics. Lucy laughed, too, as she exaggerated a couple of lavish poses for Eddie's imaginary camera. One of the poses involved licking Christian's ear. Christian smirked without protest.

He was deeply sad that Ishi wouldn't be his date, but Lucy was so entirely beautiful, and such a good long-time friend, that Christian was okay with it.

Julia chimed, "I'm going with Sieg."

Lucy's mouth dropped open, and a half-eaten French fry dropped to the ground. "Julia! Sieg from Hünfeld? That Sieg?"

Julia beamed, "That Sieg."

Julia's little sister, Cara, only two years younger, delighted in the banter of romantic arrangements, but she remained shyly quiet and smiling at everything.

Eddie hopped up to Christian like a kangaroo. "A fry for your friend?" he begged. Christian tipped the nearly empty cardboard container toward Eddie. Eddie pulled out one and then two fries. "Thanks be unto thee!"

"Ssh, ssh, ssh!" Julia waved everyone silent. She had heard a man's voice. "Someone's coming around the building."

As all five immediately stopped talking, Julia quietly walked to the corner of the large building and peeked around and saw Mister Adri walking along the paved part of the parking lot, speaking on his phone. She whispered her report, "It's Mister Adri. I don't think he knows we're here."

They all began to hear Shimon Adri's voice. The language was not German. It wasn't anything they understood. Christian and Lucy looked at each other in bewilderment. Daring to peek again, Julia could see that as Shimon Adri talked, he paced back and forth along the side of his building. When his pacing brought him nearer to the corner, where the five listened, they could, clearly, hear his foreign words — but they could not understand.

"It's Arabic!" Eddie whispered. "I know it for sure. I've heard Arabic often in Frankfurt."

Julia, still peeking carefully around the corner of the building, turned and frantically waved Eddie silent. Shimon's voice was becoming louder and angrier. The five realized that he was completely fluent in that language, Arabic, or whatever it was. Christian heard the word 'Gruber' among the strange words. His heart skipped a beat. He heard 'Gruber' again. So did the others. Worried looks spread over their faces. Shimon Adri brought his phone call to an end with more words that were somewhat familiar to Christian's ear. "Insha Allah"

Julia dared to peek around the corner again. "He's gone."

Lucy exclaimed, "That was really weird!"

As Julia stepped back toward the others, she shrugged her shoulders, "So, he speaks Arabic. Big deal. It's a free country."

Lucy replied, "Pretty fluent for someone that was born in Germany!"

Christian said, "How do you know he was born in Germany? Sebastian said that they came from Israel."

"Ishi told me. They told her, I guess. Or, right, she did say Israel?"

Lucy asked, "So, that was Israeli or Hebrew or whatever they speak there?"

Eddie educated them quickly, "Hebrew. And, no, that was not Hebrew."

Christian had been thinking about those words 'Insha Allah'. He said, "I've heard that before in films and on some news reports, I think — Insha Allah — but I don't know what it means."

"I do," Eddie stated. "As Allah wills. And that's Arabic. No Israeli is going to say; 'As Allah wills.'"

Julia asked, "As Allah wills what?" A frown enveloped her face.

Lucy added, "And what was that about the Grubers?" Lucy remembered, "Oh yeah, Ishi said Adris lived in Stuttgart for a long time."

"They did," answered Christian. "That's what they told everyone anyway."

Eddie hopped playfully, but a little less playfully, toward his Volvo. "Gotta go!" He disappeared into his car.

Julia immediately joined Eddie. "That creeped me out. Yeah, let's go! C'mon Cara." The two of them joined Eddie and climbed into the rusty Volvo. Eddie started the car, and they left.

Christian turned to Lucy. "Let's get out of here."

She nodded.

*

The Roos music was loud. The crowd, of approximately one hundred and fifty-five graduates, dates, and friends, filled the large school gym where the band's stage lights and multi-colored strobe lights at various high spots around the gym pulsed in time to the music. Everyone was having an amazing time. Two thirds of the people in the room now, near the end of the night at 2:15am, were dancing. The other third was sitting, too drunk or too worn out to dance. Everyone was happy.

The last two songs, predictably, came as slow dance songs. Three quarters of the dancing crowd, the thirty-eight grads and their dates, embraced swaying to the music. The other quarter of the dancing crowd consisted of parents of the grads — parents that had enough stamina to remain until this late hour. Horst and Dagmar Gruber were not among them. Giving Ishi and Sebastian their final congratulations, with big sincere smiles and hugs two hours earlier, they had exited for home and bed.

Forty-five minutes later, with most of the lights back on, the gym was nearly vacated as several teachers shooed the stragglers out. The parking lot was nearly empty, too. Christian and Lucy had left fifteen minutes earlier. As they had exited the parking lot, Christian caught a glimpse of Ishi and Sebastian strolling, hand-in-hand, along the far unlit side of the parking lot. Christian's heart hurt.

Sebastian and Ishi walked along the parking lot's rail fence to its end under a row of large elms. They stopped there. Sebastian pulled the slightly drunk Ishi to his body. She looked up at his beautiful face. He kissed her mouth passionately. She was consumed. While she had sporadic thoughts of Christian throughout the evening, thoughts that brought painful slivers of guilt, she was now consumed with Sebastian. They kissed long and passionately, Ishi's long dark hair hanging down her back over her scarlet red dress.

Sitting in the dark of her Skoda, on the other side of the parking lot, Leah Fromm watched. *I see what you're up to, Azim.*

A light buzzing sound! Leah looked at her burner phone sitting on the passenger's seat beside her personal phone. She took it and read the message, "I'm in."

*

A slender short figure, dressed entirely in black with a black beanie and with his face chalked black slinked carefully along the middle of Adri Foods' five aisles. He had skillfully disabled the security camera feed and alarms at the junction box outside behind the building before making his entry, with the use of a light extendable ladder that allowed him to crane open and squeeze through a very small horizontal window, just below the eaves. Once inside, he acrobatically scaled down from shelf to shelf, to counter, to the floor.

He extracted a crayon-sized device from a sheath strapped to his left leg. When the device was flicked on with a twist of the cap on one end, it would identify anything with an active electronic feed within twenty meters. Of course, the store was full of active electronics such as two cash-registers, refrigerators, freezers, smoke detectors, and more. He identified the security cameras on each of the four ceiling corners of the large room. Pointing the device at those cameras ensured him that they were, in fact, dead.

As he reached the back end of the aisle, he waved the crayon-like device in arcs to ensure that the door to the back room was purely manual. Confident of that, he passed through it and into the storage area. Immediately to his right, he saw a wide stairway leading down. On his left, there was a short stairway leading up to a landing and a closed wood-framed glass door. Stepping up to his left and arriving at that door, he again confirmed that any alarm that might've been attached to it was dead. He tried the round knob. Locked. *As expected.* From a small sheath strapped to his other leg, the little man extracted his lock set. Within less than a minute, he was inside the office.

CHAPTER 22

Ishi's head hurt. Her entire being felt saggy and like an ugly troll lived inside her stomach. Nevertheless, after a full eight and a half hours of sleep, she stumbled out of the bedroom and into the kitchen — still swooning with romantic emotions and lingering effects of wine. She saw that the front door was open, so she stepped through the kitchen to it and looked outside, instantly shielding her eyes from the daylight.

Her dad and mom were at the car, nearly finished loading a large suitcase, several Tupperware containers full of baking, and two open-top cardboard boxes of potted flowers from the garden — the multicolored blooms peeking up over the top. Knowing that, any other day, they would've expected her to be up earlier to help, Ishi realized that they gave her the gift of sleeping in 'til nearly noon after her big graduation day.

"How soon are you leaving?" Ishi called.

Her dad looked up. "Now. We were going to c-come in and wake you up and say goodbye f-first though."

Dagmar pulled her head back out from the back seat and turned to Ishi. "There you are! There are leftovers in the fridge, sweetie."

Using his cane, Horst walked toward his daughter. "You're all set to take care of the chores for t-two days? I bought some new b-bags of supplements. They're stacked b-beside the chop bin."

Ishi was still squinting against the bright June sun. "Yes dad, don't worry."

Dagmar finished loading the cardboard boxes into the car, turned and walked to the house. Ishi's head was clearing slightly, but her stomach felt awful. She sat down on the wide arm of the small sofa as her mom, and then her dad, entered.

Dagmar looked at her. "Are you okay?"

Ishi offered a sheepish half-smile. "Yeah, overdid it last night a bit, I guess. Sorry."

Dagmar suggested, "Maybe you should sit on the porch outside and get some sun and fresh air."

"Sun? Oh. No sun!"

Horst added, with a half-grin, "You have the entire day to relax. Just take it easy. You'll be f-fine. Drink lots of water!"

Ishi knew that the evening chores were easier than the morning chores because there was no milking. She glanced at the kitchen sink and saw the empty metal milk pail sitting in it. Relieved, that told her that her dad had, indeed, already done the morning milking.

Dagmar turned and said to Horst, "Okay, let's get going! We don't want to get there just in time for supper."

Horst stepped over to the kitchen counter and snatched an apple out of the fruit bowl. Dagmar stepped toward Ishi. Ishi stood and hugged her mother. Horst stepped up next and gave Ishi a big wrap-around hug. Dagmar was already halfway to the car. As Horst followed her, he called back to Ishi, "Proud of you, daughter!" Ishi felt a wave of warm love from those words. She stood in the doorway and offered little waves as the sand-colored Volvo headed up the driveway, kicking up clouds of dust.

I feel like crawling back into bed for a little longer. Taking the pitcher from the fridge, she poured herself a glass of water and drank nearly the entire glass eagerly. Then she walked into the bedroom and, not bothering to remove her baggy sweatpants and t-shirt, crawled under the covers.

It seemed like she had just dozed off when she heard a car horn. *What?* She didn't open her eyes. *Did I dream it? No, it was too real.* She opened her eyes. The horn sounded again.

As Ishi quickly got out of bed, to rush to the front door, she glanced at the alarm clock on her nightstand. 12:25pm. "Oh!" She actually slept for more than half an hour. She opened the front door and squinted at the bright sunlight. Momentarily, she focused on Sebastian. He was standing at the doorstep with a wide smile and a bouquet of roses.

"Oh!" Ishi was truly surprised to see Sebastian. "Roses," Ishi acknowledged, still trying to sweep cobwebs from her waking brain.

"For you."

Ishi had never received flowers in her life. "For me?" She was stunned.

"For you."

Ishi was without words. She spun around to try to spot a vase. *Oh, I'm rude!* She spun back toward Sebastian and accepted the bouquet. "Thank you, Sebastian!" She held the bouquet in her right hand as Sebastian stepped forward toward the doorway. She embraced him and looked again at the roses. "Thank you. Oh, wow!"

Sebastian stepped inside watching Ishi scramble looking for a vase that would fit the long stems. Sebastian said, "I have a gift for you today."

Slightly confused, Ishi said, "This is a good gift!"

"No, no. That's just for starters. What are you doing today?"

Ishi stopped her search and turned toward Sebastian, a puzzled look on her face. "Uh, not much I guess." She looked at his broad smile. "Nothing," she clarified.

"Good. Because I made reservations at Parthenon for an early dinner."

Parthenon? Parthenon was unfamiliar to her. "Parthenon?"

Sebastian explained, "Parthenon in Frankfurt."

It took Ishi a few moments for Sebastian's words to register. She squeezed out her question, "Frankfurt? Like, the Frankfurt?"

Sebastian was enjoying her wonderment. "Yes Ishi. You and I for an early dinner at a five-star restaurant in Frankfurt this afternoon."

Ishi's eyes went wide. "I've never been to Frankfurt. Ever!" She realized that she was gripping the roses too tightly. She stepped to the dining table and laid them down. "How?"

"My car," Sebastian quickly answered. "Well, my dad's car." He gestured to the black BMW 320i outside.

Ishi's mouth had fallen open. "When? I mean, when will we go?"

Sebastian pulled a dining chair out and sat. "Well, my pretty Isabella, how soon can you be ready? It's a nearly two-hour drive."

Ishi was overwhelmed as she remembered to look for a vase. A thought hit her. *Chores.* She turned to Sebastian, "I have to be home to do the evening chores."

"At what time?"

"Five. Or six. Or seven, I guess."

"That can work."

Ishi, thinking fast, said, "Well, nobody will die if it's eight. But not later than eight."

"Super! The reservation is for four o'clock. We can be on our way back by five-thirty, at the latest, and home by seven-thirty."

Stretching up onto her tiptoes, Ishi opened the double doors above the fridge and found a vase. She said, "Frankfurt! I don't have a camera." Thinking fast about what she would wear.

Sebastian quickly injected, "I do." He stood as Ishi was filling water into the vase from the sink faucet. As she put the roses into the vase, Sebastian stepped up to her. They embraced and kissed lightly.

My awful morning breath! Ishi's face flushed slightly. Then, she thought about the adventure. "Oh, I have to shower and brush my teeth." She rushed into the bedroom, opened her dresser drawers to quickly pull out a different bra and panties, then rushed back outside the bedroom toward the bathroom door. "I'll be quick," she promised, excitedly.

In less than fifteen minutes, Ishi had showered, put on minimal mascara, and rushed back to the bedroom wrapped in a big white towel — her wet, long hair messy. Sebastian heard the sound of a blow dryer. Almost six minutes later, Ishi opened the bedroom door and stepped out wearing a cute floral-patterned green skirt and a white frilly blouse, her long brunette hair perfectly framing her smiling face. Sebastian gawked at her beauty.

Ishi doubted, "Is this okay for that restaurant?" She frowned and glanced down at her skirt. "Too short?"

Sebastian chuckled. "Ishi, it's perfect. You're perfect."

*

Leah looked up at the sound of a knock on her hotel room door. Pascal was punctual. She stepped to the door, peered through the eyehole, undid the double lock, and opened the door. Small, wiry Pascal entered the plain hotel room.

"Nothing," Pascal reported, as he walked directly to the window. He pulled the drapes closed and turned to Leah Fromm. "They're good! Clean as a whistle. I went through everything. Trips to Ljubljana to buy meat, trips to Frankfurt and Munich to buy more supplies, delivery manifests, employee records. Nothing."

Leah sat on the bed. "Okay, Pascal, then you'll go through their house."

Pascal asked, "Today?"

"You bet today! They're all at work until six. Our intel said that they're acting in three days. This is day two. I want to know what's happening before it happens, not after."

"Understood. I already studied the house. I know how to get in."

Leah sighed. "If we draw a blank, Ben Dod is going to throw me to the wolves."

*

Horst and Dagmar's humble sedan cruised, southeast, along highway 81 — three-quarters of the way to their destination in Stuttgart. They did not notice the black Volkswagen Passat a kilometer behind them.

"She was absolutely beautiful last night," Dagmar expressed to her husband.

Horst agreed. "Perfection! I'm s-so proud." He turned the radio volume down slightly. "What time is Ingrid expecting--?"

"Sophie. You mean—"

"Yes. I mean S-Sophie ... expecting us?"

Dagmar answered, "Between three and four. We're right on schedule, thanks God."

*

Sebastian's black BMW cruised southeast, along highway 5 — just thirty minutes into his and Ishi's two-hour drive.

Ishi's phone erupted with a pre-set jingle. She grabbed it from where she tucked it in the corner of the dashboard and windshield. Looking at it, Ishi saw that it was Lucy.

Sebastian saw the caller's name, too.

Ishi looked at Sebastian.

Sebastian shook his head. "Let's keep this our secret — at least for today."

Ishi touched the button 'End Call' and put the phone back on the dashboard. "I agree," she smiled happily.

As Sebastian and Ishi drove through Frankfurt, Ishi's head swiveled, her eyes wide in wonder. Her exclamations of amazement at the impressive high-rises, the stunningly tall skyscrapers, and the opulent, seemingly unending, blocks of four and five-story apartment buildings made Sebastian smile.

As Sebastian and Ishi were led to their table at Parthenon, Ishi, for the first time in her life, felt the strokes of luxury. As they followed the Maitre d', Ishi whispered to Sebastian, "I feel like a VIP."

Sebastian replied, "It's nice. I've never been here before. But I heard about it."

They arrived slightly early for their reservation. Because it was only 3:45pm, the restaurant was quite empty. The Maitre d' sat them at a table dressed in white linen and a tall crystal vase with two roses. The Maitre d' pulled Ishi's chair and waited for her. She was not expecting this and hesitated, shyly, not knowing what to do.

The Maitre d' politely said, "Ma'am."

Ishi understood. She stepped into place and allowed the polite man to seat her as Sebastian seated himself across from her. A blush immediately bloomed across Ishi's face as she realized how uncultured she is. "This is new for me," she smiled, awkwardly, at her very handsome date.

Sebastian chuckled, "You're so adorable when you blush!"

Ishi's blush grew redder.

*

Inside the Adri house, even though it wasn't as dark as during his work last night, Pascal worked fast with the small flashlight clenched between his teeth.

The afternoon daylight, even though sneaking inside in small cracks between the closed curtains, offered enough light to speed up his progress.

Having rifled through all the drawers and doors in the kitchen, hall, living room and back sunroom, he had moved upstairs to the bedrooms. Choosing the master bedroom first, he inspected each dresser drawer and then moved to the closet. On the closet top shelf, he spied a hard cardboard box approximately twice the size of a shoe box. It looked like it could be a curios box. Pascal lifted it down and saw that it had a little lock. Testing it, it was, in fact, locked. He carried it to the bed and set it down, taking a few moments to think of how he would enter this box without making a mess. Momentarily, he drew a box cutter out of the small pouch at his waist. As he turned the box upside down, he heard, and felt, the tumbling of several hard, loose items.

Within a few careful minutes, he had the bottom neatly cut off. Inside the box, he saw two cell phones, several passports, three bundles of euros, and a medium-sized manila envelope. Pascal took the envelope and dumped the contents onto the bed. Neatly pulling contents of the envelope out and onto the bedspread, Pascal saw at least ten photo-scanned copies of photos, showing a variety of scenes. Sonya Katz with the young daughter aboard a luxury yacht in a harbour. A modest acreage and house. An elderly woman standing beside a chicken coop. Another photo on the yacht of Sonya Katz and Ishi playing with a dollhouse. A studio family photo of Sonya and Joseph Katz with baby Ishi on Sonya's knee. Sonya and Joseph Katz posing for a photo outside Katz Furniture entrance. Sonya Katz in a jogging outfit sitting on a park bench with a little dog on the bench beside her. An aerial photo of an acreage with a small house, a small outbuilding, and a guard tower at the edge of trees and the old German border fence. An aerial shot of the forest from the Gruber farm to Philippsthal. Dagmar and Horst Gruber walking from their house toward their barn. Two photos of Horst and Dagmar's 1996 yellow-ish Volvo. *Why the car?* Pascal wondered.

Extracting his cell phone, Pascal took a photo of each item from the box. Then he put everything back into the box. A frown crossed Pascal's face. "Shit!" He didn't know how he was going to replace the cut-out bottom. After thinking for a few moments, he raced down the stairs to the kitchen. He remembered seeing a drawer dedicated to knickknacks. After a few seconds of rifling through the drawer, he found what he had hoped for, glue. It wasn't the clear glue that he wished for, but white would still hold the secret of his break-in long enough.

*

It was almost 7:30pm, and daylight was beginning to turn to dusk. Having returned from Frankfurt, Sebastian and Ishi had just pulled up in front of Ishi's house.

"I have chores now," Ishi apologized.

"Can I help?"

Ishi looked at him, surprised at his offer. "Help? In those clothes?"

Sebastian shrugged his shoulders. "I can always wash my clothes."

Ishi began to get out of the car. "I have to change. Sure! If you want."

Sebastian immediately exited the BMW. "Good! You just tell me what to do."

As Ishi walked toward the house door, she called back, "That will speed things up. Thanks!"

Sebastian labored, hard, carrying two five-gallon pails of chop from the barn to the outside pig pen. Ishi was at the chicken coop where she had finished filling one self-feeder inside the coop and, to avoid having to tend to the chickens feed in the morning, filled the two small self-feeders in the fenced enclosure outside the coop, and was now locking the door with all the chickens inside. She looked over at Sebastian struggling with the weight of the pails. She laughed, "Ha ha! You don't have to torture yourself and fill them so full."

Sebastian replied, "I'm okay," as he launched one of the pails up to the top fence rail and began to pour it over the fence into the trough on the other side.

Finished with chores, Ishi had entered the house while Sebastian ducked into his car to grab something. Then he joined her in the house.

"What a great day!" Ishi smiled broadly, tired. Her upset stomach and hangover had disappeared earlier during the afternoon.

As he wiped at some dirt on his pant leg, Sebastian replied, "It was super!"

"I'm sorry but I only have water," Ishi apologized as she approached the sofa with two full glasses, offering one to Sebastian.

He took the water, "Perfect!"

She sat next to him.

He said, "So, now you've seen Frankfurt."

Ishi drew a breath, "Oh my god, Sebastian, it was amazing! Thank you."

Sebastian looked straight at Ishi. "I have a question for you, Ishi."

Oblivious to what the question might be, Ishi replied, "Okay."

"I love being with you."

Ishi waited.

"You trust me, right?"

Ishi, a little bit surprised, responded warily, "Yeah, why?" An instant mysterious apprehension rose in her.

"Well, you know me from school. I'm a constant rabid researcher. I research everything, you know."

"Yeah."

Sebastian continued, "I guess I'm just a curious guy."

"And a romantic guy." She gave him a flirtatious smile.

"Well, I've found some things that I think I need to show you … to tell you."

Ishi looked at him, her eyebrows raised.

Sebastian continued, "Things about you. Your parents."

Ishi's sudden, curious discomfort with this conversation appeared in her eyes. *What business are my parents of yours?*

Sebastian continued, "I need to show you some photos." He reached for a brown, large envelope that he had put on the sofa on his other side.

Ishi's brows furrowed slightly. She began to sense that these photos might for some reason not be wonderful. Sebastian dumped the contents of the envelope onto the sofa between him and Ishi. He shuffled through the photos for a few seconds, and then covered them with the brown envelope.

"Maybe I should explain first." Still looking down at the photos, Sebastian began, "What if I told you that your parents, Horst and Dagmar, might not be your actual parents?" He looked up at her expression.

Ishi had no expression. *Such a preposterous statement is not really very funny if this is supposed to be a joke.*

Sebastian continued, "Let me tell you a story … about you."

Ishi was quiet but growing more uneasy.

"Ishi, you know how I feel about you, right?"

"Yes, I think so." *What is this? What are you leading to?*

Sebastian continued, "Well, I wouldn't tell you this if I didn't think it was important for you to know." Sebastian stood up, feigning his discomfort. Then he sat back down and looked at her. "Let me start at the beginning. You were born in Tel Aviv. Isabella Katz."

Ishi laughed, "Tel Aviv! In Israel?"

Sebastian continued, "Your parents were Joseph and Sonya Katz." Sebastian took the brown envelope off the photos and selected several photos.

Ishi looked down at two photos of a man, a woman, and a young girl on a yacht and a photo of a woman playing with the young girl on the yacht deck.

Sebastian told the story, describing Katz Furniture, the cruises that the little family made quarterly to Monte Carlo, and that Sonya's mother, Ishi's Oma, lived at Philippsthal, "which was West Germany back then. Just over there on the other side of this bush," he explained, pointing west. During the narrative, Sebastian said, "Ishi, your parents were involved in crimes."

At this, Ishi looked up from the photos to Sebastian, her frown growing.

He described how she had wandered across the border and was lost in the woods, unable to find her way back.

At this point, Ishi stopped Sebastian. "How can you know all this? I mean, so much detail? I don't know who these people are, but—"

Sebastian interrupted, "I do a lot of researching of things that interest me. And you interest me."

Ishi was clearly getting upset. "Well, that girl isn't me. And," she pointed at the photos, "I don't care who that man and woman are."

Sebastian's voice softened, "Just, please, give me another minute to tell you the rest. Please!"

Ishi didn't reply. She took another drink of water, nervously drinking the glass empty.

Sebastian continued, "When you got lost and wandered across the border, you ended up here. As a three-year-old."

As Sebastian finished the story, as much as he knew it, he produced more photos including photos of Oma's acreage and the chicken coop, an old aerial photo of Oma's acreage with a guard tower next to trees and a big fence, and an aerial photo of the woods from the acreage to Ishi's farm.

Ishi stood. She was getting angry, refusing to buy any of it, her thoughts jumbling.

Sebastian added, "I looked for local birth records for you. There are none."

Ishi snapped back, "And yet here I am! Isabella Gruber. Maybe my parents didn't bother to make an official record. It's not unheard of." Her voice was rising in intensity. "Stop!" She turned and marched into the kitchen to get more water. "Stop it, Sebastian! It's none of your business anyway -- digging around on my parents."

Sebastian stood. "Ishi, I'm telling you only because you deserve it. Deserve to know it. Your real parents were involved with big crime. That's why they let you go."

"Stop, I said!" Ishi was angry. "Why would you tell me such a stupid story? Why would you—?"

Sebastian pushed it one more time, "Ishi, your real parents are Joseph and Sonya Katz."

Ishi snapped and hurled her water glass at Sebastian, the glass hitting the back of the sofa beside Sebastian, then tumbling down onto the sofa. "I said stop!" she screamed. "You're full of shit!"

Sebastian, surprised at Ishi's sudden violent act, stood and moved partway to the far window. "I'm sorry. Calm down!"

Ishi calmed down and said, "Hey, if this is meant as a joke, it's not very funny. Okay." She walked to the sofa and picked up the glass. "So, let's just not do this." As she returned the glass to the kitchen, she sighed, "I'm sorry."

Sebastian just looked at her and said, "It's not a joke."

Setting the empty drinking glass on the kitchen counter, she steered toward the door, opened it, and began to cry as she walked a few feet outside into the dark. "Why are you doing this?" she sobbed.

Sebastian stepped into the open doorway.

Through tears, Ishi apologized, facing away from Sebastian and toward the dark farmyard, "I'm sorry. I can't believe I threw that at you."

Sebastian quite calmly replied, "No, I'm sorry. But I had to tell you—"

Ishi mumbled, "I think you should go." She turned to walk back inside. "I think you should go." Pushing past Sebastian through the doorway, she added, "I should go to bed."

Given that Ishi had just hurled the glass at Sebastian, she thought that he seemed surprisingly poised. That made Ishi even more angry and uncomfortable. *The day? How could such a good day flip around like this?*

Sebastian sensed the remaining anger. "I'll go," Sebastian said. "I only told you because I care so much." As Sebastian complied, and began walking toward his BMW, he said, "Go see for yourself! It's only a short walk through the bush."

Ishi barked, "Go! Please." Ishi, confused and in tears now, called, "I'm sorry. Shit!"

Sebastian turned and looked at her with a completely composed understanding expression, "I'll leave the photos with you." He turned again and walked toward his car.

"No. Don't! Take them with you."

As Sebastian was getting into the car, he repeated, "I'll leave the photos with you."

"Go!" Ishi screamed. New sobs overtook her. From the doorway, her face red, sad, in shock, confused, Ishi watched Sebastian's car go up the driveway. She sobbed and collapsed to her knees on the front porch.

As Sebastian reached the end of the driveway, he turned to the right onto the dark road toward Vacha, his headlights cutting through the low night fog that had rolled in. Eighty meters back on the road, in the other direction from the Gruber driveway, Leah sat in her red Skoda, lights off. She tapped the back button on a little digital recorder, then tapped the play button. From the bugs inside the Gruber home, she listened to Sebastian's distant voice, "… for yourself! It's only a short walk through the bush." She tapped the stop button.

Her head on her pillow, Ishi opened her eyes and squinted at the dark wall that divided her part of the bedroom from her parents' part. The room was unusually quiet. Typically, Ishi would hear light snoring sounds of her parents. She could feel that her eyes were puffy. She remembered crying herself to sleep. *What time is it?* she wondered. Lifting her head slightly, she looked to the digital alarm clock on her nightstand. 2:14am. *Oh.* She closed her eyes again in an effort to fall back asleep.

Sebastian's words, and the images of the photos, consumed her brain. Unable to stop the thoughts and images, she let a leg droop out beside the bed. Then both legs. Two minutes later, with a bathrobe wrapped around her, she was sitting on the sofa looking through the photos one by one, her brows furrowed.

CHAPTER 23

A grey Renault sedan turned into the short driveway and approached the gate at Kiryat Arba Regional Council Building, Hebron, Palestine. Two guards emerged from the guard booth, both with AK47 machine guns slung over their shoulders. One guard walked up to the driver's window. Benjamin Sharod's driver held out an ID card as the guard stooped to look inside the car. He saw the familiar driver with Benjamin Sharod, then waved them forward as the other guard reached back into the booth to flip the switch that opened the gate.

On the second floor, Benjamin Sharod strode into the former office of Tariq Al Khalil. General Arruk, sitting behind the desk, looked up. "You're late."

Sharod threw his pack of cigarettes on the desk and sat down across from Arruk, his large body completely filling the chair. "I'm not late. It's not even seven yet."

General Arruk grabbed his own lit cigarette from the ashtray and smoked, just looking at Sharod.

Sharod tried to focus on Arruk's good eye as he spoke. "Pity about the Major-General's accident."

"Yes. I feel for his widow."

Sharod asked, "What's happening in Vacha?"

"You better hope something productive, brother. Your agents are depending on it."

Sharod asked again, "So, what is happening?"

"Three stage plan is in motion. Confront the girl with photos. Interrogate the parents. The house. Last night, Azim confronted the Katz girl. The Grubers are due to drive back from Stuttgart tomorrow. We're on track, as far as that goes."

"But" Sharod injected, "there's no guarantee that the girl will go searching."

"Correct. However, if she does not do it voluntarily, we'll make her do it. Better if it's voluntary. Cleaner."

"How much confidence do you have in Akeem?"

Arruk butted his cigarette out. "Enough. I've known him for years. He's capable, brother."

A noise in the main area caused Sharod to look around through the open office door. Arruk explained, "Desk clerks. Arriving for work."

Sharod frowned and looked doubtfully at Arruk. "What's plan B?"

"There is no plan B, Benjamin Sharod." Arruk glared at the doubter. "At least this is a plan. A plan in action. More than we've had in fifteen cursed years regarding those Katz worms."

*

A ringing phone woke up Ishi. As she opened her eyes, she recognized it as the land line. Groggy, she hurried to her feet and into the kitchen to answer the wall-phone. "Hello."

"Ishi," Lucy's voice was cheerful, "where are you?"

"Just got up."

Lucy asked, "So, did you and Sebastian spend the day together yesterday? Aaaaand perhaps more than just the day?" Lucy's voice had a playful tone.

Ishi, still gathering her wits, replied slowly, "Uh, oh, uh Sebastian went home. Yesterday. Evening."

Lucy noted a dour tone in Ishi's voice. "Girlfriend, what's up? Everything okay?"

"Just had a bad sleep."

"Oh, why? Are you feeling okay?"

"Yeah Luce, I'm fine."

"Hey, Becky and Christian and I are going to Fulda after lunch to watch the football match. We'd go earlier, but Becky is going to mass with her parents this morning. Come! Can you come?"

Ishi took a few moments to think. "Luceeee." Sigh. "I ... I don't know."

"C'mon Ishi, you gotta come. It's Sunday. There's nothing else happening, is there?"

"You know, I'd love to. But I'm not feeling the greatest. I think I'll pass this time."

Lucy's voice revealed disappointment, "Something's up. Ish, I can sense it in your voice. Okay. Too bad. We'll go to the next match, okay."

"Okay. Yeah. Have fun!"

Just as she hung up the phone, her cell phone rang in the bedroom. She hurried to it, grabbing it off the nightstand. "Hello?"

Christian's voice was cheerful. "Ishi, hi."

"Oh, hi Christian," Ishi tried to sound upbeat.

"Lucy and Becky and I are going ..."

Ishi interrupted, "I know. I just talked to her, to Lucy."

"Oh. And? Are you busy with Sebastian today, or can you come? I mean, he can come too, I guess." Christian sounded unenthusiastic about suggesting Sebastian's involvement.

Ishi answered, "No. Thanks Christian. I'm home alone. But I'm feeling quite ill today. I'm going to pass."

Christian was clearly disappointed. "Oh, Ish! You okay? Can I bring you anything or do anything?"

Ishi found genuine comfort in Christian's offer. "Thanks Chris. No, I'm just going to be a lazy sloth. I'm fine. My parents went to Stuttgart as you know. So having the house to myself will be a treat."

"Well, just chill. And enjoy it!"

Ishi replied, "Yeah, might just watch brainless television and eat ice cream." A half-smile developed as she said it.

Christian said, "Okay. I'm curious how things are going, you know, with ..."

Ishi cut in, "Christian, we can talk another time, okay. I'll just say, things aren't great."

Christian's tone indicated that he realized that he stepped outside his right to ask, "I'm sorry Ishi. I shouldn't have ... It's none of my business."

"It's okay. No problem. You can ask. Jus, not today, k."

Christian said, "Okay. I gotta go. Talk soon?"

"Sure. Have fun today!"

An old slightly rusted blue Volkswagen Passat passed the Gruber driveway slowly. Driving almost one hundred meters further along the road, it pulled off onto a small dirt-grass road that led it another thirty or forty meters into the bush. The Passat pulled up alongside Leah's red Skoda.

From window to window, Leah passed the small recorder and a square black box with a micro receiver dish mounted on top of it. Leah updated Pascal, "Nothing yet. Just a couple of phone calls from her friends about going to a football match in Fulda."

"She going?"

"No. Apparently, she's feeling ill. Oh! She did mention that something didn't turn out well between her and Sebastian. Of course, we already know that."

"Yes, pretty obvious from the recording last night. Okay, go get some sleep."

Leah started her car and drove off.

Ishi crawled back into bed and was sitting up, thinking. She grabbed her blanket and dragged it to the sofa. She shoved the photos aside, and using the remote control, turned the TV on. After a few minutes of flipping through news channels, a religious broadcast, a couple of cooking shows, a nature show, she turned the TV back off, and laid down on the sofa, pulling the blanket over her. Her eyes remained open.

She sat back up and sifted through the photos, selecting one and then another of the man and woman and girl on the yacht. After looking at them for a minute, she put those photos back down and picked up three photos of the nearby acreage. She looked at the humble house, the wider shot of the house, garden plot, and chicken coop, and the aerial of the woods from the acreage to her farm. Putting two photos down, Ishi studied the aerial photo, orienting it to her farm. She noticed the small old guard tower situated close to the acreage on the other side of the woods. She recalled the part of Sebastian's story where she as a three-year-old girl supposedly wandered from that acreage to this farm through those woods. She imagined the possible route on the aerial photo. She looked up from the photo and turned her head and thoughts toward the west. *Twenty or thirty minutes to get over there?*

The sun was higher in the sky now as Ishi hiked through the woods. This small forest beside the Gruber farm was not entirely foreign to Ishi. She'd been through here many times while growing up, but she'd never gone as far as the other side, the Philippsthal side. The nettle was very thick and difficult at some spots, causing Ishi to stop several times to remove burs from her pant legs and to backtrack slightly to go around fallen trees. After nearly thirty minutes of struggling, the bush began to thin. And then, she was out on the other side.

Her first inclination was to look for the guard tower. Looking to her left and right, she could not see it. *Maybe they tore it down? It was likely a negative reminder.* "Yeah, I would've torn it down," she muttered. "Personally, I would've burned it down!"

She noticed that there are more houses in view than the aerial photo showed, most of them new-looking. This told her that the photo definitely wasn't recent. *So, if the photo isn't recent, then maybe that acreage is gone too.* Just as she considered that possibility, she saw it! Further to her left than she had expected, but there it was! She looked at the modest house and the sagging chicken coop and a partially collapsed mesh-wire fence around the chicken coop.

As Ishi walked toward the acreage, she became suddenly aware that, with all the growth of Philippsthal houses closer to this acreage, people might be watching her. *I might be seen trespassing.* She stopped momentarily! *Do I dare?* She took several steps forward, studying the nearby houses for any people or activity. It was a Sunday afternoon, so Ishi knew that there was a good chance that families would be home. She spotted people on the back decks of two of the houses. However, those houses were quite far away. Ishi continued walking up the slight incline toward the small derelict house.

The small home was dilapidated. It was clearly abandoned for a long time. Many wooden shiplap siding boards had partly detached and fallen downward, and the windows that Ishi could see were either completely glassless or the glass was broken because of stones thrown. *Likely by neighborhood kids over the years.* Stepping up to the closed door, she turned the rusted old knob. Locked. She walked around a corner to one of the windows devoid of any glass, and standing up on her toes, she stretched her left leg through. She moved her body through and pulled her right leg after. She was in.

The inside of the house was dusty. From where she stood at the pane-less window, she saw the kitchen cabinets on the far side, two doors that led to rooms, and lots of cobwebs everywhere. *I'm trespassing*! She turned and looked back out of the window worried that someone might be coming to reprimand her. Nobody was coming.

Ishi took almost twenty minutes looking around. Cupboard drawers. Two closets in the two small bedrooms. The wide drawer in the heavy base that sat beneath the small modular fireplace. She found absolutely nothing except a black iron crank in the drawer beneath the fireplace. *This was likely for opening and closing the chimney above the fireplace.* "If I was here at some point, wouldn't I feel something familiar?" she wondered aloud. But she didn't sense any familiarity at all.

Nervous about trespassing, Ishi left the same way she came into this little house. Once outside, she slapped the dust off of her pants and stepped toward the chicken coop. *No. I've overstayed my welcome. I don't want anyone coming here and giving me grief.* She walked back down the slight hill toward the woods.

*

Pascal had quickly taken photos of the photos, making sure to leave them on the sofa just as they were. Earlier, he had deducted, when he didn't hear any activity through the receiver for more than thirty minutes after hearing the house door close, that Ishi had left. He hadn't heard a vehicle, so Pascal concluded that nobody had been by to pick her up. Cautiously he had approached the house and the barn on foot to see if perhaps she was doing the chores. Confirming that the girl was gone, he went inside the house. Because he had no way of knowing where she went or when she would return, all he dared to do was to photograph the photos that he found on the sofa, recognizing them as the originals of the photocopies he'd found at the Adri house. He then carefully extracted himself back through the trees to his car.

*

Rebecca stood at the kitchen island with her hands full of dough as she hand-mixed dough for a loaf. She intently watched the news that David was watching from the armchair in the living room.

A major news channel was describing with video a breaking news report from Hebron. Major-General Tariq Al Khalil had been assassinated. Apparently poisoned. General Arruk was shown speaking from a sitting position behind a desk, a large Palestinian Flag behind him. "Israel will pay for this terrible attack," he stated with fury! "Allah willing, we will see justice swiftly for this cowardly act by the cursed nation of the Jews. Our leader, our brother, he did not deserve this. Just another example of the evil of the cursed Israel dogs!"

The news field correspondent recapped, "If this is in-fact a retaliation by Israel, which is what it appears to be at this point from what we know, then this can only heighten the tension greatly in the region."

David looked over his shoulder to see if Rebecca was watching.

*

General Arruk, finished his lunch at his desk, tapped a button on his desk com. "Mira, send Omar Abadi in."

Several seconds later, a middle-aged trimly bearded man in civilian clothes stepped into General Arruk's office. He remained standing and didn't speak. Arruk pushed his empty dirty dishes aside and looked up at Abadi. "Are you and your team ready?"

"Yes, we have him in the trunk down in the parking garage. Hard time getting him in. So big!"

Arruk nodded his approval. "Okay, then take him to the desert immediately. Bury him deep. I don't want anyone finding him. I never want the name Benjamin Sharod connected to our cause again, to our noble cause."

"Yes, sir," Abadi bowed slightly as he turned to go.

Arruk added, "Mashallah! (as Allah wills)" As Omar Abadi energetically turned and exited, General Arruk tapped his com again. "Mira, I want my dessert. Bring it now!"

CHAPTER 24

After enjoying a good lunch with Dagmar's sister and her husband in Mannheim, Horst and Dagmar pointed their Volvo northeast toward home. They'd taken highway 43a to bypass Frankfurt and all the Monday traffic near that big city, and now they were making good time driving northeast on highway 66.

"Only another ninety or so minutes," Horst thought out loud as he glanced in the rear-view mirror. "Sure seeing a lot of black Passats on this trip! Volkswagen m-must've struck the right note with that m-model."

Dagmar asked, "What's a Passat? I don't think I'd know one to see one."

"It's a nice c-car. Never been inside one, but they look good. Expensive." He glanced up in the mirror again and noticed that the black Passat has gained on them significantly. Horst glanced down at the speedometer. 123 kph. Horst knew that, while not every highway in Germany is Autobahn, many drivers drive as if they were. So, he was not surprised at the speed of the Passat behind them. And he was not surprised as it passed them.

The surprise came as the Passat hit the brakes right in front of them! Immediately Horst reacted by hitting his brakes hard and swerving a bit. Dagmar screamed! The Passat continued to brake to a full stop. Horst was going to hit them! He swerved to the right, skidding off the highway into the ditch.

Dagmar screamed more! Horst's knuckles gripped the steering wheel hard as the Volvo came to a sliding stop pointing downward halfway into the ditch, a cloud of dust billowing around the car. As the dust cleared, Horst looked out of his side window and saw two figures running from the Passat toward them.

Their arms were outstretched. He couldn't believe his eyes! Each person was aiming a pistol at them! Dagmar continued to scream. She had seen the guns too, and held her hands in front of her face as a shield. As Horst raised his left hand in front of his face, he recognized the two assailants. "What in the--?" He couldn't believe his eyes and was immediately stunned in confusion!

Shimon Adri ran to Horst's window while Miriam Adri ran to Dagmar's window. Each pointing a gun at the window, they yelled, "Get out! Get out of the car! Now! Open the door!" As they yelled, they yanked the doors open. Horst and Dagmar were frantically trying to shield their faces with their hands. "Undo your seatbelts!" Shimon yelled. Horst and Dagmar complied immediately. Then both Shimon and Miriam grabbed their targets and dragged them out of their seats onto the coarse grass in the ditch. Complying in absolute fear and confusion, Horst and Dagmar did not resist, and found themselves face down in the dusty coarse grass, their arms and faces scratched by the stiff dry grass stalks. "Don't move!" Shimon threatened.

In less than fifteen seconds after Horst and Dagmar were face down in the ditch mute with absolute confused terror, Miriam had injected first Dagmar and then Horst in the back of their legs with a needle. It only took another fifteen seconds after those injections for Horst's and Dagmar's bodies to go limp.

They looked up and down the highway and saw that the nearest vehicle appeared to be a semi-truck approaching in the far distance from the north. Quickly without speaking a word, Shimon and Miriam each dragged a body back up from the ditch to the Passat. Shimon ran to the open driver's door, reached in and popped the trunk. Simultaneously, Miriam got into the Volvo, backed it out of the ditch, and pulled it up neatly behind the Passat. Just as the bodies were well concealed between the two cars, the truck passed. Shimon and Miriam looked and saw more traffic approaching from the south. But they had time. Together one body at a time, they hoisted the bodies of Horst and Dagmar into the trunk of the Passat and closed it.

Quickly Miriam got into the Volvo while Shimon got into the Passat. They waited twenty-five seconds for some oncoming traffic to pass, then in single file they did a 180 degree turn across the highway and drove south.

Only eight kilometers south, the Passat and the Volvo exited into the town of Altenhasslau. They drove steadily along An der Burgmühle Strässe to the train station, pulling into the train station parking lot. Miriam parked the sand-colored Volvo at one end of the parking lot, pulled a handkerchief from her pocket and wiped down the steering wheel and shifter, then got out of the car, and jumped into the Passat. They drove off with the body cargo in the trunk.

*

The next morning, Ishi slept in. Earlier when she had woken up, she thought, "On one hand, I love the silence. On the other hand, I miss the odd comfort of the light snoring and the quiet morning commotion of mom in the kitchen."

Nearly finished the chores, Ishi brought the almost full two-gallon pail of milk to the milk separator at the cleaner small room just inside the big front barn doors. There for just over eight minutes, she turned the crank steadily. The whole milk that Ishi had dumped into the big metal tub at the top of the separator ran down through the spinning separator bowl. Dividing there by the spinning device, cream streamed into a small pail from one ten-inch spout and skimmed milk gushed into a larger pail from the other spout.

As she carried the two pails toward the house, ideas of what the day could hold flitted through her mind. *It's tempting to call Christian.* She considered this thought. *Maybe Lucy or Becky would want to join me for lunch at the café.* The thought of hiking back to the acreage to explore more, maybe the chicken coop this time, danced in and out of her head.

In the kitchen, Ishi poured the cream into a large Tupperware container and put a lid on it. She poured the skimmed milk into two one-gallon plastic pails, putting lids on them both. She opened a cupboard drawer, extracting a roll of masking tape and a felt pen, tearing off a short strip, adhered it to the lid of one of the pails containing milk. "Schmidtke" she wrote on the masking tape. Then she put all three containers into the large very full fridge. The part of the whole milking process that Ishi really didn't like was bringing the separator bowl and contraptions into the house and washing them. *Such a big job! I'll do it later.*

I wonder if Christian would go to the acreage with me? She rinsed her hands under the faucet. Feelings of guilt and shame of how she had just so easily sort of discarded Christian this past week, and now so quickly wanted him back in her life. She grimaced in her shame as she tried to not think it through too thoroughly. *Yeah*, she added to the idea, *that way we could simply drive there.* Ishi knew that her mom and dad weren't planning to be back until later in the afternoon, so there was time. She also worried that she would have to share the crazy story with Christian, that crazy story that Sebastian told her. *Hmmm?*

Walking into the bedroom, she took her cell phone from the charger on top of her dresser and called.

*

The maroon-colored Jetta pulled slowly up the short gradual inclined dirt-grass driveway of the mystery acreage and stopped between the small, abandoned house and the hand-pump well. Christian and Ishi stepped out of the car.

Earlier when Christian had arrived to pick up Ishi, they sat in front of Ishi's house for quite a while as Ishi told Christian the entire events of Saturday. Christian had tried to not reveal his envy when Ishi recounted the romantic adventure to Frankfurt. He only had commented half under his breath, "Must be nice to have all that money!" As Ishi showed Christian the photos, telling him the details that Sebastian had told her, Christian found the story completely outlandish and unbelievable. "I would've ground the glass into his face instead of just throwing it," Christian had sympathized with Ishi when she told him of her violent outburst.

Nevertheless, Christian and Ishi had been close friends since before either of them could remember. So, if she wanted to explore this little acreage, he knew he wouldn't say no.

Having already looked through the house herself, Ishi let Christian go look at the house, deciding that she'd go check out the chicken coop. As she lifted the hook latch and, with some effort, pulling open the door, she was immediately hit with a waft of stale ammonia-laced air. Wiping cobwebs away, she stepped inside.

She saw three tiers of nesting boxes that lined both walls. It felt familiar. *Familiar, because it's like our own chicken coop*, she reasoned.

The door, hanging slightly uneven after so many years, slowly swung shut, extinguishing most of the light. Ishi stepped back to the door and opened it. She located a small piece of broken brick laying within reach, grabbed it and blocked the door open with it. Then she returned inside.

The one small square window at the back of the chicken coop was so caked with grime and dust that it barely allowed any light through. Ishi noticed that the straw filling each nesting box was almost grey instead of yellow because of the years of dust on it. The wooden nesting boxes' fronts were covered with a decade-old layer of grey-black dust too, so Ishi didn't see it right away. Then, she saw it! 'ISHI'. Not wanting to use her bare hands to wipe the grimy dust away, she used the bottom of her shirt. 'ISHI' It was as plain as day written in black marker on the middle nesting box. A quick wave of fright ran through her! "Christian!" Ishi stepped to the open door. "Christian!" Her heart was in her throat!

Almost twenty minutes later, without seeing anything else of significance, Ishi and Christian gave up and drove back to the Gruber farm. Ishi was mostly silent, brows knitted, thoughts pinballing in her head. As they rolled up Ishi's driveway, Christian asked, "Why would Sebastian have photos? I get it. He loves to research stuff to death. But … the photos?"

Ishi added, "You know what just dawned on me? Most of those aren't printed photos. They are actual photos, I think."

Sebastian studied Ishi's puzzled face. "And, your name in the chicken coop," he wondered aloud, knowing that he was merely repeating verbally the mysterious fact that had been the center of Ishi's consternation over the past forty minutes.

Ishi took a deep pondering breath. "I know. But about the photos. They are old. And they are originals, not photoscans or photocopies. How would Sebastian …?"

As they got out of the Jetta, Christian asked, "Can I help you with chores?"

Ishi was surprised and delighted, "Seriously? Sure, if you want to. But your clothes?"

"Oh, I don't care about the clothes." He smiled.

Ishi's head suddenly drooped. She looked at her feet, and then back up at Christian. "Chris."

"What's up, Ish?"

"Chris, I should've been your date for grad. Er, I mean, you should've been my date. What was I thinking?" Suddenly Ishi realized that she was being presumptive. "Oh, if that's something that you would've …"

"Exactly the thing that I would've wanted. I'm just sorry I wasn't on the ball with asking you first."

*

It was almost 9:30pm. Adri Foods was closed. The Monday staff had left. Sebastian stood in the dark just inside the front locked grocery store glass door peering out into the dark as he kept an ear on the activity beneath him.

Adri Foods' basement was half the size of the building above it, with a wide stairwell leading from the main floor storage area down to a landing and then down again into the middle of the main room, the larger of two large basement rooms. An open doorway to the left led to the other smaller room. The main room's walls were covered with storage shelves, shelves that were nearly full of cans and jars and many other full food containers, dozens of full carboard boxes, varieties of kitchen cleaning supplies, and much more. The basement walls and floor were constructed of poured concrete. There were no windows. In the second smaller room, a furnace, water heater, and electric wall panels took up the back third of it. In the middle of the second room near the furnace, tied to metal chairs and blindfolded, sat Horst and Dagmar in only their underwear.

A small pool of blood had collected beneath Dagmar's chair, blood that streamed down from her left hand where two of her fingernails were missing. Dagmar's head hung down as she sobbed steadily, her matted shoulder-length hair hanging like a curtain around her face.

Although there was no blood apparent under Horst's chair, his head also drooped. Half a dozen red-purple spots could be seen on his chest and neck where the electric prod had been applied.

Saadia was pacing in the larger basement room, a cell phone to her ear. "Well, we know how the girl arrived. They admitted that much. But they insist that they have no knowledge of where the girl came from." Saadia spoke in a volume quiet enough that the Gruber couple couldn't hear her from the other room over the running furnace air exchange unit there.

General Arruk hissed, "I want you to be absolutely certain first. Absolutely certain!"

Saadia replied, "Yes, sir." She tapped 'End Call' and nodded at Akeem. "One more."

Akeem and Saadia stepped back into the second room. As Horst and Dagmar heard them re-enter, Akeem said, "We just got off the phone with someone and we know that you aren't telling us everything."

Horst pleaded, "We are t-t-telling everything. There isn't anything we didn't t-tell. We d-don't know anything about her p-p-parents!"

Dagmar's sobs intensified.

Akeem stepped to a shelf and took the electric cattle prod. He stepped toward Horst.

"No!" Horst had heard the electric prod being picked up again. "We've said every s-single thing w-we …" Horst screamed in pain as Akeem pushed the electric prod against his inner thighs very near his groin!

Akeem yelled viciously, "I don't believe you."

As Horst wailed in anguish, Dagmar sobbed convulsively.

Akeem and Saadia knew how this must end for two reasons. The Grubers had seen them. And the Katz girl must be given added incentive to search for her real parents. Akeem nodded to Saadia. She stepped to the nearby wall shelf and grabbed a Hauser 9mm pistol with a silencer attached.

She stepped to Dagmar and whipped the blindfold off her.

Dagmar didn't look up.

"Look at me!" Saadia commanded.

Dagmar didn't look up. Her sobs just intensified.

Saadia yelled with a more vicious tone, "Look at me Dagmar!" Dagmar looked up through her tears and red swollen eyes.

Azim had quietly come downstairs and walked up beside his mother.

When Dagmar saw the gun in Miriam's hand, her eyes grew wide in terror. "What are you going to--"

Miriam cut her off, "Here's what will happen next if you don't tell us where Isabella came from. Tell us about her parents! Tell us where they are now! What their names are now! Tell us now!" Saadia aimed the gun at blindfolded Horst.

Dagmar tried to scream, but only crackly sounds emerged.

Horst, not realizing that a gun was pointed at him, interjected, "We've t-told you everything, you wicked d-devil …" His words were cut short by the shot of the gun. Horst's body jolted backward as a bullet entered his chest and his heart.

Dagmar fainted.

Akeem looked at Saadia. "It's no good. They don't know anything." He nodded at Saadia. She pointed the pistol at Dagmar. Her hand was shaking. Saadia Bakir might have harbored an intense hatred for the enemy, and might have been hardened through her training that included the execution of a caught Israeli soldier, but she was not cut out to be a cold killer. The fact that she had just executed Horst instantly terrorized her emotions. Azim, seeing his mother's shaking hand, took the gun from her. Without hesitation, he aimed it at Dagmar and pulled the trigger.

CHAPTER 25

Ishi was finishing labeling the milk containers and placing them in the fridge. Her face displayed her worry. She walked to the landline phone again on the kitchen wall and punched in the phone number.

"Hello," answered the female voice.

Ishi's voice was desperate, "Auntie Sophie, hi, it's me again. It's not like them to not at least call me."

Aunt Sophie asked, "Still nothing, Ishi?"

Ishi began to cry, "No."

"Well, I'm worried."

"Something is wrong, Auntie."

"Uncle Helmut already phoned the police. Oh, I don't mean to frighten you dear, but this is too long now."

"My mom has a cell phone. She would at least have called me to tell me if they … if something happened. I mean, even if their car broke down, or whatever."

"Is there someone you can call to come be with you?"

Ishi thought for a few seconds, and then replied, "Yes. My friend Christian."

"Good. Call him." Ishi heard Aunt Sophie telling her Uncle Helmut, "She's calling her friend Christian."

Ishi asked, "They didn't say anything to you? That they were going somewhere else, did they?"

"No dear. They were planning to only drive back home."

Ishi's crying turned to sobs.

Aunt Sophie continued, "Ishi, call your friend. It's okay. There will be a logical explanation, you just wait and see."

"Okay Auntie." She hung up.

*

General Arruk heard a phone ring. He instinctively grabbed his desk phone. Realizing that wasn't the ringing phone, he opened his desk drawer and grabbed a cell flip phone. He opened it and tapped the 'Answer' button. "Talk!"

Akeem Almasi reported, "They knew nothing, just as we suspected."

"So you …"

Akeem Almasi injected, "Yes. We will find a secure way to dispose of their bodies."

Arruk's desk phone rang. "Hold on! My other phone." He picked up his desk phone. "Yes?"

Omar Abadi's voice reported, "Sharod is buried."

Arruk asked, "Where even the vultures can't find him, I trust?"

"Yes, sir. He is gone. Completely gone."

"Well done." He hung up the desk phone. Arruk returned to the call with Akeem Almasi, "Did Azim push the girl sufficiently?"

Akeem answered, "Yes. Any more would have not worked. Now we must wait. If she doesn't react as we hope, especially when her parents don't come home, we'll add force."

"Two days. At the most three days Akeem. I won't rest until that Jewish worm Katz is found. Understood?"

"I understand, General Arruk."

General Arruk folded the phone closed and put it back into a drawer. He put a hand to his heart. *That Joseph Katz is going to be the death of me, even after fifteen years.*

*

Christian had just parked his car in front of the house where his father was prepping the cement mixer for a fence build. Christian was not late to the job, but always felt guilty anyway when he arrived after his father. *It's amazing*, Christian thought, frustrated! *It doesn't matter how early I show up, he's always somehow earlier.* As Christian put a leg out of the car, his cell phone buzzed. "Hello?"

Eddie's voice was full of energy. "Chris, oh Chris, wherefore art thou?"

"Just arriving at work. What's up Eddie?"

Eddie said, "Hey man, Julia and I have been sleuthing on the Internet. Hearing the Adri guy speaking Arabic made me really curious, y'know."

"And?"

"Well, you know how they said that they had a shop Adri Foods in Stuttgart before? Well, we couldn't find any trace of one. Not with that name."

"Maybe it had a different name. Could have."

"Thought of that. We looked for their personal names. We tried everything. Not a trace. Not a single thing came up."

Christian waited listening.

Eddie continued, "We think it's weirdness because, well, y'know, if someone owned a business, especially a business that would be so public as a retail store, there'd be something. Right?"

"Hmmmm? Eddie buddy, I gotta go! My dad's looking at me now wondering what I'm doing."

Eddie replied, "Go! I just think this is weird y'know. Team Adri are liars maybe?"

*

Leah's phone vibrated as it sat on the passenger's seat. She grabbed it. "Pascal?"

Pascal said, "They found the car."

"Where?"

"Abandoned at the train station at Altenhasslau."

Leah began, "Where is Alt …"

"It's a town halfway between here and Frankfurt."

Leah asked, "Who found it?"

"Local police."

"Shit!"

"What?"

Leah thought aloud, "That Gruber couple don't know anything about anything. They're as innocent as the pure driven snow. They either, hmmm … either abducted, or …" Leah was thinking.

"Or what?"

Leah pondered, "They could've been threatened and made a run for it by train." She thought a bit more. "Nah, I doubt it. Their daughter is absolutely beside herself with worry. If they were threatened and running, they would've at least got a message to Isabella somehow. They didn't."

"What now?"

"Go back into the store. This time bug their office."

Pascal pushed back, "Toto, we don't have time. They might be moving fast."

"Pascal, we have time. I suspect they're waiting on the girl to do something. I'll keep my eyes on her. Make sure she's safe. So, no trade off tonight. I'll just sit tight. You go back in!"

"Okay."

*

It was late in the afternoon, and Ishi was curled up on her bed on top of her blankets. Wrapped with worry, she didn't know what else to do. She had been trying to process everything, the photos, Sebastian's words, her name on the nesting box, and her parents being a day late without letting her know anything.

She got up and sauntered into the kitchen, realizing that soon she'll need to go do the chores. She knew that she should make something to eat because she hadn't eaten all day. But she wasn't hungry. She took a banana from the fruit bowl on the table, peeled it, and forced herself to eat it.

Nearly an hour later, the only part of the chores she had remaining was to throw hay over the fence for the cows. As she forked over the first bunch, she saw a car approaching down the driveway. Immediately Ishi recognized it as a Bundespolizei car, seeing the large black word POLIZEI on the car's side. Her heart stopped. A numb chill ran through her body. *Maybe mom and dad broke down or were in an accident, and the police are bringing them home*, she wanted to believe. As the car arrived on the yard, Ishi saw that there were only two police officers inside. She just stared, scared.

As the male and female officers stepped out of the car, Ishi forced herself to walk toward them. They saw her and began to walk toward her.

"Hello," the female officer greeted Ishi.

Ishi was too scared to say anything.

The officer continued, "Is this the home of Horst and Dagmar Gruber?"

Ishi offered a frail "yes".

The officer asked, "And, you are?"

"I'm their daughter. Ishi. Isabella." Ishi was absolutely frozen in fear of what the officers might tell her.

The male officer asked, "Did your parents go on a trip recently?"

"Yes, they went to visit my aunt and uncle in Stuttgart. Actually, two aunts and uncles. One in Stuttgart and the others in Mannheim." Ishi sensed her voice quavering.

The male officer asked, "Did they say when they would be back home?"

"Yesterday!" Ishi blurted out. "And they didn't show up."

The female officer asked, "They didn't mention going anywhere else? Did they mention taking a train?"

Ishi was now very confused. "A train? No. Nowhere else. They were just coming back home. Where are they?" Ishi felt like she was going to cry.

The male officer asked again, "Are you certain that they didn't mention going somewhere, maybe by train?"

"No! They would've told me."

"Can you wait here a minute please?" the female officer asked.

As the officers turned to retreat to their car, Ishi called after them, "Where are my parents? What happened? Are they okay?" The officers, having been briefed that the abandoned Volvo's steering wheel and interior had been wiped clean, thus leaving no fingerprints, knew that it was most likely an abduction. They also knew that telling the daughter such information would both compromise the purpose for their visit here, and also be too cruel a piece of information for the daughter.

The female officer kept walking back to the car as she held up a finger, "Just one minute."

The male officer sat into the police car and made a call with his cell phone. Ishi stood frozen on the spot, confused and scared. She realized that she was still holding the pitchfork. *This looks like a weapon!* She tossed it down. The male officer finished his phone call and stepped back out of the car. The two officers again approached Ishi.

"Miss Gruber, it seems that your parent's car was located at the train station at Altenhasslau."

"Altenhasslau? *They took a train?* Where is that?"

The male officer said, "Halfway between here and Frankfurt."

The female officer added, "It appears that the car was abandoned. None of the train manifests have your parents' names on them."

Ishi's mouth fell open. Dismay enveloped her.

The male officer asked, "Do you have any idea why your parents might abandon their vehicle, Miss Gruber?"

Ishi just stared blankly at him. They looked back at her.

"Any idea?" repeated the female officer.

"No." She felt the blood draining from her face. Ishi was desperately reaching for reason, but there was nothing but terror-filled jumble.

The male officer asked, "Is there anyone else here? Do you have siblings?"

Ishi, now in a fog, shook her head. "No," she whimpered. "No, just me." She began to cry.

The female officer handed Ishi a business card. "Here is my number. If you learn anything or if your parents show up or contact you, please call us right away, okay."

Ishi took the card with one hand while wiping her wet nose and face with her other arm.

The male officer asked, "Are you okay here? We need to go. But we'd first like to have a look inside your house, if we may."

Ishi just nodded toward the house as permission. "It's open."

As the officers walked to the house, Ishi crumpled down on the dirt, sobbing.

Leah, not having heard anything transmitted for a long time, got out of her car, and carefully made her way to the edge of the Gruber yard, staying hidden behind a thick bush. She saw the police but couldn't hear anything that was said. She saw Ishi collapsed weeping in the middle of the yard. *Ohhh.* Leah's heart broke. When the police left, Leah knew that she needed to hurry back to her vehicle to hear what Ishi might say inside the house. Leah arrived at her vehicle just in time to hear Ishi sobbing into the phone. "… at Altenhasslau, Christian. They don't know where they are." There was a silent pause as Christian was speaking. Then Ishi said, "Please. If you can." Ishi hung up. Leah listened to her weep, blow her nose, and sob more.

Less than twenty minutes later, Christian's car turned off the main road and approached up the driveway. Ishi had been waiting by the open door. As she saw Christian arriving, she walked out to meet him. Her face was red from crying. As he moved to open his door, Ishi quickly said, "No, I have a different idea."

Christian was surprised. "What?"

Ishi walked around the car and got in. "I want to go back to the acreage."

Not being able to hear anything except Christian's car coming and then going, Leah jumped back out of her vehicle and rushed through the woods. She arrived at the farmyard too late. She doubled over panting from exhaustion.

As Christian's car stopped in front of the little house at the acreage, Ishi got out quickly and headed straight to the chicken coop. Christian followed. He called after her, "What are you thinking, Ish?"

Ishi replied, "Why would she just write my name on a nesting box? And nothing else?" Ishi disappeared inside.

Although it was past 7:00pm, it was the end of June. And so, there were still a couple of hours of daylight remaining. A tiny bit of that daylight was available through the small window even though the window was covered with a film representing years of dust and grime.

Ishi walked to the box with her name. She grabbed at the front of it and pulled. It was solid.

"You think there's something else?" Christian asked rhetorically.

Ishi ran a hand underneath the box bottom the feeling, and making sure to do so slowly, aware of the potential of getting a sliver from the old wood. Then she bent and tried to see underneath. It was too dark to see, and she didn't feel anything. She stood and, wiping her hands clean on her t-shirt, looked at Christian, her brows knitted.

The day before, Shimon had installed a listening device above one of the Philippsthal acreage house window frames. Now Sebastian sat in the BMW parked a block away north on a street that didn't lead to the acreage, that, strategically so that Christian and Ishi would exit and not drive past him and see him. This was as far as the micro-receiver would work though.

As soon as he had heard a vehicle drive up, Sebastian slowly drove half a block closer peering between houses as he drove trying to get a clear visual of the acreage. He parked, got out of the car, and jogged to the end of the street where the street dead-ended and the forest began. Then he cut through the bushes toward the back of the acreage. Circling around through the woods until the chicken coop was between him and Christian's maroon-colored Jetta, he made his way quickly up the slope toward the chicken coop.

Ishi was frustrated but determined. She walked back to the open door to get some air. Christian took his turn searching. As Christian dug up the very old dusty straw from the nesting box, he felt something. He pulled up all the box's straw tossing it aside, creating a choking cloud of very stale dust. Through coughs, he said, "Ishi!" Reaching back into the box, he pulled out a sheet of very yellow old brittle paper. As Ishi stepped back inside, he handed it to her.

She took it carefully, her hands suddenly shaking nervously, and stepped back toward the doorway and better light. The wide writing was very faint, but Ishi could read it. *"Ishi my dear granddaughter; I pray you remember how you loved gathering eggs with me. That would make me so happy. If so, all is 'well'. Just look!"* Over Ishi's shoulder, Christian had read it too.

"No shit!" Christian exhaled quietly, knowing this gave credit to Sebastian's story.

Sebastian remained carefully tucked against the back of the chicken coop. He had no way to know what was happening.

Ishi read the note again. While flooded with the weight of the whole realization of what these words meant, that Sebastian's story might be true, she looked up at Christian, her bloodshot eyes wide with questions. Christian just looked back at her, also confused.

After a few minutes, a worried expression overtook Christian's face. "Ishi, there something bigger going on."

Ishi, dumbstruck, said nothing.

Christian said, "You learn all this -- you learn this exactly when your parents go missing?"

"Does anybody know we're here?"

"No."

Ishi read it again, "*Ishi my dear granddaughter; I pray you remember how you loved gathering eggs with me. If so, all is 'well'. Just look!*" Ishi repeated, "Just look! Just look! Look at what?"

Christian pondered, "… gathering eggs. … all is well. Just look!"

Ishi looked up at the hand pump well only ten feet in front of her. "All is 'well.'"

Christian turned and stepped back inside to the nesting box. He felt around more, removing more straw from neighboring nesting boxes. While he was inside, Ishi stepped thoughtfully to the hand pump. She grabbed the handle and pumped it.

Hearing the squeaks of the handle being pumped, Christian stepped back outside. "Likely dry," Christian deducted. He stepped up onto the well platform. He felt that the boards beneath his feet were loose. Realizing that the boards were old and fearing falling through, he quickly jumped back off.

Ishi, seeing that the boards were loose, pulled up on the board nearest to her. With no effort, the board lifted up. She peered down into the cool musty hole. It was black, and she could see nothing. Christian also pulled up a board, and immediately saw a little rope fastened to a little piece of rebar sticking out of the concrete platform foundation. "Look!" Christian pulled the board up further. Ishi immediately bent down and felt the rope. It seemed a little bit weighted down.

As soon as Ishi and Christian retrieved the package from the well, they hurried to the Jetta. Far too nervous to stay and open the package there by the well, Christian drove off the acreage property, pulling over at the edge of a park three blocks away.

Sebastian had been able to hear their voices through the chicken coop walls but couldn't decipher what was said. He crept along the side of the chicken coop far enough to see that Ishi and Christian had pulled a package out of the well. But he had no way to know what the package was or where the two had driven to. Hurrying back toward his car, he pulled out his phone. He dialed. "They pulled something out of the well," he reported. He listened, then responded, "I don't know. C'mon Akeem, I have no way to know!" He listened again, then responded, "I'm guessing they'll go back to the farm." He listened, and responded, "Yes, I'm going there now."

During the eight-minute drive back to the farm, Ishi wiped off spiderwebs and dust, then unwrapped the package. The wax paper was brittle and broke all over the car's floor mat. Even the plastic bags were somewhat brittle and broke apart. Slightly leery about the bag's contents, Ishi peeled the two layers of the brittle plastic back and looked in. Christian repeatedly glanced over while driving. They both saw it at the same time. Bundles of money! They looked at each other wide-eyed! "Whoa!" Christian slowed the car and pulled to a stop on the shoulder. Ishi lifted up one of the cash bundles. She was speechless!

"There's a letter," Ishi noted.

Christian was checking his mirrors. He said, "Okay, I'm seriously not comfortable! Let me find a side road." He drove ahead another half kilometer and was less than half a kilometer from Ishi's driveway when he turned off onto a small road that led into the woods. He saw a red car parked a bit further ahead where the road dead ended in the woods. "Crap!" He backed out and drove the remaining couple of hundred meters to the Gruber driveway.

"No," Ishi said panicky as Christian slowed approaching the driveway. "Can we go to your place?"

Christian replied, "Sure," understanding Ishi's nervousness.

As they drove, Ishi tucked the package behind her feet on the floor and turned to Christian. "What's happening?" Her face strained with fear and confusion.

Christian had no answer.

Ishi's voice waivered as she said, "I think my parents are ... I think something bad happened."

Neither Christian nor Ishi noticed the red Skoda that had immediately extracted itself from that dead-end road in the woods and was now following them.

Unable to wait, Ishi bent down and extracted the letter from the package. She read it silently.

> *Dearest Isabella — my sweet Ishi,*
> *I have lived under a mountain of guilt and shame since I lost you. Each day I have prayed for you and I continue to keep hope that you will make your way back to us. Should the day come where you find yourself back here looking for answers, please know that I have given you all I own. I imagine that I will no longer be here to see your beautiful face and hold you in my arms, so this is what I can do to show you my love. I hope this humble acreage, where you left with Honish so many years ago, will bring you some peace in your years and it has for me — that is, until that tragic night. I have had no peace since. It is important to me that you are the only person who receives this bequest. I have not even told your dear mother. As you will learn, and may have already, your father is not a good person; I want to make sure he can not touch what is meant solely for you. And here, too, you will find my cash savings. I know it can not make up for that horrible night — for falling asleep. I have nightmares about what you must have gone through and how you must have felt, sweet girl. I am so sorry, my dear Ishi. So very sorry. All I have is yours. I love you always.*
> *Your Oma, Ingrid Braun.*

Christian glanced at Ishi, waiting for her to say anything or read something aloud.

Ishi felt sick! "Chris, I think I'm going to be sick. Can you pull over?"

They were now nearly in Vacha. There was no more shoulder, so Christian pulled over as far to the side of the road as possible. Then eyeing an alley, he turned into it, drove another fifty meters, and stopped. Even before the car was stopped, Ishi's door was open and she was leaning out for fresh air, not sure whether she'd vomit.

Leah was caught off-guard by Christian's car suddenly turning into the alley. *What do I do?* Whether she had stopped or followed into the alley, she'd be visible to Christian's rear-view mirror. She drove past the alley, then one block later she came to a stop on the side of the road just past another alley. She then backed into that alley and waited, hoping that Christian and Ishi would continue in that direction. Christian and Ishi hadn't noticed the red car as Ishi was close to vomiting and fainting, and Christian was at a loss as to what to do for Ishi.

*

There were seven shoppers in Adri Foods. Miriam was busy behind the deli counter. Shimon was stacking boxes onto shelves in the back room. Two cashiers each tended to a customer. Shimon's cell phone rang. "Azim! What's happening?"

Azim replied with an urgency in his voice, "They didn't come back here."

"Come back where?"

"To the farm." Azim waited for a response but heard only an anguished exhale from a perplexed Akeem. "I don't know where they went. What should I do?"

Akeem thought. Then he said, "Wait. Wait there in-case they show up!" He hung up, an angry and worried frown on his face.

*

Jonathan Ben Dod picked up his ringing desk phone. "Iden," he required.

"t-o-t-o-2-4-q."

"Hi Toto. Update?"

Leah explained, "The Katz girl and her male friend Christian were at the acreage. Something spooked them. Twenty minutes ago, they left the acreage.

Instead of going back to the Gruber farm, they drove to Vacha. They're now tucked into an alley. I have no way to know what is going on with them."

"Any idea what might have spooked them, if that's what happened?"

"As I already said, no idea."

"Any progress from Pascal?"

"He's going back into the store tonight. Planting bugs this time. Pascal said that he's observed Almasi making phone calls outside his store too on the parking lot. So, he's going to put a couple of devices there."

"Why the hell didn't he do that last time?"

Leah was annoyed, "We didn't have them. Good grief! Remember, Jonathan? You were late getting them to us."

Ben Dod relinquished, "Okay. Do your best Toto! Keep me updated."

CHAPTER 26

The ZZ Top song La Grange played loudly throughout the house's main floor built-in audio system that included the large deck. David had both patio doors wide open. Four men and two women stood and sat in the afternoon heat on the deck, drinks in their hands as they talked and laughed. Inside the living room and kitchen area, another half dozen men and women sat and stood laughing and talking and drinking. David was on the deck yucking it up with a couple of guys.

Rebecca had sought harbor with Lily in a lower-level bedroom. She was not necessarily unhappy with the party upstairs, a party spontaneously created by David while at the pub the night before. She had actually mingled upstairs for some time before retreating. What did have Rebecca fuming was overhearing David recklessly bragging to his friends about the luxury yacht that he used to own and sail around the Mediterranean. And then to throw gasoline on the fire, Rebecca listened to David shoot off his mouth about having been in the furniture business and being quite a furniture expert. When Rebecca had gone to confront David on his loose lips, he had merely and crudely looked at her and said, "Fuck off!" within earshot of at least one other guest.

As Rebecca occupied herself by reorganizing the closet in the extra lower-level bedroom, she grumbled aloud, "He's going to get us blown. Moron!" She stepped over to the bed and sat. She took her phone that was laying on the bed and entered the passcode. Then she tapped the Family Tree icon that represented the ancestral genetic search. A screen opened to her account. Rebecca reviewed the screen, then seeing nothing of note, pressed the button that turned the phone off.

The bedroom door suddenly opened a crack. Rebecca, surprised, looked around at the door as it opened further, a tanned male arm pushing it open.

"Hello?" Rebecca inquired at the intrusion.

A bearded short man with bulgy eyes entered and said, "So this is where you're hiding." He grinned as he stepped into the bedroom.

Instantly, Rebecca stood. "Oh, I'm sorry, are you looking for the washroom? It's--"

"Nope." He grinned broader. "Looking for you."

Rebecca looked at him, instantly sensing danger. "I came here to-- I'm David's wife. You must've …"

"I know," the little man said as he began to close the door behind him.

Lily, also sensing danger, scampered between the two humans and barked furiously at the man.

Rebecca raised her voice, commanding, "You need to go. I don't know who you are, but I want you to leave!" She stepped toward him, intending to push him back outside through the door before he completely closed it.

Immediately he stepped toward her and attempted to grab her arms. Rebecca was faster. Squirming out of his grasp and giving him a body check, she squeezed out through the door. Lily quickly followed before the man could completely turn around.

Rebecca raced upstairs and through the guests toward the deck. The guests, recognizing her rushing as an indicator of some kind of drama, stopped their conversations to watch her enter the deck. She furiously stomped up to David. Breathing heavy and face-to-face with David, Rebecca hissed, "One of your hyena friends just tried to attack me!"

David looked at her, surprised.

"He came downstairs into the bedroom, and …"

David cut in, "Maybe he didn't know you are my--"

"He knew," Rebecca stated louder now! "He even told me that he knew."

"David buddy," the little man's voice indicated that he had stepped out onto the deck. "Hey man, I--" the man began.

Rebecca spun and pointed. "Him!"

The man continued, "Buddy, just taking the party downstairs too. No harm intended." He shrugged, palms up.

Letting his cane drop to the floor, David marched, despite the pain in his hip, to the little man, grabbed him by the shoulders, spun him around, and growled, "Get the hell out of my house!"

The man pushed back forcefully. "Hey, hey, take your fucking hands off of me!"

David pushed him harder. "Get the fuck out of my house!"

The little man, refusing to comply, pushed back.

Immediately two other men joined in the pushing and pulling. One man was trying to step between David and the little man, saying, "David buddy, easy!" The other man grabbed the little man by the back of his shoulders and was trying to haul him off the deck into the house. The little man stumbled backwards and fell, his shoulder connecting with the deck side table as he fell.

A larger sturdy man with a military haircut and tattoo on his neck stepped toward David. "You don't touch my friend like that!" He made a motion to shove David just as Rolly grabbed the man around the neck and hauled him backwards.

Within seconds, the deck erupted in violence. It was four men and three women physically swinging and grabbing and pushing in aid of David, and the little man and his friend fighting back. The sturdy man jumped toward David with a full swing of his arm. His fist grazed David's shoulder as David quickly dodged it. Instantly, David launched himself onto his assailant, collapsing him to the deck floor. Rolly and another man joined David pinning down the tattooed man while one other man and two women pinned the little man down.

David hissed at the man beneath him, "I'll kill you! If you try anything, I'll kill you!"

The man growled back, "In your dreams, you--"

David yelled over him, "I've done it before. I can do it again! Don't mess with me."

As David yelled, the two men helping David began to drag the big, tattooed man back to his feet. They hauled him from the deck, through the doors, and halfway across the living room as the other man and two women hauled the little man also toward the front door.

Halfway across the living room, the bigger man stopped struggling, shook off the hands that guided him, looked to his mate and suggested, "Let's get out of here Kenny."

"Yeah, bunch of sick losers anyway," the little man added. With the smaller man clenching his injured shoulder with one hand, they both walked out through the front door.

Rebecca stood staring at David, her mouth hanging open. She couldn't believe what she just heard him say! *Did he just say, I've done it before?* David glanced at her and saw her glaring at him.

"Sorry friends," David began to apologize to the remaining guests as Rebecca walked resolutely through the crowd and into the garage, Lily scampering along behind her. She got into the white Explorer, let Lily jump in too, past her feet and then onto the passenger's seat. Rebecca opened the garage door, and with a screech of her tires, she backed out.

*

Lucy's left hand gripped the steering wheel of the white Citroen Xsara as her right hand shifted into fifth gear as they ramped onto the highway southbound toward Frankfurt. Ishi sat in the passenger's seat, her lap full of papers. They drove with no music. The mood in the car was serious.

Lucy asked, "If they kept your parents' car for the investigation, did they say that they were ever going to return it?"

Ishi replied, "No, they didn't tell me anything." Wanting more comfort, using her feet one at a time, Ishi pushed her sneakers off. "After signing that missing persons police form the other day, they told me that they'd update me on everything. But nothing. Nothing!" Ishi slid down in her seat to as low a slouch as her shoulder belt would allow. "Thanks for doing this Luce."

Lucy chimed back, "Of course. Ishi, this is all so crazy! Are you absolutely sure you want to do this?"

Ishi just looked at her friend with a stern 'My mind is made up' look.

"Well, I'm with you. I support you. Right decision!"

Ishi's phone buzzed. "Hello?"

Christian's voice calmed Ishi slightly. "Are you on your way?"

"Yeah, just filled up with gas. On the highway now."

"I'm glad Lucy's parents let her use their car. I'm sorry I couldn't …"

Ishi interrupted, "Christian, I've already made you skip work enough. I didn't want your parents getting upset with me too."

"Okay Ish, call me when you're back, okay."

"I will. Oh and, I told Julia that I'm going to Frankfurt to register for the search. Just so you know who all knows." Just before Ishi tapped the 'End Call' button, she heard Christian say something. She put the phone back to her ear. "Sorry. What did you say?"

"I drove by the store today. Saw Sebastian working inside."

Ishi said, "Oh. Okay. Thanks. Bye." Again, just as Ishi raised her hand to tap the 'End Call' button, she heard Christian again.

"Ishi! Ish!"

She returned the phone to her ear. "I'm still here."

"You're applying for your passport too while you're down there, right? Like you said?"

"Yes. I have all my documents along for that."

Christian said, "Good. The more official documents you have, the less hassle you'll have for the title on that acreage, I think. Y'know, like we talked about."

"Yep. Talk to you later Chris."

Lucy asked, "When we get back, do you want to stay a few more days? Or do you want to go back home? You can stay over more. My parents are fine with it."

Ishi answered, "Can I stay a bit more? I don't feel comfortable at home right now."

"Oh, sure. But what about your chores?"

"Christian is doing them for a few days." As a qualifier, Ishi added, "I'm paying him."

"You have enough money to pay him? I can help, you know."

Ishi hadn't divulged the entire contents of the package or the letter to Lucy. She had only told her about the letter, and portions of its contents, and her desire now to try to find her biological parents. Ishi had also lied to Lucy saying that a passport was required as official documentation for such a search, something Lucy hadn't questioned. "Yeah, it's tight. But I can pay him. He's amazing! His work with his dad. Helping me." As an afterthought, Ishi asked Lucy, "When we're back, do you mind if we go by my house though? I need to get some clothes."

"Sure. No problem."

As Lucy and Ishi drove along a Frankfurt street, Ishi was intently studying a map app on her phone. "Next intersection, turn left," Ishi instructed.

Lucy signaled.

"They told me that it'll take at least an hour, Lucy. What are you going to do?"

"I'll just wait. It's okay Ishi. I'm sure they have a waiting room or something."

Ishi smiled at Lucy, "Okay."

Lucy was craning her head, gawking at the office towers while driving. "Ishi, look at that one! Wow! It's all glass."

Inside a Family Tree small side-office, a male attendant with a cotton swab was taking a saliva swab from Ishi's mouth. The attendant then snipped off the end of the Q-Tip with a scissors and dropped the sample into a little glass container. The attendant said, "Okay. You can go back to the front desk now. They'll help you install the app on your phone.

Ishi replied, "Okay." She got up and left the small room.

After finishing at the Family Tree front desk, Ishi turned and stepped over to Lucy who was waiting sitting in a chair.

Lucy asked, "To the passport office now?"

"Yep. It's about ten minutes nearer to the city center."

"Pitter patter, let's get at 'er!" Lucy rose to join her friend as they left the office. Lucy was determined to be a strong and good friend for her hurting dear Ishi.

*

Jonathan Ben Dod was finishing lunch at Café Shapira when his phone buzzed. Quickly putting down his fork and knife, he stepped outside the café and answered, "Iden!"

Leah sighed and recited, "t-o-t-o-5-8-9-b."

Jonathan looked at his phone screen and put the phone back to his ear. "Repeat iden."

Leah's voice was clearly frustrated. "t-o-t-o-5-8-9 … d."

"Iden confirmed. What's the problem, Toto?"

"The problem is -- we don't know where the girl is the past day and a half. We put the tracker on her boyfriend's car, but he hasn't been picking her up or meeting her. Pascal didn't find anything new at the store. He planted the bugs. But as he says that while keeping eyes on them, he sees Shimon Adri taking some of his calls on his cell phone outside in the parking lot, but further away from the building lately. So, they aren't audible."

"And the Grubers?"

Leah replied, "Gone. Just simply gone. And the girl isn't even showing up to do the chores on the farm. Her boyfriend Christian is doing them."

"Who are her other friends? Maybe she's with …"

Leah interrupted, "We're working on it. Not easy without actually having conversations with one or more, for example, with the boyfriend." … *something we're likely going to have to do.*

Ben Dod suggested, "Can Pascal simply be a store customer, and get into a conversation with the Azim guy? Never mind! Scratch that thought. Pascal's face can be IDd on cameras."

Leah suggested, "I think we should give it the rest of the day. And if the girl doesn't show up, Pascal can get into a conversation with the boyfriend. That'd be safer."

"Agreed. Did you hear back from Washington Motor Vehicles about the vehicle?"

"Plates were stolen. They used stolen plates. Smart! Dead end."

Ben Dod sighed with frustration, hit the 'End Call' button, and re-entered the café.

*

"You don't get to tell me that," General Arruk yelled into his phone! "You don't have the freedom to not know where she is! I want to hear by the end of the day that you have things under control! The Finance Committee is auditing Yitzhak Biton's bank next week. The last thing we need is for this ship to have leaks!" He angrily slammed the receiver down on his desk phone.

*

Shimon Adri put his cell phone back into his pocket and walked from the parking lot back into the store, carelessly bumping two customers that were exiting, and out of character for Shimon, not apologizing. Sebastian looked up from his position stocking a shelf in the middle aisle. His and Shimon's eyes met, and with a small gesture Shimon let Sebastian know that he needs to talk with him. They both quickly walked through the storage room doors and up the few steps into the office.

Shimon said, "Arruk is furious."

Sebastian listened with an unfocused gaze down over the store through a one-way glass window.

Shimon continued, "Okay, you know all her friends. Approach them. Find out what's going on. Where she is."

Sebastian turned and said, "I don't know if they'll talk to me anymore. Ishi has told at least some of them that I made her very uncomfortable. She might have told them details. I don't know."

Shimon hissed at Sebastian, "Do it, Azim! Find a way!"

Sebastian instantly quickly glanced around at Akeem's use of his real name, hoping nobody was within earshot, already knowing that to be impossible in this private office. "What about my shift? Who's going to come in to cover me?"

"I'll figure it out."

"Who's covering Ishi's shifts?"

"Miriam is doing double duty."

Pascal sat on the seat of a rented moped at the rear corner of the parking lot. He rented a moped to switch things up so that Shimon Adri wouldn't see the same Passat in the Adri Foods parking lot so often. Pascal watched Shimon walk back into the store after the apparently tense phone conversation. Pascal's helmet and shield kept Shimon from being able to identify him even if he had noticed him there. Pascal, having listened to the exchange in the office between Shimon and Sebastian, learned nothing useful. He started his moped and drove to a spot across the highway to watch, and so that the Adris wouldn't see him watching.

Five minutes later as Sebastian left in the black BMW, Pascal followed.

The three PLO agents knew trade craft. They hadn't employed any trade craft in an effort of losing a tail here in Vacha because of the town's small size. And, the Adris had no reason yet to suspect that any other agency would be present in Vacha. So, it was easy for Pascal to keep track of the BMW as it drove directly to the site where Christian was working with his father building a patio and a fence.

Christian looked up as Sebastian parked at the curb. Sebastian got out of the car and walked up to Christian.

Christian frowned, "Can't talk, Sebastian. Working." Christian glanced over at his father who was peering in his direction.

Sebastian conveyed a humble apologetic air, "No problem, buddy. Just a quick question."

Christian, soaked in sweat, didn't look away from his work of pouring a measured amount of cement from a cement bag into the slowly turning mixer.

"Hey, I said some things to upset Ishi the other day. I feel terrible. I want to apologize to her. Do you know where I can find her?"

Christian kept working without responding.

Sebastian tried again, "I went to the farm. I tried calling. Nothing. Is she out of town with friends or something?"

Christian didn't respond. *Please just go away!*

"Look, I just want to apologize. I don't like to have bad blood."

Christian finally paused from his work and looked at Sebastian. "You know her parents are missing, right?"

"Yes of course. Everyone knows. That's why we're covering her shifts at the store."

Christian said forcefully without taking his eyes off his work, "Then leave her the hell alone!"

Sebastian's expression immediately changed as his eyes grew narrow with dark-spirited rejection. Sebastian saw that Christian's father had begun to approach. Without any more words, he walked back to his car and drove away.

Pascal continued to follow as Sebastian drove seven blocks to the other side of Vacha. The BMW pulled up outside a large two-story wood and stone house. Sebastian walked up to the front door and knocked. There was no answer. He knocked again. Then he walked around the side of the house to the back yard where he saw Julia and her mother weeding in the vegetable garden.

"Hi," announced Sebastian, trying to not startle them.

Nevertheless, they were startled. Julia's mother exclaimed, "Oh, you startled me! Hi! Sebastian!"

Sebastian smiled warmly. "Hi Julia."

Julia glanced up at him but said nothing.

Pascal had crept along the side of the house close enough to listen in on the exchange between Sebastian and the others.

In as pleasant a voice as Sebastian could muster, he asked, "Hey Julia, have you seen Ishi?"

Without looking up from her weeding, Julia asked, "Why?"

Sebastian, recognizing the intentional unfriendliness, explained, "I might've said some things to her the other day. I was stupid. Shouldn't have. Anyway, I want to apologize to her."

Julia looked up at him, her mind racing with potential reactive words. She said nothing.

Eddie had done more sleuthing, from around the back corner of the building, listening to Shimon Adri talk in Arabic. He had reported that to Julia. Now Julia was tempted to confront Sebastian by saying, *Are you going to apologize to her in Arabic?* But she held herself back. Instead, she said spitefully, "You do know that her parents are missing, right?"

Sebastian, with a sheepish expression, answered, "Yes. Okay, sorry. I just thought an apology might help."

"It won't."

She returned to weeding as Sebastian retreated to his car mumbling angrily under his breath in Arabic.

Pascal had scurried around to the other side of the house and behind a chimney to remain unseen.

CHAPTER 27

Christian's work with his father had gone late. So, it was extra late by the time Christian made it out to the Gruber farm. Sebastian crouched in the dark against a tree just far enough into the woods beside the Gruber farm to watch as Christian finished the chores. As Christian drove off the Gruber farmyard and turned toward Vacha, Sebastian stood up and walked to the farmhouse. It took him only half a minute with his lock set to pick the front door open. He walked inside, flicked on a flashlight, and began rummaging through drawers in each room starting with the bedroom. Both Sebastian and Miriam had searched the house before, but they'd decided that Sebastian should do it again, and this time put trackers in Ishi's clothing.

Leah Fromm, sitting half asleep in her car tucked into the woods, perked up when she heard noise coming through the monitor. She turned up the volume as far as it would go and strained to listen. The noise from the Gruber house was sporadic and quiet. Leah immediately realized that someone was in the house covertly. After listening for nearly two minutes and learning nothing to indicate who it might be, she got out of the car and hurried quietly on foot through the dark woods toward the house, using a penlight to expose her path.

Approaching the bedroom rear window in the dark, she saw the beam of a flashlight inside. Creeping up to the window, she peeked past the window frame and saw Sebastian working a device into Ishi's sneakers. *Why didn't we think of that?* Leah wondered to herself, slightly ashamed.

Before continuing his search beyond the bedroom, he took Ishi's sneakers and, with a small knife, sliced a tiny crack into the ankle support side of the shoe. He slid a dime-sized tracker in. Then pulling a small tube of glue from his pocket, he sealed the crack shut. He repeated the process with two of Ishi's pullovers, putting the dime-sized trackers in the lining, and then with Ishi's only two pairs of casual pants, inserted the trackers into the waistbands.

Sebastian had just started searching through the bathroom drawers when he heard a car outside. He flipped off his flashlight and saw the headlights of a car circling the yard and coming to a stop in front of the door. He sprinted quietly to the front door and locked it.

Leah also saw the car arrive on the yard. Covered by darkness behind the house, she noticed Sebastian's flashlight go off. Leah concluded immediately that the car's occupants were not in league with the PLO agent inside the house. Careful to make no noise while she reached behind her waist to produce her Browning pistol, she moved around to the side of the house where she could peek inside the living room window.

Mossad had guessed that their objective was the same as the PLO agents in-so-far as letting Isabella Katz lead them to her parents. And, if the PLO were going to spur Ishi to search, Mossad decided to let them do the seeding and then Mossad would do the harvesting. So far, this had been the learning part of Leah and Pascal's mission, learning the PLO agents' likely strategy. However, when the Gruber couple went missing and the car was found abandoned, Leah deducted that Ishi was being pushed hard and quickly, being cruelly motivated to act. Jonathan Ben Dod had agreed with Leah that, should the PLO strategy work, Leah would need to eliminate the PLO's ability to follow the girl. That might come down to eliminating the PLO agents themselves. She could. And she would! And Leah would not fail to follow the girl. But how this would unfold, she still didn't have a clue. So, she waited, patiently observing.

Momentarily, Leah saw Ishi and her attractive brunette girlfriend, perhaps Lucy, enter the house and turn on the light. Ishi's face was distraught. As she began to weep, the other girl wrapped her up in a hug.

Ishi cried, "I was hoping against hope, I guess …"

Leah listened as the other girl finished Ishi's thought, "That they'd be home."

Ishi whimpered, "Yeah."

The girlfriend continued to hug her.

Letting her embrace go, Ishi said, "Okay, I'll get some things." She turned and disappeared into the bedroom.

As Ishi pulled several items of clothing out of dresser drawers and a pair of sneakers from the closet, she was unaware of Sebastian hiding under her parents' bed. Because the house was so small, Sebastian had nowhere else to hide. Sliding under the parents' bed was not easy because of the various boxes that the Grubers stored under it. But Sebastian had tucked himself on the far side of the bed, the side that Ishi couldn't see him.

Leah watched as the car drove away. There was no way that she could have retreated to her own car fast enough to try to follow them. But she had another idea. The PLO agent inside the house would surely have a means of transportation tucked away nearby. As he would follow his tracking sensors, she'd follow him in order to find out where Ishi is harboring. And because that tall brunette friend looked like Ishi's friend Lucy, *that's likely where she's staying.*

*

July 12 was scorching hot in Vacha, too hot for Christian and his father to be working outside with bricks. Christian had called Ishi to ask how she is. She asked him if he could come by for a bit.

As Christian's Jetta pulled up in front of Lucy's house, he saw Ishi wearing a bikini top, shorts, and barefoot sitting waiting on Lucy's front steps. She immediately walked to the car and got in.

Christian smiled. "Hi."

"Ohhh, I'm glad you have air conditioning!"

"Just curious, what are you going to do about your job at Adri Foods?"

Ishi answered immediately, "That's one reason I needed to talk to you. I need to pick your brains a bit. What should I do? I mean, I think I know what I'll do. But what do you think?"

"Is it okay … do you just want to sit here? Not go anywhere?"

Ishi nodded. "Yeah, it's good to just be out of that heat."

"Ish, I've thought about this, wondering what you were going to do. I think you should just drop it."

"The job?"

"Yeah. It's too uncomfortable and weird around Sebastian. You're a mess because of …" Christian hesitated to remind Ishi of her parents. "…because of your parents missing. Plus, you have all that money now."

"Exactly what I was thinking."

"What have you told Lucy?"

"Oh, I've been so so tempted to tell her more. I'm so glad that I have you to talk to. I've only told her about my parents missing and the abandoned car and the possibility of other biological parents. Not anything about the money or even inheriting the acreage. But I've sure wanted to! I mean, of course she went with me when I applied for the passport. I just told her that I wanted one now that I'm eighteen and that it was required for that genetic search thing."

Christian replied quickly, "Don't tell her more! Keep it hush hush for now."

Ishi's eyebrows lowered, "Why? I mean, I know why I want to keep quiet. But why do you say that?"

Christian tapped the steering wheel rhythmically and gazed unfocused forward down the street. "Something is not right." He looked at Ishi. "I mean … Let me explain! Eddie came and talked to me. He's been sleuthing more on Mister Adri, hearing lots more hush hush parking lot conversations in Arabic. He said that he and Julia have been digging, you know, doing a ton of research on the Adris. It's like they lied about their Stuttgart life. Lied completely!"

"But I saw all their photos." Ishi stared at Christian while his words bounced around in her head. She attempted to make it all make some sense. Finally, Ishi said, "Okay, well you know that I have to go get the passport from the Frankfurt office at some point. They won't mail or courier it."

"Really?"

"Yeah. Gotta do it in person. But as soon as I have it, I'm going to do what I need to do in Philippsthal about getting my name on the acreage title."

"Of course. Sooner the better."

"And I've been thinking. Well, sort of doubting, I guess. What if that letter and everything was planted? My name in the chicken coop. Not by my so-called Oma? What if it's all fiction? A set up? There never was another set of parents. There was no Oma. What if someone is trying to trick me into something for some insane reason? Oh and, no acreage inheritance?"

Christian was astonished at the thought, so stunned by it that he took a full ten seconds to speak again. "Why? What would anyone have to gain?" They sat in swirling thoughts while watching a neighborhood yellow cat warily cross the street just ahead of the car. "Just thinking … the package wrapping was old. Brittle. Remember? How do you plant that?"

Ishi breathed out deeply. "I don't know. I don't know anything except that something horrible happened to my parents." Her voice quivered as she said those words.

Christian reached over to embrace her. Ishi sank into his embrace. Still embraced, Christian said, "Well, if you get a hit from that genealogy thing, that'll confirm something one way or the other. Right?"

Sitting back up, more composed, Ishi said, "I think I'll go back home tomorrow. You can still come help me with chores if you want. I'll still pay you. Or not. It's up to you. But I feel like I need to go back home."

"Okay," Christian said, "just let me know when. I'll drive you. Unless I'm working. But if it's this hot again tomorrow, I won't be working."

As Ishi walked from Christian's car back up to Lucy's house, nearly a block back and backed into the start of an alley, Sebastian and Shimon sat in a white delivery van, watching. Unknown to Sebastian and Shimon, another half block further back, Leah and Pascal sat in the red Skoda, watching.

*

Rebecca sat with her hands folded on her lap. Pastor Henry Forster and his wife Dorothy had pulled chairs up facing her. Suzanna sat next to Rebecca, all four chairs on the visitor's side of the pastor's large office desk. Rebecca had been explaining to them that she is very depressed, that her home situation is terrible, and that she worries for her safety because of her abusive husband.

Rebecca hadn't been attending North Shore Alliance Church regularly. But because of her involvement in some church activities with Suzanna, she met Dorothy Forster. Suzanna had shared with Dorothy that Rebecca might need some spiritual and emotional support. So, when Suzanna asked Dorothy to reach out to Rebecca, Rebecca, distraught and feeling quite desperate, had easily agreed to meet at the church to talk about it, although intimidated by the prospect of it.

And they had talked, the pastor's office air heavy with emotions and moist eyes. Rebecca hadn't disclosed anything about her lost daughter. She only described her home life. And now Dorothy asked, "Rebecca, do you mind if I pray for you?"

Rebecca looked at Dorothy, not sure what to answer. Actual verbal prayer was foreign to Rebecca, something Rebecca had actually never been involved with except for rare graces before meals decades ago. Not really knowing what to answer, she said, "Okay. Sure."

Dorothy moved her chair close to and at an angle mostly facing Rebecca's chair, and gingerly took both of Rebecca's hands. This was very strange for Rebecca, but the human contact and the sense of genuine caring was comforting.

Dorothy prayed, "Our heavenly Father, our loving caring heavenly Father, we come before you with heavy hearts for our dear friend Rebecca. God, I sure don't know all the details, but I do know that she is in pain." Already only two sentences into the prayer, an emotional dam broke in Rebecca's heart, and she began weeping as Dorothy prayed. "Father, we know you love her. We know you want the best for her. And we know that you understand her heart, and that you love her dearly."

Rebecca's weeping turned into heaving sobs as her emotions released involuntarily.

Dorothy continued, "Gracious loving God, I ask that you give me an attitude of love and care for Rebecca, that you help me to give her the words that she needs and even help that she might need … if she wants it. Please touch her heart. Wrap your loving arms around her. Please comfort her."

Suzanna put an arm around broken sobbing Rebecca.

Dorothy continued, "Thank you for Suzanna's friendship for Rebecca." Dorothy paused as she considered her next words and as her husband offered a quiet "yes" of agreement in the prayer. Dorothy continued, "Lord, we depend on you. We know you love us. And so, we ask all of this humbly and eagerly. In Jesus precious name, amen."

Rebecca was hunched over sobbing. Suzanna's arm was still around her. Dorothy still held her one hand as Rebecca used her free hand to wipe tears from her face. Pastor Henry quickly grabbed a tissue box from his desk top and passed it toward Rebecca.

An hour later, Rebecca approached their driveway. The garage door was open. A sea kayak was upside-down using most of the garage floor space beside David's Infiniti. David appeared to be applying poxy to the kayak. Rebecca parked on the front circular driveway and began to walk to the front door, bypassing the garage.

David stepped out of the garage. "Where have you been?" His tone was suspicious as usual.

Rebecca answered while she continued to walk, "Church."

"Jesus Christ!" David's tone was sarcastic as he turned to step back into the garage, not even recognizing the irony of his cursing expression.

*

At 2:00am in the dark, it took Pascal only seconds per vehicle to place trackers on Christian's maroon Jetta and Adri's black BMW. Pascal would have liked to bug both cars' interiors, but with their closed windows, he was sure that he'd trigger alarms by Slim-Jimming the doors, so he decided to be satisfied enough with just the tracking sensors. He had intended to put a tracker on Adri's Passat too, but it wasn't to be found. Strange!

CHAPTER 28

First thing in the morning, Ishi went back home as planned. Almost immediately when she arrived home, her mind raced. Christian only dropped her off and then had to quickly leave to run an errand for his mom.

Most of the thoughts racing through Ishi's mind pointed to the Philippsthal acreage.

Hungry, but not wanting to take time to eat, Ishi snatched a small satchel from a front door coat hook and tossed an apple and a bottle of sparkling water into it. Then she trekked back through the woods twenty-five minutes to the acreage. Her progress was slightly slower because, with the heat of the day, she wore only shorts, a t-shirt, and sandals. As a result of her minimal attire, she suffered several small scratches along her trek through the woods.

Ishi stood at the edge of the acreage analyzing the neighbors' homes, their locations and sizes, then looking again back at this acreage. Her phone dinged to indicate an incoming email. She looked at it. It was not an email, but rather an indicator of a new notification on the Family Tree icon. So far, Family Tree had not proactively communicated to her. She tapped it nervously.

Quite quickly, Christian had finished running the errand for his mom. He settled down in his bedroom at the desktop computer, happy to be in an air-conditioned house.

A ding from Christian's phone indicated that he had a text message. He looked. "They're in Vancouver, Canada."

Christian's phone buzzed. He quickly answered, "Hi."

Ishi's voice was hysterical, "I sent you a text. There's a hit! They found my parents! Christian, it's actually confirmed."

"Which parents? What hit?" Christian already assumed which parents Ishi was talking about from the Vancouver, Canada text.

"No, no. My biological parents! They found them. A connection. They're in Canada. David and Rebecca Weiss."

Christian was mind-struck, "I just saw your text. Canada!"

"I can't believe … I'm so confused right now. I …"

"Where are you?"

"I walked to the acreage. I'm at the acreage."

"Stay there! I'm coming."

He jumped up from his computer, and grabbing his keys, hurried out to his car. As he passed through the front hall, his mother called, "Where are you going?" Christian was already outside and didn't answer his mother as the sound of the door closed behind him.

As Christian drove quickly out of Vacha toward Philippsthal, he saw grey plumes of smoke ahead. As he continued west, the smoke appeared bigger and thicker rising into the sky. One kilometer from the Gruber farm, he saw that the smoke was coming from exactly where the Gruber farm is. *Oh no! Something big is on fire.*

As he neared, in horror, Christian saw Gruber's yellow house engulfed by flames. Panicking, he began to turn left fast onto the dirt driveway, but then skidded to a stop. The house was already hopelessly burning! He grabbed his phone and quickly called Ishi. Ishi answered.

"Your house is burning!"

"What?"

Christian repeated, "Your house is burning. It's already too late. It's completely on fire!"

"Whhhat?"

Christian quickly said, "I have to call one-one-two." He hung up and quickly called to report the emergency.

Having called for help, he realized that he should stay until firetrucks arrive. He drove his car a little bit closer but stayed back on the side of the driveway. After another anxious minute of waiting, he saw the house roof begin to collapse. His phone rang. It was Ishi.

"Christian, what's happening? I can't believe …"

"The roof is already collapsing. I called one-one-two. They should be here…"

"My house! My house! Christian!" Ishi was yelling frantically!

Christian cut Ishi off, "Ish, I'll wait just two more minutes for the firetrucks. Then I'll come get you, okay."

Christian waited almost four more minutes until he heard the sirens. His phone buzzed.

"Christian I can see the smoke. It's bad!"

"It's terrible, Ishi! The house is destroyed."

Ishi wailed, "What's happening to me? The barn? The animals? They're okay?"

Christian assured her. Suddenly a terrible thought hit Christian, "Ishi, where is your money?"

"In the bank."

"Good," Christian sighed relieved.

"But, I had almost two hundred in the house."

"Well, that two hundred is gone. Okay, I'll come to you right away."

His phone buzzed two more times while he waited. It was Ishi panicking. Each time Christian quickly answered and told her that he'll be on his way to her as soon as he sees the firetrucks. He looked east and could make out the flashing red lights of the trucks approaching. Immediately, he spun the Jetta around and raced up off the driveway and west to get Ishi.

*

Miriam Adri finished bagging Missus Schultz's items at the cash register and offered her a pleasant "Have a good morning!"

Missus Schultz looked toward Sebastian who was busy behind the deli counter. As she grabbed up her two bags, she asked, "Where is Mister Adri today? Day off?"

Miriam replied, "Yes, a well-earned day off."

Missus Schultz, walking toward the exit, said, "Well, good for him. He's such a hard worker!"

"He is. Bye now."

It had taken no effort to start the fire. Shimon had simply placed two oil-soaked rags, one under the wooden front porch and the other tucked into the chopped wood pile that leaned against a side of the house. With the hot and dry August temperature and age of the old house siding, it took only minutes for the flames to be raging up the walls.

As soon as Shimon was confident enough that the fire would grow, he began jogging past the barn and east through the small pasture behind the barn, then further east through fifty meters of trees to the black BMW that was tucked there out of sight. By the time he was driving past the Gruber driveway westbound toward Philippsthal, he could see the flames licking their way up to the roof's eave at the front door of the house.

Shimon didn't drive directly to the acreage at Philippsthal. Instead, he slowly drove and then pulled over to a stop where between houses he could view the acreage, that, from the same street just north of the acreage and just as Sebastian had done days before. He saw Ishi standing beside the little old acreage house, phone to her ear. Her arms were animated with frantic gestures as she talked. Her gaze was toward the big grey plumes of smoke just on the other side of the woods. Shimon looked toward the smoke that was growing darker and larger as it rose into the sky.

Suddenly, Shimon saw the maroon Jetta storm up onto the acreage, skidding to a stop just in front of the chicken coop in a cloud of dust. He watched Christian jump out of the car as Ishi ran toward him. Shimon instantly grabbed his Makarov handgun and exited his car. He tucked the gun into his belt as he ran the three house lengths to the end of the dead-end street, and then turned to his right, and raced past the far side of the last house toward the wooded acreage perimeter. He made sure that he was far enough behind the edge of the trees to remain concealed as he raced, hurdling over fallen branches and nearing the acreage behind the chicken coop. With the chicken coop as cover, just as Azim had done days earlier, Shimon raced up the slight incline out of sight from Ishi and Christian. He desperately wanted to get close enough to hear what the two teenagers were saying.

Ishi and Christian stared at the growing black and grey cloud of smoke in disbelief.

"Ishi, this can't be an accident. Not coincidence."

"Let's go!" Ishi was in a panic to go and try to salvage anything.

"Ishi, I don't know if we should." *You might not want to see. And you won't salvage anything anyway.*

"Too much! Someone is trying to kill me."

Christian looked at her wide-eyed, his reaction to her words. "Kill you?"

Ishi was crying now, "Yeah, kill me. I don't know. I could've been inside the hou-- it's-- just so many things!"

Christian's face showed grave worry. "Then, let's not go there. You can't salvage anything anyway. You wouldn't want to see it either, Ishi. Would you?"

While Christian and Ishi were talking, Shimon snuck low from the chicken coop to the car. He still couldn't hear what the two were saying. He poked his head up just above the passenger's closed window. He saw Christian's cell phone laying on the middle console. Shimon wanted that phone! He realized that the emails and text messages on that phone had potential to reveal a lot. He also knew that he wouldn't be able to open the door and take the phone without being noticed. Shimon considered his gun. *No. Harming the girl would defeat the push tactic on her. And I don't want her to see my face.*

In fast movements, Shimon opened the door, grabbed the phone, and before Ishi and Christian turned to look clearly, Shimon pulled his shirt up over his head as he rose into view, spun, and raced back past the chicken coop, down the slope, and toward the woods.

"What! Who was …?" Christian, realizing that someone had just been in his car, instantly raced after the fleeing person.

Ishi yelled, "Christian, no! Don't!"

Christian continued to chase after the mystery thief until Christian was halfway to the woods. The man was already completely invisible inside the bush.

Ishi, chasing Christian, yelled again, "No! Christian! He might be dangerous."

Christian heard Ishi's words. *She's right.* He turned back and raced back to his car. Ishi spun around and followed. Arriving at his car, he looked in and confirmed that his cell phone was gone from where it sat on the console. "My phone! Aaaaaaa!" Christian yelled, spinning around and looking again toward the trees where the thief had run to.

Ishi, catching up, asked, "What?"

Christian instantly seething, said, "My phone. He got my phone."

"Christian!" Ishi reached a conclusion.

Christian, wiping the back of his neck in anxious frustration, looked at her.

"Christian, this is all … I have to hide. We have to hide. This is all," she searched for words, "connected." Her face lost its color. She looked at Christian. "I'm scared!"

Suddenly she jumped as the phone in her hand vibrated and buzzed! She looked at the caller ID. 'Eddie'. She answered, her voice frail.

Eddie spoke immediately and frantically, "Your house! Ishi, where are you? Your house is burning."

"I know. I'm not there." She could hear Eddie's instant sigh of relief.

"Your house is burning to the ground! Where are you?"

"I'm close, Eddie," Ishi answered, now too overwhelmed for tears.

Eddie continued, "I'm here. The police are just arriving now. Your house. It's completely gone!"

Ishi said, "We're coming." She tapped 'End Call' as she and Christian were already getting into the car.

Christian was still circling around to leave the acreage yard when Ishi's phone vibrated and buzzed again. She answered, "Hello."

"Ishi!" Lucy's voice was hysterical. "Ishi, the police were just at my house. They were demanding to know what you were doing in Frankfurt."

"Frankfurt? Lucy, my house is burning down. Right now!"

It took a few moments for Lucy to realize that Ishi was being literal. "What? Ishi, your house?"

"Yes, right now. It's burning to the ground!"

Lucy gasped. "Are you okay? Where are you?"

"With Chris. Yeah, I'm …"

Lucy interrupted, "Ishi, this policeman was really pushing me for information … Okay, go! Your house! Oh crap, Ish!" The call ended.

They were just a few minutes from the farm now. The cloud of smoke was still growing into the sky. A thought struck Ishi as she remembered Sebastian's words, "Your real parents were involved with big crime. That's why they let you go." Ishi looked at Christian. "Stop!"

Christian, confused, looked at Ishi as he continued to drive.

Ishi screamed, "Stop! Stop the car! Please, Chris!"

Christian slowed and pulled to the shoulder, then stopped.

Wide-eyed, Ishi said, "We have to go. Now! We have to go where they can't find us."

"Why?"

"Because! Everything Sebastian said is coming true. It is! And he said that my real parents were into big crime." Ishi looked through the windshield at the billows of smoke that were now less black and more grey. She looked at Christian. "I don't know why, but we're in the middle of a mess. Or, I am. I don't know. Chris, we have to go hide. Somewhere where I can think."

Christian was shocked at Ishi's words but knew that they were rational. He had never known her to be dramatic. Actually, quite the opposite. He furrowed his eyebrows. "I don't know how Sebastian could have known all that. I mean, curiosity is one thing. But?"

"Maybe my parents are already hiding," Ishi looked at Christian, wide-eyed. She wailed, "Maybe that's … I don't know!"

"Okay," Christian resolved, "I don't know either what's going on. Let's get out of here!"

Immediately, he wheeled the car around from grassy shoulder, across the pavement, partly across the opposite grassy shoulder, and sped back toward Philippsthal. They passed through Philippsthal and continued twenty-five minutes west to Friedewald. Friedewald still felt too close for both Ishi and Christian. They continued on another twenty minutes west to the small city of Bad Hersfeld. Approaching Bad Hersfeld, Ishi spotted a MacDonald's restaurant ahead. She pointed at it and said, "Let's just stop here for a bit, okay. I need to think."

Christian turned left off highway 62 and parked in the MacDonald's parking lot.

*

Less than two hours earlier, Pascal had dressed up in a German Police uniform. He and Leah knew that they'd spook the Katz daughter too much if they confronted her forcefully or even directly and more softly. They decided to try to press Lucy because Ishi had stayed at Lucy's house for several days.

Pascal walked up to the door of the nice two-story brick house. He knocked. Momentarily, Lucy's mother opened the door. Surprise was obvious on her face when she saw the Bundepolizei officer standing there.

Pascal asked, "Is your daughter Lucille Dauber home? I need to ask her a few questions."

Lucy's mother, immediately a bit panicky, answered, "Oh, yes she is. She's umm, she's tanning in the back. I'll get her."

Ten seconds later, Lucy appeared at the doorway. She had thrown a long light button-up shirt over her bikini.

"Miss Lucille Dauber?"

Lucy nervously confirmed, "Yes."

Pascal said, "We have a record of your Citroen Xsara driving twenty-eight kilometers over the speed limit through Dorndorf three days ago. An officer attempted to flag you down, but you failed to obey."

What!? Lucy's expression was of pure surprise! "That can't be! I wasn't anywhere near Dorndorf. I was two and a half hours away in Frankfurt."

Pascal made a note on a pad. He looked at Lucy. "You say that you were in Frankfurt. Can you prove that?"

Lucy thought quickly. *I don't think so. Well, there must be a way.* She struggled to find a way to prove it, as the officer asked another question.

"Were you in Frankfurt alone Miss Dauber? Can anyone else corroborate it?"

Lucy thought of something. "I have a gas receipt. It's in the car," she exclaimed pointing to the white Citroen on the street.

As Lucy's mom watched concerned from two meters back inside the house, the officer stepped aside indicating that Lucy may go to her car. Locating the gas receipt from the car's console, Lucy, quickly looked at it, realized that it was from a gas station in Hanau just outside Frankfurt. *Close enough*, she assumed. She walked quickly back to the waiting officer and handed him the receipt.

He took it, looked at it, and handed it back to her. He then jotted again on his pad.

"Did you travel to Frankfurt alone Miss Dauber?"

Lucy answered quickly. "No, I went with my friend."

"And, what is the name of your friend?"

"Ishi. Isabella Gruber is her full name. People call her Ishi."

Scribbling a note, the officer asked, "And what was the reason for your trip with this friend Ishi?"

"She is looking for her parents. For her biological parents." Immediately Lucy felt like she was saying too much. *But it's the police. What else can I do? I can't lie.*

"Her biological parents? Your friend thinks that they are in Frankfurt?"

Lucy shifted on her bare feet, wondering how to backtrack on this package of information. She didn't find a way out, so she explained, "Ishi went to an ancestral genealogy search office to create a search."

Pascal knew that he had to make this seem legitimate. He said, "Just give me a minute." He walked down to the sidewalk mostly out of earshot of Lucy, pulled a radio mic from his belt, and talked into it pretending to be talking to someone. Then he returned to Lucy. "So, Miss Dauber, you weren't driving through Dorndorf three days ago at all?"

Lucy nodded eagerly. "No sir. Nowhere near Dorndorf."

The officer asked, "And regarding your friend's genealogy search, what was the name of the office she went to?"

Lucy really wanted this questioning to be finished. She answered reluctantly, "Life Line. Or Family Tree, I think. I'm pretty sure. No, I can't remember which one of those."

The officer smiled now and seemed to soften. "One more question. Was your friend's trip a success? Did she find her parents?"

Lucy, relieved that the questioning is nearly done, answered, "Not yet. They said they'd contact her if there's a match."

The officer asked, "Will your friend let you know?"

"I hope so. She's a good friend."

He smiled warmly.

Lucy was somewhat put at ease by his smile. "She would tell me. I'm sure of it."

The officer turned to leave. "Apologies for the mix up. Have a good day!"

As he left, Lucy retreated back inside, closing the door. *Dorndorf?*

*

As Christian and Ishi sat parked outside MacDonald's, Ishi was sobbing. Through her sobs she blurted out, "I'm scared! What if they take me too, like they took my mom and dad? I bet that's what happened. They burned down our house!"

Christian was scared too, but tried to console Ishi. "Ishi …" He honestly didn't know what to say. Then he remembered, "That guy took my phone. Stole it right from in front of us! What crazy person would steal a phone right in front of someone?"

She looked at him. "Chris, I have to hide."

They both took a few moments to think, to assess the situation with the random pieces that they knew.

Ishi said, "Let's drive to Frankfurt. They won't find me there. The city is so big."

Christian's eyes widened, astonished at the idea! "Frankfurt?"

"I don't know," Ishi blurted out while trying to keep from crying.

Christian tried to process everything fast. "Actually Ish, that's a good idea."

As Christian began to shift the car into first gear, Ishi looked at him with slight astonishment that he is actually going to drive them to Frankfurt. Right now!

"Can you? Do you have time? Money for gas?"

Christian replied firmly, "Yes. Yes. And no. I have enough on me to get there, but …"

"I'll give you money," Ishi quickly inserted. "I have almost three hundred on me." Immediately she dug into the front pocket of her shorts.

CHAPTER 29

As Christian and Ishi pulled back onto the highway heading south, they were completely unaware of Akeem Almasi in the black BMW and Leah Fromm in the red Skoda separately racing east along highway 62 toward Bad Hersfeld, both spy agencies tracking the censors on Christian's car, both spies unaware of the other in this pursuit, both just four and five minutes respectively behind Christian's maroon Jetta.

Along the way south toward Frankfurt, Christian and Ishi discussed a plan. Ishi was overwhelmed that in less than a week, her entire world had been turned upside-down and changed. *Ruined. I have no parents, no home, no job.* Increasing fast, Ishi had gone from the elation of her graduation to losing everything and being scared for her life. The weight of the sudden changes catapulted her during this drive to kick into a mental gear, a survivor mode of strength that she didn't know she had.

Christian was overwhelmed and bewildered by the rapidly unfolding circumstances. But he loved Ishi fiercely. They had been such close friends for so many years. *Can I find some solid way to be an anchor for Ishi right now?* So, although his thoughts continued to make little sense, he was determined to protect her. *I don't even know if Ishi is a target. Better to play it safe though.* He pushed the speedometer from 120 kph to slightly over 130.

They were completely oblivious to the fact that less than three kilometers behind them, the PLO and Mossad were following and closing the distance.

Both intelligence agencies wanted the same thing out of the Katz girl, for her to lead them to her parents. But each spy agency intended a different outcome for Joseph and Sonya Katz.

The PLO wanted to eliminate the Katz couple to erase any possibility of them exposing their nearly two-decade old network in Israel.

Mossad wanted to find the Katz couple to learn details of that network in Israel. Finding Joseph and Sonya Katz had been a priority but an elusive target for too long. And now with the daughter racing toward Frankfurt, there was real hope that progress might be at hand.

Ishi and Christian decided that Ishi would tuck away in a small hotel for a few days at least. Christian wanted to stay with her but waffled on that notion because his sudden absence would create panic with his parents. "I'll buy a new phone as soon as I get home," Christian had said. "Then at least we'll be in contact." Ishi assured Christian that she'd be fine money-wise because she'd have access to bank machines. Twice as they neared Frankfurt and the hotel, Ishi gave way to her emotions, tears streaming down her face. "I'm sorry for crying," she twice apologized to Christian. The thought of Christian leaving, and of her being all alone in the strange big city suddenly hit Ishi hard! "Chris, we have to stay in regular phone contact. Please!"

Christian assured her fear and her thoughts. "We will. Constantly. And if necessary, at any time, I'll come back down here." To show his care and connection to her, he put his hand over her hand that she had resting on her left leg. Momentarily, he drew his hand away again.

"Thanks, Christian." *Why haven't I at least got my drivers license by now? Then, at least I could rent a car if I needed to. I'm so stupid!*

While following the Jetta, Akeem Almasi reached for his cell phone and dialed.

Saadia answered eagerly, "Hello?"

Almasi reported, "Seems like the fire worked faster than we thought it would. She's on her way to Frankfurt right now."

Saadia exclaimed, "Oh wow! Thanks be to Allah!"

"Saadia, I'm nearing Frankfurt soon. I don't want to make a scene. I'm just going to keep following to see where she is going. The sensors are working well, so I won't have a problem even if I stay safely back."

Saadia replied, "Okay Akeem. Keep us updated."

"Well, I do have an update. A big update! I got the boyfriend's phone. Text messages. Ishi found her parents."

Saadia gasped, "What?"

"They're in Vancouver, Canada."

Sadia asked, "Names? What are their names?"

"Don't know names. Just know where. Saadia, inform Arruk right away! Immediately! I'm too busy right now to communicate with him."

The PLO had little to no intelligence on the ground worldwide. Compared to other larger intelligence agencies such as CSIS, DGSE, Mossad, CIA, and others, they had only the manpower to be singular mission oriented. And so, if the Katz girl would try to travel by train or plane, one of the PLO team would need to be eyes-on. They must see the details. And if it would be a flight to any country, they must follow.

Although Christian felt safer now in the traffic and congestion of the big city, he continued to nervously check his rear-view mirror. He saw a black BMW that looked too familiar. He had noticed it far behind them along the highway earlier, and he noticed that it remained behind them as they navigated through the Frankfurt streets. *Should I tell her?* He considered how overwhelmed she already was. *It could be something worth mentioning anyway.*

"Ish," he said as calmly as possible, "I think we're being followed."

"What?" Ishi instantly swiveled around to look.

"No! Don't look!"

Instantly more terrified, Ishi restrained herself, and slouched down in her seat. "How do you know?"

"Black BMW. Been behind us since long before Frankfurt."

Ishi knew immediately. "Adri!" She turned to Christian, "That's what Adris drive. That's what we, Sebastian and I came to Frankfurt in!"

As Christian continued driving, he thought for a minute, then responded, "But Ish, that's also what a lot of people drive."

As they came within half a dozen blocks of their chosen nondescript 2-star small hotel, Stolpern Inn on Schmidtstrasse and Christian was still seeing the black BMW in his rear-view mirror, he vocalized an idea to Ishi. "Ishi, when we turn off of this main street at the next intersection-- don't be shocked." He added, pointing, "I'm going to drop you off as soon as we turn at that intersection. And I'm going to keep driving. The black BMW is still behind us."

Ishi looked at him, stunned, scared!

Christian continued, "Jump as soon as we stop. And run through some stores or something! The hotel Stolpern Inn is three blocks up the street. You'll find it on your map app."

Ishi carefully peeked over her seatback and through the rear window. She didn't see the BMW.

Christian said, "It's nearly a full block back, but it's there. If you jump as soon as we turn the corner, they won't see you."

Ishi immediately scrambled to gather her handbag. The look on her face was absolute terror.

"Where are you going to go?"

Christian thought for a few moments. He answered, "Home. I don't know. Home, I guess. Aaahh," he exhaled stress. "I don't know. Home. I'll call you … or call me."

They were nearing the intersection.

Christian said, "I'll get another phone right away. I know your number."

They began the turn at the intersection. Ishi said, "Oh shit! I … okay, I'm ready." Christian made the turn and immediately pulled to the curb. Ishi launched herself out of the Jetta and ran desperately toward the first shop door that she saw. She was wearing only summer sandals, so running was not as easy, but she passed quickly through the shop door of a travel agency. She glanced over her shoulder to see Christian's car already half a block racing away. As she was looking back, she saw the black BMW rounding the corner and then accelerating fast to catch up to Christian's Jetta. By seeing the black BMW, Ishi was penetrated with the harsh reality of the circumstance! Ishi was fully making her way through the travel shop before the red Skoda also raced past following the black BMW. She didn't notice it.

Akeem Almasi had counted on being able to track the sensors in the girl's sneakers. Or at least the sensors in her pants waistline. Ishi was wearing neither, nor did she have them along. All Ishi had was her handbag, sandals, shorts, and a white t-shirt. Completely unaware that the girl was no longer in the Jetta, Akeem continued to follow the boyfriend's car. Leah followed Akeem only three cars back. With two separate trackers beeping in her phone app, she had identified well back along highway 66 that the black BMW was following Ishi and her boyfriend. Leah had quickly identified that the BMW was an Adri vehicle and was content to fall behind it. Even now in the middle of Frankfurt, Leah followed without panic.

As Leah drove navigating lane changes and turns, she dialed Jonathan Ben Dod.

Ben Dod answered, "Iden?"

Leah responded curtly, "Forget it! I'm racing through Frankfurt following Almasi. And I don't remember."

Ben Dod sighed, "Okay. Name then?"

"Toto."

"What's happening?"

"Almasi burned down the girl's house. The girl with her boyfriend fled to Frankfurt."

Ben Dod jumped in, astonished, "Hold it! Hold it! Almasi did what?"

"Pushed the girl past her limit. Burned down the house. I think it worked. The girl is in Frankfurt. Can only be to catch a flight or a train. Or maybe to pick up a report from the ancestry DNA agency. I don't know. But right now, I'm racing through city streets behind Almasi who is following the girl and boyfriend."

"I want you to take both of them. The Katz girl and the boy. Take them before Almasi does!"

Leah listened, waiting for more.

"We'll find a way to put the screws to the girl. But that has to be us before Almasi. Understand?"

"Yes." She stepped on the gas. *A little offer of assistance would've been nice,* she thought snidely.

Christian had circled back to the Hanauer Landstrasse that they had arrived along. Heading east, he knew that this would lead him back to highway 66. Monitoring his mirrors, he continued to see the black BMW behind him, but closer now.

Fifteen stressful minutes later with the BMW still in his rear-view mirror, Christian was just east of the city and navigating the large, complicated stacked multi-layer intersection that would put him back northeast along highway 66. While anxious, he had strained relief that the BMW was still trailing him. *That means that Ishi's exit went undetected.*

Approximately six kilometers after Christian merged from the onramp heading north, the black BMW suddenly raced past him. Glancing sideways, Christian identified Shimon Adri as the sole occupant, and Shimon Adri was also glaring back at Christian. The BMW pulled back into the lane in front of Christian. Suddenly, the black car's brake lights came on! The BMW was slowing very quickly! Christian slammed his foot onto his brake pedal. Both cars came to a stop with tires screeching. Christian's heart banged against his chest!

Shimon Adri launched himself out of his car and marched toward the Jetta with a handgun aimed at Christian.

Reverse? But he didn't put his car into reverse, knowing that a bullet from that gun would make such a move irrelevant.

As Adri approached the Jetta, he yelled, "Where's the girl?"

Christian sat frozen.

Adri, furious and eyes bulging wide, yelled again, "Where's the girl?"

Two cars were approaching from the south at a distance while Shimon Adri was aiming the pistol at Christian. Before they neared, he tucked the gun against his other side, hiding it. Once the cars passed, he quickly pointed it again.

Adri reached the car door now, pulled at it to open it, but the door was still auto-locked from driving.

Terrified with the gun aimed straight at his head, Christian opened the door. "Take off your seatbelt," Adri yelled furiously! Christian complied. Immediately, Adri grabbed Christian's hair and dragged him from the driver's seat, along the side of the car, and threw him down on the pavement between the two cars where he'd be more out of sight of passing traffic.

Akeem Almasi looked up and saw that one of the cars that had passed in their lane had pulled over to the highway's shoulder and stopped, and had begun to reverse from approximately two hundred meters ahead. Akeem thought fast! *I could force the boy into my car and just drive -- but that would look like kidnapping. That would have German police on top of me quickly.* "Shit!" he hissed. Not thinking of any good solution, he decided to try to scare the car away.

Aiming at the pavement beside Christian, Akeem pulled the trigger firing a round near Christian's head as a threat to not move. Christian lurched in shock, also, because of asphalt shrapnel spraying his head. Then Akeem ran to the front of his BMW and marched toward the reversing car, arm outstretched, pointing his Makarov. Immediately, the Good Samaritan hit the brakes, and began to drive forward again accelerating quickly.

A red Skoda approached, and instead of passing, it screeched to a stop behind Christian's Jetta. Akeem, still minding the Good Samaritan, spun around just in time to see a woman stepping out of the red car. She instantly crouched behind her open car door.

Akeem, unaware that the newcomer was armed, ran toward the crouching woman, gun pointed. He yelled as he ran, "Get out of here! Get out of here or I'll shoot you!" As he passed where Christian lay, Akeem's voice was more hysterical, "Get out of here or I'll shoot you!"

Leah, her Browning pistol in her right hand, had enough room by the car door hinges to take a fairly good shot through that crack. Without any other options, she aimed at the approaching threat and squeezed the trigger. The 9mm bullet slammed into Akeem Almasi's chest and heart, dropping him on the spot.

Christian hadn't dared to move until now. The sound of the gunshot pierced him with terror! All he could think to do is to try to quickly shuffle a few feet sideways under the front of his car. Pried as far under his car as possible, Christian heard the car door close behind him. Then he heard a combination of dragging sounds mixed with grunting and more vehicles approaching and passing at highway speed.

Twenty seconds later, Christian saw a pair of fairly small hiking shoes and the bottoms of pantlegs that appeared to be female.

Leah ordered, "Come out! I won't hurt you. Come on!"

Christian was frozen in fear and didn't move. Leah tried again, "Come on out Christian! I'm here to help you, not hurt you. I've put my gun away. Don't worry! Come on!" After several moments, Christian conceded and slithered out from under his car.

As soon as Leah knew Christian could view her properly, she held up her empty hands. "See, no gun."

"Where's the …" Christian began?

Leah quickly answered, "Dead. He's no longer a threat. Don't worry!"

Christian sat up and looked at the small woman with the stocky build. Her word "dead" not really sinking in thoroughly. "Who are you?"

"Don't worry about that. I'm here to take care of you."

Christian, completely overwhelmed and confused, remained sitting on the asphalt in front of his car. He failed to sort out his thoughts enough to form any more questions. *Dead?*

"Just sit there a minute!"

Christian watched her pull a cell phone from her pocket and tap a button. She turned her back to Christian to make her voice less audible to him. "T-o-t-o-2-4-4-t".

A pause.

"Who do we have in Frankfurt? I'm a few minutes northeast of the intersection of highways forty-five and sixty-six on highway sixty-six. I need someone out here immediately to clean up a car and body."

Another pause.

"Black BMW. Vic in the trunk. Almasi. I can wait on site for five minutes tops. No longer."

Another pause.

"Okay." She ended the call and turned back to Christian. Christian missed some of the woman's words because of noise from passing cars. But he heard enough to know that she was not Bundespolizei.

Leah, somewhat confident that Christian wouldn't try to make a run at her, walked to the open door of the Jetta, reached in, and grabbed the keys. She stepped back far enough toward the front of the Jetta that Christian could see her. She dangled his keys from her fingers, letting him know that he can't make a run for it. Then she walked to the ditch side of her red car.

After just under a minute of heaving and dragging, pausing twice as vehicles passed, Leah had opened the BMW'S trunk and had deposited the bloody body into it. She fished through the dead man's pants pockets and found his cell phone. She put it into her own pants' front pocket. Stepping back to the BMW's open door, she looked in to confirm that the keys were still in the ignition, flipped on the car's emergency flashers, then closed the black car's door and walked back to Christian. Christian simply watched, unable to make sense of the overwhelming events, but noting how calm and efficient this woman was.

"Christian, you can stand up." She had tucked her gun back under her belt to show the young man that she didn't intend to harm him. Christian stood up, wondering how she knew his name.

Leah said, "You are going to do as I say! Here's what you are going to do."

Christian, scared and helpless, listened.

"You are going to get into your car and drive until you get to the next country road turn-off. Turn right. Go one kilometer. Then stop. I'll be right behind you. Do not think you can make a run for it. I'm not alone." Leah was bluffing. She was alone. But she wasn't worried. The kid was scared witless. He was going to do as she told him to do. She tossed Christian's keys to him.

He was too nervous to catch them. They fell on the pavement. He picked them up.

"First, you're going to give me your phone!"

Christian looked at her. "I don't have it. It was stolen back at, back at …" Christian hesitated to mention the acreage, not knowing how much this woman knew.

Leah paused to think. Then she walked around the BMW to the passenger door, opened it, looked, and then spotted the cell phone on the passenger floor mat. She grabbed it. Holding it up, she asked, "This?"

Recognizing it immediately, Christian nodded, "Yes." He watched as the woman carried it with her to her car. *My phone. That was Mister Adri?*

Christian got back into his car. Well aware that there were big dangerous elements at play here, he was absolutely willing to comply. After-all, he just witnessed Shimon Adri getting gunned down. *Mister Adri is dead.* With shaking hands, he put the key into the ignition slot. He wondered if Ishi was okay. *Did she find the hotel? What's going to happen to me?* His mind raced.

Christian started his car and drove, seeing in his rear-view mirror that the red car followed immediately behind him. Identifying a small gravel road up ahead, he turned onto it and drove one kilometer as instructed. There were two farmyards close to where Christian stopped. He wondered if anyone from those farms would notice them.

The woman tapped on his side window.

Christian lowered it.

"Keys," the woman demanded, her hand outstretched.

Christian obediently surrendered his keys to her.

Then she walked around the front of the car to the passenger's door, and got in, shocking Christian a little by her close and casual proximity. "Where's your girlfriend?" Leah asked.

"What's going on? Who are you? Did you burn down her house?"

"No," she pointed her thumb over her shoulder, "that man in the trunk back there did."

Christian asked again, "What's going on? Who are you?"

Leah paused, then answered, "I'm here to see that Ishi finds her real parents. And to protect her. The Adri family are here to hurt her. That's all you need to know. So, where is she? Where did you leave her?"

Can I trust or believe this woman that just shot someone and was so cool and collected about it? He thought fast.

Leah sighed. "Oh Christian, I get it. You want to protect her too. You're a good friend. But if you don't tell me where she is, more of the people that the

Adris work with will come after her, and I won't be able to protect her, or you. Or your parents. Or Lucy, Julia, Becky, or anyone."

Christian's heart jumped into his throat as he learned of this woman's knowledge of everyone dear to him. He simply gawked at the woman in shock! Relenting, he admitted, "She's at the Stolpern Inn." *How does she know everyone?* "I hope," he added quietly.

Leah pulled her phone from her pocket, looked up Stolpern Inn in Frankfurt on the Internet, and called. After a short conversation with Stolpern Inn, it was confirmed that Isabella Gruber had checked in. She ended the call.

Leah looked directly at Christian. "Why is Ishi in Frankfurt?"

"She's hiding. She's scared. Her parents go missing. She thinks they'll try to take her too. Her house is burned down. She's told wild stories about her past. She's terrified, scared that they're going to hurt her or kill her. So, she's trying to hide."

"So, why didn't you stay there with her?"

"Because if I did, my parents would be freaking out," Christian explained. "They don't even know that I'm not in Vacha right now. And, I have to work."

"Bit hot for masonry, isn't it?" Leah offered a calmer voice. "Did Ishi find her real parents?"

"No," Christian lied. "Not yet. She's done a genetic search. But nothing yet." *She even knows about my work!*

Leah brought Christian's phone to life and began scrolling through the text messages. Over the next several minutes, Leah scrolled through many text messages and noting the most recent one in which Ishi informed Christian that she found her parents, and that they are in Vancouver, Canada. "You lied to me," Leah quietly informed the boy as she continued to scan the messages.

Before leaving Ishi's text messages, Leah tapped on Ishi's name icon. A new screen showed Ishi Gruber's phone number. Leah committed it to memory. "What's your phone number?" the woman asked.

Christian hesitated.

Leah gave him a don't-screw-with-me look.

Christian complied and gave her his number.

Leah committed that to memory too.

Leah wanted to listen to voice messages. "What's your voicemail ... never mind," Leah handed the phone to Christian, "Here, dial up your voicemail for me." Over the next several minutes, Leah heard no messages containing any information about Ishi's parents. She handed the phone back to Christian. "Okay, here, you can have your phone back." Surprised, Christian took the phone.

CHAPTER 30

All afternoon at Adri Foods, customers had been exclaiming in astonishment and sadness about the fire at the Gruber farm. Most townsfolk weren't aware that Horst and Dagmar had been missing, so they also voiced their concern about their welfare due to the fire.

Miriam had called Ingrid, who was labelling items in aisle two, up to run the cash register, explaining that she needed to make some phone calls. Then, Miriam grabbed her cell phone and stepped outside and around to the side of the building. She had been calling Akeem, but not getting an answer. After trying four times, she walked back into the store with her phone clutched tightly in her anxious hands. Sebastian, standing behind the deli counter, looked at her. Miriam met his eyes and shook her head.

*

Ishi's walk to Stolpern Inn had been a careful and stressful myriad of back alleys, going through several cafés' front doors and out back doors, and everything she could think of to avoid being tracked or seen by anyone in a black BMW or potential accomplices on foot. As luck would have it, she found herself passing right by an ATM. Stopping, she quickly withdrew her daily limit of fifteen-hundred euros.

Ishi had never booked into a hotel in her life. But she'd seen the procedure often enough in movies, so she had no problem going through the motions at the old musty front desk. The four-story hotel put Ishi in room 208 on the second floor. Wary of being cornered in an elevator and traveling extremely light, Ishi opted to use the creaky wide carpeted stairs. Just as she began to slip her key card into the door, her phone dinged with a notification of an email.

With the whirlwind of events and the weight of everything that had unfolded in the past several days, Ishi assumed that any email was an important email. Quickly closing the door behind her, she rushed to sit on the queen-sized bed and looked at her phone. *From Christian*, she wondered, assuming that he'd be well on his way back to Vacha by now, forgetting that he had no phone. Instead, the email was a notification from the passport office that her passport was ready for pick-up. *Oh wow! That's faster than the five business days that they said it could take.*

Ishi took a few moments to look around the room. A TV sat on a wide low chest of drawers. A large frameless nature print hung above the TV and another one above the headboard. A corner small table, lamp, and chair to the right of the large, heavily curtained window. Another small corner table with a coffeemaker and condiments to the left of the window. *Why choose such a ghastly mauve with grey circle patterned bedspread cover? Eeeack, horrid!* The room smelled strongly of pine cleaner.

She got up, walked over to the window, and parted the heavy curtains the width of her arms' reach. Immediately, sunlight brightened the room. "Oh," Ishi realized, "I can't let anyone see me." She pulled the curtains closed again, sat on the bed and allowed images of the clouds of smoke from her burning house to fill her mind. She was too overwhelmed to cry. *Everything!* The jumble of it all nearly cauterized her thoughts now entirely. *I'm so tired,* she realized.

She stood up and walked into the bathroom. As she sat on the toilet, she looked at the tub-shower unit with the cheap plastic white-ish shower curtain with yet more patterned circles, this time blue, the old white marble sink and counter, and the small square metal box ant trap device on the floor at the corner by the door. *This is what hotels are like?*

Walking back into the bedroom, she laid on the bed. "These are good pillows," she noticed. But her mind was too busy with images and thoughts and confusion to just lay there. Stacking both large pillows up behind her to cushion her, she leaned up against the headboard.

After almost twenty minutes of sitting there trying to sort out her thoughts, Ishi began to feel very tired. In her shorts and white t-shirt, she slid back down into a horizontal position and tried to pull the blanket and tightly tucked sheets up so she could crawl in. The sheets were too tightly tucked. *Why do they do this with the sheets?* Aggravated, she stood up from the bed and angrily yanked the tucked sheets up and out from where they were solidly tucked under the mattress. "Grrrrr …!" Ishi pulled violently at the sheets, ripping the corner at least half a metre long as she emitted a supressed scream of angst! With the angst scream released and out, Ishi claimed a little sense of relief, enough to notice how much the sheets smelled like laundry detergent. That made her think of her own bed, a bed that she'll never sleep in again. Tears welled up as she crawled in under the sheets and blanket and closed her eyes. Even though it was just late afternoon, this day had felt so long already. And, confusing. Within two minutes, Ishi dozed off.

The buzzing sound of the moped chasing her told her that it was catching up fast! She tried to run faster, but her legs hurt. Everything around her was on fire. She had nowhere to run! The buzz got louder. Ishi snapped awake!

The nightmare dissipated immediately as she quickly searched for and then saw the source of the buzzing sound. *Where am I?* She quickly desperately glanced around. She was in a completely dark room. *Oh*, she remembered as she grabbed her phone, *in the hotel room*. She answered, "Hello?"

"Ishi," Christian's voice was urgent, "are you okay? Are you in the hotel?"

"Yeah. Fell asleep. What day is it? It's night?" She looked toward the draped window, seeing through the middle slightly cracked opening that it was dark outside.

"Still Tuesday. Hey, are you okay? I have things to tell you. Important things. Big. You awake?"

Ishi swung her legs out off the side of the bed and sat up, instantly full of fear. "Yeah. What? Are you okay?"

Christian began, "Adri in the black BMW forced me to stop and was going to shoot me. I was just heading north from Frankfurt."

Ishi gasped, "What?"

"A woman showed up and shot Adri. Shimon Adri."

"He's dead?"

"Yes. And she made me drive to a side road and …"

"He's dead?" Ishi's mind was blown. "Mister Adri?"

"… and she grilled me. I'm okay now. But I thought I was going to die. Ishi, I seriously thought …"

"What … Oh god! What was …" she was trying to take this all in, "Who was the woman?"

"I don't know. But it's all connected. They're all connected. It's all around you somehow. You!"

Ishi sat mind-numb waiting for more, not knowing what to say or ask next.

Christian continued, "I think they're all spy agencies. But I don't know why they …? I know Mister Adri burned your house down. I know that for sure. The woman said that she's trying to protect you. But she also said that -- oh Ish, I don't want to scare you."

Ishi asked in a blur, "What? Tell me! No, don't tell me! No, tell me!" *Mister Adri burned down my house.* The drastic thought-pile was so huge now, that Ishi mentally simply shelved this piece of information as data.

"She also said that more people that are associated with Adris will come after you."

Ishi just listened. She could literally feel her heart beating quickly. She put the cell phone down on the bedspread, stood up, and paced across the room, her hands up to the sides of her head.

"Ishi, you there? Ishi?"

Ishi returned to the phone and picked it up. "Sorry. I'm here."

"Oh, I got my phone back, obviously."

"How did you get your phone …?" Then she remembered the email about her passport. "Where are you now, Christian?"

"I'm back in Vacha. I haven't told my parents anything. I wouldn't know what to tell them. But I think I'm going to just go drive into some hiding spot somewhere. There are still two more Adris around here, and they'll come after me too."

Ishi announced, "I got my passport. Well, I didn't get my passport … I mean, I didn't pick it up yet obviously. Not yet. But I got the email notification."

"How will you get it? Can you get it in the morning?"

"Do you think it's safe to leave the hotel?"

It was silent while Christian assessed. He said, "Well, the only two people that know where you are, besides me that is, well, one is dead, and the other one, the woman, says that she's trying to protect you. She forced me to say where you are. She followed me all the way back to Vacha, by the way."

"Wow! Mister Adri is dead." Ishi vocalized the information as it was sinking in! Ishi heard shuffling on the other end of the call. "What's that noise?"

"Just changing my shoes. I'm going to take my car and hide for a while like I said."

"What should I do?" As an afterthought, she asked, "How did you get your phone back?"

"The woman. She got it back out of Adri's car."

Ishi breathed in sharply, "Oh! That was …" *Mister Adri!*

Christian said, "Just stay where you are, I guess."

"Who is the woman," Ishi asked, confused and worried?

"I do not know."

After a long pause, Ishi said, "Okay, I'm going to take a shower."

"Do you have a TV or something?"

Ishi replied gruffly, "Chrrristian, after today? My house! Guns! I'm in hiding for my life? My parents? Not much in the mood for TV. What, a cooking show? Or …"

"Okay. Okay. Yeah, I know. Sorry. I know. Well, sleep if you can, Ish."

Ishi was struggling to screw the cap off the small bottle of shampoo provided for the shower when her phone buzzed again. She opened the plastic curtain, leaned toward the buzzing phone by the sink, saw that it was Christian again. Dripping all over the bathroom floor, she answered it, "Hi."

Christian's voice was urgent, "Ishi, I think I know what you should do."

"What?"

"Tomorrow morning, book into another hotel. I'll find one for you tonight and email you details. That way, only I will know where you are."

Ishi thought, then replied, "Good idea! And you know what else I'll do?"

"What?"

"I'm going to go by the ATM and withdraw another fifteen hundred euros. And I'm going to go get my passport. I wish I had a drivers license."

"Good idea!"

Ishi saw another 'unknown' number calling. A chill ran through her. "Chris, an unknown number is trying to call."

"Ishi, do not answer if you don't recognize it!"

"Okay. So where are you now?"

"Backed into a bush across the road from Adri Foods. I'm invisible here in the dark. I can see them though. I mean, they're closed. But anyway …"

"Okay. Stay invisible, Chris!"

"I'll text you every few hours. You text me too. Just to know that we're okay."

Ishi said through a yawn, "I might be sleeping."

"Okay, text me when you go to sleep and when you wake up, okay."

"Okay."

"Promise?"

"I will. I promise."

Christian quickly added, "Ish. Block Sebastian's number. And any Adri number."

I can't believe that I didn't think of that already. "I will right after I finish my shower."

*

General Arruk was livid as he slammed his desk phone down. He stood up so abruptly that he pushed his chair over backwards. He stomped to his office door, opened it, and shouted at his secretary, "Get Omar Abadi in here. Now!" As he returned to his desk, he slammed the glass-framed office door behind him so hard that the glass rattled dangerously close to shattering.

Fifteen minutes later, Arruk was no less furious as Abadi stood across the desk from him. Arruk had been bringing him up to speed. "Akeem Almasi has vanished into thin air. They've lost track of the girl. They can't find the boyfriend. All we know is that she is in Frankfurt. This is a disaster, Omar!"

Abadi asked, "What about the house?"

Arruk explained, "Akeem burned it as planned. The girl and the boyfriend raced to Frankfurt. Akeem followed. And then …?" Arruk threw his hands up in the air. "We went to all this trouble in Germany with Akeem and Saadia and that boy Azim! And now what!?"

"Brother, Akeem Almasi would not just go missing."

Arruk and Abadi looked at each other for a few moments. Then Arruk spoke, a new painful realization evident in his face. "Mossad."

Abadi thought, then suggested, "Let me go to Frankfurt. I'll find her. If nothing else, I'll monitor the airport and catch her there if she tries flying anywhere. And train stations. Of course I'll need men."

"How," Arruk raised his voice? "Frankfurt is not a small town."

Omar Abadi calmly responded, "Yes, I'll need a team. I'll monitor the airport, train stations, and I'll have a couple of agents go to Vacha. We'll find out how to find the boy. I think that if we find the boy, we'll find the girl."

Arruk stood and walked to his big window, gazed out, thinking. Calmer now, he said, "Okay. But I want constant reporting. We can't get this close to tracking down that Jewish Katz serpent and lose the trail because of being so inept as to lose his daughter." He turned around to face Abadi. "Do not let Mossad see you! Mossad will be there in Frankfurt. I know they're there. Do NOT let them see you!"

Abadi agreed, "We'll see them before they see us."

*

Leah no sooner arrived back in Vacha trailing Christian to his home, then she returned to her hotel. As she had been driving behind Christian, she had called Pascal with instructions for him to go to the Neufeld house to keep an eye on the Jetta, to bug the house, and to report anything and everything back to her. She had also updated Jonathan Ben Dod on everything.

As soon as Leah arrived at her hotel, she packed up and checked out. The night manager was surprised, asking if everything was alright in her room. Leah had offered him a cheerful reply by explaining that there is a sudden business emergency at the head office, and that she needed to get going right away.

When Leah was only sixty kilometers south of Vacha on her way back to Frankfurt, her phone alerted her of an incoming call. It was Pascal saying that the Jetta was in-fact not at the Neufeld home.

"When did you get there," Leah asked accusingly?

"When you called, I was at the acreage, looking for anything. I got back to Vacha as fast as I could, and no Jetta."

Leah's voice raised with frustration, "Use the tracker!"

Pascal replied that the tracker is good for twenty-five kilometers, but even so, he was not raising a signal.

Leah snapped back, "Well I followed him to Vacha myself. I know he's there somewhere." She thought for a moment. *Or* … Then she said, "Maybe he headed straight back to Frankfurt. If that's the case, I'll pick him up there. I'll update you, Pascal."

"Listen Toto, I don't understand why, if the girl is using the ancestral genetic office to find her parents, we can't just tap in on that."

Leah sighed and explained, "Look! BND don't even know we're here. We have no system in place neither here nor in Canada to monitor those encrypted files at those agencies."

"Yeah but, a little pointed pressure on a desk clerk of the genetic company could get us into their system."

Leah couldn't believe her ears. "Pascal, really? Apparently, you were born just yesterday." Leah was angry. "Force our way in. Create a ruckus that would be an alarm to the daughter, the Katz couple, CSIS, BND? You're kidding me, right?" Frustrated, she punched 'End call.'

*

An hour earlier, Christian had a realization that, because of his involvement with Ishi, he was being sought after too, and might be in greater danger than he had previously thought. *I need to get out of Vacha altogether and hide!*

Immediately starting up his car and then driving carefully without his headlights, he headed east toward Dorndorf. Once on the highway, he turned his lights on. Just before Dorndorf, Christian somewhat randomly chose a much smaller highway heading south. Three kilometers along that highway,

Christian saw a dirt approach off the paved road into a half-kilometer-wide tall-standing barley field that was framed on the north side by thick bushes. Navigating the small dirt approach in the dark, he pulled off the highway and then drove north along the front edge of the field, the barley standing taller than his car, and arrived at the bushes where he stopped and turned off his lights. He cranked the steering wheel to the right and backed up a car's length beside the edge of the field.

He checked his phone to make sure that he had a signal. He did. It was weak, but it was there. From his landing spot with the Jetta's rear tucked into the field and his front view facing the adjacent small highway, the bushes hid his car from southbound traffic and the tall barley hid his car from northbound traffic. He lowered his driver's side window all the way and marvelled at the night's silence around him in his hiding spot.

Christian, then, spent twenty minutes online on his phone searching for another hotel for Ishi. Finding a good one, he texted Ishi. "Sternenlicht Hotel. Just off Osloer Strasse at 2718 Rheinstrasse. Just three and a half blocks south-southwest from Stolpern Inn."

She texted back quite promptly, "Okay."

Two hours after having checked out of her hotel in Vacha, Leah approached Frankfurt.

Pascal had been scouring Vacha, driving his rusted blue Passat up and down every street and alley. Coming up empty in Vacha, he began to check rural roads just outside town. Just after 11:00pm, Pascal slowly drove in the dark, lights off, through the Adri Foods parking lot and stopped at the front double glass doors. Seeing a piece of paper taped to the inside of the doors, he stepped out of his car and turned on his flashlight to read it. In wide felt pen it read, 'Closed for renovations until further notice.' Pascal called Leah to report this.

She said, "Could be that they're on their way to Frankfurt. Or exfiltrating. But I'd put my money on Frankfurt. Anyway, you ended up getting trackers on their Passat, right?"

"Yes. But remember, only good for twenty-five kilom--"

"I know, I know. But if they're in Frankfurt, I'll pick them up. If they're in Vacha, you will. What about the boyfriend?"

Pascal answered, "Nothing yet. Like you said, if he's in Frankfurt, you'll see him. If he's here, I'll find him."

Leah had arrived in Frankfurt and was driving the last ten minutes to Stolpern Inn. She intended to find a perch where she could monitor the hotel entrance visually. As she drove, she called Pascal again, "Spoke with Ben Dod. We're coordinating with Frankfurt Station for extra eyes on the airport and train stations."

"Good."

"I'm arriving at the target's hotel in a few minutes."

Earlier as Christian had relocated from Vacha to the field just south of Dorndorf, the gravity of the entire situation began to sink in more. *Whatever this is, it's international and big and ugly. Something that involves Arab Intelligence and God knows whom else. I'll bet it has to do with Ishi's biological parents.* He phoned Ishi.

"Christian! What's happening?"

Christian replied with an urgency in his voice, "Ishi, this is bigger than we could possibly know. You have to move! Tonight! Right now!" He could tell that he was scaring her. "Ishi, I don't know what's going on. But these are big forces. International forces. They're up to something, and I don't know how or why it involves you, but it does."

Ishi's voice whimpered back, "Chris …"

Christian continued, "You have to move tonight. Even though that woman says she's trying to protect you, I don't know if that's true. But she does know where you are. Ish, I saw her gun down Mister Adri without batting an eye. Cold as ice. So, go!"

"But Chris …"

"Now! Immediately! Don't even check out. Just go to the other hotel! I texted you the name and address."

Leah Fromm drove past Stolpern Inn slowly. As she searched for a good place to park along the street, she noticed two spaces on the other side of the street that would furnish her with a clear view. She needed to go to the next intersection, do a U-turn, and slide into the vacant curbside parking spot nearest the hotel door.

Ishi, scared, immediately grabbed her tote and phone, exited the hotel room, taking the stairs down to the lobby. At the lobby, she glanced sideways at the night manager.

He looked up at her quizzically.

"Out to see the city," Ishi offered spritely. Ishi exited the hotel and walked south, unaware of the red Skoda driving north in the opposite direction just behind her. Leah did not notice Ishi in her rear-view mirror.

*

Azim was behind the steering wheel of the black Passat. His mother sat beside him as they drove south toward Frankfurt. As they had explained to Arruk, they hadn't heard anything from Akeem. They had also explained that, because there are tracking sensors on Christian's car and in Ishi's clothing, and because they picked up no signals in Vacha of either, they have to conclude that the pair are in Frankfurt, especially after Akeem had reported tailing them to Frankfurt. They had put their store on hold with a notice of closure due to renovations, determined to take a day or two to track down their targets.

Arruk had responded with a perplexing mixture of anger and complacency, perplexing to Azim and Saadia, as they expected the anger but not the complacency. Arruk had not told them of Abadi and his team that were due to arrive in Frankfurt the next day.

As far as Arruk was concerned, Akeem Almasi, Azim Bakir, and Saadia Bakir were incompetent, incapable of finishing the assignment. *But,* Arruk had reasoned to himself, *there is power in numbers. So let them try.* At this point though, he certainly put more stock in Abadi and his team.

"Have you simply tried phoning her?" Arruk had asked in a mocking tone during a phone conversation just ten minutes earlier.

"Yes. She has blocked me and our other phones."

Arruk shouted, "Then use another phone!"

Azim replied, "General Arruk, I did. She doesn't answer."

Their schedule had been so pressure-packed and erratic lately that Saadia and Azim hadn't been able to talk. The drive to Frankfurt finally gave them that opportunity.

"Mama …"

Saadia turned to look at her son, waiting.

"Mama, what if we don't do this? I mean, what if we'd just stop, wash our hands of everything?"

"Son, what are you talking about?"

Azim cleared his throat. "Mama, I made friends. I've seen what a normal life can be."

"Azim, give your head a shake! What craziness is in your head?"

"Haven't you seen it too mama? The nice people that come into the store. Even just running the store is good, isn't it? The Grubers were nice people too."

"Son," Saadia repositioned her entire body to face her son. "Do you forget your father, peace be upon him, and your sisters, peace be upon them, so quickly? Shame on you! You mock them."

"I didn't forget. I just …"

"There are casualties in war," Saadia stated. "This is war! These Germans aren't innocent. Son, they are aligned with our enemy Israel. And so, they are enemies of Allah."

"I don't think innocent individuals like my classmates are aligned with Israel, mama."

"Azim, they are not aligned with Palestine. That's for sure. And don't forget that they are infidels! All of them. Has your soul fallen out of your body in less than a year? So easily? Son, do not break my heart! My heart is already too broken."

"Mama, I am still committed. Don't judge me so hard."

"Son, if you have character and are true to Allah, you will, instead of getting soft and being enticed by things of the world and losing your will, you will avenge the murders of your father and sisters. Yes?"

"Yes, mama." Her words did actually inspire him again and changed his attitude to one of more determination. He put his hand on hers. "Mama, 'ant masdar 'iilham li (you inspire me)."

*

Although Ishi put no priority at this point in the nice-ness of the hotel, she did notice that the Sternenlicht Hotel was notably a better quality than Stolpern Inn. Even so, the nice-ness of a hotel and even all the crazy events of the past days … Ishi compacted those thoughts into the back of her mind as she now concentrated on her own safety.

As soon as she was checked into room 157, a ground-floor room facing a back alley, she sat down on the bed and called Christian. He answered immediately.

"I'm in," Ishi reported.

"Good! Did you have to give your name when you checked in?"

"Of course! How else?"

"Uhmmm, yeah, I guess so. I have no experience with hotels."

Ishi replied, "Yeah, well me neither. But I'm getting experience pretty damn fast. Where are you? Are you hiding?"

"Yeah. I'm in a field outside of Dorndorf."

Ishi asked, "What about your parents?"

"I texted them and told them that I'm on a road trip with friends for a couple of days. Asked my dad if that was okay for work. He didn't like it, but … what could he do?"

"Chris, I gotta sleep. I'm so tired!"

"Yeah, nobody knows where you are now. Go to sleep."

"Are you going to sleep there? In your car?"

"Yeah. It's okay. No problem. Ish, call me as soon as you're up, okay."

Ishi suddenly realized how much she cherished her friendship with Christian. "I will, Chris." Just as quickly, a wave of shame ran through Ishi as she remembered how she detoured from Christian to Sebastian only less than two weeks ago. She was amazed and ashamed at her own shallowness. After ending the call with Christian, she muttered to herself, "I need to see a shrink.

CHAPTER 31

A black cargo ship moved as if in slow motion toward the dockyards at Vancouver's Coal Harbour. But that wasn't the ship that Rebecca was watching. From the restaurant's slightly elevated perch on the North Shore, she was watching the big cruise ship just behind the cargo ship, a gigantic white cruise ship that would dock beside the Pan Pacific Hotel on the far opposite side of the harbor. After more than two years in Vancouver, Rebecca was still often stunned by the beauty of the city, its glimmering high-rises bordering the curves and juts of the Pacific's shores.

"Becky," Katherine tried to bring Rebecca back into focus! "Rebecca, oh Rebecca! Earth to Rebecca," Katherine continued in a friendly musical tone. Rebecca snapped out of her fixation and turned back to the three ladies at the table with her.

Suzanna, Katherine, Dorothy, and Rebecca had frequented mid-afternoon late lunches at Pier 6 Restaurant. Because of the restaurant's close proximity to both the waterfront and the huge Public Market Station, and especially in high tourist season as it was now in the middle of July, Pier 6 was usually very busy. So, the ladies learned that the easiest time to get a table with a view was mid-afternoon. They'd made a habit of it, meeting here on the average two or three days each week.

"So, you've tried for a second mortgage?" Dorothy asked Suzanna.

Suzanna sighed in despair. "We already have a second mortgage. We're out of options." Suzanna's face showed deep worry.

Suzanna's home business of medical transcription came to a screeching halt nearly three months earlier when the company she was employed by was bought out. At the same time, her husband Mark went on medical leave from his work as a self-employed carpenter because of his heart's triple bypass surgery. Mark was fine and healing. But now their house faced foreclosure, and Suzanna was very worried and depressed.

Over the past two years, Rebecca's and Suzanna's friendship had grown very deep and strong. Rebecca struggled viciously with whether to help Suzanna or not. There were two massive roadblocks to such help. Firstly, David would refuse. Besides the fact that he had no charitable personality, he has never really liked Suzanna, or any of Rebecca's friends. Secondly, digging into the funds might open up a can of worms; questions about how Rebecca has access to large amounts of money. Nevertheless, Rebecca was on the verge of doing it anyway. She couldn't bear the thought of Suzanna losing her home.

A waitress arrived at the table. "Desserts for you ladies?"

The women began to muse among themselves, "My mouth wants dessert but my hips don't."

"Oooo, I love their dark chocolate tart."

"I should say no, but I'm gunna say yes …" Just then Rebecca's phone dinged letting her know of an incoming email. She checked it. Her heart skipped a beat as she saw that it was from Family Tree.

Rebecca had resigned herself to the likelihood years earlier that little Ishi was likely not alive, although her internal war of surrender versus hope always continued to some degree. The weight toward surrender hadn't stop her from registering the search, however. But she had refused to get her hopes up.

Rebecca opened the email and read. "A positive match has been made for your genetic/DNA Autosomal search. Please press "Continue" if you wish to have your search result opened for you." Rebecca stared at her phone in disbelief! The other three ladies were busy considering desserts, and so they didn't notice Rebecca's expression.

With a suddenly quivering finger Rebecca pressed 'Continue'. Immediately Rebecca self-prepared for the search to have found something that wasn't right and likely way off. *Perhaps a girl in Denmark or in South America or somewhere.*

Strangely, Rebecca almost hoped for a wrong result to justify her many years of mourning.

A new page opened. "Autosomal Genetic/DNA match 99% for Isabella Gruber. Age 18. Currently living in Vacha, Germany. Registered at Family Tree in Frankfurt, Germany." The report had more, but upon seeing Vacha, Germany, the town a mere six kilometers from where Ishi vanished, Rebecca knew! "Oh," Rebecca breathed out the word as she felt her head go light! "Ohhh," she uttered again as she felt so very light-headed. The phone dropped from her hand as she slid off her chair onto the floor, thoroughly fainted.

Rebecca opened her eyes. "Where am I?" Someone was holding a cool wet towel against her forehead. She tried to focus. *What am I looking at?* She was looking through, *what? Legs of tables and chairs?* Quickly her scenario began to make sense. She was sitting on the floor beside the restaurant table. Her friends and at least three servers were doting on her, trying to revive her. Rebecca managed a weak smile as she regained her wits.

She got up, and shakily sat back onto her chair.

"Honey," Katherine cooed, "you fainted. Are you okay?"

Suzanna asked, "Becky, what's happening? How are you? Did you eat something …?"

Rebecca interrupted, straightening out her blouse, "I'm good. I'm okay. I'm okay."

"Are you sure?" Katherine continued. "You're still quite pale, Honey."

Dorothy chimed in, "Should I take you to a doctor?"

Rebecca's mind was clear now. She straightened herself in her chair and thanked the restaurant staff with gestures that they could leave her alone now. Then she realized -- *Where's my phone?* "Where's my phone?" Rebecca asked.

Suzanna had picked it up off the floor. "Here." Suzanna handed it to her friend.

Rebecca immediately looked at the phone screen. The Family Tree page closed when the phone dropped. Rebecca looked at her friends and then at Suzanna and then glanced to other restaurant patrons who were staring. "I have to go. I'm sorry. Just got some news that I guess hit me … well, news," she sputtered. "I have to go."

Rebecca stood up, collected her small handbag, and began toward the exit. Suzanna immediately stood to catch up with her friend.

"Becky," Suzanna called after her eagerly, "what's happened? Becky?"

Rebecca suddenly stopped walking, spun around, and returned to the table. In her retreat, Rebecca had left Suzanna still walking toward the exit, stopped, turned, confused as Rebecca returned to the table. Rebecca rifled through her handbag, produced a small wallet, quickly dug out the first bill she could find which was a fifty-dollar bill, dropped it on the table, and turned and walked briskly again toward Suzanna and the exit.

Katherine and Dorothy were speechless as they watched Rebecca exit. Minutes later, Suzanna returned to the table of confused friends.

Dorothy asked, "What did she say? What happened?"

Katherine asked, "What news?"

Suzanna sat and said, "She wouldn't say. I don't know. She was just mumbling; "If only my mother knew." Suzanna shrugged palms up, "I don't know what that's about." Suzanna's posture indicated her desire to rejoin Rebecca.

Dorothy said, "Suzanna, I've got this," referring to the bill. "Go!"

"Thanks." Suzanna stood up again and turned to follow again after her friend.

*

Azim and Saadia spent the entire evening and night driving around Frankfurt. They had not picked up a tracking signal at all. They were frustrated, angry, and worried at their lack of success. They were scared to call in a report of failure to General Arruk. Absolutely exhausted and in need of sleep, by early-morning, they found a small tuck-away under trees in the large parking lot of the Sportanlage Recreational Center just east of the international airport. The Passat's seats reclined nearly fully, so they'd be able to get some sleep here.

Reclined, eyes closed, both Azim and Saadia could hear the excited morning chirping of birds in nearby trees and the dull hum of general city traffic. Azim's overall exhaustion included a deflated spirit. "Mama," he mumbled, "I will honour papa and my sisters, peace be upon them. Don't worry!"

"Good!" Since the death of Mohammad and her girls, the fire of revenge had become Saadia's mental foundation. "Never forget your father, boy!"

"Never! We will avenge him and Aisha and Akilah, of course. And we'll do our part helping find that Katz couple. But we are not succeeding. We must pray for success."

"Sleep, Azim! We only can take a few hours here."

Azim breathed in deeply, knowing sleep was moving in quickly. He murmured one last thought, "Why are people born where they are born? Why couldn't we have been born in Vacha?"

Saadia murmured, "Allah knows. I don't know. One day when you meet him, you can ask."

*

Halfway through the night, Leah still hadn't seen any coming or going from Stolpern Inn by Ishi. That was expected though, as Leah understood that the girl was likely exhausted and sleeping. Leah did, however, get a tracker sensor notification on her phone! She immediately called Pascal. She explained that she couldn't leave her post, so she couldn't follow the tracking sensor. Confirming that he still has had no tracker notifications in or around Vacha, she instructed him to drive to Frankfurt immediately so that he could pick up on the tracking here. Pascal agreed but stressed that he is in desperate need of some sleep. Leah replied, "I know Pascal. I am way beyond my limit too. Just get here first. Nail down locations from these tracking sensors, then we can tag-team with a bit of shut-eye. Right now, I can't take my eyes off this hotel's doors, not even for one minute."

*

General Arruk had just arrived at Al-Aaam Saleeh restaurant for lunch with two of his PLO Majors. As he was being ushered to the table where the two Majors waited, his phone rang. *Timing!* "Who is it?" he growled into the phone. The anxious voice belonged to Yitzhak Biton, Governor at Kiryat HaMenshala Bank in Jerusalem.

"General Arruk, I'm sorry to disturb, but ..."

Arruk snapped back, "Where are you calling from? Is the line secure?"

"Yes, from my car. Listen! Ben Dod from Mossad has been here at the bank two days in a row. The first day, yesterday, he was inquiring about any existing accounts past or present for Joseph or Sonya Katz."

Just having arrived at his table, but not yet seated, Arruk stayed standing, rigid. "And?"

"Today he was inquiring about any money transfer history to Canadian banks and Vancouver banks."

Arruk's face grew immediately red with frustration. "And of course you have none, correct? You proved to him that you could produce nothing of the sort, even when showing him your history? Right?" Arruk's questions were more like statements. Arruk stepped farther away from the table and out of earshot of the Majors.

Biton replied, "Well of course that's right. But the very fact that he's here asking …"

Arruk interrupted, "Listen! I suspected that if we knew those Katzes are in Vancouver, Canada, Mossad would know too. Their intelligence is far more complex than ours." *Ah hah! I'll bet Mossad caught Akeem Almasi and squeezed the Vancouver, Canada information out of him.*

Biton's voice was stressed, "But General, the very fact that they're here! Here at my bank!"

"Listen! If you have no compromising records -- and why would you have anything that would connect your bank to those Katz devils -- then you don't need to worry, brother. The important thing is that we find that Katz couple and close that loose end before they talk. And if Mossad gets to them first, they will talk!" Arruk heard the sigh of fear in Biton's reaction to his words.

"Ben Dod spoke to me directly yesterday. He threatened to have me subpoenaed to a hearing to explain unaccounted for money. General, this is not good! The audit obviously identified the gaps!"

Arruk continued, "Listen, we've got the girl on the move now. I mean the Katz daughter. We believe she's going to make a run for her parents in Canada. So, hold tight Biton! After so many years, we're on the verge of ending this loose end. And, about that threat of subpoena from Mossad, it's just a trick. Listen to me, Yitzhak Biton! It's just a trick. Mossad can't subpoena anyone into a finance hearing any more than I can make it snow in July." Arruk hit 'End Call' and with considerable effort to unfurl his worried eyebrows, returned to his table and the curious waiting table guests. "Apologies, Majors."

*

By following the tracking sensor, Pascal had located Adri's black Passat tucked into the corner of the parking lot. He parked his old blue Passat on the shoulder of the main street directly adjacent to Adri's car. The two cars were divided and made invisible from each other by a thirty-meter-wide berm of landscaped hedges and grass that separated the street's shoulder from the parking lot. Pascal reached into his cargo pants leg pocket and extracted a heat sensor.

Carefully sneaking up over the berm through the hedges, he approached to within four or five meters of the black car. He aimed his heat sensor at the vehicle and peered through the monocular eye lens. Pascal could clearly see two bodies laying in the car. Because he could see that the heat outlines were reclined, he dared to creep up closer to try to see through the back window. Crouched behind the car, he slowly raised his body to look, but realized that the back window was too tinted. He took a step to his right to try to see through a side window. Aided by some light from the parking lot's lights in the still half-light dawn, he saw Azim Bakir clearly asleep in the reclined driver's seat. And he saw some longer black hair from the head on the passenger's seat, concluding that it was Saadia Bakir sleeping. Quickly and carefully, Pascal extracted himself back over the berm to his blue car on the main road.

Pascal drove a few hundred meters forward past the entrance of the parking lot, then when the passing traffic slackened, he did a U-turn and parked against the curb on the opposite side of the street facing back toward the parking lot entrance so that he could see if the PLO agents would exit. Pascal grabbed his phone from his console and called Leah.

"Pascal?"

"Leah, it's the two Adris. They're sleeping in their car in a parking lot. That's the only tracking sensor alert I picked up here in Frankfurt."

Leah exclaimed, "Damn it! You're sure that tracking sensor that you put on Christian's Jetta is reliable? I've only picked up one signal myself."

"One hundred percent."

"You're sure that Christian couldn't have located it and removed it?"

"Impossible."

Leah sighed, "Okay, let me think."

*

Christian woke up several times through the night. His sleep in the Jetta was sporadic and poor. Even though not many vehicles had driven past on the road during the night, each vehicle's sound alerted him awake. By now at nearly 8:30am, he had been awake already for more than three hours. *I hope the farmer doesn't come by here.* In the morning sunshine, Christian could see that the tall stand of barley wasn't yet ripened yellow. So, he felt confident that no farmer would be coming around. He had texted Ishi twice to ensure that she was okay. She texted back reassuring him that she was.

His phone buzzed. "Hey Ishi."

Ishi's voice revealed her general fatigue and fear, "Christian, I've been thinking. I can't go back home."

Christian listened.

"I mean, there's no home to go back to. I don't know where mom and dad are. There are people, dangerous people after me."

"Did something happen in your hotel? Are you okay there?"

"I'm okay. But I keep thinking about what Sebastian said about my parents being involved with crimes. And I think about my Oma's letter that said that my biological father was horrible." Ishi began to whimper into the phone. "And they … what happened to my mom and dad? What will happen to me?"

"Should I come down there?" *I don't care now what my parents might think. This is more important.* "I should come down there."

"No. I think it's too dangerous if you drive anywhere. Just think of what happened to you yesterday. Hang on!" Ishi walked into the bathroom and pulled two tissues from the dispenser there. Wiping her nose and her face, she said, "Aaach, I've been a crying mess. Can't seem to stop. I didn't bring anything with me. Thank God I don't have my period this week."

"Whoa! Too much information."

Ishi chuckled slightly amidst her whimpering. "Anyway, I need to go to get my passport. Then, seriously, I think I should fly to Vancouver. It's not safe here, anywhere here. At least I'll be out of the country."

"Wow, Ishi!" Christian hadn't yet allowed thoughts that entertained such huge steps.

Ishi continued, "So, I've been thinking about it. What if my mother, I mean my biological mother isn't evil? Just my biological father. I mean, I don't know. But it's not safe here. And I could go meet with my biological mother. At least meet her. Maybe it would be safe, or safer there."

This was a lot for Christian to take in! He opened his car door and stepped out into the tall grass that bordered the barley field. Running his hand through his hair as he quickly processed his thoughts, he said, "So, maybe. How would you book your flight? I've never flown in a plane. I don't know how that's done."

"I've never flown either. I don't know. Just go to the airport and buy the ticket, I guess." She began to pace in her hotel room. "I need to go to the passport office anyway to get that. So, I could just keep going to the airport. I'd have my passport and cash, so I should be able to buy a ticket, don't you think?"

Christian took a few moments to think. *What if I lose complete contact with her?* "Would your phone still work in Canada?"

"I don't know. But there's always email. I can get a phone there too, I guess."

"Did the Family Tree email give contact information for your parents? What are their names again?"

"Rebecca and David Wiess. Yes, it gave me their street address, phone, and email."

Christian was thinking as fast as possible of all possible scenarios. He asked, "What about ATMs? Can you use your bank card there?"

Ishi's reply had a note of pent-up frustration, "Chris, I don't know? You're asking all these things that I don't know. But Christian, I'm scared to death here."

After at least ten seconds of neither saying anything more, Ishi knew that Christian was thinking about it. She needed his honest opinion on this, so she gave him time to think. Finally, Christian said with confidence in his voice, "Go! Go do it! It makes sense."

Ishi's voice became frail with fear. "Do you really think so? Chris, I'm scared. I've never … This is all so," Ishi paused searching for the word …

"Scary."

"Yeah. And big."

It was mid morning, and Leah hadn't seen any trace of Ishi at the Stolpern Inn. She had thought up a plan. She ordered Quick Eats to deliver a pizza and soft drink to the address on the door beside where she was parked.

Exactly seventeen minutes later, she saw the delivery driver pull onto the side of the extra wide part of the hotel driveway. As the young female delivery driver hopped out and opened the back door to grab the food and drink, Leah was already standing beside the door of the given address up on the first of two wide stone entrance steps.

"Hi! Thanks!" Leah chimed. "I'm starving. And you were fast. Thank you."

The girl smiled, handing her the food and the bill.

Leah set the food down on the steps and dug money from her pocket. Then Leah looked at the girl's Quick Eats cap admiringly. "I love that hat!" Leah exclaimed. "Where can I get one of those?"

"Oh, they're not for sale. Just for us delivery people."

"But I need to have one of those!"

The girl gave Leah a quizzical look.

"Can I buy your hat?"

The girl chuckled, "Oh, no ma'am. It's not for sale."

"Fifty euros?" Leah held a fifty bill out.

The girl, confused, asked, "For the pizza?"

"For the pizza and your hat."

"I don't know. No, I better not."

Leah tried again, "A hundred euros?"

She pulled another fifty out of her pocket.

The girl giggled nervously, then gave in and traded her hat for the cash.

"Tell your boss that it blew away in the wind. Or someone stole it," Leah offered as the girl quickly walked back to her car.

Within minutes, Leah had entered the Stolpern Inn lobby with the cap on and food in-hand. She walked up to the front desk. "Ishi Gruber, one of your guests ordered this but she forgot to give us her room number. Which room is she in please?"

The older woman behind the counter looked up at Leah, then down at a book, leafed a page, scanning with her index finger, "Ishi … Ishi … Ah! Isabella Gruber. Two o eight."

Leah chimed, "Thanks," as she immediately headed for the wide stairway.

With the food set down on the hallway floor, Leah first put her ear to the door for nearly half a minute. She heard nothing, no noise at all coming from the room. She knocked. "Room Service!" Nothing. Again, "room service! Hello?" She knocked more insistently now. Nothing. Quickly, Leah pulled a lock set out of her waist pouch and went to work on the rather simple lock. Within fifteen seconds, she was inside the empty hotel room.

Pascal's cell phone buzzed. He quickly answered, "What's up?"

Leah's voice betrayed her anger! "She's gone. The girl isn't in her hotel room."

"Shit! Leah, how?"

Leah didn't have an answer for "how". Instead, she said, "I'm calling Tel Aviv. Stay with those PLO agents!"

Within the next few minutes of frantic phone calls, Mossad had dispatched two agents to the airport and an agent to each of the three train stations. Leah had offered to rush to the main bus station. Pascal would stay with the two Adris.

CHAPTER 32

At Terminal 1 of Frankfurt International Airport an older couple that looked to be in their mid-sixties sat near a coffee kiosk in the general area of the ticketing-departure level of the giant concourse. The slumping frowning man was in a wheelchair and his stick-thin wife sat on a café chair next to him. They were both nursing their morning coffees that were in take-out cups with lids.

It was a massive concourse with many airlines' designated counters stretching one after the other the amazing length of a football field. The couple had positioned themselves in a central point and strategically as close as possible to United, Delta, Air Canada, KLM, and airlines that would most frequently fly to points in North America. The couple continuously monitored the flight boards identifying all flights that were scheduled to go either directly or indirectly to Vancouver.

But because those two Mossad agents were on the departure level, they were oblivious to the five Palestinians that had just cleared Customs and were making their way to the arrival concourse one level below.

Omar Abadi walked with one agent while ten meters behind them, three other PLO agents walked completely independent of Abadi toward the baggage carousel area for their flight.

The two PLO parties stood on opposite sides of the carousel as their luggage slowly appeared. They did not exchange glances or anything that would indicate that they were together. However, Abadi had given the other three agents their orders. They knew that two of them would take a taxi to the main train station while the other one would rent a car and drive northeast two hours to Vacha.

Just over an hour earlier, Azim and Saadia Bakir had been awakened with a phone call from General Arruk. He updated them on the incoming support, detailing the coverage of the airport, train stations, and Vacha. With a stern warning, Arruk had instructed them to scour through every hotel guest list possible within a two-kilometer radius of the airport and to also keep monitoring the tracking sensors. They were also told that they would now be reporting to Omar Abadi. After giving them Abadi's contact information, Arruk had ended his call with a threat. A threat that made clear that failure to find the Katz girl would result in very unsavoury consequences for both Azim and Saadia.

As Azim and Saadia drove away from the parking lot to begin scouring the city, they were not aware of the old blue Passat following some distance behind them.

Ishi was terrified! She was taking a massive step, bigger than she would've ever dreamed she'd take. *A week ago, I thought a daytrip to Frankfurt with Sebastian was a huge deal. Now, I'm going to buy a one-way ticket across the ocean to a country that I know nothing about!* Intimidation of this set of actions didn't even begin to describe Ishi's general psyche and mood. If, however, she knew what was waiting for her at the airport, she would have likely reconsidered this plan of action all-together.

Ishi knew she was hiding from dangerous people. But Isabella Gruber had no idea of how central she was to the interests of at least two entire nations.

Having no bags to pack, she had again thought of leaving the Sternenlicht Hotel without checking out. She actually wasn't clear on whether an official check-out was required. Then, she remembered the hundred-euro deposit that the front desk had required because she couldn't give them a passport as insurance, something that hadn't been asked of her at all at Stolpern Inn.

Getting the deposit back was simple and fast. Five minutes after leaving her room, she was walking west toward Osloer Strässe where she hoped she'd easily be able to flag down a taxi.

In the efficient thirty-five minutes that followed, she had been to the passport office, received her passport, and was back on the street trying to flag down another taxi.

Once in a taxi's back seat, she tried to sound confident. "To the international airport please."

The taxi driver looked at her in the mirror and replied, "Right away, Miss."

"How far is it? I mean, how long to get there?"

"About fifteen minutes. Maybe twenty."

This was only Ishi's second time in a taxi. *Feels weird, like I'm in a movie or something.* She knew how the taxi thing goes, what to say and ask because she'd seen it countless times in movies. But now that she was actually doing it, it felt surreal.

As they progressed toward the airport, Ishi finally took time to look at her new passport. *It looks so official!*

Having never been to an airport, much less, such a massive international airport, confusion and an overwhelming feeling swept through and gripped Ishi as the taxi rolled slowly toward the Departures gates.

"Which airline?" the driver asked.

"Oh no," Ishi thought, panicking! *I don't know. Okay, just pick one. Sound confident.* Seeing United on a gate ahead, she said "United." She didn't know. She was instantly aware that this was much more complicated than just walking into an airport and buying a flight.

Standing outside the double set of revolving glass doors, she called Christian. Christian answered instantly, "I was just calling you."

Ishi said, panic in her voice, "I don't know what I'm doing! I don't know how this works, how to buy a flight to Vancouver. And this airport is enormous! More than enormous!"

Christian said, "That's why I was calling you. I went online and searched for flights. There are so many options, it's a bit confusing."

"What did you find? How do I do this?"

"Well, there are two that are the best price. One is United Airlines."

"Okay, good. That's where I am right now."

"They connect through Chicago O'Hare Airport and then to Vancouver.

You have to change planes in Chicago."

Ishi sighed her exasperation at the complexity.

"And there's Air Canada. They connect through Toronto. And you have to change planes there too. Also, there are other direct flights, but they are crazy expensive."

I'm so confused! It's all too much! Ishi asked, "What do you think?"

Christian said, "I thought about it just before I called, or, before you called. I think you should connect through Toronto, Canada. That way you're only involving Germany and Canada. The other way, you'd be throwing USA into the equation. Anyway, they're both about sixteen hours total."

Ishi gasped, "Sixteen hours! Wow!"

"Yeah, but Ishi, you want to know the cool thing about that?"

"What?"

"You're flying with the sun. With the rotation of the Earth. So even though you'd be on a sixteen-hour flight, you leave at eleven. Oh yeah, I should tell you the flight times. Anyway, you leave at eleven-o-five o'clock this morning and arrive in Vancouver at four-thirty in the afternoon. Like five or six hours later. Plus, the time to change planes, I guess. Cool, heh?"

Ishi was not thinking about "Cool" right now. "So, what do I do next," she asked?

Christian thought he knew from movies he'd watched. "Go inside. Find the Air Canada ticket counter. Buy the ticket. I'm pretty sure they'll give you instructions from there."

"Can I still use my phone inside?"

"I have no idea."

Ishi had located the Air Canada section and followed the slowly moving queue to the ticket agents. She was as nervous as she looked. She felt naked. Besides being dressed only in a t-shirt and shorts, everyone around her had lots of luggage. She had none. She had only the small tote and her phone.

The older couple had identified the PLO agents immediately. The man quickly texted the sighting to Leah. Minutes later, the Mossad older couple saw Ishi approach the ticket queue for Air Canada. With his carry-on luggage in his lap, he quickly gestured to his female Mossad associate who immediately got off her stool and pushed his wheelchair while towing her carry-on luggage behind her. Pushing his wheelchair, they went out through double revolving doors to the outside of the terminal where rows of taxis sat awaiting customers. There, the man stood up and pulled a cushion down and out from under his shirt bottom, thereby immediately transforming him from an overweight pot-bellied frowning man to an in-shape astute man. Tossing the cushion onto the wheelchair, he pushed the wheelchair aside toward the terminal exterior wall. The woman produced a sport coat for him out of her handbag. He quickly put it on. While he was putting on the coat, the woman quickly called Leah letting her know in one short sentence that the target is at the airport in the Air Canada ticketing queue, and to get the whole team here immediately. The man slipped on glasses while the woman stepped over to the discarded wheelchair and pulled a wide-brimmed hat from its back pouch and put it on. Producing a fashionable silk scarf from her handbag, she slung it around her neck, and they walked back into the airport appearing unrecognizable from their former appearance, each wheeling their one piece of carry-on luggage, walking briskly.

Two PLO agents, both men in their thirties who could pass for dark-skinned German citizens, saw Ishi too. They had been keeping a suspicious eye on the older couple and had seen them leave the terminal. Quickly, the two agents got into the queue approximately fourteen people behind Ishi. Because their focus was on the girl, they did not notice the refurbished older couple re-enter the terminal.

The Mossad couple did not join the queue but instead hoped Leah would arrive soon so that she could.

The realization hit both agents of both teams quickly. They had no way to know which flight she'd book. They looked up at the massive flight board and saw that there are two direct flights to Vancouver over the next three hours. But they also realized that she would likely buy a connecting flight because of the price differences. They looked at the other flights to Montreal, Denver,

London, Atlanta, Toronto and realized that any of those flights might connect to Vancouver.

Ishi had progressed to third in the queue waiting for the next ticket agent. Both the female Mossad agent and one of the PLO agents were typing furiously on their phones, both realized that they need to get someone on the other side of screening to see which gate she goes to.

The Mossad agent typed frantically to the operations lead agent Toto, "Do we have access to flight manifests? We need to know which flight."

Leah used voice-to-text as she was racing toward the airport in her car, "No. I'll be there in ten minutes. We can't involve the Germans. They don't know we're here. Well, they know we're here, but they don't know that we're running an operation without telling them. I'll buy any flight just to get me through screening."

Mossad agent typed, "2 PLO in the ticket queue just behind target. 30s. Could pass as dark-skinned Germans."

Leah instructed, "Get photos. Send to me."

As nervous as Ishi was, the whole ordeal was not as bad as she feared. Going through screening was a bit nerve-racking. *Really? My flip flops? I have to remove my flip flops?* But now on the other side walking down seemingly endless long corridors toward her gate, she was stunned by the completely different nicer world in this part of the airport terminal, an array of cafés, shops, and even moving sidewalks! The agent had told her to hurry because her flight was going to start boarding in less than ten minutes. So, she took advantage of the moving sidewalks, half-jogging most of the way, and reached Gate 11a. She saw that boarding had begun.

Afraid that the plane might leave without her, she rushed past the line up of boarding passengers to the male boarding agent. She held out her ticket for him to see. "Am I late?" she inquired, flustered, intimidated by the entire procedure.

The man smiled at her and replied, "You're fine Miss. We're boarding disabled and first class right now. You'll be next."

Ishi breathed a sigh of relief! She walked up to the massive floor to ceiling windows and looked out at the huge airplane and at other airplanes nearby. She had never seen anything like this!

Suddenly remembering Christian, she dug her phone from her handbag and texted him. "Boarding now. I'll text again during the flight. If I can. Don't know if I can?"

Christian's reply text appeared seconds later, "Try! If not, text from Toronto if you can. Or email."

"I will. Still hiding?"

"Yes. Bored out of my mind."

Ishi texted, "Be safe. Bye. Thanks! Bye. Btw, this airport is amazing! The planes are huge! I had no idea. Bye."

The two Palestinian men hit a dead end when they were informed that they'd need to provide a visa to pass through Customs into Canada. They had not anticipated the visa requirement for a Palestinian to visit Canada. Stunned at first, they tried to bribe the ticketing agent. When that was met with a warning, they became furious and hurled insults. That was met with another more severe warning and a phone call by the ticketing agent to airport security. The men quickly relented and retreated into the concourse where one of them immediately called Omar Abadi to report the failure.

Leah Fromm had anticipated the visa requirements. Because she had recently been in Washington State, she was also furnished with the required paperwork to enter Canada. Jonathan Ben Dod had made sure of that. But she too did not know which flight Ishi had purchased. However, she had studied the flight options on the Internet on her cell phone while waiting in the queue, and she knew that the more expensive direct flight, even though it would leave almost two and a half hours later than the other flights, would arrive in Vancouver nearly an hour earlier than any other connecting flight. That was essential for her!

Ben Dod knew too that Toto would be going to operate for Mossad in Canada without the knowledge of CSIS, the Canadian Security Intelligence Service, Ben Dod knew that, if CSIS would be informed, they would want to play in on the operation, and that would just clutter up and possibly jeopardize

Toto's effectiveness. So, Leah Fromm and the one other agent that Ben Dod would send up from Denver Station would have to ensure that they stay cleanly off any CSIS radars or else CSIS would be furious with Israel for running an unsanctioned operation on Canadian soil.

*

General Arruk's relationship with Mahmoud Ramaki the Minister of the Iranian Prime Intelligence Ministry was dicey. They were sometimes on speaking terms and often too angry with each other to communicate. But lately, they had cooperated on an arms negotiation with Moscow, so they were on speaking terms again, but barely.

When General Arruk learned of the miserable failure by his agents at the airport, he was furious and desperate! He realized that, without anyone to follow the girl or to pick up her trail in Canada, years of efforts to eliminate the Katz couple would be destroyed. In desperation, Arruk phoned Iranian Minister Ramaki.

General Arruk waited on the phone at his desk while Minister Ramaki's Assistant transferred his call. Ramaki answered in his usual controlled, cool tone.

Arruk chimed, "Minister Ramaki, how are you? How are your wife and children?"

Ramaki replied coldly and abruptly, "General Arruk, what do you want?"

Arruk got right to it. "Minister Ramaki, I have to ask for a little favor. Of course, I'll return the favor ten-fold. You know I will."

"What is it?"

Arruk explained while trying to remain vague, "Well, it's nothing big. But it's important to Palestine and to me."

"Not big you say? Well, if you want to tour our nuclear enrichment facility or something like that, the answer is no!"

"No, no," Arruk kept his tone light. "We have a rogue agent that we've been looking for for a long time. We think we've found him in Vancouver, Canada, and …"

"Joseph Katz."

Arruk was somewhat shocked at Ramaki's knowledge! So shocked that it took Arruk a few seconds to recompose himself. "Yes, Joseph and Sonya Katz. We've been tracking someone—"

"Their daughter," Ramaki interjected.

Arruk paused for a stunned three-second shock at Ramaki's intelligence. "Yes. The daughter that is flying there now to reunite with her parents. We have no boots on the ground in Canada, but I know that you do. We know they live in Vancouver. But we don't know their new names or address. Or do you also know that too?" Arruk's question carried an icy tone of cynical suspicion.

"No, Arruk. I do not."

I ask that you provide a tracker from the airport in Vancouver so that we can bring the Katz couple back into the fold, my brother. We're quite sure that Mossad will be there too, and we need to ensure that we stay ahead of Israel on this. I can have my agents there shortly. But not for a day or two. A lot depends on this, my brother. I'll owe you favors, like I said, ten-fold if Iran will give us aid with this."

Iran did in fact have a secret presence in Canada. After another minute of terse conversation, Ramaki agreed to help Arruk for several days until Arruk could get his own agents there. But Ramaki made it clear that, for the highest interest of Iran, word of Iran's involvement must never find its way to either CSIS or the CIA.

*

Having had a lot of time to run all the past weeks and days events through his mind over and over, Christian had decided that it was not he that was the ultimate target of the search, but Ishi alone. *Likely because of her biological parents.* And now that she was safely on her flight, he decided to come out of hiding.

On his way home, he detoured past Vacha to the Gruber farm. He knew that the animals were at least a full day overdue for attention. So, he decided to go do the chores. As he turned onto the driveway, the sight of the completely burned rubble that used to be Ishi's house sickened him in his stomach.

The pigs, chickens, cows, and horse were all very eager for food. But milking was the trickiest part of it all because one of two milk pails had been inside the burned house. So, Christian milked one pail full, then made a little more room in the pail by fetching his travel mug from his car and filling that, then filling the pail again from the third of the three relieved cows. But, what now to do with all this milk? He put the full pail into his car on the passenger's side floor, and driving extra slowly and smoothly, he went home spilling a bit of milk onto his passenger floor mat along the way.

*

Azim and Saadia were almost back in Vacha. Earlier that afternoon, Abadi had informed them of the failure at the airport, and that the Katz girl was en route to Vancouver. Abadi had also said that General Arruk was arranging people at the Vancouver International Airport to pick up the girl's trail. "Drop Vacha. Drop the other kid, the boyfriend. Leave the store. You're going to be exfiltrated back to Palestine. Just stand by for instructions," Abadi had ordered. "Oh and," he had added, "we are assuming that Akeem is no longer with us."

To that, Saadia had gasped and asked, "What do you mean, no longer with…"

"Has been eliminated."

It was a kick in her stomach! Saadia instantly felt the energy drain completely out of her. After a few moments of absorbing the news, she asked feebly, "By who?"

Abadi replied, "We're trying to find out. Best guess is Mossad."

After the call ended and after Saadia had relayed its contents to Azim, the realization hit them both at once … *We were not alone in Vacha that entire time. Mossad was there!* Azim and his mother, deflated and sickened about Akeem, continued the last sixty-five kilometers toward their house with thoughts of their leader, their beloved recruiter, front and center in their sad minds, thoughts combined with embarrassment at their professional sloppiness of not anticipating the presence of Mossad in Vacha. Azim just gazed unfocused out of the passenger window as his mother drove. *What a disaster!*

*

Christian laid on his back in his bed, his head propped up slightly by two pillows, his hands folded behind his head. Even though he was now back in the comfort of his home, with the intention of grabbing a needed nap, he couldn't get to sleep. He glanced at the digital clock radio on the side table. 2:18pm. His brain wouldn't stop. There were so many details! It was hard to make them make sense. *Where are the Grubers? Ishi's unknown past, … and the Adris knew about it. Mister Adri speaking Arabic. The woman shooting Mister Adri. Burning the house down. Why burn down the house? Were they trying to kill Ishi? Why?* As he repeated these thoughts over and over, it impacted on Christian again how big these forces likely were. *Why Ishi?* He remembered that woman simply making a quick phone call to have Mister Adri's car and body cleaned up.

They're not just going to let Ishi fly away, Christian suddenly realized in horror! He jumped out of bed and paced his bedroom, trying to put his thoughts together. He pulled on his pants and walked down the hall to the kitchen to get a drink of water. *She's alone! She's completely alone now!* That thought ran through him with a chill of anxiety.

Christian assumed that he wouldn't know how to explain this to his parents anyway, especially since he couldn't even make sense of it himself, so he just decided that he'd call them from along the way. He put some clothes and toiletries into a suitcase, made sure that he had some cash and his bank card in his wallet, and pulling on a shirt, a light jacket, and his shoes, he quietly exited the front door and walked to his car that was parked on the street in front of the house.

*

Despite everything swarming through her mind, the take-off in the Boeing 767 was amazing, exhilarating! She desperately wanted to call her mom and dad and explain the experience to them. That thought and desire, though, ushered back brutal reality.

Now, even though Ishi had been awestruck by all the elements of the flight to Toronto, she easily resisted the mild temptation to watch an inflight movie. Instead, she slept quite solidly for nearly four hours. An in-flight attendant had politely awakened her for a meal. After the meal, Ishi slept another two hours.

Clearing Customs in Canada was smooth, and she was proud to get a first official stamp of a foreign country in her passport. *I wish I could show this to my mom and dad,* she thought painfully.

The layover at Toronto's Pearson International Airport was scheduled to be only seventy minutes before she was due to board at Gate 4c for the flight to Vancouver. As she walked through the huge airport, she stopped in at several shops, marvelling at the high prices of items in those shops. She knew that she had been wearing the same shorts and shirt, a dirty white t-shirt for several days. Plus, she hadn't been outside in Canada yet, and had no clue about Canadian summers. "Are they hot, cool, cold?" So, despite that it was July, she decided to play it safe. Quickly browsing through two shops in the concourse, she found a cute minty green t-shirt without any Canadian or touristy insignias. She also selected a ruby-red pullover hoody. She bought them both.

Ishi didn't know what Canadians should look like. She didn't know anything about Canada really. She found it interesting and actually somewhat bewildering that all the people she was seeing looked just like all the people back home in Germany. Seeing a restaurant called Flight Deck, she decided to plant herself there for fifteen minutes to eat a burger or something.

English was a mandatory course in school in Germany. That, together with having watched countless English-language movies and also having sometimes spoken English for practice with her peers ... all together gave Ishi enough confidence to try ordering her burger in English. Ishi was pleased how well she did.

With the burger and Caesar salad eaten, she looked at her phone and realized that she still had thirty-five minutes. She glanced at her phone again and wondered if it would work here away from Germany. The thought that crossed her mind filled her with nervous excitement. *Should I try to call her? What will she think? Will she even answer?* Ishi hesitated, wondering if she should find a more private spot to do this. After paying her café bill with euros, she realized that she should go back a small distance through the concourse to the exchange kiosk that she had seen and change her remaining seven-hundred and forty euros into Canadian dollars.

Finished at the kiosk, she looked at her phone again to see how much time she had left. Twenty-two minutes. She found a spot near a big sculpture where there were no people. She opened her email. "Good!" she thought. "My email works here. So, I guess my phone might work too?" She scrolled down and found the email from Family Tree. Opening it, she memorized the phone number for Rebecca Wiess.

With shaking fingers, she entered the phone number and hesitated before hitting 'Call'. *What if she doesn't want to hear from me?* Ishi ran an anxious hand through her long brunette hair. *No, that's crazy! She registered for a search just like I did. Of-course she wants to hear from me. But maybe she registered years ago, and has forgotten about it or regrets it? What if ...* With no further hesitation, Ishi tapped the 'Call' button.

CHAPTER 33

Rebecca Wiess had answered on the fourth ring. Ishi was almost speechless, not in surprise, but in the gravity of that "hello".

They had talked, both of them stressed and excited. But they had talked for nearly eight minutes. Ishi had informed Rebecca that she was arriving from Germany via Toronto to Vancouver at 2:15pm Vancouver time, and could they meet either at the airport or somewhere? Rebecca had ecstatically assured Ishi that she would meet her at the airport. Rebecca had described her appearance briefly so that Ishi would recognize her. Ishi then did the same. "… long dark brunette hair, white t-shirt, shorts."

Before the Toronto-to-Vancouver flight, just as the airplane was taxiing to take off, her cell phone dinged announcing a text message. It was from Christian. "Ishi, do NOT meet your parents at the airport!! I've been thinking. It's not safe. Please!" Instantly, a wave of terror rushed through Ishi's body.

She texted back, "Okay. Thanks???" Immediately after that, the flight attendant instructed everyone to turn their phones off.

Disobeying that order and pushing her luck, immediately, she called back to Rebecca. "I can't meet you at the airport."

"Why?"

Ishi admitted, "There might be someone, umm … I think some people are following me. I know, I know I sound paranoid, but …"

A wave of fear streaked through Rebecca too. Even though there were so many years between them and past events, Rebecca knew well what large factors might still be in play. Rebecca replied, "Okay, I understand. I'll think of a place to meet. Can I text that to you once I think of it?"

"Yes, of course. But I might not get your text while flying."

Rebecca responded, "But you'll at least see it once you're on the ground before passing through the Arrivals Gate. Alright Ishi, be sure to check for the text message!"

Rebecca, horrified, realized that she likely in-fact opened Pandora's Box by doing the ancestral genetic search!

Ishi had butterflies in her stomach as the airplane soared westward over the mountains of British Columbia. The pilot had just announced that they'd be landing shortly. *Oh, I'm so nervous!* Suddenly she felt very far from home. *But I don't have a home.* To her relief, for most of the last eight hours of flying, she had mostly not thought about all the horrible events that led up to this moment but instead while enjoying her window seat, had marvelled at the landscapes below, and had slept a little bit more.

With only twenty minutes of flight remaining, butterflies began to flap harder in Ishi's stomach. *If Christian's instincts are right ... He wouldn't send such a frightening text for no reason. If his instincts are right, then I'm no safer here than back in Germany.* The butterflies turned into a sickening clench in her body.

From having looked at maps online while at Toronto Pearson Airport, she knew that the next airport near Vancouver is in a city called Abbots-something. *Oh!* The tension in her body was making her nauseous. She waved at a flight attendant that was approaching up the aisle.

The flight attendant, a middle-aged man with slick blonde hair asked, "Yes, how can I help you?"

Ishi asked, "Is it possible to book a connecting flight from here? I mean, right now while I'm flying?"

"Yes, you can book it online as soon as we're on the ground. But you'd just need to go to the ticket counter to get your ticket."

Ishi knew immediately that that wouldn't solve anything because she'd be exposing herself by going to the ticket counter. "Okay, thanks." She frowned.

Ishi was thinking fast! *What can I do to somehow be unseen?*

As the Airbus A321-200 taxied to the gate, Ishi turned her phone back on.

Immediately, the phone dinged. She checked. "Take a taxi to Granville Island. Farmer's Market. I'll be waiting at the north side at the meat section. See you soon!" Ishi put the phone down and thought. Another ding! "Text me when you're in the taxi, please."

"I will. Just getting off the flight now."

There was no way, of course, for Ishi to know that her mother was sitting in her white Ford Explorer on the second level of the airport parkade.

Leah Fromm had cleared Customs just fifty minutes earlier and was sitting at a table at the edge of the large food fair area monitoring one of several nearby flights screens that displayed arrivals. With her taco salad on the table, mostly eaten, and her luggage sitting beside her, she appeared to be a typical traveller. She felt well rested after the desperately needed sleep that she got during her non-stop flight.

Ten minutes earlier, she discreetly received a small belt-clip microphone and a Sig Sauer P938 9mm handgun from Mack Ture while they waited in line next to each other at the food fair Taco Bell.

Athletically built mid-forties Mack Ture stood tall next to Leah at six-feet four-inches. His demeanor was always one of easy charm. His curly dark messy hair and his shirt worn out of his jeans only added to his casual demeanor.

After the gun hand-off to Leah in the Taco Bell line up, Mack had exited the main terminal and taken a position on the parking ground level between two SUVs where he had a clear view of all four main double glass entrance doors into the Arrivals level of the terminal. He also had a Sig Sauer P938 tucked into his back waist.

Leah spotted the Iranian as soon as she sat down at the table. She had let Mack know right away by pretending to check her phone for messages and mumbling toward the microphone clipped to her belt. Leah's and Mack's microphones were better than phone connection because it allowed them to stay in constant live contact. Although Leah was aware that there is a large Iranian population in Greater Vancouver, she recognized this agent. His name escaped her at the moment, but she had studied his profile in past years.

"What are the Iranians doing here?" she whispered to Mack.

"Iranians? You sure?"

"Yes, I'm sure. And I recognize this one. He's standing by the window on the opposite side of that big Indigenous sculpture. You might even be able to see the back of him through the window."

"I can't see anything through the windows. The sunlight out here."

"Well, keep your eyes open out there for more of them!"

*

Omar Abadi had just finished a call to Azim Bakir. He had instructed Azim and Saadia to go through Adri Foods and their house very thoroughly today, cleaning up anything that could be incriminating. Then by the end of the day, they must drive to Frankfurt for exfiltration back to Palestine. Abadi sat alone in a Frankfurt café bakery with his tea and scone. Earlier that day, he had sent his team back to Palestine via a flight through Damascus, Syria.

His phone buzzed and vibrated. "Hello?"

General Arruk's voice was serious as usual. "Omar Abadi, I want you and Azim Bakir to fly to Vancouver, Canada today. Your papers are being prepared and will be ready within the hour."

"But, my English?"

Arruk rebutted, "That's why Azim is going with you. Azim's English is good. You need to manage him. Saadia Bakir can return to Hebron as planned."

Abadi asked, "But we don't have their new names or an address."

Arruk replied, "We will. I have people there at the Vancouver airport as we speak. As soon as you land in Vancouver, get a burner, text me the number, and I'll text all the details to you on that. Then destroy it and get another one. Understand, Omar Abadi?"

Abadi replied, "Yes, General."

Arruk's voice grew angrier, "After so many years, let's finally clean up this mess. Bring it to an end!"

"Yes, General Arruk."

*

"Can he see you?" Mack asked Leah.

Leah mumbled back, "I think so. Easily."

"And?"

Leah answered, "I'm a hundred percent sure that I'm not on the Iranian Prime Intelligence radar. I'm confident that I'm okay just like this."

She took her phone and after going through the double-code screening process, sent an update text to Jonathan Ben Dod.

Mack asked, "See any PLO signs?"

Leah replied, "No. Iran might be stepping in as a proxy. That's my guess."

As Ishi walked out of the airplane and through the ramp, she quickly punched in a quick text. "Chris, I'm in Vancouver. Exiting the plane." She wasn't completely confident that the text would get through to Christian. But the text tag read 'sent', so she assumed that it worked.

Along with other passengers, Ishi exited the gangway and turned left into a long plain corridor that was lined along the left side, the runway side, with massive floor to ceiling windows. After thirty or forty meters, she followed the corridor and the other passengers as it turned right and led deeper into the terminal building. Ahead, she saw two restroom doorways, one for each gender. Relieved, she walked into the woman's restroom. Sitting on the plastic toilet seat, she sent another text. "I don't remember if I mentioned their names. David and Rebecca Wiess. Bye. Miss you." The text tag read 'sent'.

After pulling her new t-shirt and the ruby red pullover out of the bag, ripping the tags off, and putting them both on, she stuffed her dirty white t-shirt back into the bag and turned back into the corridor to continue into the terminal. All her thoughts went to her situation. *How can I get to a taxi without being recognized?*

Passing the baggage carousel area, Ishi stopped to think. As she saw several single young men waiting for their luggage, an idea was forming.

She spotted a man who appeared to be in his mid-twenties standing by a carousel waiting for his luggage. Ishi's shaky nervousness gave way to desperate action now. She approached the man as confidently as possible. The young man, seeing the beautiful young woman approaching him with a smile, smiled back and turned to her.

Ishi tried hard to speak English with as little German accent as possible, "Hi. You just arrived too, I see."

He replied, "Yep. Luggage takes a while though."

"May I ask you a favor? It's a bit strange though."

His smile immediately faded as he instantly remembered all the TV shows he'd seen about border contraband-related arrests. Skeptical, and also suspicious of the detectable German accent, he asked, "Okay?"

"Listen, while I was away in Toronto, I found out that my boyfriend was cheating on me. Now he's out there," she pointed toward the exit, "waiting to meet me. I'm pissed! I don't want to go with him. And I want to rub it in a bit."

The young man's face showed his interest in what she was saying. He was relieved that she wasn't asking him to carry anything for her, but wary about her accent, he asked, "Do you live here?"

Oh, my accent worries him! "Yes. Moved a while ago from Germany. Can we exit together through the terminal as far as a taxi so that I can just get past him and take a taxi? I mean, together, like we're madly in love?"

The man liked her suggestion. *It'll be fun to help this gorgeous girl give her cheating boyfriend some karma.* He smiled. "Sure!"

Nearly four minutes later, as he towed his suitcase with his right hand, the young man and Ishi passed the official and handed in their declaration slips, then walked through the exit together embracing and laughing. Ishi, her red hood up over her head, was clinging to him closely, trying to bury her face in his shoulder as much as possible without being completely weird about it.

Both the Iranian agent and Leah had been trying to get a good look at the girl snuggled into her boyfriend's side. As the young couple passed through the concourse and were nearing the outside double doors, Leah thought she recognized Ishi. Instantly Leah said to Mack, "Target exiting with boyfriend in five seconds! Red pullover. I'm following." Leah jumped to her feet and walked quickly, following.

The Iranian saw the young couple too, and had also been trying to get a look at the girl's face. But he had his doubts until he noticed the woman from the food fair jump up and follow them. *Oh, oh! Mossad are here just as General*

Ramaki warned. While instantly following, he raised a small hand mic to his mouth, "Girl exiting now with boyfriend. Red hoody. Bring the car up!" A short squelching sound on the mic offered confirmation that the Iranian's accomplice was complying. The Iranian added, "And, we're not alone. Unknown agents. Could be CSIS or Mossad. Woman. Light green jacket. Short. Black luggage. She's in pursuit of the girl."

Ishi and her new friend had exited and were now just outside the main doors at the nearest taxi. Ishi quickly kissed the young man on the cheek. "Thanks!"

As she dove into the back seat of the yellow taxi, she heard him say, "That was fun."

"Where to, Miss?"

Ishi quickly instructed, "Granville Island. Farmer's Market."

The taxi driver responded, "Okay."

"Please rush. I'm terribly late."

The cab jerked from its standing position, and they were on their way.

Rebecca had parked on parking level 2 at the only available stall near the middle of the floor that was packed full of vehicles. She had walked to the concrete second floor ledge overlooking the three-lane-wide avenue that runs past the airport's main Arrivals entrance. Approximately ten meters to both her left and her right were two elevated glass-enclosed walkways that bridge from parking level 2 to the Departures level of the terminal. She had a good view down to the entrance from there.

When she saw the young couple come out through the doors below, she had to look twice because she didn't anticipate Ishi being with a guy. *That girl is wearing a red pullover, not a white t-shirt.* But Rebecca got a pretty good look at the girl's face. *It's Ishi!* Rebecca was instantly smacked with mixed emotions of love and a desire to call out. *Why didn't she mention the boyfriend?* Then when she saw Ishi get into the yellow taxi alone, she began to understand. *My daughter has grown up to be clever.*

Just as Rebecca began turning to run to her SUV, she saw a woman race out of the airport to another taxi. The woman almost recklessly tossed her suitcase in and then jumped in after it. That red taxi sped away trailing Ishi's yellow taxi.

Less than five seconds later, Rebecca saw that close behind the red taxi, a black sedan lurched out of the spot where it sat. The sedan stopped as a middle-aged dark-featured man ran out of the airport and jumped into the sedan. It sped ahead seemingly to catch up to the taxis.

The horrible realization that major forces were following her daughter seemed to in-fact be confirmed. She sprinted to her vehicle and jumped in. Before she started up her white Ford, she realized that, by the time she could get out of this parking lot, she'd be far behind the three cars. She grabbed her phone and called.

Ishi answered cheerfully, "Hi!"

Rebecca's voice was urgent. "Ishi, there are at least two teams in separate cars following you right now."

She heard Ishi gasp.

"Don't panic! I'm behind you too, just a bit farther back."

"Ohhh, what is happening? What should I do? What do they want with me?"

Rebecca's voice was firm, "Listen, this is serious. But listen to me! Keep going to the Granville Island Farmer's Market as planned. Your taxi driver will know exactly where it is. Listen carefully, Ishi! When he drops you, pay before you're completely stopped! Pay in cash. Overpay if you have to … just to be quick. When he drops you, walk into the market. Then as soon as you're inside, run all the way through and out of the back of it. That will put you on the waterfront right where tiny little ferries go across the channel. Take one of those as fast as possible. Did you follow all that?"

Ishi answered, her voice frail, revealing her fear, "Yeah, I think so."

"Okay. Repeat it back to me!"

Ishi recited, "I pay in advance. I go to Granville Island Farmer's Market. Walk in. Then run out of the back and take a little tiny water taxi. Where?"

Rebecca answered, "They only go across to one spot. Sunset Beach. I'll be waiting there. If you don't see me standing waiting, I'll be in a white Ford Explorer SUV."

"Okay. I think I got it."

Rebecca added, "One more thing Ishi. Text me I'm here or something just before or when you're on the little water taxi, okay."

"Okay."

Ishi cautiously sneaked a peek over her shoulder through the taxi's back window. There were many vehicles. There was no way she could tell which ones would be following her. She clenched her hand tightly around her phone, absolutely terrified!

"I'm really late. And I'm going to be in big trouble." Ishi pleaded to the cabbie, "Is it possible to go just a bit faster, please?" Ishi had leaned over slightly to pull her small, folded wad of dollars from her shorts' front pocket, and dissected three twenty-dollar bills out. She handed the twenties over the cabbie's shoulder. The taxi driver looked at her in the mirror, took the money and said nothing. However, Ishi sensed that his driving became a bit more aggressive.

As Leah continued to put pressure on the taxi driver to follow that yellow taxi, she saw that they were falling behind. She was desperate! To lose Ishi now would be to lose altogether. She pulled the Sig Hauer pistol out of her handbag.

Keeping the gun concealed, Leah shouted, "Pull over! Pull over! Stop the car!"

The taxi driver wide-eyed looked in the mirror. "It's Granville Street. I can't …"

Leah yelled, "Stop the car! Let me out!"

The driver protested, "But it's a busy street."

Nevertheless, he slowed and pulled over to the curb. Instantly, horns began to blare behind him. Leah put the gun to the back of his head. "Get out!" The driver didn't have to be told again. He frantically undid his seatbelt, opened his door, and nearly fell out of the car in his panicked rush, while at the same time trying desperately to avoid busy traffic in the next lane. As he was exiting, Leah was already climbing over the seat and struggled to quickly get into the driver's seat. Once there, she threw the car into 'Drive' and sped forward as she plopped the gun down on the passenger's seat.

The black sedan with the Iranians were caught in the jammed traffic behind the incident ahead. But they were only three cars back of the red taxi, so they had a visual on it as it sped forward. Without time to wait for confused cars ahead of them to get going again, the Iranian at the wheel cranked the steering wheel to the right and drove up onto the grassy tree-belt between the street and the sidewalk. Dodging several trees by lurching around onto the sidewalk twice, the Iranians managed to leapfrog ahead of at least two other cars. There was now only one car between them and the red speeding taxi ahead. And they had a visual of the yellow taxi almost a full block ahead.

Approximately ten or twelve minutes along Granville Street, Leah was only two cars behind Ishi's yellow taxi as it suddenly took an off-ramp to the right. The ramp was a sharp decline down to Marine Drive. The yellow taxi merged aggressively onto Marine Drive and then immediately merged again into the center and then the far-left lane. Leah could see that it was going to be turning left where the huge overhead green sign read Granville Island with a large black arrow pointing left. Aggressively pinching the car between traffic, she followed merging left, earning angry blasts from horns. Now there were three cars between Leah and the yellow taxi, but Leah assumed that not all of them would be turning left into Granville Island.

The black sedan followed two cars behind Leah's red taxi, merging rudely and dangerously, drawing long angry horn blasts.

Both Mossad and the Iranian agents had clear instructions to not apprehend, hurt, or even spook the Katz girl. Their objective was to follow her to her parents. But they absolutely could not lose her. And right now, trying to not lose her altogether definitely included the strong probability of spooking her. Neither Mossad nor the Palestinian Authority had been able to learn the new names of Joseph and Sonya Katz. So, desperation to not lose the daughter won as the only remaining conceivable option.

Assuming that there was no way that her live mic with Mack would've kept connected at such distances, Leah grabbed her phone and hit a speed dial button.

Mack Ture answered instantly. "Where are you?" he asked eagerly.

"Driving onto a place called Granville Island. Where are you? What are you driving?"

"White Camry. I ran to my rental in the parkade and got out too slow. I'm nearly all the way downtown along Granville Street. Crossing over False Creek now."

Leah tried to remember the city map that she had studied during her flight. "Then you've over-shot. Use your map app. Navigate back to Granville Island. I'll need a lift. I stole the taxi."

"You stole the ... You what?!"

The car lurched and Leah's head hit the roof as she took a speed bump far too fast. The phone tumbled from her hand onto the passenger's floor. As the yellow taxi ahead was pulling up in front of a huge Public Market, she glanced to the passenger's seat to see if the gun also fell to the floor. It didn't. It was still on the seat.

The yellow taxi had stopped, and quickly the hooded girl stepped out and was walking into the market. Leah arced to the right, then pulled a hairpin left and drew up with her passenger door mere inches from the yellow taxi driver's door. She lowered the passenger's window to catch the attention of the other driver.

"Is she coming back?" Leah shouted.

The other taxi driver looked bewildered at first, and then shook his head.

"Shit!" Leah hissed. She tried to bend down to grab her phone, but the shoulder strap wouldn't let her. Frantically she undid her seat belt, bent way down and grabbed the phone, then grabbed her gun. Just as she was straightening back up, she saw the black sedan driving straight at her door picking up speed. Nimbly and desperately, Leah launched herself over the console to the passenger's seat. The black car kept coming! She aimed her gun and fired three shots straight at the driver of the black sedan. As blood blew from the driver's head onto the sedan's windshield, the black car rammed the red taxi, throwing Leah hard against the passenger door. Shocked and stunned, Leah opened the door, banging it hard against the yellow taxi as the yellow taxi lurched forward and away from the mayhem. Leah fell out onto the pavement, landing hard.

Ouuw! My shoulder! Despite the immediate pain in her left shoulder from crashing down onto the asphalt, Leah knew that she must follow that girl into the market. With pure adrenaline, Leah launched to her feet and raced into the market. *My gun!* With her gun visible in her right hand, she instantly tucked it into her belt at her waist as she ran. Realizing that the gun was still somewhat visible, she continued to rush desperately into the market.

The Iranian in the passenger's seat was momentarily dazed by both the collision and the death of his partner. But five seconds later, he too was on his feet and running into the market.

Ishi had sprinted quickly through the market. It was bigger than she had anticipated, and with many shoppers. She bumped through a lot of people as she pinballed her way to the rear of the building. Suddenly, she was out of the rear at the waterfront. Ishi bent over momentarily, panting, trying to catch her breath. She had barely heard the gunshots and the car crash behind her, but she had heard them. It filled Ishi with desperate energy. She didn't, however, notice her phone bounce its way out of her red pullover pocket somewhere in the market.

Just as Rebecca had said, there were tiny water taxis there at the end of the dock. Two of them. Ishi sprinted toward the one that was nearly full of people and jumped on, drawing frowns of disapproval from other boarded passengers.

Looking toward the pilot, she asked, "Wie viel kostet es?" Quickly catching her mistake, she repeated in English, "How much?"

He answered with a grin, "Drei dollar." She handed him a ten while looking back toward the rear of the market to see if her assailants had come out through the back. The pilot handed her back a five-dollar bill and two coins. She waived off the coins.

Less than fifteen anxious seconds later, the miniature water taxi put out to water. Ishi hunched down among the other riders, keeping an eye on the rear of the market. When they were two or three minutes away from the dock, Ishi finally pulled the hood off her head and looked around to see where they were going. She saw that they were approximately halfway across the channel heading under a huge bridge and toward a dock at a wide sandy beach. Behind the beach Ishi saw a parking lot. *Oh! I'll be too easy to identify in this red pullover!* She whipped it off. At the same time, she realized that she couldn't feel her phone in her pocket. She reached down. It wasn't there! Panicking, she went through the pockets of the pullover and of the bag with her old t-shirt. It was gone! The sudden despair made her feel like she would have a heart attack!

After zig zagging through the market, Leah had to constantly duck down below vendors' bins for the first twenty seconds to avoid being seen by the searching Iranian. Then, she watched the Iranian run back out of the front of the market.

The Iranian agent realized that he had to get the car and his dead partner away before police arrive. He saw a crowd of horrified onlookers near the car, two of them right at the driver's door. He pulled his handgun. Waving it back and forth like a wand, he sent the crowd running for cover, screaming. He assessed the damage to the front of the car. It was bad enough, but he hoped that most of the damage stayed with the squashed bumper. He hoped the car would start. Opening the rear door and then the driver's door, he undid the driver's seatbelt, then pulled the bloody dead body out and dragged and heaved it into the back seat. Glancing around, he saw several people cowering back into the market, many of them with their hands over their mouths, wide-eyed. They were not just watching. Some of them were holding up their phones taking pictures and video. *Shit!* Quickly, he pushed accordion-style the legs of his dead partner all the way in, slammed the rear door closed, and jumped into the driver's seat. He turned the key. There was a loud scraping grinding noise. Instantly he realized that the car engine was still running. "Good!" *Thank you, Allah.* As the car lurched backward, he heard some car pieces falling off the front and onto the pavement. Five seconds later, with rising steam and a constant screeching noise growing quickly louder from the car's damaged radiator fan, he had driven off Granville Island and was gone.

Leah realized that she had lost track of the girl. Also, it was obvious that Ishi would now know for sure that she was being followed. Leah remembered that she just shot a man in front of many onlookers. *This whole thing is an unmitigated disaster*, Leah knew!

Seeing that a number of people were pointing at her and also on their phones, no doubt calling nine-one-one, she disappeared quickly out through the open rear of the market. Finding herself at the waterfront exactly where Ishi had been minutes earlier, Leah quickly scanned right and left, but saw no sign of Ishi. Then, she turned to her right and ran along a narrow sidewalk that ran along the very edge of the small island along the water. She hurried along, a waterside concrete rail to her left and tall walls of buildings on her right, her shoulder screaming at her in pain! As she ran, she passed a few docks on her left, a café entrance on her right, what appeared to be an office entrance to her right, and then after approximately a hundred meters, the sidewalk abruptly ended where the buildings ended. She found herself at a grassy park with a children's playground. Ducking to her right into an architectural recess in the last of the row of buildings that she had just run past, facing into the playground, she felt behind her at her waist to ensure that she hadn't dropped her gun. It was still there, but as she moved her arm, the shrieking pain in her left shoulder shocked her! She grabbed her phone out of her pants pocket and called Mack Ture. Mack answered instantly.

Heaving for breaths, she explained, "The Iranians -- made me. They -- rammed my car to try to -- to try to disable me. I shot one of them. It's a mess. There's a crowd. I'm at a small park. Playground. Just east of a bunch of five or six-story buildings. Try a different street. Avoid the crowd!"

CHAPTER 34

Rebecca was nearly a collapsing wreck from nervous fear as she stood at the dock waiting. Ishi hadn't texted. She saw the little water taxi getting closer, but she couldn't yet see faces of the group onboard. Rebecca was looking for the ruby-red pullover, but not seeing it. She began to panic. *Oh no! They caught up with her on the other side.* She walked fearfully halfway along the dock as the tiny ferry got close.

Moments later, Ishi, red pullover draped over an arm, was walking toward Rebecca looking at her analytically. Ishi had seen her photo on the Family Tree email, but with fear and doubt of everything now permeating Ishi, she needed to be absolutely certain. She viewed the woman looking at her. The woman then took several quick steps toward her, stopped and put her hands over her mouth. Unsure why the woman stopped and put her hands over her mouth like that, Ishi quickly and fearfully glanced behind her to see if there was danger. With most of the other taxi riders already past her, there seemed to be nothing of concern. She looked again toward Rebecca.

Rebecca had now fallen to her knees and was weeping, her eyes up and trained on Ishi. Ishi's steps slowed as the significance of this occasion began to impact her.

"Ishi!" Tears of joy and relief streamed down Rebecca's cheeks.

Waves of confusing emotions swept through Ishi. She walked to Rebecca who stood up, stretching her arms forward. Rebecca embraced her daughter passionately. Ishi hugged in return, but there was little passion. Ishi did not know this woman.

As Rebecca and Ishi drove quickly out of the parking lot and onto Pacific

Boulevard, Ishi's mind raced. *Am I still in danger? Did they see me? This is my mother? Where are we going?* Feelings of shame of betrayal begin to needle at Ishi's mind. *What about my real mother? Where is my real mother? I'm so far from home!*

Checking her mirrors constantly, Rebecca drove aggressively two blocks one way, one block another way, suddenly pulled into an available parking space at the curb and waited for fifteen seconds, then repeated the seeming same zig zags, and then approached a bigger street that led toward a bridge that led out of the city center.

Rebecca said, "I'll get us to a place where we can talk, okay."

"Okay." Emotions of affection hadn't surfaced for Ishi. It had all been far too much for her brain to take!

Rebecca sensed Ishi's bewilderment at the zig zagged route. "Just taking an extra few turns to make sure we're safe. Don't worry!"

After having entered the only street onto Granville Island, Mack Ture, saw the throngs straight ahead by the Farmer's Market. He chose to turn right at the first of three streets on the small island to avoid the mayhem ahead. His GPS indicated that he could circle around the perimeter of the small island that way and still get to the location that Leah had described. The island had two parks, one beside a small boutique hotel on the island's far end, so he assumed that it would be the other one closer to the market, although he couldn't be sure because it was quickly obvious how very tiny Granville Island was.

As Leah saw the white Toyota Camry appear around the curve at the far end of her little park, she began jogging toward it, her shoulder throbbing with pain. Mack was relieved to see that the little road that circumnavigates the island, while narrow, was actually a two-way street. He immediately turned around and drove them out the same way he had arrived.

As they were exiting Granville Island left onto Marine Drive, they saw the lights and heard the sirens of police cars rushing toward the island from both directions.

"Ben Dod know?" Mack asked.

Leah gave him a sour look. "I guess I better call him." She winced and groaned in pain as she reached under her lap belt and pulled the phone out of her pocket, shaky hands fumbling the phone to the floormat. She retrieved it as she realized that her nerves were just now succumbing to the chaos. "He's not going to like this," she muttered the understatement.

As Rebecca drove the white SUV, she asked, "Did you book a hotel?"

Sheepishly Ishi replied, "No. I didn't think of it. I sort of didn't have enough time …"

"I did. Nothing amazing. Just a three-star. Maybe not even that. But it's close to our house. And it looks comfortable."

"Thanks. I can pay you back."

"Oh, no! I'd let you stay with us but," Rebecca quickly searched for words, "ummm, there might be an issue with your father."

It was strange, a kind of blasphemy to Ishi's senses, to hear anyone other than the father Ishi knew and loved to be referred to as her father. Ishi looked at her quizzically. "Issue?"

Rebecca said, "I'll explain as soon as we get to a spot where we can talk." Rebecca could hardly believe that her beloved Isabella was back from the dead and sitting right beside her. *Right here! Right now! Beside me!*

*

Apex Chalet Hotel, on the north side of Seymour Parkway, backs immediately onto the densely forested south slope of Mount Elsay. Rebecca chose this chalet-styled thirty-two room hotel because of its less-than-ten-minute distance to Rebecca's and David's house. When she booked it, Rebecca made sure to inspect the available second-floor room at the back side of the hotel to ensure that Ishi would be comfortable here. She was happy that the room wasn't in the front facing the main street, that, so Ishi would be able to enjoy peace and quiet.

Rebecca had gone home. Ishi stood gazing out of her hotel room window into the night at the dark forested North Vancouver mountain slope. She was looking at nothing really, unfocused on any mountainside there, but rather, attempting, but not succeeding, to process and compartmentalize both the drastic events of the day and the residual emotions. She drew the drapes closed.

Then she walked to the bed, climbed on, and positioned herself leaning against the square thick wood-panel headboard. *Exhausted! Even with all the sleep I got during flights.* Her face was red from crying for nearly the entire three hours that she and her mother talked. The entirety of all the information that had been shared was an insurmountable mountain of thoughts in her head. The weight of the information was too overwhelming! Her heart hurt. Her soul ached.

Earlier on the way to the hotel, Rebecca had stopped at a Shoppers Drug Mart where Ishi bought a set of necessary toiletries. She had scanned the store for cell phones too, but saw none.

After a few minutes, Ishi got back off the bed to take a desperately needed shower and to brush her teeth.

As the warm water poured over her, Ishi considered, *I'm now involved,* now familiar with the fact that her parents fled from a life of crime. *The fact that I even know now …* Her head hurt when she considered this. *I'm now an accomplice in a way.* She rubbed shampoo into her long hair. *If I keep it secret …* Aware now of Rebecca's -- her mother's story and two-decade-long plight, Ishi had an immediate goal to keep her protected. *But how? What if all these people looking for her find her? She'll absolutely be arrested or worse. Then I'll be arrested. But,* Ishi also realized the worse fate that likely awaited Rebecca if she went to the police and turned her in.

Ishi laid on her side, her head on the too-hard pillow. She had closed her eyes some time ago, but her thoughts raced. *I miss my mom and dad. Those evil cursed Adris! I'll bet mom and dad were kidnapped.* She turned over onto her other side, hoping that would stop her thoughts. *I'll bet mom and dad were …* She refused to finish that thought! She thought of the house burning down. She pictured her dad forking hay over the fence. Her mom in the kitchen. Emotions brought light sobbing as she laid there. She pictured Christian milking. *Oh, Chris!*

With all that she and her mother … her mother, her Sonya mother had talked about, and then stopping to get toiletries, since arriving here at the hotel, Ishi hadn't needed her missing phone. *I have to get a phone in the morning,* she thought! *I have to contact Christian.*

Can she and I run away and hide together? And then, what if we both get caught? What is the penalty in Israel for treason? Life in prison? Death sentence? Ohhh! Ishi's thoughts were all sad, heavy. The more she thought about it, the more she realized that there was no winning option. No way out of this.

And then, sleep rescued and relieved her.

*

General Arruk sat at his ornate teak desk. The morning sun shone brightly into his big window illuminating his cold angry deeply lined face as a uniformed desk clerk gently placed a tray with a tea set in front of him. As the desk clerk was exiting the General's office, he suddenly heard a crash against the far wall. Spinning around, he saw that Arruk had hurled the full tea pot against the far wall with white hot rage!

Arruk then picked up his phone and dialed. He knew that Abadi and Azim Bakir had just left Frankfurt and were in the air now, so they might not get this until they land in Vancouver. "Our so-called help in Vancouver has created a disaster. Call me the second you arrive! And," he yelled into the phone, "Omar Abadi, I want you to turn up every stone and pebble until you find that girl. Do you understand? If you fail, I will …" he restrained his words slightly. "Do not fail!"

*

Ben Dod had just had his nose, ears, and neck hair trimmed, and a shave. He walked out of the barbershop onto a bustling street in Tel Aviv, his bald dome shiny. His phone buzzed in his pocket. He put it to his ear.

"Iden."

He listened as Leah recited the identity code.

Calmly Ben Dod said, "Toto, we know who they are. Our tap on the airport cameras paid off. I knew eventually it would be worth having that tap. Iranians. We've had our eye on those two for some time. Well, I guess now thanks to you, there aren't two anymore."

He listened to Leah for a few seconds, then replied, "No Toto. We don't have quite that many tentacles into Canada. So, I want you and your agent to contact every hotel in Vancouver. I mean every single hotel big or small. Every single one!"

He listened again as Leah protested.

"Leah, we have no other good options. It's hard work, yes. What? Did you think you were taking a holiday to Vancouver?"

He listened for a few seconds more.

"Ah ah! Watch your tone, Toto! I still like you. I hope to keep it that way." Ben Dod heard the ding of an incoming text. He glanced at the screen and then put the phone back to his ear. "In the meantime, we're going to be reviewing parkade cameras for ins and outs sixty minutes prior and ten minutes after. By the way, it's only seven in the morning there. But you sound like you're at a café. Cafés are open so early in Vancouver?"

Perched at an elevated open window counter looking two steps down and out to Robson Street, Leah answered, "Yes, some are. Coffee is apparently a drug of choice for people here."

Jonathan Ben Dod put his phone away, turned to look at his clean bald head in a shop window's reflection, frowned, and walked toward his office.

With the call ended, Leah flicked a small dead moth from the counter near them out and down onto the patio lower and in front of where they sat at the window counter. She looked to her right at Mack Ture.

While she and Ben Dod were talking, Mack had come up with a burning question that he couldn't wait to ask. "Leah, you said you have her phone number."

Leah nodded.

"Well then, why don't you just call her?"

"I'm thinking about it. But I have a question for you first."

"You're thinking about it?" Ture's face revealed surprised exasperation. "Okay. What? Shoot!"

"Do you think," Leah began, "that you'd have enough pull with Ben Dod to bring one of our Denver techs up here? Someone that can get into the local phone system enough to triangulate a phone signal to its location?"

Mack gave Leah a look of astonishment. "No." He laughed out loud.

They both glanced at the other couple below them on the far side of the patio to ensure that they hadn't drawn undue attention. "No," Mack repeated quieter. "No can do."

Leah sighed and said, "Okay. I'll call her. I'll figure out a way to make it work."

Mack had an idea. "You have the boyfriend's phone number, right? From your little encounter on the highway in Germany?"

Leah nodded.

"Well, give him a little friendly 'How are you doing ole buddy?' call. Maybe let him know that for the protection of his girl from big bad enemies, he needs to keep you updated on what he knows."

Leah thought about this for at least fifteen seconds while she sipped her coffee. Then she said, "That might be worth a try." She nursed her left shoulder with her right hand while thinking.

Leah put words together in her head for several moments, then tapped Christian's phone number. It rang four times and then went to an answering message, "This is Christian. Can't make it to the phone right now, so please leave a message. Thanks."

Leah said, "Christian, this is the woman from the incident on the highway just outside Frankfurt. Listen Christian, I'm still trying to protect your Ishi. I'm in Vancouver where she is. But her enemies are here too. Please call me back at …" she quickly tried to remember the number of her burner phone, "… at one-six-zero-four-four-two-two-nine-nine-seven-eight if you hear from her. I can't reach her. But I fear that she might be in danger."

*

Omar Abadi and Azim Bakir sat next to each other in business class. Unaccustomed to being afforded such luxury, Azim ordered a second pillow from the attractive flight attendant. As she walked away toward the galley that separated economy from business class and disappeared past the curtain, Abadi said, "Okay, there's no point checking hotels. We don't even know if she's staying in a hotel. We might just waste our time." He grinned, "But do you know what we do know?"

"No. What?"

Abadi grinned, "We know that there are only two ancestral genetic-DNA search offices in Greater Vancouver. And we know that they will have all the contact information for her parents."

Azim shook his head, rejecting the idea, "They will be sworn to confidentiality. I'm sure."

"Yes brother, sworn to confidentiality. And we'll be persuasive. I'm sure."

As Azim considered Abadi's intent, he too began to grin.

The flight attendant returned and handed Azim the pillow. "Thank you," Azim said with his handsome and charming smile.

Abadi continued, "This flight doesn't have the Internet. But as soon as we land, I'll get addresses for both of them. We'll rent a car tonight. And first thing in the morning, we'll go fishing."

"You -- We will need," Azim lowered his voice, "guns. What about that?"

Abadi replied in a hushed voice, "We'll find guns. That's the easy part."

"How is that the easy part?"

"Brother, I didn't get into this line of work just last week. I know someone who knows someone who can do us a favor or two almost anywhere. We Palestinians have sympathizers all over the world you know, good men who also want Israel to sink to the bottom of the sea."

CHAPTER 35

Ishi was awake much earlier than she wanted to be. Besides her general skittishness from her overall situation, she had had bad dreams, jumbles of negative storylines that merged, but were nonsensical. Nevertheless, those dreams startled her awake just after six. She was not wide awake, though. A grogginess enveloped her.

Rebecca had given her clear and emphatic instructions to not use the phone in her room for security reasons. Without a phone, she had no way to call or text Rebecca or Christian. Ishi frowned at the prospect of simply waiting until Rebecca showed up at 11:00am to pick her up. *Why so late?* Ishi sighed in frustration. *First, absolute first order of priority is to get a phone!*

Ishi was waiting in the hotel lobby watching for the white SUV to appear. As it pulled up, Ishi ran out to it and jumped in. She looked at Rebecca. Ishi's eyes widened in shock! Rebecca's face was bruised and there was a gash on her right cheekbone.

"Oh!" Ishi couldn't believe what she was seeing. "What happened?"

As Rebecca began to drive forward, she said, "Ishi, sometimes your father is not a very nice person. You already know that from our talk yesterday …"

"Don't call him my father. Please!"

Rebecca paused a beat, and then continued. "When I came home after being out for so long yesterday, he was angry. So, to play it safe this morning, I chose to wait to come here until he had gone out, which I knew would be around ten-thirty."

Anger welled up in Ishi.

Yesterday, Ishi had learned of Rebecca's years of unwilling involvement in the criminal activity more than a decade ago. Rebecca had also briefly described the challenges with David since then. But this! Ishi's anger boiled! Then, in stark contrast she was struck with the memories of her mom and dad, how they were so peaceful and loving toward each other. *Oh,* Ishi thought in despair. *Where are my mom and dad?*

As they drove, Ishi's face showed the despair, the anger, the fear, and grogginess.

Rebecca could clearly see it. She asked, "Bad sleep?"

"Yes!" Suddenly, Ishi burst into tears.

Rebecca looked at her and placed her right hand on Ishi's leg, "What, sweetheart?"

Through sobs, Ishi uttered what she had already realized immediately yesterday even when arriving at the airport. "I shouldn't have looked for you," she blubbered.

"Don't say that! No, no, don't say that!"

"I've only brought trouble now. They followed me to find you." Her sobs intensified.

Rebecca didn't respond for some seconds as she gathered words. All yesterday afternoon, evening, and all night, Rebecca had been weighing too whether it had been worth it. She said, "Ishi, I went into searching for you with my eyes wide open. I knew the risks. But I had no way to know that you'd be in harm's way. I'm so so sorry, Sweetheart!"

Ishi continued to sob.

Rebecca tried to console her daughter, "I shouldn't have put you in danger. It's my fault. The last thing I wanted was for you to be in danger." Rebecca pulled over to a vacant spot at the curb. She put the vehicle into Park and turned to face Ishi. "We'll figure this out. We'll figure this out together. We will! I promise."

"How?"

"I don't know yet." Rebecca began again to drive. Several blocks later, she navigated the vehicle off the main street onto a smaller street toward a small shopping center where she knew of a phone store. "First though, you need to have a phone. It'll be a new number that only I will have."

Ishi shook her head. "I have to text Christian right away. He'll be losing his mind wondering if I'm alive."

Rebecca agreed, "Oh yes, of course."

As they drove through the huge mostly empty parking lot toward the phone store, Ishi looked at Rebecca's bruised and cut face. "I can go in and get a phone," Ishi offered, wanting to spare Rebecca the embarrassment.

Rebecca took a few moments to consider it. "Ummm, no," she finally said, "they'll need an address for billing and a credit card. It's okay. I'll go in too."

Almost half an hour later, Ishi and Rebecca walked out of the phone shop. As they walked across the parking lot, Ishi said, "It's amazing to me! The people here in Canada are just like the people back home … in Germany." Rebecca glanced at Ishi, not quite sure what to reply. Ishi continued, "I thought Canadians would be, umm, you know, different."

"Well, lots of Canadians came from Germany you know. And also lots of other countries from all over, including all the European countries."

"I had no clue. I guess I'd heard that Canadians spoke French and lived with lots of snow and mountains and in cold forests. Huh! What did I know?"

The moment they were back in the white Ford, Ishi immediately entered Christian's number as the first entry in her contact list, then typed out a message. "In Vancouver, but not safe. They followed me. Very scary! Met Rebecca. Nice. Love her! Not David. Lost my phone, so just now got a new phone. Did they leave you alone in Vacha yet? I'm either at my hotel or at my parents' house at …" Ishi turned to Rebecca. "What's your address again?"

"Four two eight Badger Road, Deep Cove." The moment after she recited it, Rebecca had second thoughts about giving out the address and about that address being texted. But she said nothing.

"428 Badger Road, Deep Cove. Call me or text me. Love you!" She tapped 'Send'.

Ishi had taken a step! A significant step. She had never used the word 'love' with Christian before. Ishi actually thought about it as she had intentionally typed it. Now, she was glad that she did it.

Rebecca smiled, "I think I'd like to buy my daughter some clothes." She glanced at Ishi with the big smile on her damaged face. "There's a good shopping center about ten minutes that way," she pointed.

Ishi smiled. "Sounds good!"

As they drove toward the shopping center, they said almost nothing. Both Ishi and Rebecca's minds were racing with tough considerations. There was so much to talk about, to catch up on. But right now, crucial methods for strategic safety needed to be focused on. Rebecca thought, *Okay. Ishi is here now. Where does this go now?*

As they drove, the sickening realization that locating and meeting her own biological parents and the crazy dilemma it created repeated itself in Ishi's brain. *If I keep it secret,* she kept thinking repeatedly, *then will I become an accomplice?* And now that Rebecca had confirmed in detail the criminal past, even if she was an unwilling participant, Ishi was quite sure that she is already an accomplice. *What are the odds of hiding from international intelligence agencies? Not good at all,* Ishi assumed. *On the other hand, if I would go to the authorities, if for no other reason for Rebecca's safety, then it would be guaranteed that Sonya and Joseph Katz would be extradited back to Israel to face justice. In that case, justice might end up being severe for Rebecca whether or not she was a willing participant all those years ago.* Ishi picked at her fingernails. *If they'd be caught and sent back, does Israel have the death penalty for treason? Plus, there was that agent that they killed back in Israel,* Ishi recalled that chilling part of Rebecca's story. Ishi didn't know. She shuddered at the thought! *Why in the world did I come here? This is an impossible situation!*

This dilemma had been heavy on Ishi's mind, but not as heavy as it might have been if her emotions and mind weren't already so jumbled up with the chaos and horrors of the past week beginning in Vacha immediately after her graduation. *Oh wow, graduation. That seems like ages ago!*

Rebecca knew that she must somehow tell David about Ishi. She was quite sure that he'd be very upset. But because enemies, God knows who they all are, had followed Ishi to Vancouver, David and Rebecca and Ishi might all be in jeopardy. *It would be reckless to not give David a heads-up,* Rebecca considered. *But then what might his anger look like?*

She asked Ishi, "What first? Shoes, shirts, or pants?"

Ishi and Rebecca found several good shops right beside each other inside the Capilano Shopping Center. As they approach them, Rebecca grabbed Ishi lightly by the arm, "Ishi, go ahead and start finding what you need. I'll catch up to you. I urgently need to call David. He'll be wondering where I am."

Ishi said, "Okay," but frowned as she walked toward the first shop, remembering the reason for the bruises and gash on Rebecca's face.

*

David, Rolly, and two other men sat at a table at Fat Friar's Pub. It was early, only just before 2:00pm, but there were back-to-back football games on. And the guys had been looking forward to this, especially because the Chiefs were playing.

The first game started nearly two hours ago, and David was halfway through his fourth beer. His phone emitted a tune indicating a call. He answered in a half-drunk slur while standing, grabbing his cane, and stepping away from the table, "What's up?"

Rebecca said, "David, something big has happened. Are you in a place where you can talk very privately?" She heard the pub noise in the background.

David instantly didn't like her question. He stepped toward the door and out into the parking lot and the bright July mid-day sun. "Yes. I'm outside now. What's up?"

Rebecca didn't know how to dance around it. She announced, "Ishi is alive."

David was silent. Rebecca listened to his silence, imagining his shock and anger.

"And, David, she is here."

Silence.

"In Vancouver."

Waves of emotions and thoughts and questions raced through David's mind all together. Rebecca could hear his breathing quicken with, what she assumed, was shock and probable fury. Still, he said nothing.

She added, "And, people have followed her. Uh -- people we wish didn't follow … People Ishi wishes didn't follow …"

"Fuckkkk!" David exploded. "Aaaaaaah! Aaaaaaaahg" He swung his cane hard against a nearby vehicle, causing a scar on the vehicle's fender.

"They've lost track of her. So that's good."

David hissed, "Why the …? How did she find us?" At the top of his lungs, he released a shrieking roar, "Aaaaaaaaaagh!"

Giving him a few moments to get his expletives out, Rebecca said, "It doesn't matter right now. The fact is, she's here. And …"

David yelled, "Why did you let her find …?" He suddenly realized-- *She's with her right now!* "She's with you right now, isn't she?"

"Yes. Listen David--"

"Damn it, Sonya!" immediately realizing and not caring about the name he had just yelled.

"Listen David, we need to come by the house in a bit. She's staying in a hotel. But I need to get her some things."

David snarled, "You're bringing her to our house? No! No, you're not!"

"Yes, I am!" Rebecca replied stubbornly. "It'll be quick. It's okay. Nobody knows where she is now. I know you're out, likely at Fat Friars. Just stay there!"

David ended the call with an angry punch of his finger. He stormed back into the pub, grabbed his keys and his beer, swigged the last half of it, and without explanation, in a not very straight line, with the aid of his cane, rushed back out of the pub, his friends watching him go.

CHAPTER 36

Christian walked through the Vancouver International Airport carrying his one piece of carry-on luggage. While he walked, he turned his phone back on. Ding! Ding! Ding! He saw that two text messages were from his parents. Christian knew that they'd be freaking out. *Oh, I can't. I'm just not ready to try to explain this to them yet.* One text message was from a number he didn't recognize, but he could see the beginning of the message. *Ishi?* He tapped on it and read. As he read, he stopped walking, and his mouth fell open as he murmured, "Oh no!"

He put his luggage down and immediately called Ishi. It rang six times, and then went to an automated message that said, "This customer has not set up voice mail yet. Goodbye." Christian groaned in frustration. He tried calling again. Same message. He texted, "Ishi, got your message. What!! They followed you?!! You okay? I tried calling you. You didn't set up voice mail yet. I'm going to drive to your parents' house now. Using the address you gave me. Btw, I'm in Vancouver. Surprise!"

Christian picked up his luggage and, following the signs, began sprinting toward the car rental section of the huge concourse.

*

An olive-skinned middle-aged man in construction clothes, a safety vest, and a hardhat walked from a back-alley into the small parking lot behind a Starbucks. He carried a green reusable grocery store bag. He walked through the parking lot, then sidestepped to an old-ish dark blue Dodge Caravan that was backed into a parking stall. Without a word, he passed the bag through the open driver's window, and continued walking through the parking lot and disappeared along the sidewalk to the right.

Omar Abadi peered into the bag and saw two Glock 19 handguns, four individual cartridges, and two boxes of bullets. He handed the bag to Azim, slid the shifter to D, and started forward out of the parking lot. As he drove, Azim pulled out the contents of the bag and began loading the cartridges.

*

In their hotel room, Leah and Mack had been calling hotels all morning and so far into the first part of the afternoon. Their line was "I'm looking for my cousin Isabella Gruber. She goes by Ishi. We know she's on a little holiday in Vancouver. But there's a family medical emergency back home, and we need to reach her right away. She's not answering her phone. Is she booked into your hotel?" So far, Leah and Mack had been coming up absolutely empty.

At 2:08pm just as Leah was stuffing a bite of a submarine sandwich into her mouth, she heard Mack say, "Oh, she is! Is she in her room now? Can you put me through?"

Leah frantically waved her finger 'no'! Mack corrected himself to the hotel clerk, "On the other hand, this is a very delicate bit of news that I need to tell Isabella. It's better I do it in person. I'm sure you understand. Is she in?" He waited for the response as he looked at Leah, her eyebrows raised. Ten more seconds passed. "She's not answering? Okay. Then I think I'll just come down there and wait for her. Oh, just a sec! Here's her sister."

Thinking it would help remove any sinister suspicions from the desk clerk by adding a female to the equation, he handed the phone to Leah who was trying to clear her mouth of the bite of submarine sandwich as fast as possible. Leah said, "Hi. Thanks. I'm her sister Kristy. We're on our way over. Thanks."

Even though it was a hot July day, Leah quickly slipped on a light jacket. Then, grabbing their handguns from where they lay on the bedspread, checking that they were loaded, Leah stuffed her gun into her jacket pocket. Mack tucked his gun into his belt at his back under the big shirt that he wore over a t-shirt and out of his pants, thus conveniently covering his belt and gun. They exited quickly.

*

Azim found a parking spot less than half a block from the Heritage office downtown. He and Abadi rode up in the elevator to the fifth floor. They exited the elevator and turned right to office door 523. They passed a young man exiting as they walked into the office. Pausing a few moments and glancing back ensuring that the young man successfully boarded the elevator, they approached the receptionist's desk.

The middle-aged woman greeted the men, "Hi there. Welcome to Heritage. How can I help you gentlemen?"

Azim replied, "Hello. I hope you can help us. Our friend has matched with her parents. She's coming here from her home in Germany, but we came ahead to set up a bigger formal surprise reunion for her. We don't have her parents' contact information though, so I'm wondering if you can give that to us so we can get started on organizing the party."

The woman looked at him skeptically. "That information is confidential, sir. I can't give that to anyone but the actual parties that registered their searches."

Azim sighed and muttered mostly inaudibly, "I hoped you wouldn't say that."

"Why don't you ask your friend for that information?"

Azim replied, "She's on the long flight now. There's no way to reach her. And by the time she lands here, it'll be too late for us to organize the party."

"I'm sorry sir. But I can't help you."

Azim employed his charming handsome smile. "Miss, can you at least let us know if our friend is on your system? We're not sure if she registered through you or through the other agency Family Tree."

The woman, frowning, looked at the young man for several moments. Then she asked, "What's her name?"

"Isabella Gruber. She also goes by Ishi Gruber. Nickname."

The woman typed and looked at her monitor. She typed again and looked at the results. She typed again and looked at the results. Then she looked up. "That name is not on our system."

Omar Abadi and Azim Bakir both frowned and looked at each other. Abadi looked back to the receptionist. "Thank you, Miss." They walked back toward the elevator.

*

Mack Ture had backed the white Camry into a parking stall opposite Apex Hotel's front door where they had a perfect view of any activity going in and out of the hotel.

"How long?" Mack asked.

Leah thought. Then she said, "No more than twenty minutes."

"Good! Enough time to order Quick Eats or whatever delivers around here."

Leah gave him a 'not funny' look. "So, it seems force is on the table. Your opinion? Will force be more productive with the hotel clerk or with the Katz girl?"

Mack answered immediately, "The clerk for sure."

"Why?"

"Because, if something goes wrong with the clerk, we haven't played our Ace. But if …"

"Agreed!"

*

The Family Tree office in North Vancouver, entirely different than the office Omar Abadi and Azim Bakir had just visited downtown, was on the ground floor of a four-story brown stone building. The front door was directly facing the spacious half-filled parking lot. Azim had parked the minivan just to the right out of direct view of any Family Tree windows.

Azim used the same line that he tried at the previous place. He finished, "…so I'm wondering if you can give that to us so we can get started on organizing the party."

The young woman behind the counter looked at him apologetically. "I'm sorry sir. I can't. I'm sorry but that information is strictly confidential to the registrant."

Azim tried his charming smile, "Please. It's so important to us."

The young woman just smiled back sheepishly and said again, "I'm so sorry. But I just can't."

"But you can confirm if a name is registered with Family Tree?"

"No, I'm sorry. I can't even do that."

Azim raised his gun so that it was visible over the counter. The woman's eyes went wide in terror! Azim threatened, "Oh, I think you can." The young, terrified woman wanted to scream. She quickly glanced left and right to see if anyone else was watching. "Do not scream!" Azim hissed. "Or it'll be the end of you." The woman was on the verge of fainting. Her face went ashen immediately.

"Now, you will confirm if Isabella Gruber or Ishi Gruber is on your system."

The young woman, petrified, didn't move.

"Now!" Azim seethed while controlling the volume of his voice. Immediately, the young woman began to type. While she typed, Abadi moved toward the left side short hall to ensure that nobody was watching.

"Yes, she … she is on our system."

"Good! Okay, now you're going to tell us the name of her match here in Vancouver."

In his very limited English, Abadi added, "And address."

The woman typed desperately with shaking hands.

Abadi stepped closer after checking the left-side hall. "Fast!" he hissed.

She found it. "Okay, I have it here."

Azim asked, "What is the name?"

"Rebecca Wiess. And she has …" She stopped herself from telling more.

Azim jumped on this hesitation, "And she has what?"

The woman relented, "And, she … she has another name on file too. Sonya Katz."

Azim and Abadi looked at each other, pleased. Azim said, "Write down the address!"

The woman grabbed a notepad and pen. She scribbled the address down with her trembling hand and handed it across the counter to Azim.

Then, Abadi began to move around the counter.

The woman shrieked, "What are you doing?"

Azim cursed, "Shut up or I'll blow your head off!"

Abadi also stepped closer and pulled a zip tie out of his pocket as he reached for the whimpering terrified woman. He grabbed her wrists and wrenched her arms behind her chair. She squealed in pain. As Abadi was finishing tying the woman's hands together and then to the chair, Azim heard a noise to his right.

A bearded middle-aged man wearing a business suit, having heard the commotion, came out of his office door and toward them. "Hey, what are you doing?"

Azim spun around toward the intruder and, without hesitating, shot him in the chest. The man fell on the spot.

The woman screamed in terror!

Abadi and Azim, note in hand, raced out of the office and toward the minivan.

*

Mack had waited long enough as far as he was concerned. He looked at Leah who was studying the local area streets on her map app. "I don't think we'll gain anything by waiting more."

Leah looked up toward the hotel. "Yeah, I suppose you're right."

They got out of their car and walked to the entrance and inside toward the front desk. They were surprised to see an older quite wrinkled thin white-haired woman behind the desk.

She glared at them, her face stern but not unfriendly. "Hello. Welcome to Apex," she said in a gravelly voice that reflected a likely lifetime of heavy smoking.

In a cheerful voice, Leah said, "Hi. I'm Ishi Gruber's sister Kristy. We called earlier. Is Ishi back yet? Have you seen her?"

The elderly clerk had seen the pair sitting outside for most of the past twenty minutes. She looked straight at Leah and answered, "I don't think so."

Slightly bewildered by the answer, Leah asked, "You don't think you've seen her yet?"

"No. I don't think you're her sister."

Leah and Mack stopped in their tracks, surprised! They certainly did not expect this kind of cold rebuke as a reception.

Already aware of their surroundings and that they were alone, Mack rolled his eyes, sighed, and pulled the gun out from behind his loose shirt at his waist. "Oh dear," he complained dryly, "you are a smart one aren't you."

The woman's eyes grew wide when she saw the gun. She was feisty enough to call things as she saw them, but she hadn't been confronted by a gun before. As Leah and Mack stepped up closer to the counter, the woman collected herself and bravely asked, "What do you want with that girl?"

Mack quipped, "Why? You want to join our little team? You certainly seem to have the personality for it."

The woman repeated the question louder and more assertively, "What do you want with her?"

Leah replied, "We're here to protect her."

"Yeah right!" she guffawed, followed by a raspy cough.

As Mack moved around to the back side of the counter, the woman said, "I guess now you're going to shoot me. Or tie me up, or something. Isn't that how it goes?"

Mack glanced toward Leah. "See, she would make a good member of our team." He chuckled as he reached for the woman's arms.

While Mack constrained the woman's hands and feet, Leah asked, "Who booked the hotel for Isabella Gruber?"

The woman didn't reply.

Leah saw a framed photo of three young children sitting on the inside of the counter. Leah pointed at the photo. "Grandchildren? They're so beautiful."

The elderly woman understood the threat.

"Her mother," she admitted in anger.

"Her mother," Leah repeated.

Mack had tied the woman to a heavy wooden highbacked stool, and was dragging it and the elderly woman from the reception area to a side file room. While the woman was being dragged away, Leah asked, "And where would I find the contact information for that mother?"

The woman shouted, "And you're here to protect the girl? Like hell. You are not!"

Leah turned and looked at the woman. "Actually, we are. We're here to protect her from her mother."

"Bull shit!"

Mack commented, "Gawd, I love her spirit!"

Leah pulled another stool to the counter and sat down at the computer. The screen was already up, so Leah saw that thankfully she'd avoid any need to convince a password out of that defiant blustery woman.

The woman shouted from the file room, "The information is in a drawer. And it's locked. So, you're out of luck."

Leah began to type on the computer keyboard. "Pretty sure I found the drawer," she quipped back. As she typed, Leah noticed a vehicle stopping at the entrance. "Oh no!" she groaned. She saw that the vehicle contained two women that appeared to be in their twenties or thirties.

As Mack quickly stepped into the file room and closed the door, he looked around for anything to gag the woman with. There was nothing. Bending down, he untied his shoes and slipped them and his socks off. Very quickly, he tied his socks together to make them long enough, and gagged the woman while both his and the elderly women's facial expressions showed their mutual unpleasantness of him taking this measure. He stayed barefoot for the time being, listening carefully through the file room door. The woman moaned through the sock gag, but her volume was not enough to make a difference.

Momentarily, a very overweight young woman and a very bubbly happy young woman entered and approached the reception desk. "Do you have any rooms?" the bubbly young woman asked. "The sign outside says that you do."

Leah smiled at her and responded, "I'm so sorry ma'am. I just haven't had time to change that sign yet. Just booked up. I'm so sorry."

The young woman's face drooped into disappointment. "Everywhere is booked solid. Okay. That's okay. Thanks." She turned and left. Momentarily, the car drove away.

Less than twenty seconds later, Leah and Mack were looking at Rebecca Wiess's home address, phone number, and credit card number. Mack, having put his shoes back on over his bare feet, pulled out his phone and clicked two photos of the computer screen's information.

Leah and Mack were heading for the front door. Mack called back loud enough for the elderly woman to hear through the closed filing room door, "Thanks for having us! We enjoyed our stay."

CHAPTER 37

David was furious, more furious the more he thought about it! Having arrived home, he turned into the driveway, came to an abrupt squawking stop outside the garage while hitting the remote device to open the garage door. He leapt out of the black Infiniti, grabbed his cane, and hobbled quickly through the garage into the house.

As he'd been driving and now as he hurried through the house to the master bedroom, David had been thinking of ways that he could remove the cursed threat of Ishi. He muttered as he moved toward the bedroom, "She might be my daughter. But she has never been anything but trouble." *And now, she represents big fucking trouble!* He hobbled quickly into the walk-in closet, reached up to a shelf, felt under a blanket for his gun. "There it is." He took the Sig Hauer P938 handgun down, then felt up on the shelf again for the magazine. Finding it with his fingertips, he stood to his tip toes, grabbed it, and took it down. *How did she find us?* He quickly checked that the magazine was loaded, then clicked it into the gun. *If she found us, anyone can find us*, he reasoned quickly.

Can I just shoot my own daughter? "Yes," he admitted, the four consumed glasses of beer undergirding his rage! He felt the blur on his mind and body from the combination of alcohol, emotions, and panic. *If she led Mossad here*, he stepped toward the bathroom, the thought of Mossad horrifying him, *then I have to run. I'll just disappear.* He put his cane on the counter, quickly dropped to his knees, opened the vanity door, shoved the shelves aside, and turned the dial on the safe. *Screw Sonya! I'll just disappear.* He began to pull packets of cash out, then glanced around wondering what to put the money into. Quickly he hobbled back to the closet, located one of Rebecca's larger handbags on the floor, grabbed it and scurried back into the bathroom.

With the handbag half full of cash, David began to think how much he could get into just one bag. *Maybe two million dollars*, he approximated. "Should've grabbed two bags," he muttered. More thoughts raced through his head! *Where will I go? I can fly to South America.* He continued to stuff cash into the bag. *The damned girl! Clothes? I can buy clothes. I'll fly out of Abbotsford,* he thought, assuming Mossad or whomever will be monitoring the Vancouver airport.

He heard a noise! *Sonya is here!* He stopped stuffing the bag and listened more closely. *Maybe just someone driving by. Or maybe a neighbor?*

As Rebecca pulled into the driveway, she saw David's car parked outside the open garage door. She frowned, thinking quickly, *Why is he home? Why is he home so fast? Why is he parked outside with the garage open?* Rebecca turned to Ishi, "Wait here for a sec."

Rebecca got out of the SUV and quietly walked through the garage and into the house. Looking slightly to the left into the kitchen, and directly ahead into living room area, she didn't see David. Stealthily, she steered to her right down the short hall toward the master bedroom. Perfectly quietly she entered the bedroom and heard shuffling noises coming from the ensuite. Through the crack on the hinge side of the door, Rebecca saw David stuffing money into one of her large bags. Then she saw the gun above his head laying on the bathroom sink countertop. "Oh no!" she gasped quietly. Rebecca turned and quietly retreated quickly through the short hall and toward the garage. Exiting the short hall, Rebecca stopped short in shock when she saw Ishi standing near the kitchen island facing her.

Ishi, having read Rebecca's body language, assumed that something was very wrong. She couldn't just sit there in the vehicle. She had walked through the garage and into the house. Still not seeing Rebecca, Ishi stepped left toward the kitchen. And now, Rebecca was standing there in the hall staring at her, eyes wide with fear!

Rebecca heard a noise behind her in the direction of the bedroom. It was the sound of quiet shuffling. Then she heard the metallic click of the slide loading the gun. Rebecca instantly calculated two things. *David is furious. He is a lethal threat.* Noticing that Ishi stood closer to the stairs than to the garage, Rebecca whispered in a panic while she pointed toward the stairs, "Go downstairs!" Immediately Ishi ran for the stairs. Rebecca followed.

As David stepped from the bedroom into the hall, he saw the top half of Rebecca as she descended. Furious, half drunk, and desperate, he aimed the gun and fired. The bullet hit a wood baluster and ricocheted past Rebecca's head. Two small slivers of smashed baluster splinters pierced Rebecca's shoulder and lower neck, evoking an instant scream from Rebecca. Lily, who had been sleeping in her doggy bed just inside the deck doors, barked and scurried across the room toward the stairs hoping to join Rebecca downstairs. In his furious craze, David aimed at the dog and fired. He missed. The dog yelped and continued to scurry down the stairs.

Rebecca put her hand up to the painful tiny spear in her neck as she reached the bottom of the stairs. *We don't dare try to escape out through the patio doors to the back yard-- We'd be easy targets if David had moved onto the deck above.* Terrified, she yelled to Ishi, "Get into that room!" She pointed at a door that led into the furnace room. Ishi raced to it, opened the door and hurried inside, her mother and the little dog right behind her. Rebecca flipped the light switch on.

Rebecca and Ishi both quickly looked around for something heavy to push in front of the door. They only saw cans of paint, some half-full cardboard boxes, and some loose baseboard on shelves. They were aware that simply pushing with the weight of their bodies against the door from the inside would be deadly because David's bullets could easily go right through the hollow door and hit them. Rebecca looked at Ishi with an expression of pure despair.

"Fuck 'em!" David hissed. He turned back to the master bedroom.

Quickly tossing cash into the bag until it was almost too full to zip closed, he grabbed the heavy bag, the cane, and his gun and walked quickly out of the bedroom, through the short hall, and toward the garage.

With the bag and gun beside him on the passenger's seat, he started the car. Slightly blocked in from behind by the SUV, he backed up making light contact with the SUV's front bumper. But now he had enough room to steer out. He shot ahead, and quickly circled out of the driveway, onto the street, and sped away. Just as he was accelerating along the street, he passed a white Camry that was slowing as it approached his driveway. As he continued down Badger Road, David glanced into his rear-view mirror and saw the white car stopping at the side of the street along the row of tall cedar hedges just short of his driveway.

Mack and Leah, guns in hand, quietly stepped out of the car. They walked along the thick row of hedges that ended at the driveway, peered around and saw the white SUV and the open garage door. They had both noticed the black car driving away but weren't sure if it had come from this driveway or from along the street. The open garage door was interesting though.

"I'll go to the back," Leah said, identifying a cobblestone path that led downward along the near side of the house. Immediately, using brief cover of the white SUV, they both crept to the side of the garage. Leah continued on down the side of the house while Mack stayed preparing to enter through the garage.

Having flipped the light back off, Rebecca and Ishi cowered silently in the dark room behind the furnace, listening for anything. The furnace was silent because it was shut off for the summer, but the water heater made a small constant noise, just enough noise to make it impossible for either Rebecca or Ishi to hear as they wished they could. The tension was almost more than either Ishi or Rebecca could bear!

Big Mack Ture entered the garage, gun ready. He then quietly opened the door into the mudroom and moved through it to the open doorway that led into the main area. He peaked around the doorway and was able to see the kitchen to the left. Nobody there. Taking one careful step forward, he arrived at a corner of a wall. He analysed the empty living room area directly ahead, and the vacant large deck beyond the living room. He saw immediately to his right a short hallway that, Mack assumed, led to bedrooms. Sliding quietly around the corner, he moved smoothly along the short hallway to an open door on his left and a closed door on his right. Peeking in through the open door on the left, he saw that it was the master bedroom. He deducted, considering that the closed door's room location on his right was against the garage, it was likely a laundry room.

Leah crept along the lower back deck crouching under two separate bedroom windows and toward the wood-framed glass patio door. She scowled when she saw that the glass patio door was flanked on each side by floor to ceiling windows. She dared to peek into the first large window. The contrast of bright sunlight outside versus the darker interior made it impossible for Leah to see in. *What now? Do I just rush for the door and risk being seen too early?* Unable to think of any better options, Leah took two quick steps to the glass patio door, grabbed the handle and pulled. *Locked!* And she had made noise trying to pull the door open!

In the furnace room, Lily had heard that noise. Instantly, she barked frantically! She scurried to the door and kept barking. Rebecca rushed to her dog, feeling for it in the dark, grabbed her up, and covered Lily's mouth. Ishi's heart was pounding out of her chest!

Leah paused to think whether to retreat back up along the side of the house.

Mack had frozen in his tracks just two steps into the bedroom. He had heard the barking! It came from directly below him. As he turned to quickly exit the bedroom and head for the stairs, he caught a glimpse into the ensuite and saw the open vanity door with an open heavy metal door inside protruding out past the vanity door. *A safe*, he realized as he continued toward the stairs!

Thinking nothing of the white Camry parked street-side near the driveway entrance, Azim steered the dark blue minivan into the driveway, slowly coming to a stop behind the white Ford SUV. Abadi had guided Azim to the address by using the map app on his phone. But to make sure, Abadi quickly got out of the vehicle, slinked around the front of it while concealed by the white SUV. He peered toward the front door and saw the number 428 mounted on the wall beside the door. He turned and nodded confirmation to Azim.

Immediately, Azim grabbed his gun from the center console and stepped out of the vehicle. Neither Omar Abadi nor Azim Bakir were very concerned with stealth. This was a kill mission. With their shoot-on-sight attitude and with guns held at waist height in front of them, they strode into the open garage.

They froze in their tracks though momentarily as two cars in succession passed by on the street. Confident that the two parked vehicles outside the garage mostly hid them from the street, they proceeded through the garage to the open door that led from the garage into the house.

Rebecca was thinking fast! She didn't know if David had left or if he is simply being quiet and waiting them out. *He's too angry and bombastic to be quiet and wait like this. He must have left.* She considered telling Ishi to make a dash for the back door with her. She turned and whispered to Ishi, "If we make it through the patio door, we'll be able to run down the slope and hide in the bushes."

Ishi, terrified, didn't know whether that was a good plan or not. She simply whimpered, "Okay."

Just as Lily tried to bark again, the door flew open. Ishi and Rebecca stared at a big man standing in the doorway aiming a gun at them! "Do not move!" he snapped at them. Reaching in, he flipped the light on.

"Toto!" the big man called loudly.

Rebecca moved backward in an attempt to shield Ishi. The man raised his voice, "I said; Do not move!" Rebecca stopped moving.

He shouted again, "Toto!" Seeing that the two women were unarmed, he relaxed a little.

Leah had reached the top of the grade and the front of the house. She saw the new vehicle parked behind the white SUV. She didn't hear Mack calling.

Abadi and Azim, halfway across the main area of the main floor, stopped moving when they heard the man's voice shouting from below them. They looked at the baluster stairwell and realized that they'd be exposed by simply waltzing down the stairs.

Assuming the voice belonged to Joseph Katz, their target, Abadi whispered to Azim, "I don't know if he has a gun. But we have to assume."

They stepped quietly to the top of the stairwell. Azim looked at Abadi and mouthed, "How?"

Abadi was thinking fast. He whispered, "I'll go around to the bottom and shoot out windows. When I have their attention, come down the stairs."

Azim quickly put a hand to his pants pocket to reassure himself that he had the extra magazine with him. Abadi turned and stepped quickly and quietly back toward the garage.

Leah was halfway through the garage as Abadi entered from the house. They were both shocked at the same instant, and both raised their guns. Leah yelled, "I'll shoot!" Abadi did not stop the motion of taking aim. Leah pulled the trigger, sending a round into Abadi's forehead. He jerked backward and fell hard, his torn skull clunking against a red tool chest behind him where he fell. "Shite!" Leah squeezed out the word, at first thinking she just killed their witness. But just as quickly, knowing well what Joseph Katz looks like, she realized that it was not him. *Iranian or PLO*, she assessed.

Assuming that this man was not alone, Leah quickly and carefully entered the house with her gun prone in front of her, her left shoulder screaming in pain from the frantic jerking motions in the garage.

Azim was already sneaking down the first few steps when he heard the gunshot. He turned his head momentarily back up toward the sound. Instantly recognizing danger was coming from the direction of the garage, he hurried further down the stairs.

At the same moment, Mack, hearing the gunshot too, turned to the stairs. He saw the man halfway down turning his gaze toward him and aiming the gun. They both fired at exactly the same moment. And both Mack and Azim reeled backwards, Mack Ture collapsing back against a basement wall and Azim folding down halfway down the stairs.

Azim felt nothing. He frantically regained his feet and scrambled upward on the stairs, desperately running his hands over his body feeling for a wound.

Mack felt the hot spear run into the side of his torso. He had fallen backward against a wall. As the dark-skinned man scrambled up the stairs, Mack quickly attempted to stand back up and chase after him. But he couldn't get up. He looked down to his waist and saw a blood stain forming on his shirt. "Ohhh, I hate it when that happens," he muttered painfully as he pushed his hand against the wound, blood beginning to drip onto the floor.

Azim reached the top of the stairs and came face-to-face with the business end of a handgun being pointed directly at his face by a short stocky Caucasian woman. Abruptly stopping, Azim's eyes went wide.

Leah screamed, "Put the gun down!"

Azim just stood there.

Leah yelled louder and more forcefully, "Put the gun down or I'll blow your head off like I did to your partner!"

After a few seconds, he realized that he had no options. Azim dropped his gun. It bounced down several steps.

Rebecca and Ishi saw their chance. They made a dash past the fallen man for the patio door.

"No, you don't!" They heard the voice just as they reached the door. "No, you don't! No, no, no!" Mack repeated. Rebecca and Ishi turned around to see the wounded bleeding man pointing his gun at them from where he slouched against the wall.

As Christian drove along Mount Seymour Parkway toward the address that Ishi had given him, he passed a hotel where there was a parking lot full of police cars, their lights flashing. He drove on. *This is what it's like in Vancouver?* He had entered the address on the car's GPS system when he left the rental parking lot at the airport, so he could see that he was now only minutes from his destination.

Leah's gun was still trained on the young dark-skinned man. She ordered, "Put your hands behind your head!"

Azim hesitated as he frantically tried to think of any option.

"I will blow your damned head off!" Leah wasn't kidding.

Unable to think of any recourse, Azim complied and put his hands up behind his head.

"Now," ordered Leah, "turn around and walk down the stairs!"

Azim realized that, with no more interaction or sound from Omar Abadi, that this woman must have in-fact killed him as she had claimed. He reluctantly walked down the stairs. Leah followed.

As Leah descended, she saw the scene. Ishi and a woman, likely Sonya Katz, stood at the glass patio door. Mack was shot and injured laying against a wall, his gun trained on the two women. Leah's eyes widened when she saw Mack and the blood soaking his shirt! Mack immediately tried to calm her down, "Superficial." However, he groaned as he spoke the word. Leah immediately knew that his wound was not superficial.

Ishi gasped as she saw Sebastian! She put her hands over her mouth in shock.

Both Azim and Leah having reached the bottom of the stairs, Leah barked at her captive, "Lay on your stomach!"

Azim sat down and then rolled into a face-down prostate position. With his free hand, Mack reached into a pouch on his belt and pulled out two zip ties. With a groan, he tossed them toward Leah. She quickly secured her captive's hands and feet. Once the young man was secured, Leah looked up at Sonya Katz. "Hello Sonya."

Ishi glanced at her mother and saw fear in her eyes.

Leah looked at Ishi. "Nice to see you again Ishi."

Ishi looked back at the woman with surprise, and whimpered, "Again?"

As Leah moved over to Mack to examine him, Leah replied to Ishi, "I was at your graduation. Saw you smooching with this guy." She pointed at Sebastian with her gun. "Actually, been camped out just beside your farm."

Ishi was instantly furious at the strange woman! "Where are my parents? What did you do to my--?"

"Nothing," Leah cut in. "We're looking for them too. Perhaps we should ask Azim Bakir here," Leah said pointing her nose toward the restrained man on his stomach. Leah glanced back at Ishi to enjoy Ishi's expression of shocking education.

Azim was astonished to hear his real name used by the woman. Fear instantly struck him. *How does she know my name?*

"Aa!" Leah winced in pain from her shoulder as she lifted Mack's shirt and checked the extent of the wound, she asked, "Or Azim, should we call you Sebastian? Both nice names."

Ishi aimed a blood-curdling scream at Azim, "Where are my parents? What did you do with my mom and dad?"

Azim said nothing intelligible, but only muttered inaudibly in Arabic.

Ishi took a step toward Azim.

Mack lifted his gun more threateningly at Ishi. "Ah uh! Don't!"

Ishi screamed hysterically at Sebastian, "You piece of shit! You sick piece of shit!"

Rebecca said calmly to Leah, "May I know who you are?"

As Leah helped Mack remove his shirt, bunched it up and compressed it against the wound to slow down the bleeding, she without looking back at Sonya, replied, "No."

Sonya tried again. "I think it's my husband Joseph that you really want."

Leah replied, "Oh Sonya. Good try. But we want you too." She handed off the task of holding the compress to Mack and stood back up turning her gun toward the two women. "Sit! Please."

Ishi and Sonya sat obediently on the floor beside the exterior door. Lily, completely confused by the activity but feeling her owner's fear, circled quickly and then jumped on her master's lap.

Leah looked at Sonya. "Where's Joseph?"

Sonya answered immediately, "I have no idea. All I know is that he tried to murder us." She pointed at Ishi, "Both of us!"

Leah was surprised by this bit of information and chose to believe her. Leah said, "Okay, I need you to tell me where you think he would likely go."

Mack interjected, "We need to go. The police will have been at the hotel by now. And, Wonder Woman there will have updated them."

Leah glanced at Mack.

Mack added, "… and sent them to this address."

Leah realized that Mack was right. "Can you get up?"

Through groans and muted cries of pain, Mack struggled, and with assistance from Leah, stood, his compressed shirt now red and soaked.

Leah pulled a small knife out of her shoe, walked over to Azim, and cut his feet free of the zip tie. "Stand up!" she ordered. "And don't think I won't shoot you in the head. In-fact, it would be my absolute pleasure to see justice done," she added menacingly. Azim stood.

Christian turned onto the driveway, pulled up beside the white SUV, and stopped. *So many cars,* he thought in mild surprise! He got out of the car and walked toward the open garage door, then froze in his tracks as he saw the body of the dead bloody man at the far side of the garage. "Oh, no!" he gasped. *Ishi,* he thought in horror! *Are you inside? Are you hurt?* He rushed past the grotesque sight of the body and into the house.

The first thing Christian saw upon rushing from the mudroom into the main area was, to his left, the top half of Sebastian coming up the stairs. Both young men stopped and looked at each other in absolute shock! While Christian remained standing there, his mouth agape, Sebastian began again to proceed up the stairs. Quickly Christian saw the face of a middle-aged woman and then Ishi.

"Ishi!" Christian gasped in relief.

Ishi was absolutely stunned when she saw Christian! "What?" Ishi began, completely bewildered. "Christian? Christian? What …?"

By now the procession had brought Leah's gun into view.

Ishi shouted, "Christian run!"

Christian turned to race back outside. Leah barked, "Run, and you're dead!" Leah didn't actually mean it but knew it would work. Christian stopped. As Christian turned around, his mouth dropped open as now he recognized the same woman that he had encountered on the highway near Frankfurt. Leah gave him a little wry grin, "Hello again, Christian."

"Oh, Chris," Ishi started crying. "What are you doing here? How …?"

Leah shouted, "Okay, everybody into the garage!" She looked behind her to ensure that Mack was able to follow. He was. Slowly and painfully one labored step at a time up the stairs, gun tucked into his belt.

Ishi was still crying. "Why did you come?"

While Mack struggled up the final few steps, with her gun still trained on the group, Leah took a few side-steps into the kitchen and whipped the two dishtowels from the oven handle. She assumed that Mack would need those as fresh compresses.

As they streamed into the garage, Azim glanced down at Omar Abadi's body while Sonya looked at Ishi. "Who is he?"

Before Ishi could reply, Leah shouted, "No words! Shut up, everybody!" She turned to Mack. "Can you drive?" She saw that he was leaving a small trail of blood and realized that he was in serious trouble from blood loss alone.

He squeezed out his words while looking forward and analyzing the vehicles, "Yes. Caravan."

Leah looked to see which vehicle was a Caravan. Seeing it as the dark blue van behind the white SUV, she ordered everybody to get into it. She looked at Mack again, "Can we all fit?"

"Those contraptions were made for times like these." He immediately followed his words up with severe groans of pain.

"I don't like it," Leah said as she observed how full the vehicle would be with only her gun to secure it. "Christian," Leah pointed her gun at Christian. "You'll drive! Mack," she looked at her injured partner, "front seat! Don't anybody slow down. I might not shoot to kill, except you," she pointed her gun at Azim, "but I'll have no problem blowing your kneecaps off … any one of you."

As Leah ordered Azim, Sonya, and Ishi to sit in the second of the van's three rows, she heard sirens in the distance. "They're coming!" she muttered. She hurried to the side door, slid it closed, then ran to the back hatch, opened it, and quickly climbed in. Perching behind the empty third row of seats, she trained her gun on the group in front of her while Mack held his gun on the group from the front seat. "Drive!" she yelled at Christian. "Drive!"

As Christian turned left off the driveway onto the street, Mack said, "I need everybody's phones. Give me your phones!" His left hand was still holding the bloody compress to his wound, and his other hand was holding the gun. "Just toss them onto my floormat," he added. Sonya, Ishi, and Christian all struggled to pull their phones out of their pockets, and as they could, they tossed them as instructed. Azim's hands were still tied behind his back, so he couldn't comply. Instead, Azim muttered threats in Arabic under his breath.

Leah instructed Sonya who was sitting in the middle between Azim and Ishi, "Get his phone out for him!" Sonya uncomfortably dug into Azim's front pocket and with some effort, produced the phone. That drew more vicious

Arabic from Azim. During the process, Azim spit on Sonya's face. Repulsed, Sonya instantly wiped the spit away.

As Sonya was tossing it forward, Leah shouted up to Mack, "Keep track of which phone that is!"

One block down the street, they passed police cars racing up the street, lights on and sirens blaring. More police cars followed. When they were two blocks away, Leah looked around through the van's rear window and saw the police cars stopping at angles at the intersection behind them to block off the street. Leah breathed out. *Just in time!*

"Where am I going?" Christian asked.

Leah had been looking at her map app and identified two ways out of Deep Cove. There was Mount Seymour Parkway which was the road she and Mack used to arrive on, and there was Dollarton Highway. Leah saw that Dollarton Highway looked more major and thus perhaps a safer route. "Go another three blocks. Then turn right onto Dollarton Highway."

Mack disagreed, "No. No, don't!" It took some effort for him to get his words out so that Leah could hear all the way in the back. "That's exactly what they'll be expecting."

Leah realized that Mack was right. She looked back down at her phone hoping to find a better solution.

CHAPTER 38

Sonya didn't know what she wanted less, to be in the hands of Israel's Mossad or the Vancouver Police. Sensing that she might at least have the possibility to try to negotiate with Mossad but certainly not local police who would likely eventually hand her off to Israel anyway, she spoke up, "There's a park. It's down by the water about eight or nine blocks from here. It'll be pretty empty right now. Cates Park." She glanced around to try to see Leah's reaction. But Leah, directly behind Sonya, was impossible to view. So, Leah's reaction remained unknown.

Leah and Mack looked at each other, considering Sonya's words. Mack nodded. Leah said, "Okay Sonya, tell Christian where to go!"

As Sonya directed Christian, Leah sent Ben Dod a text, "Fleeing scene/police. PLO 1 dead 1 with. Katz 2 with, 1 missed. Mack shot stomach. Need medic, no hosp. Urgent! Will text address in 15."

Five minutes later the van rolled into Cates Park. Mack pulled the bloody shirt away from his wound, tossed the shirt down by his feet, and put a dishtowel that Leah had set on his lap against the wound. It seemed that the bleeding was slowing. *It must've missed vital organs,* he assessed with relief. But he was beginning to feel faint.

As Sonya had predicted, there was almost nobody in the heavily treed park despite it being a sunny afternoon. Mack looked and saw a small road leading to a tree-rimmed parking lot on the right where there were two cars and some people on the grass. As Christian continued to roll ahead, Mack looked down a small road that led off to the left. He saw no vehicles there. "Go left!" he instructed Christian.

Christian turned left, then drove down the short, paved lane and continued to the back of the empty round parking lot. Leah instructed, "Stop here! On the right. At the side by the grass!" Christian pulled over into a stall near a thick group of bushes. Leah lifted the back hatch and jumped out. She walked to the driver's door and opened it. "Give me the keys!" Christian obeyed, that particular command from that particular woman becoming a bit too familiar.

Leah quickly marched around to the other side of the van and pulled the sliding door open. With her gun leveled at the group, she said, "Okay, Sonya, you're going to move to the front seat. Get out!"

Ishi had begun to cry. *This is where they kill us,* she was concluding.

Leah tucked her gun into her belt and opened the front door to help Mack out. Sonya began to climb over Ishi to get out. She whispered to her daughter as she climbed past, "It'll be okay in the end. Don't worry!"

Nobody noticed that Azim, with his long arms, was now sitting on his zip-tied hands. He had managed to slide his tied hands under his butt. Along the way, using his feet, he had also removed his shoes.

As Mack was helped out of the passenger's seat and as Sonya exited the van, in one quick movement, Azim squeezed his legs up and slid his hands around his feet. Instantly, he lunged against and past Ishi and out onto the grass. Then he lunged at Leah, taking her by surprise and knocking her down. With his hands still zip-tied together in front of him, he reached for her gun and yanked it out of her hands.

Azim's push had knocked Ishi out of the van too, but she had fallen out after he was already fully out and attacking the woman. Christian leapt from the driver's seat and ran around the back of the van, coming around just as Azim lifted the gun toward Leah. Sonya, seeing the opportunity, reached for the gun that Mack was holding in his hand. She clenched onto the gun. Mack and Sonya each struggled for a best grip. But Mack was too weak and began to lose his grip.

Leah, seeing the gun aiming toward her, rolled sideways just as Christian plowed into Azim from behind. Azim and Christian went flying together onto the grass. They struggled, but Azim still had the gun. As Leah was quickly getting back to her feet, the gun in Azim's hand fired, digging up sod just inches from Leah's feet, causing her to instantly scamper backwards.

"Chris," Ishi screamed, terrified that he was going to lose his struggle and be shot!

In-fact, Christian was losing the struggle. But with the gun waving wildly during the struggle, neither Ishi nor Leah dared run toward the wrestling pair. Azim kicked Christian in the groin and then sideswiped him across the face, instantly gouging his cheek with the gun. Christian fell to the side. Azim freely lifted the gun toward any most immediate person directly in front of him, Ishi. A shot burst through the air!

Sonya had won her struggle with Mack and had immediately turned the gun on Azim. Azim's body went limp. He fell onto his back, his eyes looking around in bewildered terror. He put his tied hands to his clavicle at the bottom of his throat. Blood oozed through his fingers.

Thinking she was being shot, Ishi's hands instantly flew to her chest where she anticipated the bullet. Ishi was frozen in shock! After several moments, she snapped out of it and realized that she was still alive. She looked at the young man with his life oozing out of him. While Sonya trained her gun back and forth from Leah to Mack to Leah, Ishi instinctively raced forward and fell on her knees beside her dying classmate. She held her hand to the hole where blood streamed out. The blood quickly filtered between and through her fingers. Christian, his cheek bleeding, joined Ishi. He whipped off his button-up shirt, popping all the buttons, bunched the shirt up and held it against the wound.

"Leave him," Leah suggested. "It's no use."

Azim's eyes, full of fear, looked past Ishi, then shifted and looked in the direction of Leah's voice. He tried to say something in Arabic, but only gurgled air mixed with blood came out of his mouth. Ishi wailed in horror! Then Azim's body relaxed as he surrendered.

Christian pulled the gun out of Azim's grasp. He stood up, his face and hands dripping with blood. He stepped a couple of meters away, shaking. He let his gun hand drop to his side as he tried desperately to collect himself.

Ishi, sobbing, ran toward the nearest bush and collapsed onto the grass in a sobbing heap.

Leah began to step forward. Instantly, Christian raised the gun toward her. "No!" he said with as much determination as he could muster. Leah stopped.

Mack had slowly laid down on the grass beside the van. His face was pale. Leah pointed at her partner and pleaded, "You have to let me get him help, or he will die too."

Sonya and Christian looked at the female Mossad agent and then at the dying male Mossad agent laying on the grass, considering the situation.

Both Sonya and Leah had been glancing occasionally toward the main park road to see if anyone had stopped or seen them. It had remained clear. Keeping the gun generally ready on both Mossad agents, Sonya stepped to the van and leaned in to scoop up her phone.

As she was leaning into the van, Christian commanded, "I want your gun."

Sonya looked up and back at Christian in surprise. "What?" She began to straighten up, "Why would you--?"

"I want your gun," Christian repeated the request. With shaking bloody hands, he pointed his gun with more determination at Sonya. "Now!" he bellowed.

As Sonya tossed the gun toward Christian onto the grass, Ishi turned to see. "Christian!" she gasped. "What are you doing?"

Christian stepped forward and picked the gun up with his free hand. Ishi yelled again, "Christian! What are you doing? Christian?"

Christian answered, "It's okay. I'm just being safe."

Ishi got up and stumbled back toward the van. "But Christian, she's my mother."

"It's okay. I'm just playing it safe. She might be your mother, but I don't know her ..." Christian shook his head from side to side. "This is all so crazy!"

Sonya, having already assessed Christian as being good and trustworthy, looked at her daughter, and tried to calm her, "Ishi, it's okay." Sonya was both physically and emotionally spent. She walked a few steps away from the group and sat down on the grass.

Azim's body was laying in a spot mostly blocked by the van so that anybody simply driving into the first part of the parking lot would not easily be able to see it.

Ishi was slowly regaining her composure. She said, "Christian, come talk to me." They stepped toward each other while Christian kept the gun generally raised toward both Leah and Sonya, both of those women now kneeling exhausted on the grass. He was not worried about the big man laying on the grass at this point because he saw that he didn't have enough strength left to be a threat.

Ishi knelt on the grass and pulled Christian into a kneeling position facing her and so Christian could also keep an eye on the others. "My mother is not a threat, Chris."

Christian replied immediately, "Yes maybe. But she has a criminal past. You told me yourself. She has a lot to lose if she doesn't escape."

Ishi considered Chris's words. Then she looked at the injured man. "He's going to die if we don't do something."

Christian looked toward the man laying on his side on the grass. His brows furrowed. "I know."

"Chris, me too! I have a lot to lose if she doesn't escape!" Ishi's face showed desperate confusion. "I didn't know you were coming here. How did you …?"

"The minute I realized the actual danger you were in with those forces following you, I drove to Frankfurt and applied for my passport. Same-day turn-around for extra money."

Ishi looked at him with bewilderment, "How …" Ishi didn't know where to start. "How did you pay for the flight?"

Christian offered her a little weary grin, "Sold my car in Frankfurt during the day that I waited. Didn't get what it was worth, but here I am. Had to buy one of those crazy expensive direct flights too. I was in a hurry."

Leah called over to them, "Hey lovebirds, my friend is dying here!"

Ishi and Christian looked over again at the man on the grass.

Ishi sighed, "I've known that I'd face this dilemma even before I actually met her." Ishi pointed her nose in her mother's direction.

Christian raised his eyebrows, not understanding.

Ishi explained, "If I turn her in, she'll be taken back to Israel and charged with her crimes. Treason, murder of a federal officer, and who knows what else. Maybe a death sentence! I don't know." Ishi remembered, raising her voice into a loud hate-filled hiss, "Oh and, my biological father, the one that got my mother into this in the first place, is still out there somewhere," she swung a pointing finger in a semi-circle, "on the loose."

"Oh yeah. Completely forgot about him."

"And, if I don't turn her in, let's say we try to run or something, well, then I'm an accomplice. Then I'm a criminal too."

Christian's sudden wide eyes and face showed his shocked understanding. He gasped, "Oh, no! Oh wow! Ish, what …?"

"And we're talking about spy agencies. Big! We'd never be able to hide. For sure they'd find us sooner or later. Likely sooner." She looked toward Sonya who was looking back at her daughter. "Maybe I'm already an accomplice. Likely." Ishi slouched in despair. "I can't live trying to hide like she did."

Leah called again. "Listen Ishi, let me at least call for medical help. This is serious!"

Ishi stood up and walked away to the bushes again, thinking, she knelt down as she tried to wipe some of the blood off her hands onto the grass.

Leah pleaded, "Please. He'll die! It'll be on you."

Christian kept an eye on the others while he waited for Ishi. He watched Ishi stand up again, her hands moving up and down in front of her animated as if she was having a tense conversation with the bush. Thirty seconds turned into a full minute. Crumpling again to her knees, Ishi continued to contemplate in animated angst.

"Please," Sonya pleaded for the dying man too. "Ishi!"

Christian added to the pleas. "Ish!"

Ishi stood back up, turned, and walked back to Christian. Her eyes were red with tears. She stepped toward Leah. Standing facing the woman, Ishi stated resolutely, "I want to make a deal."

Sonya, hearing her daughter's words said, "Ishi, she's Mossad. Deals are worth nothing."

Leah glared at Sonya, "Sonya, you don't know."

Ishi persisted, "I want to make a deal."

Leah replied from where she knelt on the grass, "I'm listening."

"My biological father forced her into it," Ishi pointed at her mother. "He's an asshole. Threatened her right from day one, right from when I was …" Ishi screamed her next words, "… from when I was just a little baby!" Toning it back down, Ishi continued, "… if she ever tried to leave or not cooperate throughout all those years …"

Leah stood to her feet, listening.

"I want clemency for my mother. I want you to guarantee me that. And I don't want to be charged as an accomplice in any way. I want it in writing. Officially!"

"I'd have to get that approved. I can't make that decision."

"And there's more. I want my sick sperm-donor of a biological father found! If he's not found, he's going to come and try to kill me and her again." Ishi pointed at her mother.

Leah replied, "Well Ishi, we want that too."

Ishi continued, more forceful as she spoke, "But he has a lot of money, enough to hide with. The only way you're going to find him fast enough is to get the local police involved. To find his car. Track his phone." Ishi pointed to the south as emphasis, "Airports. Borders."

Leah painfully took in Ishi's words, knowing that there would be hell to pay for Israel because of Mossad operating unsanctioned in Canada. But Leah feared that Ishi was not being unreasonable. Leah was impressed with the eighteen-year-old's prowess.

Sonya stated, "That means that it's going to be egg in Mossad's face here in Canada. But it'll save your friend's life."

Ishi continued, "That'll get your friend to emergency in a hurry," she said motioning at the big man on the grass. "I want it in writing. On government letterhead. Signed by Israel's government."

Leah looked at Sonya, then back at Ishi. "I'll need my phone," she held out her hand.

Christian quickly ran to the van, grabbed the remaining phones from the floor mat, and held them up one by one. "That one," Leah identified her phone. Christian brought it to her.

Leah immediately tapped through the security codes process and began typing.

Ishi said, "I need to see your message before you send it."

Leah looked up at the girl, again impressed. "Okay."

As Leah continued typing out her message, Ishi tried to justify her last order, "Just need to be sure that you're not ordering up surprises for us."

Leah answered, "I understand," as she typed.

After more than a minute of fast typing, Leah handed the phone to Ishi. Christian stepped over and they read it together. Ishi handed the phone back to Leah. "Okay, send it." Leah tapped 'Send'.

Christian still had a gun loosely trained on Leah. While they waited one, then two, then three minutes for a response to Leah's message, Sonya finally said, "Listen Ishi, how about while we're waiting, Christian and I at least get this body into the van."

Ishi nodded approval. Christian handed Ishi the second gun.

Just as Sonya was closing the rear van hatch and Christian was walking back toward Ishi, blood still running down from his cheek, Leah's phone dinged! She read. She looked up at Ishi, "No deal."

Ishi let out a blood-curdling scream! "Why? Why wouldn't you do that?" Ishi began to wave the gun back and forth in Leah's direction. She aimed another louder scream at Leah, "Why!?"

Leah answered flatly, "They said that we can get all the information we need from Sonya."

Mack groaned as he heard the result, "I'm dying here. Damn you to hell, Ben Dod!"

Sonya chimed in, glaring at Leah, "No you can't. I don't know the contacts in Israel, much less any contact information. Never did," she lied.

"Joseph wouldn't tell me. Didn't trust me with it."

Leah glared at Sonya, weighing whether to believe her, that, as she processed all that was immediately at stake including Mack's survival. Then Leah typed a new message quickly, knowing that Mack's life hung in the balance.

One painful minute turned into two and then three and four. Ishi had handed the guns back to Christian and stomped off again to the nearest bush. Fifteen meters away, she released a blood-curdling scream of anxiety as she paced back and forth!

Just then, Leah, Christian, and Sonya saw a vehicle turn toward the parking lot. As the topless Jeep drove closer, everyone held their breath. Christian rotated his body so that the guns remained hidden. The Jeep parked approximately ten stalls from them. Two girls and one guy jumped out, the guy slinging a pack onto his back. The three young adults chose a well-worn trail and followed it into the woods and disappeared from view.

Seven minutes had passed since Leah sent her second message to Ben Dod. Leah's phone dinged!

Ishi held her breath as Leah read. Leah raised her phone screen toward Ishi in triumph and without saying anything, smiled at Ishi.

Ishi asked, "Really? What?"

"They'll do it."

CHAPTER 39

Standing on the top step of the three-step painter's ladder, Christian reached as high as possible to place the star at the top of the beautiful full Douglas Fir. "That good?" he asked.

Ishi, lounging back in the cozy crème-chenille loveseat analyzed it. "Perfect!" she clapped her hands like an excited little girl. "Okay, let's plug it in."

Christian stepped back down, grabbed the ladder, placed it aside, and then ducked behind the tree to plug it in. With the tree lights on, he joined his girlfriend on the loveseat.

He looked at her adoringly. The crackling fire in the big new stone fireplace added a glowing color to her face that enhanced Ishi's beauty.

Christian and his father had put the finishing touches on Ishi's house by building a gorgeous brick courtyard both in front and out back of her renovated and expanded house on the acreage. Both courtyards were framed on the outside by handsome brick waist-high walls. That was, of course, before winter arrived with blankets of snow.

To punctuate Ishi's improvement to the acreage, she had also renovated the chicken coop. That, she did herself. She bought herself the necessary tools including a table saw, skill saw, air compressor and nail gun, and much more. Sure, Christian had given her some tutoring. But Ishi had taken over quite eagerly and with quickly acquired expertise. She even managed to get all the red vinyl siding on before the snow arrived.

Having sold the farm where she grew up, the home that held so many beautiful and also some terrible memories, she had made sure to migrate the hens from there to this refurbished chicken coop. She insisted on being able to gather her own fresh eggs each day.

She missed her mom and dad Gruber thoroughly and intensely. Even though everyone, especially Ishi, held up hope that they'd reappear, as one month led to another month, sadly it became clearer that they weren't going to ever show up again. During a long phone conversation with her mom, Sonya had carefully and gingerly advised Ishi of the high probability that the Adris had done something terrible and permanent to Horst and Dagmar.

Sonya was allowed to call Ishi once each week for a supervised phone visit. That's all the Israel National Prison would permit.

But those phone visits with her mother were better than nothing while both Ishi and Sonya waited for the Court Hearing in March. Both Ishi and Sonya had been reassured multiple times by Israel's Minister of Internal Affairs that keeping Sonya incarcerated until the hearing was a necessary and typical matter of legal protocol in situations like this, and that Sonya was guaranteed to be released after the court date. Sonya considered it a reasonable price to pay, considering that things could have gone much worse.

When Sonya referred to "things could have gone much worse", she was comparing her fate to that of her ex-husband Joseph Katz. With coordination of Vancouver City Police and the RCMP, Joseph had been found in the Vancouver area within one day. It took only one month to have him extradited back to Israel.

Joseph Katz would have faced a possible death sentence if he had not given up the names of the PLO moles, thus collapsing that entire long-standing covert network. In exchange for Joseph's information, the State was pursuing only life imprisonment with no chance of parole instead of the death penalty.

With excited anticipation, it was both Ishi's and Sonya's expectation that Sonya would come to Philippsthal to live with Ishi after her release in March.

Ishi, loving the Christmas tree lights and the mood in her living room, snuggled against Christian. She looked up at his face, then brushed a finger tenderly along the healed scar on Christian's cheekbone.

Christian slung an arm around her as they both reclined back into the loveseat. "Is Lucy still coming for dinner tomorrow?"

Ishi answered happily, "Not just Lucy. Eddie, Becky, and Julia. Oh, did you know that Eddie got into Insead?"

"No. Wow! I heard that Julia got into Columbia though."

"And," Ishi excitedly announced, "Julia and Sieg got engaged!"

"Saw that one coming. What are you making?"

Ishi looked up at him with a what's-wrong-with-you look. "Turkey. What holiday do you think it is?"

Christian grabbed a cushion and tried to bop her with it as she raised a hand in time to block it. "Could've been a ham, y'know. You're the turkey."

Ishi grabbed the cushion out of Christian's grasp and wacked him with it, giggling. "You're the turkey!"

They playfully jostled a few more seconds. Then a more serious expression appeared on Christian's face. He reached out with one hand behind Ishi's head and combed with his fingers through and down Ishi's long hair, gazing at her adoringly as she looked longingly into his eyes.

Ishi pushed him onto his back and laid on top of him. "You might be the turkey. But I'm the dressing." She grinned, then kissed him deeply.

The End

ABOUT THE AUTHOR

Glen Peters, having lived in 5 countries on 3 different continents, has gained personal insight into many various mindsets and behaviors. Such understanding furnishes him to write more accurately diverse characters and scenarios into his literary works because of the better understanding of worldwide differences and commonalities.

Besides authoring short stories, screenplays, and a nonfiction book Am I Nephilim, Glen Peters is also the author and producer of award-winning feature films including The Fanny Crosby Story (Netflix, Amazon Prime) and 20 documentaries of Kichwa, Waorani, Secoya, and Siona Indigenous peoples in the Amazon Basin.

Glen Peters is home at beautiful Kelowna, BC, Canada, and can be found most days in his home office gazing across his gorgeous lake and mountain view, drawing inspiration for more writing.

To discover more about Glen Peters and his writing, please visit:

glenpeters.info

Made in the USA
Columbia, SC
16 April 2023

14933545R00214